# DEATH BY HOROSCOPE

# DEATH BY HOROSCOPE

Edited by

## Anne Perry

CARROLL & GRAF PUBLISHERS, INC.
NEW YORK

Carroll & Graf Publishers, Inc.
A Division of Avalon Publishing Group
19 West 21st street
New York, NY 10010-6805

Library of Congress Cataloging-in-Publication Data is available.
ISBN: 0-7867-0845-X
Manufactured in the United States of America

# CONTENTS

# INTRODUCTION

DO YOU BELIEVE in horoscopes? No, neither do I, not really. Only when they tell me that I am unique and exciting and my destiny is full of wonderful things. That, of course, makes perfect sense, and I shall believe this one absolutely, and quit reading them while I am so far ahead—until next time! In case tomorrow tells me I am quite ordinary and must apply myself to all the daily trivia of life and attend to a pile of jobs I should catch up with, domestic chores and paying bills, etc.

If your horoscope tells you to have fun, that a little relaxation and entertainment would be good for you—and if it doesn't, try another one—then take a little time out to read these stories of believers and unbelievers, light and shadow, humour, violence, love and hate. There is a terrific variety, but every one has vivid and individual writing. They are set in many different places, most in the present day, two earlier last century (1900's—not 1800's) and one medieval, but all have a zodiac core to bind them together. With some the thread is slender, no more than an artifact or an idea, with others it is an inescapable fate.

Meet professional hitmen (more than one!) whose destiny is written in the stars, very funny, compelling, and one even carrying in it the seeds of redemption. Visit New York, Texas, Las Vegas with all the atmosphere and colour, none of the hard edges spared.

Meet police officers who discover that astrologers come in all sorts of shapes and guises, with all the human passions and fallibilities of everyone else. They fall in love, they commit crimes, they get caught,

sometimes they even get killed! Now why did they not see that coming? Or perhaps they did—but the stars are inescapable.

Meet adventurers and profiteers by land and at sea, caught up in
the tangle of belief and skepticism, love, greed, and the subtle plots
of others. Meet would-be predators neatly enmeshed in their own
snares, and lovers with the tables turned on them. You will hesitate
to make a pass at a stranger, believe me!

And if you are married and have thoughts of cheating on wife or
mistress, the stars also look down on some fiendishly Machiavellian
people who, when they believe themselves wronged can kill, and
smile, and frame you for the crime.

And of course there are lovers who are gentle and easy to like, who
use knowledge of astrology in brilliant deduction. There is plenty of
humour, dry or broad, open laughter, or the subtle smile of satisfaction at parody of the familiar, at wit and a sharp and joyous turn of
phrase.

Meet those who care passionately about the real stars, and the astronauts who journey towards them. Perhaps dream a little of what
the future may bring, far beyond our own time.

Or in the past! Astrology has been with us since we first looked up
at the heavens and wondered who we are and where we came from,
and if our lives are reflections of a greater plan. Vanity, greed and
opportunism were with us in Medieval times as they are now.

Spend a little time with wounded soldiers recovering in war-torn
England. Immerse yourself in the atmosphere until you walk every step
of the way with them, in their loves and loyalties, pities and beliefs.

Or perhaps share the same emotions after the Great War, the soul-
weariness of men who have seen too much horror, and the women
who love them, the frightened, the greedy and the confused, in a
world which will never be the same again.

Whatever you believe of the stars, you believe in people, and here
are scores of them in all their wealth of life—and death.

Enjoy.

—Anne Perry
Ross-shire, Scotland
August 2001

# THE ASTROLOGER WHO
# PREDICTED HIS OWN MURDER

## A Sister Fidelma Mystery

### Peter Tremayne

"I CAN APPRECIATE why the Bishop has sent you to defend Abbot Rígán, Sister. However, I think that you will find this is an open and shut case. The abbot is demonstrably guilty of the murder of Brother Eolang."

Brehon Gormán was a tall, dark man, swarthy of complexion. He sat back regarding Sister Fidelma, seated across the table opposite him, with a look of cynical amusement. He had an arrogance of manner which irritated her. They were using the chamber of Brother Cass, the steward of the abbey of Fota, who stood nervously to one side.

"As I understood the circumstances, there were no eyewitnesses. How, then, can the abbot be demonstrably guilty?" she asked coldly with an emphasis on the words he had used.

The sharp faced Brehon smiled even more broadly. The smile made Fidelma feel a coldness at the nape of her neck. It had all the warmth of a shark about to snap at its prey.

"Our law takes cognizance of the words of a man uttered before his death," remarked the Brehon in the manner of a teacher explaining something to a backward child.

"I do not follow."

"The victim named the abbot as his murderer before his death."

Sister Fidelma was stunned into silence by his calm announcement.

It had been only that morning when the Bishop of Cashel had

1

called her into his chambers and asked her if she, being a *dálaigh*, an advocate of the courts, would undertake the defence of Abbot Rígán, whose abbey of Fota stood on an island in a nearby lake. The abbot had been accused of killing one of his own brethren. Brehon Gormán was to hear the case and it was known that Gormán was no lover of the religious. The Bishop of Cashel was concerned for the abbot, who, by all accounts, a man with a reputation for kindliness and largess, was a man whose good works had distinguished him among the brethren. However, the abbot was also known to be a man of strict obedience to the Rule of Rome which brought him into conflict with many of his fellow religious.

The community of the Abbey of Fota was a small exclusive brotherhood of leather workers and a few scholars. They were a self-sufficient community. As protocol requested, Fidelma had introduced herself to the worried looking steward, Brother Cass, who had then introduced her to Brehon Gormán who had ensconced himself in the steward's chamber. She had asked to be informed of all the facts of the case.

The facts seemed simple, according to the Brehon. Brother Eolang, a member of the community, had been found by the lake under a wooden landing pier. He had evidently been drowned but there was bruising and cuts to his head. The community's apothecary, Brother Cruinn, had expressed suspicion about the death. Brother Eolang had not been an elderly man. He was in the prime of his life and the bruising seemed to indicate that he had been struck on the forehead and pushed into the lake where he had drowned.

Brother Gormán had been sent for. After some initial inquiries he had placed Abbot Rígán in custody pending a full trial.

For a moment or two Fidelma sat gazing at Brehon Gormán in astonishment.

"My understanding of what I have been told is that Brother Eolang was dead when he was discovered in the lake? Is this not so? But you say he was able to name the abbot as his killer. How was this miracle accomplished?"

"He was certainly dead when his body was found," agreed the Brehon.

"Then explain this riddle which you have set me."

"It is quite simple. Brother Eolang told several of his brethren a week ago that he would be murdered on a particular day and that the abbot would be responsible."

Fidelma found herself in the unusual position of being unable to comment for a moment or so. Then she shook her head in bewilderment, trying to control the growing sarcasm in her tone.

"This is the evidence? He predicted he would be murdered by the abbot?"

Brehon Gormán smiled again, even more coldly.

"Brother Eolang also foretold the exact manner of his death," he added.

"I think you need to explain more precisely, Brehon Gormán," Fidelma said. "Was Brother Eolang a prophet?"

"It would appear so for we have the accusation and prediction written in Brother Eolang's own hand."

Sister Fidelma sat back and folded her hands in her lap.

"I am listening attentively to your explanation," she said quietly. "Please tell me the facts so that I do not make any assumptions."

"There was no love lost between Abbot Rígán and Brother Eolang," replied the Brehon. "There are witnesses to several arguments between them. They arose because the abbot did not agree with some of Brother Eolang's beliefs and activities . . ."

Fidelma frowned, still feeling lost.

"Activities? What activities?"

"Brother Eolang was the assistant to the apothecary of the abbey and an adept at making speculations from the patterns of the stars."

"Medicine and astrology were often twins in the practice of the physician's art," conceded Fidelma. "Its use is widespread throughout the five kingdoms of Éireann. Why was the abbot so condemning of the practice?"

Fidelma herself had studied the art of star charts and their interpretation under Brother Conchobar of Cashel who had once told her that she would have made an excellent interpreter of the portents. However, Fidelma placed no great reliance on astrologers, for it was a science which seemed to rely solely on the interpretive ability of the individual. However, she did accept that much might be learnt from the wisest among them. The study of the heavens, *nemgnacht*, was an ancient art among the people of Éireann and most who could afford to do so, had a chart cast for the moment of their children's birth which was called *nemindithib*, a horoscope.

The more ancient forms of astrology used by the Druids before the coming of Christianity had fallen out of use because the New Faith had also brought in new forms which were practised among the Greeks and Romans and originated in Babylon.

"The abbot did not approve of astrology, Sister," interrupted the steward of the community, Brother Cass, who had been standing quietly by during the initial exchange. "The abbot disliked Brother Eolang on account of his practise of astrology. The abbot had read a passage in one of the Scriptures which denounced astrology and so he took his teaching from it. He tried to forbid its practice within our community."

Fidelma smiled softly.

"Forbidding anything is a sure way of encouraging it. I thought we were more tolerant in such matters? The art of the *réaltóir*, the astrologer, has been one that has its origins from the very time our ancestors first raised their eyes to the night sky. It is part of our way of life and even those who have accepted the New Faith have not rejected the fact that God put the stars in the sky for the obedience of fools and the guidance of the wise."

There was a silence then Brother Cass spoke again.

"Yet there was an animosity between Eolang and the abbot over this matter."

"Over a week ago," commenced the Brehon, "according to certain members of the community, and as they will testify, Brother Eolang became so worried about the animosity that he cast a chart, what is a called a horary chart, to see if he was in any danger from the abbot. He did this because the abbot's language had grown quite violent in the denunciation of Brother Eolang's beliefs."

Fidelma did not make any comment but waited for the Brehon to continue.

"Eolang told certain of his comrades among the brethren that within a week from the time he had cast that chart, he would be dead. The chart, he said, showed that he was powerless against the abbot and would suffer death at his hands either by drowning or poisoning."

Brehon Gormán sat back with a smile of triumph.

Fidelma regarded him with some skepticism.

"You appear to believe this."

"I have seen the chart. I am an amateur in such things but my knowledge is such that the accuracy of the prediction becomes obvious. I shall accept it into evidence along with the testimony of those of the brethren to whom Brother Eolang discussed the meaning of it before his death."

Fidelma considered the matter silently for a moment. Then she turned to Brother Cass.

"Do you have someone available who could take a message to Cashel for me?"

Brother Cass glanced at the Brehon, who frowned.

"What do you propose, Sister Fidelma?"

"Why, since this chart is apparently central to the abbot's supposed guilt, I would send to Cashel for an expert witness to verify its interpretation."

"What expert witness?"

"Doubtless, as someone who has dabbled in the art, you have heard of Brother Conchobar, the astrologer of Cashel? He was taught by the famous Mo Chuaróc mac Neth Sémon, the greatest astrologer that Cashel ever produced."

The Brehon's frown deepened.

"I have heard of Conchobar, of course. But do we need worry him when everything is so clear?"

"Oh, for the sake of justice," smiled Fidelma, without humour, "we need to ensure that the abbot has the best defence and that implies someone who is an expert in the evidence against him. You have admitted to having only an amateur's knowledge. I also have but a passing knowledge so it is best to consult a real expert."

The Brehon examined her features carefully. A suspicion crossed his mind as to whether she was being facetious. Then he glanced to Brother Cass and inclined his head in approval.

"You may send for Brother Conchobar."

Sister Fidelma smiled briefly in acknowledgment.

"And if we are to take this star chart seriously as evidence," she went on as Brother Cass departed on his mission, "then I shall want to have proof that it was drawn up by Eolang at the time it is claimed. I shall want to examine those brethren with whom he discussed it and its conclusions. And, having some slight knowledge of the art, I shall want to see it for myself."

Brehon Gormán raised an eyebrow.

"It sounds as if you do not trust my judgment?" There was a dangerous quality to his voice.

"You are the Brehon," Fidelma replied softly. "When you sit in your court and pronounce your judgment, having heard all the evidence and the plea from myself, as a *dálaigh* defending my client, then your judgment demands and receives respect. Until that time, I shall presume that you have not made any judgment for if you had that would have been contrary to law."

Her features seemed inscrutable but he noticed her green eyes glimmering with an angry fire as they returned his stare.

The Brehon's cheeks crimsoned.

"I . . . of course, I have made no judgment. All that I have done is point out to you that I have accepted this chart as essential evidence. Also that the people to whom Brother Eolang spoke about its conclusions are satisfactory witnesses. They chart and witnesses will be presented to the court."

"Do you have the chart here?"

"I have it and written on it is testimony as to when it was written and its interpretation in the very hand of Brother Eolang and witnessed."

"Show me," demanded Fidelma.

Brehon Gormán drew a vellum from a case and spread it on the table between them.

"Note the date and time and Eolang's signature in the corner. You will also note that a Brother Iarlug has signed his name as witness and dated it on the same day."

"This Brother Iarlug is available to testify?"

"Of course, as is Brothers Brugach, Senach and Dubán to whom

Eolang spoke of his prediction. They all will testify when this chart was drawn up and when he spoke to them."

Fidelma pursed her lips skeptically.

"With five of the brethren, including the victim, forewarned of the day when the abbot would commit this alleged murder, it seems a curiosity that Brother Eolang was not given protection against the event."

Brehon Gormán shook his head, his face serious.

"You cannot alter fate. Fate has no reprieve."

"That is a concept brought to us by Rome," Fidelma rebuked. "Our own wise men say that whatever limits us, we call fate. Fate is not something which is inevitable whether we act or not. It is only inevitable if we do not act."

Brehon Gormán glowered at her for a moment but she was oblivious to his stare.

"Now, let us examine this chart. You may explain it to me as you confess to be something of an amateur in its deciphering."

It took a moment or two before Brehon Gormán became involved in the task and, in spite of his antagonism to Fidelma, his voice took on an enthusiastic tone.

"The chart is easy to follow. See here," he thrust out a finger to the symbols on the vellum.

Sister Fidelma bent over it, silently thanking the time she had spent with old Conchobar learning something of the mysteries of the art.

"It seems that Eolang was so worried that he asked a question 'Am I in mortal danger from Abbot Rígán?' This is called a horary question and the chart is timed for the birth of the question. It is like looking at a natal chart but, in this case, it is the birth of the question."

Fidelma suppressed a sigh of impatience. She knew well what a horary question was. But she held her tongue.

"It seems from the chart that Eolang was ruled by Mercury ruling the Virgo ascendant with the moon as co-ruler. His enemy, the abbot, is represented by the ruler of the seventh house, signified by Jupiter in the seventh house in Pisces."

"Very well. That I can follow. Continue."

"Brother Eolang's first impression was that Mercury was very weak in Pisces, being in detriment and fall and also retrograde. Also Mercury was close to the cusp of the eighth house of death. Jupiter on the other hand was powerful. It was in its rulership and angular and disposed Mercury. Jupiter, importantly, also ruled the eighth house of death."

Sister Fidelma followed the Brehon's pointing finger as he indicated the positions on the chart.

"Now, see here: the moon applied to the sun, ruler of the twelfth house of self-undoing and was combust. We astrologers . . ." he smiled deprecatingly, "have long regarded this as the worst condition for any planet. The sun and moon were in the eighth house and the moon in Aries is peregrine or totally without power."

Fidelma now found herself struggling to understand the various angles which were depicted on the chart. Her knowledge was insufficient to discern the nuances.

"In Brother Eolang's interpretation, what did all of this mean?" she asked.

"All these indications told Brother Eolang that he was powerless against Abbot Rígán. It told him that he would suffer death at the abbot's hands either by drowning or poisoning. Drowning was more likely with Pisces being a water sign. And, see, Jupiter in Pisces indicates a large, powerful man, religious and well respected in the community. Who else did that identify but the abbot?"

"And from your knowledge, you find this interpretation acceptable?" Fidelma asked curiously. Certainly, from her own limited knowledge of how astrologers worked, she could see no flaw in his presentation.

"I accept it completely," affirmed Brehon Gormán.

"Very well. Let us now send for these witnesses to see what they have to say. Firstly, Brother Iarluq who signed the chart as a witnesses to its provenance."

Brother Iarlug was thin and mournful and had no hesitation in verifying that he had witnessed Eolang drawing up his chart. Eolang had also explained what the chart portended. That within the week Eolang would be dead and at the hands of the abbot.

"Why, then, was nothing done to protect Eolang if he believed this knowledge," demanded Fidelma, not for the first time.

"Eolang was a fatalist. He thought there was no escape," Brother Iarlug assured her while Brehon Gormán smiled in satisfaction behind him.

One after the other, Brothers Brugach, Senach and Dubán all told how Brother Eolang had showed them his chart over a week before. He had predicted the very day on which he would be found in the lake. Each of them confirmed that they believed in inescapable fate.

Fidelma was exasperated.

"Everyone here seems a slave to predestination. Has no one free will?" she sneered.

"Fate is . . ." began Brehon Gormán.

"Fate is the fool's excuse for failure," she snapped at him. "Am I to believe that you believed this event would happen and simply sat down and waited for it?"

"It is the fate of the leaf to float and the stone to sink," intoned Brother Dubán. "We cannot change our destiny. Even the New Faith tells us that. In this place we have all studied the writings of the great Augustine of Hippo — De civitate Dei, The City of God. Does he not argue that we cannot escape our fate? Our fate was predestined even before we were born. Even before God made the world, the Omnipotent One had decreed the fate of the meanest among us."

"On the contrary. Did not our own great theologian Pelagius argue in De Libero Arbitrio — On Free Will — that meek acceptance of fate is destructive to man's advancement? We are given information to make choices upon, not to sit back and do nothing. Doing nothing, as Augustine suggests we do, imperils the entire moral law of mankind. We have to take the initial and fundamental steps for our salvation. If we are not responsible for our actions, good or bad, then there is nothing to restrain ourselves from indulging in sin."

"But that's a Druidic teaching . . ." protested the Brehon.

"And Pelagius was accused of trying to revive the Druidic philosophy," interrupted the Brother Dubán in annoyance. "That was why he was declared a heretic by Rome and excommunicated by Pope Innocent I."

"But that judgment was not accepted by the churches here, nor in Britain nor Gaul nor even by many of the Roman bishops," answered Fidelma sharply. "Even Pope Zosimus, who succeeded Innocent, rescinded that degree and declared Pelagius innocent of heresy. Only the African bishops, the friends of Augustine, refused to accept the Pope's ruling and persuaded the Roman Emperor Honorius to issue an imperial decree denouncing him. It was for political reasons, not those of faith, that Pope Zosimus had to reconsider and change his ruling which lifted the excommunication."

Brehon Gormán was studying Fidelma with an expression of suspicion and annoyance.

"You seem well informed on this?"

"As lawyers, is it not our duty to imbibe as much information as we can?" she demanded. "Our knowledge must surely be as wide as we can make it, otherwise how can we profess to set ourselves up as judges of other people's actions?"

Brehon Gormán seemed confused for a moment.

Fidelma continued in a confident tone: "Now, I shall want to see the person who found Brother Eolang's body, the apothecary who examined it and, of course, the abbot."

"The body was found by Brother Petrán," the Brehon responded sourly. "The apothecary is Brother Cruinn and you will find the abbot confined to his chamber. I do not think there is need for me to accompany you for I an conversant with their evidence. It is of little importance."

Sister Fidelma raised an eyebrow but said nothing. She glanced at the surly Brother Dubán.

"Then perhaps Brother Dubán will show me whether I may find them?"

Brother Dubán reluctantly led the way to the herb garden of the community. There was a single brother working in it.

"Petrán tends the garden and you will see our apothecary's shop in the far corner. There you will find Brother Cruinn."

Brother Dubán turned and walked swiftly off without another word.

The rotund, red faced religieux who was tending some bushes in the garden, turned as she approached. He frowned for a moment and then gave a friendly smile.

"Sister Fidelma?"

"Do you know me?" she asked, puzzled by the greeting.

"Indeed. But you would not know me. I was in the court when you defended Brother Fergal from a charge of murder. Have you now come to defend our abbot?"

"Only if I believe him to be innocent," agreed Fidelma.

"Innocent enough," the man was now serious. "I am Brother Petrán and I found the body of poor Eolang."

"But you do not believe that the abbot is guilty?"

"I do not believe that a man should be condemned on the evidence of a claim based on obscure maps of the stars."

"Tell me what happened?"

"I was going to go to market to buy new plants for the herb garden. This involved crossing the lake," he added unnecessarily. "I went to the pier where our boat was tied up. It was then that I saw the body of Brother Eolang in the water under the pier."

"Under the pier?" Fidelma asked quickly with emphasis.

"The pier is made of thin wooden planking. Some of it is loose and missing. You have to look down to make sure you step surely. That was how I was able to see him. I was keeping my eyes on where I was placing my feet. I saw the body between a gap in the planking. Mind you, I do not suppose I would have looked down so closely at that spot had it not been for the man calling to me and pointing down."

Fidelma tried not to show her surprise.

"What man?" she asked slowly.

Brother Petrán did not seem perturbed.

"There was a man on horseback on the far bank. As I came onto the pier he started to shout and wave to me. I wondered what was up. It was too far distance to hear any words distinctly. He kept gesturing with his arm towards the water and that was when I looked down and saw the body."

"Are you saying that this man might be a witness to what happened?" she asked quietly.

Brother Petrán shrugged.

"He certainly spotted the body and drew my attention to it."

"Did you tell the Brehon this?"

"He thought it was irrelevant because of the evidence that showed the abbot's involvement."

"Can you describe the man on horseback? Did you know him?"

"He was a stranger. But he rode a fine horse and was dressed as a warrior. He carried the standard of the King of Cashel."

"Then he must have been a messenger of the King, passing on his way to Cashel," Fidelma cried in relief. "We can find him." Fidelma paused a moment and then continued: "What then? What happened after your attention was drawn to the body?"

"I raised a cry for help and, being a good swimmer, I jumped into the water and brought the body ashore. By that time Brother Cruinn, our apothecary, had arrived to help me."

"And the man on the far bank?"

"When he saw that I had brought the body out of the water, he raised his hand and rode off. There was little else he could do for there was no boat on his side of the water."

"You say that you could swim?" Fidelma went on. "Do you know if Brother Eolang was a swimmer?"

Brother Petrán shook his head immediately.

"He came from a small fishing community, islanders, who believe that it is wiser not to know how to swim for it is best to be drowned outright, falling into heavy, merciless seas, than prolonging the agony and torture of the body and soul by vain struggle."

Fidelma suppressed a shiver at the idea.

"I have heard the philosophy although I do not agree with it. Was there no one else who came except the apothecary?"

"No one."

"Do you know how long Brother Eolang had been in the water?"

"I do not. But the apothecary, Brother Cruinn said . . ."

Fidelma held up her hand to silence him.

"Perhaps we should leave Brother Cruinn to recount what he said," she advised. "You can only give evidence as to your own views."

Brother Petrán's glance wandered past her shoulder and focussed.

"Then there is no better opportunity to hear his words for here is Brother Cruinn."

Fidelma turned and saw an elderly man coming through the garden. He was strongly built, the arms of his robe rolled up around the elbows showing strong, muscular forearms. His hair was grey and eyes deep blue. He seemed puzzled at seeing the female religious in the herb garden.

Brother Petrán introduced her and the apothecary's face relaxed.

"I was the one who noticed that this was no mere drowning, Sister," he said with complacency. "Poor Eolang. He assisted me as apothecary, you know."

"Perhaps you will accompany me to the wooden pier and explain, on the way, the circumstances which aroused your suspicions?"

They left the herb garden and passed through a small door in a high stone wall which led immediately onto the bank of the island. Fidelma saw that the lake was very wide at this point. The pier, standing on wooden piles was certainly old. Some of the planking was rotten and did not seem secure.

"This is in need of repair," Fidelma commented.

"Indeed. It is only used for landing materials for our garden. The primary landing stage is at the main gate as you will have doubtless observed when you arrived."

"Was there a specific reason why Brother Eolang was here?"

The apothecary rubbed his chin.

"He had gone out in the boat that morning to deliver something to the mainland and so, I presume, he was returning it so that Brother Petrán could use it to go to the market. Brother Petrán found his *marsupium*, his purse, still in the boat."

"His purse was found in the boat?"

"He had probably forgotten it when he climbed onto the pier."

"I understand that Brother Petrán retrieved the body of Brother Eolang from the water and then you answered his cries for assistance. Is that so?"

"I heard Brother Petrán from the herb garden and came straightaway," confirmed Brother Cruinn. "I saw immediately that poor Eolang was dead."

"How long had he been dead? Could you tell?"

"I am proficient in my work, Sister." The apothecary was proud of his professional capabilities which made him sound a trifle haughty in manner. "He had not been dead long. The blood was still flowing from the wound on his forehead and that was when I realized that murder had been committed."

"Because of the wound? What was it like."

"It was on the forehead, between the eyes. It was clear that someone had picked up a cudgel of some sort and smote the brother who fell into the water and drowned."

"And had you heard the story of how Brother Eolang had predicted that he would be murdered on that day?"

Brother Cruinn shook his head firmly.

"It was only afterwards that I learnt this story from Brother Senach."

"But you worked with him. He was your assistant apothecary. Is it not strange that he did not mention this prediction?"

"He knew my views. I knew of Eolang's reputation as an astrologer. Personally, I did not think much of it. I am a practical man but there are many in my profession who use it as an aid to their medical arts. However, it seems that this time, Eolang was right."

"This time?" queried Fidelma.

Brother Cruinn smiled deprecatingly.

"I have known many of Eolang's predictions to fail. That is probably why he did not raise the matter of the prediction with me."

Fidelma nodded thoughtfully.

She made her way back to the chamber of Brother Cass, the steward of the community, and found him in conversation again with Brehon Gormán.

"Have you sent for the messenger of the King of Cashel to hear his evidence?" she asked the Brehon without preamble.

Brehon Gormán looked bewildered.

"The man on horseback who drew Brother Petrán's attention to the body," she explained impatiently.

"Oh, that man? How did you find out he was a King's messenger?" He paused at her expression and then added defensively: "I did not think his evidence would be relevant. After all, we have evidence enough about the incident."

Fidelma scowled in annoyance.

"Don't you realise that he might have witnessed the entire incident?" She turned to Brother Cass. "You must send another messenger to Cashel immediately to find this man. He is one of the King's messengers so his identify should be easy to discover. He must be brought here as an important witness." She turned on her heel but at the door she paused and glanced back at the scowling Brehon and then looked at the unhappy steward. "I shall expect my orders to be carried out, Brother Cass. I shall now speak with the abbot."

Abbot Rígán was, at first meeting, a likable man; friendly, concerned and bewildered at the situation in which he found himself. Only after talking to him for a time, did Fidelma find that he was, indeed, rigid in his beliefs and a passionate supporter of the Roman Rule of the Faith.

"Did you killed Brother Eolang?" Fidelma demanded in opening the conversation after she had introduced herself.

"As God is my witness, I did not," replied the abbot solemnly.

"Have you heard the nature of the evidence against you?"

"It is ridiculous! Surely no reasonable person would countenance such evidence as worth considering."

"Brehon Gormán does. There is much to be explain in that evidence. Over a week ago Brother Eolang foretold that on such a day he would be killed by either drowning or poisoning. No one can deny that he did die in such circumstances."

The abbot was silent.

"Brother Eolang said that if that circumstance happen, you would be responsible for his death."

"But that is rubbish."

"The Brehon says that if one part of the prediction is true, why not the other?"

"I refuse to answer the prattling of superstition."

"I am told, Father Abbot, that you and Brother Eolang were not friends. That you criticized him because he practised astrology. Superstition, as you have just called it."

Abbot Rígán nodded emphatically.

"Doesn't Deuteronomy say—"Nor must you raise your eyes to the heavens and look up to the sun, the moon, and the stars, all the host of heaven, and be led on to bow down to them and worship them . . . ?" "

Fidelma inclined her head.

"I know the passage. Our astrologers would say that they do not worship the stars, but are guided by their patterns for that very passage of Deuteronomy continues where you left off ". . . the Lord your God created these for the various peoples under heaven." If He created them, why should we be afraid to follow their guidance?"

The abbot sniffed disparagingly.

"You have a quick tongue, Sister. But it is clear that God forbade star worship. Jeremiah says "do not be awed by signs in the heavens" . . ."

"Our astrologers would say that they don't worship the stars. They would point out that Jeremiah is actually admitting that there are, indeed, signs in the heavens and he merely admonishes us not to be awed by them with the implication we should understand them and learn by them."

"Not at all!" snapped the abbot. "Isaiah says: —

Let your astrologers, your star-gazes
who foretell your future month by month,
persist, and save you!
But look, they are gone like chaff;
fire burns them up . . .

"Isaiah was addressing the Babylonians during the exile of the Israelites in Babylon. Naturally, he would belittle their leaders. The point is, abbot, whether you like it or not, astrology accuses you and astrology must, therefore, defend you."

"I will not be defended by that which my Faith denies."

"Then you cannot be defended at all," said Fidelma, rising. "If a man comes with a stick to beat you, would you say that I will not defend myself for that man has no right to use that stick as a weapon?"

She was at the door when the abbot coughed nervously. She turned back expectantly.

"In what way would you defend me?" he muttered.

"Where were you when Eolang was drowned?" she asked.

"That morning I was engaged in the accounts of the community. Our brethren make leather goods and sell them and thus we are able to sustain our little community."

"Was anyone with you?"

Abbot Rígán shrugged.

"I was alone all morning until Brother Cass came to report the finding of Brother Eolang to me. I detected a strange atmosphere in the community for I was unaware of this nonsense about a prediction. I was therefore surprised when Brother Cass informed me that he had already sent for a Brehon based on information he had received. I was more surprised when the Brehon arrived and I found myself accused of killing Eolang."

"The prediction is damning," pointed out Fidelma.

"Could it be that Brother Eolang killed himself to spite me?"

"In my experience, suicides do not hit themselves over the head and drown nor is spite considered a sufficient motive for killing oneself."

"It sounds as if you believe this prediction and therefore my guilt."

"My task, Father Abbot, is to investigate the facts and if the facts show you to be guilty, then my oath as a *dálaigh* forbids me hide your guilt from the court. My task would only be to explain any special circumstances which caused your guilt. A *dálaigh* cannot intentionally protect the guilty before the courts. But, I emphasise, judgment must be based on facts."

When the abbot tried to speak again she raised her hand to silence him.

"At the moment, I have no judgment one way or the other. I have a suspicion of what happened but I cannot prove my suspicion before the Brehon. I am not, therefore, in full possession of the facts."

Twenty-four hours had to pass before Brother Cass announced that his messengers were returning from Cashel.

Sister Fidelma went to the main gate to watch the boat crossing the lake towards the pier. Her sharp eyes immediately spotted the bent figure of the elderly Brother Conchobar in the stern of the boat. Her anxious eyes found a second figure, a young warrior, seated next to him.

"Brother Conchobar, I am glad that you have come," she greeted as they stepped ashore.

The old man smiled, a slow, sad smile.

"I heard of your curious case from the messenger you sent. This is Ferchar, by the way."

The young warrior bowed to Fidelma. He did not forget that Fidelma was sister to the King of Cashel.

"Lady, I heard that the man drowned. I am sorrowful that I was not able to do anything more than I did. Alas, it was too far for me to swim across the lake to his rescue."

Fidelma glanced anxiously from Ferchar to Conchobar as a thought struck her.

"Have either of you discussed this matter with one another on your journey here?"

Brother Conchobar shook his head. It was Ferchar who answered.

"Lady, we know that the method of giving evidence says that no witnesses may confer with another about the event. We have kept our silence on this matter."

One of the brethren, whom Brother Cass had sent to bring them to the abbey, came forward.

"I can swear to this before the Brehon if need be, Sister. These men have not spoken of the matter since we found them and brought them hither."

"Excellent," Fidelma was relieved. "Come with me."

Fidelma led them to Brother Cass's chamber where Brehon Gormán was waiting impatiently.

"This judgment on this matter has been delayed a full twenty-four hours. I hope this has not been a waste of time."

"Justice, as you must known, Brehon Gormán, is never a waste of time. I have asked Brother Conchobar to wait outside while we now hear from an eyewitness."

She motioned to Ferchar.

Brehon Gormán examined the young warrior.

"State your name and position."

"I am Ferchar of the bodyguard of King Colgú and act as his messenger."

"What is your evidence in the matter of the murder of Brother Eolang?"

Ferchar looked puzzled and Fidelma intervened.

"He means the death of Brother Eolang, the brother found by the pier."

Brehon Gormán scowled in annoyance at her correction.

"That is what I meant," he said tightly.

"I was riding along the shore on my way to Cashel," began Ferchar.

"Across, on the island, I saw a religieux mooring his boat at the end of one of the side piers of the abbey."

"I do not think we need bring forward evidence that this was Brother Eolang bringing the boat to the herb garden pier where he was found," intervened Fidelma.

Brehon Gormán motioned Ferchar to continue with an impatient gesture.

"The religieux had moored the boat and was walking along the pier when it seemed that he stopped abruptly and turned back to the boat. This meant that he was facing toward me. Then, curiously, he started back as if something had stopped him. I heard a crack. He staggered back and fell off the edge of the pier. I started shouting to attract attention. I shouted for some minutes and then I saw another religieux exit from a gate. He heard my voice but I doubt if he heard my words. I gestured to where the religieux had fallen in. He must have seen him for he waved acknowledgement and jumped in and started to haul the body to the shore. Seeing that another religieux had arrived, and that there was nothing else I could do, I continued on my journey, not realising in that short time, the first religieux had met his death."

"Are you sure there was no one else around at the time the religieux fell into the water? The religieux was by himself on the pier?"

"No one else was there," affirmed Ferchar.

"But you heard a crack?" intervened Brehon Gormán.

"I did. Like a branch breaking."

"Perhaps someone had cast a spear at him to make him fall back or . . . yes, a sling shot perhaps?" suggested the Brehon.

"He was facing towards me on the shore. The distance was too far to cast a sling shot nor any other weapon. No, there was no one around when the man fell into the lake."

"Are you claiming that this was the act of some supernatural force?" demanded the Brehon turning to Fidelma. "What of the prediction? You cannot explain away the accuracy of the prediction."

Fidelma smiled at Ferchar.

"Wait outside and ask Brother Conchobar to enter."

A moment later the old man did so and Fidelma asked the Brehon to spread the astrological chart before him.

"Conchobar will you examine this chart and give me your advice?" she invited.

The old man nodded and took the chart from her hands. He spent some time pouring over it and then he looked up.

"It is a good chart. A professional one."

Brehon Gormán smiled approvingly.

"You agree, then, learned Conchobar with the conclusions of Eolang?"

"Most things are correct . . ." agreed the old man.

Fidelma could see the Brehon's smile broaden but Brother Conchobar was continuing.

". . . except one important point. Brother Eolang appears to have predicted that within a week following his drawing and judging his horary question that he would die. It would happen on the day that Mercury and Jupiter perfected conjunction."

"Exactly. The first day of the month of Aibreán. And that was the very day and that he was killed, exactly as he predicted," the Brehon confirmed. "You cannot deny that."

The old man tapped on the chart with his finger, shaking his head.

"The error, however, is that he failed to note that Mercury turned direct a few hours later and never perfected the conjunction. Brehon, as you have some knowledge of the art, you should know that we call this phenomenon refranation. Alas, I have seen this carelessness, this overlooking of such an important fact, among many astrologers. To give Brother Eolang his due, perhaps he was too confused and worried to sit and spend time calculating the planetary movements accurately."

"But he was accurate. He did indeed die on the predicted day. How do you explain it?" protested Brehon Gormán.

"But he was not murdered," insisted Brother Conchobar. "The chart does not show it."

'Then how can it be explained?' demanded the Brehon in bewilderment. "How did he die?"

Fidelma intervened with a smile.

"If you come with me, I will show you what happened."

At the end of the old pier, Fidelma paused.

"Brother Eolang brought the boat to the end of the pier. He

climbed onto the pier and started to head to the abbey. He forgot something in the boat. His *marsupium* to be exact. This was found by Brother Petrán later. So, halfway along the pier, he turned back for it. This much did our friend, Ferchar, observe from the far shore."

There was a murmur of agreement from Ferchar.

"Now, look at the condition of the planks on the pier. Some are rotten, some are not nailed down. He stepped sharply towards the boat and . . ."

Fidelma turned, examined the planking critically for a moment, stepped sharply on one. The far end rose with a cracking noise and she had to step swiftly aside to avoid being hit by it as it flew up into the air. She turned back triumphantly to the onlookers.

"Brother Eolang was hit by the end of the plank between the eyes, causing the wounds found by the apothecary. It also knocked him unconscious and he fell back into the water. Drowning does not have to be a long process. By the time he was hauled out of the water he was dead."

"Then the prediction. . . . ?" began the bewildered Brehon.

"Was false. It was an accident. It was nobody's fault."

Sometime later as Ferchar, Conchobar and Fidelma were being rowed back to the mainland, the old astrologer turned to Fidelma with a lopsided smile.

"I can't help thinking that had Brother Eolang been a better astrologer, he would have made a correct prediction. It was all there, danger of death from water and he was accurate as to the day such danger would occur."

Fidelma nodded thoughtfully.

"The fault was that Brother Eolang, like our friend, Brehon Gormán, believed that the patterns of the stars absolved man from using his free will; that man no longer had choice and that everything was predestined. That is not how the ancients taught the art of *nemgnacht*."

Brother Conchobar nodded approvingly.

"So you do remember what I taught you?"

"You taught that there are signs that serve as warnings and give us information from which the wise can make decisions. They are options, possibilities from which we may select choices. The new

learning from the east seems more fatalistic. Even the Christian teachings of Augustine of Hippo would have it that everything is predestined. That is why I am more happy with the teachings of Pelagius."

"Even though Augustine's supporters have sneered at Pelagius as
being "full of Irish porridge?" "

"Better Irish porridge than blind prejudice."

Brother Conchobar chuckled.

"Have a care, Fidelma, lest you be accused of a pagan heresy!"

# THE EYE OF THE BEHOLDER

## Lillian Stewart Carl

BY THE TIME Jake turned into the driveway the bombs were already falling. He stood beside the car and watched the flashes play along the bottom of the clouds like lightning. It was going to rain again — the wind was gusty, damp, scented with earth, weighing down the collar of his uniform. But lightning? No. The Luftwaffe was hammering the shipyards at Bristol again.

Not that he could do anything about it, not now. He stabbed his cane into the mud. The movement jolted the patchwork that was his gut and he winced. He should be glad he was out of it, safe, tucked away at this old house in the Somerset countryside. He should be glad to be alive.

The conical shape of Glastonbury Tor stood in black outline against the distant fiery glow. Jake had crawled like a worm along the dark, narrow roads to get from there to here. He could've flown those few miles in seconds.

He felt again the throb of his Spitfire, full throttle, nose up, the patterns of fields and roads falling away behind him and clouds streaming over the wings — he'd break free of earth and cloud alike and see the stars strewn across the night sky, constellations marching from horizon to horizon — the sound of his engines, of his thoughts, would be lost in the mighty vastness. . . . He crash-landed in his own present.

He'd drunk too much scrumpy cider in Glastonbury, Jake told himself. The Brits hadn't been joking, it was powerful stuff.

The surrounding trees creaked and thrashed in the wind. Cold rain sifted down on his face. Awkwardly he felt his way up the unlit steps and opened the front door of the house. Once a butler had answered this door. Now Jake was greeted by the acrid hospital smell of disinfectant and overcooked cabbage.

A musical feminine voice asked, "Did you enjoy your leave?"

He looked around. There was the one bright spot in this dark, cold, wet, besieged country. Nurse O'Neill. Bridget. Tonight the starched wings of her cap contained her tightly-bound red hair. Last night, during her birthday party, her hair had tumbled down over her shoulders and he'd caught a flowery whiff more intoxicating than any alcohol.

"I'd have enjoyed my leave a lot more if you'd come along," he told her with a smile. "Country boys like me, we need native guides."

"You manage well enough, I'm thinking."

Jake could see her breath leaving her parted pink lips. He leaned forward. "All those narrow lanes, night coming on fast—I was expecting a Roman soldier or a medieval knight to step out in front of me."

"I shouldn't be surprised to see one myself, not here."

"The car heater was acting up. Feel my hands." He grasped her warm hands with his icy ones.

She pulled hers away, but not very quickly. "You're thinking it's cold? Just you wait, it's autumn now, winter's round the bend. . . ."

"Well, well, well." Harry Davenport's nasal bray echoed from the high ceiling.

Bridget's face went rigid and she stepped back abruptly. She hasn't done anything wrong, Jake told himself. I'll be damned if I'll let anyone make her feel like she's done something wrong.

Harry's nose and teeth thrust forward like a predator's. A red scar creased one cheek. "So you fancy foreigners like yourself, is that it, Bridget? Can't resist our Yank's Hollywood handsome face? No accounting for tastes, is there? But then, I hear beauty is in the eye of the beholder."

"And handsome is as handsome does." With a tart glance at Jake, Bridget walked off down the hall toward the kitchen.

Harry's dark beads of eyes followed her. Jake stepped in front of him. "She told you last night she wasn't interested."

"Why should I be interested in her, she's nothing but a bog-trotter's daughter." Harry pivoted on his crutch and started heaving himself up the staircase, one thudding step at a time.

Jake wanted to shout after him, *Pick on someone your own size.* But the other airmen were already Harry's favorite targets, like Taffy with his Welsh accent and tin ear, and serious, literal-minded Dicky.

Jake took off his coat. Outside a rush of wind threw raindrops like shrapnel against the mahogany panels of the door. The fanlight was blocked by cardboard. The marble flooring of the entrance hall would have gleamed if it hadn't been smudged by muddy footprints—and if more than two bulbs of the chandelier had been lit.

This was a hell of a place, Jake thought, and amended, had been a hell of a place. Now the carved wood and marble trim was roughly boxed in. Now pale rectangles on the wallpaper were the ghosts of paintings taken away for safekeeping. Anthony Jenkins-Ashe was trying to preserve his ancestral home. He'd told Jake his family had lived at Lydford Hall for centuries.

Jake had grown up in a bungalow in Kansas City and was hard-pressed to name his grandparents. While the other airmen might call the elderly estate owner "Dotty Andy," Jake found him both educational and entertaining—not least because he refused to let anyone call him "My lord" or "his lordship" or however a baronet was supposed to be addressed.

Jake pulled a paper and twine-wrapped package out of his coat pocket and headed for the back parlor that was now Andy's sole domain. He knocked. After a long moment Andy's reedy voice answered, "Come."

The room was cold and dark. A small fire provided the only light. The old man would rather strain his eyes than close the blackout curtains, even though tonight his view was of blank darkness. His chair sat on the hearth, so close to the fire that the flames illuminated the hills and furrows of his face as harshly as the folds in his old tweed suit. He was scraping the mud off a boot.

"Have you studied Herodotus?" Andy asked. " 'In peace, children inter their parents; war violates the order of nature and causes parents to inter their children.' "

He was thinking of his son, dead at Dunkirk. "I was scheduled for a classics seminar," Jake answered. "Then the war started, and suddenly history and literature seemed mighty useless."

"Useless? No, history and literature are never useless. Glastonbury, now, is proof of that."

"It's an interesting little town with a heck of a history—I looked at some of the books while I was waiting for the clerk to fill your order. Here you go." Jake handed over the package.

Andy put the boot down next to his rack of pipes and used his knife to cut the twine. "Thank you, Pilot Officer Houston. Very kind of you."

"Seems only fair, I was using your car."

"The car belongs to the hospital now. There's a war on." Paper rustled and Andy held two books to the firelight.

Jake squinted at their spines—*The Company of Avalon* by Frederick Bligh Bond and *The High History of the Holy Grail*. Those names were vaguely familiar, which was more than he could say of most of Andy's books. He'd barely heard of heraldry and astrology and De-Brett's Peerage before he'd come here.

With a weary sigh Andy stacked the books by his chair, next to his omnipresent notebook and pen, and picked up the boot again. "Please, sit down."

Jake glanced over his shoulder, but Bridget was probably back under Matron's watchful eye. He pulled up a footstool and lowered himself onto it. The wind whistled a low note in the chimney and rain streamed down the windows. "Did you get out for your walk this afternoon? Find any more Roman ruins?"

"Perhaps a trace or two by the Brue, between the bridge and the apple orchard. If this rain ever lets up I'll give you a tour. Although we're unlikely to see any improvement so late in the year. It's the equinox, you know. Virgo giving way to Libra . . . What is that commotion? Are they playing cricket in the gallery again?"

Voices spoke urgently in the distance. Footsteps drummed overhead. A door slammed. "I don't think so," Jake answered. "I'll take a look."

He got up, opened the door, and peered out. Now several voices were talking at once. Foggy Dewar was stumping along the hall as though he was working his way through deep mud. "What's happened?" Jake called.

"Another poor sod's bought it. Randy last week and now . . ." Foggy disappeared around the corner.

Hell, Jake told himself. Losing a colleague on the mend was worse than losing him in the midst of battle.

Behind him Andy said quietly, "Fate can be cruel, can't it? Damnable war, too many young men lost."

Jake agreed, but he didn't see any way of stopping the war other than sacrificing even more men. With a half-salute to Andy, he followed Foggy toward the library.

Its double door was clotted with his fellow patients. Using his cane, Jake levered himself high enough to see Doc Skelton, the flight surgeon, kneeling on the floor. "Yes, he's dead. Has been for over an hour."

A murmur ran through the group. Jake pushed his way through the gathered men until he could see Bridget. She was standing alone next to the massive Victorian desk. Her normally rosy cheeks were pasty white and her arms were laced across her chest.

Skelton stood up and brushed off his trousers. He turned toward the door, shoulders coiled and head down like a bull searching for a china shop. "As you've no doubt noticed, gentlemen, his head's been bashed right in, by that bit of sculpture, I should think. He was murdered."

*Murdered.* Jake's mind tripped over the word and went sprawling. In the sudden silence he could hear the wind howling outside, rain sluicing down the tall windows behind the heavy black curtains, and the ragged breaths of the men around him. Then someone swore, softly. Each airman inched a bit farther away from the man he was standing next to and Jake found himself popped like a cork into the library.

Stretched out on the bare planks of the floor lay Dicky Richardson. A rust-red puddle pillowed his head and his blond hair was mottled with crimson. His face was as white and still as the plaster cast on his left arm. His blue eyes looked purple. Maybe, Jake thought, they'd stared yearningly into the sky so long they'd bruised.

A fist-sized lump of gray stone lay between Dicky and the desk. Even in the dim light Jake could see the half-dozen drops of blood spattering its weathered surface.

He braced himself on his cane. Dicky. He'd liked Dicky, even though the man had no sense of humor. Which was hardly reason to murder him.

So what, then, would be enough reason to murder him? Or anyone, for that matter? Hadn't there been enough death already? Jake looked up at Bridget. She bit her lip, and for just a moment fear dulled her eyes.

"Has anyone been seen going into or coming out of the library in the last hour?" asked Skelton. "Save Nurse O'Neill, who fetched me."

Some of the men looked off into space, some at the floor, some at each other. No one answered.

"Has anyone had a row with Richardson, lent him money, anything of that nature?"

Silence.

"Right. Houston?" Skelton pronounced it "Hooston," like everyone except Andy, who knew better, and Bridget, who'd asked.

Reluctantly Jake turned away from her. "Sir?"

"You were on leave."

"Yes, sir."

"When did you get in?"

"Fifteen minutes ago. Maybe twenty."

"Anyone see you?"

"Yes, why?"

"Because it appears you're the only person in the house who couldn't have done Richardson here in. He died whilst you were away."

"Twig and I've been playing cards all evening," said Epsom, his moustache bristling.

Foggy added quickly, "I've been reading, Taffy looked in on me."

Harry's voice overrode the others. "A bit hard to sneak up on a chap and bash him when you're lumbered with a bloody great crutch, isn't it?"

"No one here is incapacitated," Skelton told him.

Jake nodded. "And the wind is noisy enough to hide footsteps."

"Very observant," said Harry acidly.

Matron thrust her way through the door, parting the men with her cantilevered bosom like a ship's bow parting the waves. A clean white sheet hung from her arm. "I phoned for the police, but the line's dead. A tree's gone down in the storm, I expect. Good job the electricity's from our own generator. I've sent the orderly with the car round by West Pennard, in case the road's blocked or the bridge over the Brue is awash."

"Slow going, but needs must," said Skelton.

Taffy asked, "What if the orderly's the murderer?"

"Then he'll be in the hands of the police, won't he?" Matron beckoned to Bridget. "Come along, Nurse."

"Aren't you going to pick him up and lay him out properly?" asked Foggy.

Skelton shook his head. "The police will want to see him like this."

The women unfolded the sheet, stretched it out over Dicky's body like a canopy, then lowered it. His outstretched arm and hand lay at an angle to his torso and Bridget bent down to pull the fabric over them. She looked like a ministering angel in a Renaissance manuscript, Jake thought. . . . "Wait a minute. What's he holding?"

Skelton brushed Bridget aside, knelt, and inspected the tightly curled fingers of Dicky's right hand. "A pen. His fingers have ink on them. Was he writing something?"

Jake walked the dozen paces to the desk. A bottle of ink stood in the center of the blotter, its lid beside it. Next to that lay a partly crumpled piece of paper. When he smoothed it out Jake saw several smudges looking like badly-drawn heiroglyphs straggling across its top. The only words he could read were "Lydford" and "suspected t . . . ," the rest of the word trailing away and ending in a blotch. The letter "B" nestled beside another blotch.

"Dicky was left-handed," said Bridget at his shoulder. "He was learning to use his right, but still I was writing the letters home to his mum."

"This one he wanted to write himself," Jake said, handing the paper to Skelton.

"Lydford," Skelton read aloud. "Suspected, followed by a word beginning with T. Another word beginning with B. Anyone have any idea what he was on about?"

Jake looked back at the men crowding the door. Funny how clear his mind was now, the last vapors of the cider burned away. He saw each face as clearly as a dial on his control panel. Everyone's expression ranged from puzzled to blank except for Twig's and Harry's.

It was, of course, Harry who spoke up. "The word is traitor. A suspected traitor."

"Traitor?" Matron repeated.

"Out with it, man," ordered Skelton.

Harry drew himself up, the center of attention. "Last night, after the party for Nurse O'Neill, Dicky said he suspected someone here of handing information to the Nazis."

"Too much to hope he gave you a name?" Jake asked, wondering whether Harry's sneer had made his face look like a gargoyle's even before it was scarred.

"He started to do, then was interrupted when Matron called lights-out."

"Harry's having us on, isn't he?" Taffy's freckled face peered over his neck brace like a fox from his hole. "He was always having Dicky on, Dicky being such an easy target and all—positively gullible at times."

"No," said Twig, shuffling forward. "I heard what Dicky said, too. He had evidence of a traitor at Lydford Hall."

Jake exchanged a look with Skelton. The doctor knew as well as he did that Twig was a former divinity student who made George Washington look like a liar and a cheat.

"B." Skelton repeated reflectively. "That might be the initial of a name. The person Richardson suspected."

"It's bleeding obvious, isn't it?" demanded Harry. "B as in Bridget. Bridget O'Neill. She's the traitor."

Jake stepped forward, his fist already raised. "Why you . . .'"

"Steady on," murmured Skelton.

Bridget's slender body swayed. Jake thought she was going to fall back against the desk and changed course. But she caught herself.

The look she shot toward Harry would've disintegrated anyone made of flesh and blood.

"Think," Harry went on. "She found Randy dead last week, didn't she? Lying in the bathroom, not a mark on him. She's the one goes about with tablets and injections—what if she slipped him a few grams of poison?"

"Pilot Officer Randolph had two broken femurs," said Matron, stepping closer to Bridget. "The cause of death was a pulmonary fat embolism."

"Are you questioning my competence?" demanded Skelton.

Harry plunged on. "And today Bridget finds Dicky."

"I'm a nurse," said Bridget. "My job is watching the patients."

"So she watches well enough she catches Dicky writing a letter that'll expose her for what she is. You said yourself, Tex, normally she'd be writing his letters for him, but this one he was writing on his own."

"My name isn't Tex," Jake said. "And it's bleeding obvious to anyone with half a brain that just because Dicky wanted to keep his suspicions to himself doesn't mean he suspected Brid—Nurse O'Neill. Unless you planted the whole idea in his mind to begin with, as another of your stupid jokes. Maybe you wanted to get back at her because she refused your advances."

"And accepted yours?" asked Harry.

Matron shot a swift look at Bridget, who suddenly grew very interested in her shoes.

"No," Jake snapped. "There's nothing between us."

Harry's voice was taking on the same shrill note as the sound of the wind in the chimney. "She's a foreigner, just like you are. Worse. She's Irish. Ireland's sitting out the war. It's not only letting the side down, it's filthy with Nazi sympathizers who'd do anything, commit any crime, to defeat us."

Jake wanted to reach out and pry Bridget's fingernails loose from where they were sunk into her palms, but he didn't dare touch her. Was that what frightened her, that Harry's constant slanders about her homeland would eventually stick? "America's not in the war, either," he said. "Are you accusing us of being a fifth column, too?"

Harry made a dismissive gesture that was almost an obscene one. Jake doubled his fist again. He'd knock the chip off the man's shoulder whether he was wounded or not.

Skelton stepped between them. "Stop it. We're getting nowhere with this. The police have been notified, they'll sort it."

"She needs locking up," said Harry, pointing his crutch at Bridget. "In the linen closet or pantry, so she'll keep. The police'll take her away, and good riddance."

Frowning, Matron took Bridget's arm. "We'll sit in my room and have ourselves a cuppa, won't we? Come along."

With a look over her shoulder at Jake—whether pleading for help or warning him to keep out of it, he couldn't tell—Bridget let herself be led away. The police, he thought. The police might well take Harry's accusations seriously. Everyone in the country was damned touchy right now. And with Hitler's armies poised right across the Channel, who could blame them? But if Bridget was arrested, no matter how quickly she was cleared, she'd have a blot on her record dark enough to cost her not only this job but any other one. That wasn't right.

Not that Dicky's death was right, Jake told himself, not by a long shot.

"The rest of you lot, clear off!" directed Skelton.

The other men shuffled away silently, burdened by deep and discomforting thought. With one last glare over his shoulder, Harry brought up the rear.

Bridget hasn't done anything wrong, Jake told himself. I'll be damned if I'll let anyone make her feel like she's done something wrong. . . . Skelton was looking at him, waiting for him to leave, too. He wanted to lock up the room.

"Sir," Jake said, "sir, you said yourself I couldn't be the murderer. Let me stay here, look the place over, see if I can come up with something that'll exonerate Nurse O'Neill. The evidence against her is no more than prejudice and coincidence."

"You rather fancy Nurse O'Neill, do you, Houston?" Skelton allowed himself a thin smile. "But yes, you could well be quite correct about coincidence. And the prejudice as well, sadly, although you have to recognize that we have our backs to the wall just now, which does rather alter one's viewpoint."

"Yes sir. I understand. Just give me until the police come."

"Very good then. I'd hate to lose Nurse O'Neill."

"Just one thing, sir. Do you have a copy of the roster—a list of . . ." Jake almost said "inmates," ". . . patients and staff both?"

"The initial B, is that it?" Skelton reached into his breast pocket, pulled out a small notebook, and tore off a page. "There you are. You have one thing on your side, Houston—we discharged a group of patients last week and several staff are on leave, so there aren't many people here tonight."

"And I have one thing working against me. Time. Thank you, sir. I'll do my best."

"Lock up when you've finished." With a firm nod, Skelton walked across to the doorway and pulled the double doors shut behind him.

Jake turned in a slow circle, trying to see the familiar room with new eyes. The library had been his sanctuary against the outside darkness both literal and figurative. He'd spent many hours here, reading and writing letters and listening to Andy's half-baked but always interesting musings—*the fault, my lad, is not in ourselves but in our stars*. Now the comforting smell of books, paper and ink with an afterglow of mildew, was overwhelmed by the reek of mortality.

Between the books the shelves were cluttered with Andy's collection of art and artifacts—a bust of Athena, a set of apothecary's scales with a stuffed dove nestling in one bowl, a model ship, a Roman amphora. Several of his rolled-up maps lay on the mantel. . . . Andy. After he looked over the library he'd talk to Andy. If the old man had just come in from his daily walk maybe he'd seen or heard something.

Jake leaned up against the desk and unfolded Skelton's list. Of course Skelton himself might be the murderer. While it was stretching it a bit to think a doctor would kill one of his own patients, if Skelton was the traitor then he'd have a motive to kill. Assuming Dicky actually had reason to suspect a traitor. As much as Jake wanted to think the entire scenario was another of Harry's malicious jokes, he couldn't see how a joke would lead to murder. Neither could he see Harry himself killing Dicky, more's the pity.

And what information would a traitor find at Lydford Hall, anyway? Killing off a few recuperating airmen wouldn't damage the war effort.

He read down the list, looking for names beginning with B. No, Skelton's first name was Trevor, for what that was worth. Matron was Geraldine White. The orderly was William Graves. . . . Someone named William was often nicknamed Bill, but Jake couldn't remember hearing anyone ever call him that.

The Brits with their mania for multiple names. Harry wasn't the only one who called Jake "Tex," even though the closest he'd ever been to Texas was Tulsa. His surname was Houston, that was enough. At least Tex was better than some of the others' nicknames, which made them sound like characters in a Wodehouse comedy—Epsom Downs, Foggy Dewar, Twig Smallwood, Taffy Evans. Harry Davenport should've been "Sofa," Jake supposed. But then, no one liked Harry well enough to give him a nickname.

Jake glanced down at Dicky's shrouded shape. He was—had been—a big man. Jake had often wondered how he managed to pleat himself into a cockpit. Now he was no more than a pile of meat to be disposed of. If he owed Bridget the truth, Jake told himself, then he owed Dicky, too.

He looked at the list. Dicky's name was Donald Richardson—not that he'd have been writing about himself. The only "B" on the list besides Bridget was Twig, whose name was Bernard. Even if he could believe Twig was a spy and traitor, which he didn't, Jake knew the man had only to keep his mouth shut about Dicky's suspicions and every one else would've discounted Harry's wild story as just that.

Jake folded the paper into his pocket. The storm seemed to have eased a bit—at least the wind was moaning rather than howling and the rain was more a patter than a roar. A draft played along the floor, stirring the edge of the sheet and exposing Dicky's clenched hand. Jake shivered. From the cold, he assured himself. The fire inside the massive fireplace with its marble mantelpiece had died down, not that it had been very big to begin with. Looking into that fire Jake could see burning cities, exploding flak, Spitfires spiraling down into the cool but unforgiving water of the Channel. He'd sat in the pub in Glastonbury staring into its fire and seeing the same visions. The pictures weren't in the fire at all, were they, but in his own mind.

The small stone—the murder weapon—lay on the floor. Jake knew what it was, a lion's head from Glastonbury Abbey that usually sat on the desk. Andy had rescued it from a spoils heap when he was helping with the excavations before the war. The first war.

And that, realized Jake, was where he'd heard the name on one of Andy's books. Frederick Bligh Bond had been the archaeologist in charge of the excavations. He'd been discredited in later years for saying the spirits of dead monks had told him where to dig.

Painfully Jake lowered himself down beside the sculpture. Except for the flecks of blood the stone looked all right, not damaged at all. Andy wouldn't be happy one of his prized possessions had been used to kill someone. He'd had a wooden pedestal made especially for that lion's head. . . . Jake glanced back at the desk. The pedestal and the sculpture had stood on the edge of the desk. Now the pedestal was lying on its side.

Cursing both the feeble light and his own injuries, Jake sat down on the floor and leaned as close as he could to the sculpture. Yes, it was spattered with a few drops of blood. But several drops lay on the floor as well. And as far as he could tell not one strand of hair clung to that rock, not one blood smear. What if it wasn't the murder weapon at all?

He clambered clumsily to his feet and peered down at the bottom edge of the desk. Yes, beside it lay a long triangle of clean wooden plank. The desk had been moved, very recently. And there—yes. The upper corner, closest to where the sculpture had stood, was sticky. The color of drying blood blended with the cherry wood so well it was almost invisible. But the two strands of blond hair that were matted in the sticky patch were apparent enough, if anyone looked.

Jake let himself down into the desk chair. That was it. Dicky hadn't been hit with the sculpture at all. He'd pitched forward for some reason, hitting his head on the corner of the desk. A sudden jolt could've both moved the desk and toppled the sculpture. Then, dazed, Dicky could've crawled a few paces and then collapsed. Head wounds bled profusely. When Dicky's head hit the floor blood spattered all around.

Jake supposed an autopsy would show that the indentation in Dicky's head was sharply angled, not rounded, to fit the corner of the desk but not the sculpture. Which was all well and good, except for one very important point. Unlike Harry, Foggy, or Jake himself, Dicky had been perfectly steady on his feet. Why had he fallen? Had he been knocked over in a struggle?

The door behind him burst open and Jake jumped, jamming his belly into the arm of the chair. The pain shot stars and comets across the room. When they cleared he saw Harry standing in front of him, wearing a triumphant smirk and holding out a piece of paper. On the whole, Jake thought, he'd rather have the stars and the stitch in his side. "What do you want?"

"I found this in the sideboard in the dining room. Dicky and I both saw Bridget put it there last night. I daresay he had himself a look after the party. Perfectly damning evidence against your little Irish . . ."

Jake lashed out with his cane, striking Harry across his good shin. He cried out, dropped the paper, and staggered backward to crash heavily against one of the bookcases. Several books fell to the floor.

Apologizing silently to the books, Jake leaned over and picked up the paper. On it was drawn a circle with lines radiating out from the center. Other lines angled across them. Letters and symbols were grouped in different sections. *Oh, for the love of. . . .*

"What's all this?" demanded Skelton from the doorway.

Harry's words came in staccato bursts, like a machine gun. "Bloody Yank tripped me up. Found proof that O'Neill is the traitor. Some sort of navigation chart. Guiding the Jerry bombers to Bristol. Maybe more. An invasion plan."

"This is perfectly innocent," Jake told them both. "It's not even Bridget's handwriting."

Skelton levered Harry away from the bookcase and draped him over his crutch. Then he took the paper from Jake's hand. "Whose handwriting is it, then?"

"It's Andy's. He cast her horoscope for her—her birthday was yesterday, remember?" Jake reached down and picked up one of the books that had slid to his feet. He opened it. Across the top of the flyleaf, in calligraphy worthy of a diploma, was written, *Anthony Jenkins-Ashe, Lord Brue.* He handed the book to Skelton. "You don't see penmanship like that any more."

"A horo-what?" asked Skelton, looking from the book to the drawing and back again.

"A horoscope's a way of predicting the future by charting where certain constellations were in the zodiac on the day someone was born. Like in the Bible, when the three wise men follow a special star to Bethlehem. Astrology's just a mathematical game, if you ask me, but Andy believes in it. He told me he knew he'd never see his son again because he read it in his horoscope, and that made his death easier to accept."

Skelton shook his head doubtfully. "Spiritualism?"

"No, he's not claiming he can communicate with the dead. He's claiming he can predict, maybe even control . . . Oh, hell." Jake suddenly remembered the purchase order he'd given the bookshop owner in Glastonbury, signed with just the one word, *Brue*. That was another of Andy's topics, how titles were based on landscape features. *Anthony Jenkins-Ashe, Lord Brue*.

He could see it all now, and he didn't like what he was seeing. "I remember reading an English history book when I was a kid, the author kept referring to Robert Dudley, Earl of Leicester, as both 'Dudley' and 'Leicester.' I thought he was talking about two different people. What I didn't think was that Dicky's 'B' could be Andy. But he always tried to call Andy by his title, didn't he? If he was referring to him in a letter he'd call him 'Brue.' "

Skelton leaned over and pulled the letter closer. "Yes, the word could be 'Brue,' right enough. Richardson may well have thought this, this horoscope business was something underhanded. He borrowed Andy's books, he'd recognize the handwriting."

Jake looked at the sheet laid so carefully over Dicky's body. Blood from the puddle on the floor was seeping through, staining the white linen with a brownish-red blotch. Dicky had been prepared to die for his country in battle. Even here he'd thought he was helping his country by turning in a traitor.

Harry kicked petulantly at the books lying at his feet. "Who's saying this horoscope rubbish isn't underhanded? Maybe the traitor isn't O'Neill—I'll reserve judgement on that—but what about Dotty Andy, eh? He's out and about the countryside every day, isn't he, always writing in that notebook of his, always at his maps. I shouldn't be a bit surprised if he is helping the enemy, him and his supernatural bunkum. The Nazis believe in the occult, don't they? Everyone knows that!"

"It doesn't follow that because Andy's interested in astrology he's a traitor!" Jake spat.

"I've said before and I'll say again," insisted Harry, "that there's something seriously wrong with that man. Wrong enough to sell us all out. Wrong enough to murder Dicky here."

Jake heaved himself to his feet and with his cane started pushing the fallen books into a pile. "Look. I don't think Dicky was murdered at all. He fell against the desk — see, how it's been moved? And there's blood and a couple of hairs on the corner. The sculpture fell over when the desk was pushed. Andy wasn't even here."

Skelton inspected the desk. "I see. Very good."

"So how did he fall, eh?" Harry asked.

"I don't . . ." Beside the book that lay next to the door were several little brown lumps. Jake slowly knelt next to them, but he already knew what they were. He picked up first one lump and then another, rubbing them between his fingers. His heart dived like a rudderless airplane.

"What do you have there?" asked Skelton.

"Bits of mud and leaf mold."

"Someone tracked it in from the outside, I expect."

Jake looked out the door. Footprints smudged the entrance hall, but he didn't see any between there and here. Only the suggestive little clots of mud, as though someone had put a pair of muddy boots down just inside the door. Put them down because they had to do something in the library.

Gritting his teeth, Jake pulled himself up. "I have to talk to Andy."

"Right," said Skelton. "I'll come along, shall I? No, Davenport, I'll see to it."

Jake could feel Harry's glower on the back of his neck as he and Skelton knocked on Andy's door. Again the old man's voice said, "Come."

He was still sitting by the fire, holding a rolled paper across his knees. The scent of tobacco smoke hung in the air and a ghostly wisp of it wafted across the silvery pale rectangles of the windows. The storm had passed, and the moon and the stars were starting to peek through the clouds. A full moon was a bomber's moon, Jake thought. Under the full moon no blackout could hide a target. Only camouflage could do that, making factories look like fields and gun emplacements like barns.

"I hope we're not intruding," Skelton said.

"Not at all," returned Andy. "Please, sit down."

Jake sat on his stool. With a sharp glance at Jake, Skelton moved Andy's clean boots aside and pulled up a light chair.

"Have to valet myself, don't you know," Andy explained. "There's a war on. Mustn't complain."

"Too many young men lost," Jake said quietly, repeating the words Andy had dismissed him with earlier. "Were you thinking of your son? Or were you thinking of someone else?"

Andy's face sagged as though pulled down by a heavy weight.

"You put your dirty boots down inside the library door," Jake went on. "What happened? Why is Dicky—Pilot Officer Richardson—why is he lying there dead?"

The dying fire crackled. Skelton's chair squeaked. Andy said slowly and precisely, "Upon returning from my walk, I wished to consult a reference book. When I pushed open the door of the library I saw Richardson sitting at the desk. He was muttering and splashing ink about, having a spot of bother, I expect, writing with his right hand and holding the paper steady with his left. I asked him if I could be of assistance. He crushed the paper, leapt from the chair, and spun round as though I'd shot him."

"Ah," said Skelton softly.

"Then he went positively ashen and toppled over, striking his head on the desk. I dropped my boots and hurried forward to help, but he propelled himself across the floor away from me. And then he collapsed, quite dead. Quite. Horribly. Dead." Andy closed his eyes. One bright teardrop traced a zigzag path down the creases in his cheek.

Skelton nodded. "Richardson was still convalescing. Leaping up in alarm like that caused his blood pressure to plummet. He blacked out briefly. Rotten luck he fell against the desk."

"Rotten luck he hadn't been taking Harry's spitefulness with a grain of salt, the way the rest of us have," Jake said. "You never looked at the letter he was writing, Andy?"

"Read another man's private correspondence? I should hope not!"

"Why didn't you fetch Matron or me as soon as it happened?" Skelton asked.

"Ah. Well then. . . ." Turning away from the fire, Andy drew his fragile body to attention. "I've been sitting here having a smoke and thinking it all over. I've decided I should put you in the picture. The full picture. You see, Richardson had one of my maps unrolled on the desk beside him, held open with one of my notebooks. He'd found both there in the library. I'm a bit disappointed that he'd take it upon himself to read them, but I imagine the other gentlemen's talk of 'Dotty Andy' and the like had piqued his curiosity."

"Not to say his suspicions," muttered Jake.

"Yes, his suspicions. What was he thinking, do you suppose? That I was making maps to guide the German bombers? An appalling misconception, if so, for I've been doing the exact opposite."

"I beg your pardon?" Skelton asked.

Andy's face struggled with several expressions, doubt, distress, determination. "I didn't tell you Richardson had been injured—had been killed—because I knew there'd be a lengthy investigation that would in all likelihood draw me away from Lydford tomorrow. Tomorrow being the equinox. Virgo is moving into Libra, you see. That segment of the zodiac must be walked."

"The zodiac," repeated Jake.

"I've hesitated to speak of it openly. Look what happened to Bligh Bond when he spoke of his spirit guides—he was removed from his position, completely discredited, left to die in shocking obscurity." Andy shook his head. "But personal considerations aside—and they must be put aside in wartime, mustn't they?—I had an even better reason for keeping my own counsel. While Richardson and Davenport had the wrong end of the stick in regard to my loyalty, in one area they were quite correct. Loose talk must be avoided. The more people who know about the Zodiac and the importance of the equinoctial walk, the more opportunity the enemy will have to hear of it, to realize its importance, and to try to destroy it!"

Jake groped for solid facts. "You didn't tell anyone Dicky was dead because you were afraid you'd have to explain why he was startled, even frightened of you. And then you might be prevented from— walking?"

"Richardson was suspicious of the horoscope you made for Nurse O'Neill," said Skelton. "But what's all this about a zodiac?"

"Have a look." Andy handed over the rolled paper. Jake opened it up and turned it to the firelight. Skelton leaned closer.

Jake had no trouble recognizing a map of Somerset. Or of this part of Somerset, at least. There was Glastonbury, West Pennard, Street, the River Brue, Lydford itself. But on top of the usual lines of roads and field boundaries were drawn black borders, in some places inter-connecting, in other enclosing angular shapes. One at the bottom of the paper, beyond Charlton, looked like a rough approximation of a dog—or a lion.

"The symbols are quite distinct, really, once you know where to look," Andy assured them. "The Glastonbury Zodiac has been marked out by hills, trackways, watercourses, and the like. It was rediscovered very recently, by Katherine Maltwood whilst she was researching the quest for the Holy Grail as enacted here in Somerset. The chance of such patterns being found on the ground randomly, patterns that har-monize so closely with those in the sky, is on the order of 149,000,000 to 1 against."

Skelton looked at Jake. Jake looked at the map. Only by a stretch of his imagination could he see any likeness to real objects in the indicated shapes.

But Andy's eyes were shining with his vision. "This house was built betwixt Virgo and Libra. At the equinox. But the Glastonbury Zodiac uses the dove of peace instead of the traditional symbol for Libra, the scales. See, there it is in the center of the circle, just above Barton St. David. St. David's symbol, you'll remember, is the dove. And Glas-tonbury itself is in Aquarius, the beginning of the year, which here is not a water-bearer but a phoenix rising from the ashes. How better could the ancients have signaled to us the importance of this site in wartime than by using such symbols?"

He'd put together a string of coincidences the same way Harry had done with his evidence, Jake told himself. Give either of them a map of Missouri and they'd find Mickey Mouse between Kansas City and

St. Joseph. "I've flown over this area. You can't miss the Tor and the square of the ruined abbey, but I've never seen any of these outlines."

"One always sees patterns in the earth," Skelton cautioned.

"But the Temple of the Stars is a pattern in time as well as space," said Andy. "It's the world's greatest feat of engineering, repeating in the natural forms of the earth's surface the patterns of the stars themselves. For the earth and heavens are linked, and the forces of one affect the other. As above, so below."

"You mean streams, roads, and so forth were engineered to form the shapes of the zodiac?" asked Jake. "But streams and roads change course. People build by-passes, that sort of thing."

"Who's to say whether the minds of the surveyors are being directed by planetary forces? The Roman road to the east, for example, the Fosse Way, has a kink in an otherwise dead-straight stretch just at Virgo's clasped hands. Hands clasped in prayer, no doubt."

"Planetary forces." Skelton was looking dazed, but then, he wasn't used to talking to Andy.

Not that Jake wasn't starting to wonder if he were experiencing some bizarre after-effect of the cider. "So this zodiac was built by the Romans?"

"Oh no, it's much older than that. Older than the ancient temples of Stonehenge and Avebury. Once we believed in such spiritual matters and were sustained by them. Now we place our trust in rationality and science, and look where we are—bombs are raining down upon our cities!"

Muted lights flashed across Andy's windows. A car. More than one car. The police. Jake looked over at Skelton.

With a grimace almost of embarrassment, Skelton stood up. "Your Lordship, would you be so kind as to join me in the entrance hall? I'm afraid the local authorities must be told about Pilot Officer Richardson's—tragic accident."

"Yes, yes, of course." But Andy made no move to get up. The light in his eyes winked out and his face went cold and bleak as moorland beneath a sleet storm.

Jake got to his feet, watched Skelton walk out of the room, then turned back to Andy. His symbols were only shapes in the fire, in blotches of ink—or in blood. But he saw those symbols because he had to. "Why do you need to walk over part of the zodiac pattern tomorrow, Andy? What are you trying to do?"

"I'm hoping to raise the powers of England's ancient soil, the soil from which we sprung, to repel a German invasion. Some prayer is a laying on of hands. This is a laying on of feet."

"A prayer? Or a magical rite?"

"Both," Andy replied. "Even such an enlightened Renaissance prince as Elizabeth the Great kept an astrologer, John Dee. He lived here at Glastonbury. Here he raised the power that repulsed the Spanish invasion of the Armada."

The ships of the Armada were dispersed by a sudden storm, Jake knew, but he'd always thought Dee was a charlatan.

"And here, in the Vale of Avalon, is where Britain's greatest warrior, Arthur, was laid to rest. Because in life he, too, walked the zodiac, and so defeated the invading barbarian hordes at Mount Badon."

Jake didn't mention that the invading Angles were the ancestors of the English, and that they won their war in the next generation.

"During the eighteenth century Glastonbury became, briefly, a spa. People came to drink the healing waters of Chalice Well. How many of them were then inspired to walk through the countryside and, however unaware, trace the zodiac? Soon afterwards Napoleon threatened to invade England, but never did so."

Jake could only shake his head in something between astonishment and admiration.

"This evening, this accident—fate can be cruel and capricious— perhaps it's written in the stars that England should fall." Andy looked up, his face twisted in pain. "And yet fate is balanced by free will, isn't it? Jake, my lad, you've told me your date of birth, you're an Aries, active and courageous. Why else would you volunteer to fight here when your own country isn't at war?"

"A lot of people volunteered," said Jake.

"But you are here now. If you could possibly see your way clear to volunteering one more time, to making one more effort for your old and beset mother country. . . ."

Jake looked down at the map he was still holding.

"The notebook beside my bed, the pages devoted to Virgo and Libra," Andy went on, his voice winding tighter and tighter. "They list the exact paths to take, the places where you must stop and make small offerings — a bit of food, a drop of wine or beer, a flower. The going isn't difficult, you'd manage quite well even with your cane. Jake, I know you're thinking I'm daft, but. . . ."

He'd come this far, thought Jake, from the Great Plains of America to the antique landscape of Somerset. He'd offered to lay down his life. Why shouldn't he lay down his feet, too? What difference would a few more steps make?

According to Andy, a big difference. If he didn't walk the zodiac tomorrow, Jake asked himself, would the Germans invade? If he did, would they stay back? And he answered, no one would ever know what was cause and what effect. If you see the future and then do something to alter it, then it wasn't the future that you saw. The future, like much of the past, was a matter of perception.

If Andy wanted to perceive meaningful symbols in the spilled blood, the death in war, of so many young men, let him. The tragedy wasn't that a troubled old man saw symbols where there were none but that the unimaginative minds of people like Dicky couldn't see symbols at all.

Jake said, "I'd be honored to walk the zodiac in your place."

"Thank you." For a moment Andy went limp with relief. Then he pulled himself together, stood up, seized Jake's free hand, and wrung it between his own. "Most kind. Very good of you."

"Seems the least I can do," Jake said with a wry smile.

Brisk male voices echoed from the entrance hall. Bridget hurried down the corridor and stopped in the door. Her voice was music compared to the crow-like clamor of the others. "Doc Skelton just told us what happened. Andy, I'm so sorry."

Andy's skin crinkled in Jake's hand like the paper of the map. Inside his tweeds he seemed very old, very small, sucked dry. But still he summoned up a hint of a twinkle. "Thank you, Nurse O'Neill. You and Pilot Officer Houston make quite a handsome couple, don't you now? Did I tell you, Nurse, that your horoscope predicts a long happy marriage to an Aries? Houston here is an Aries."

Jake opened his mouth to protest. But the words were spoken — the die was cast. He stole a glance at Bridget.

A log collapsed in a shower of sparks and a sudden flame shot upwards. But the rosy glow in Bridget's face, he decided, wasn't from the fire. Releasing Andy's hand, he slipped his arm around her waist and told himself that some prophecies just might be self-fulfilling.

She leaned against him. Together they watched Andy walk, slowly but as erect as a soldier, out the door and down the hall.

"Thank you, Jake," Bridget murmured. "I was seeing myself sacked and deported. But that poor old man, now, will they be sending him to a home?"

"This is his home," Jake told her. "And sometimes I think he's more sane—and more sober—than anyone else in this crazy world."

"Do you now? With him reading the future in the stars and all? Or is he reading the past this time round?"

"A bit of each. Here, let me show you." Jake unrolled the map and angled it so she could see. "The storm's lifted. I think we should take a walk tomorrow morning, follow some of these paths and have us a picnic in honor of your birthday. The exercise will do me good, shake out the knots in my side."

She eyed the distorted shapes of the zodiac, her head tilted, then turned her face up to Jake's. "I'd like that. Especially if you're after explaining it all to me."

"I'll try," Jake assured her. "I'll try."

The flare of light from the fireplace died down. Shadows oozed in from the corners of the room, but still the windows gleamed faintly. An airplane droned overhead, making the panes of glass reverberate. Jake looked toward them. Even though he couldn't see the Tor he imagined it reaching toward the stars, steady, solid, reassuringly permanent, a bridge between earth and heaven.

Bridget took his cool hand in her warm and capable one and tugged him toward the door. "Let's get on with it, then. There's a war on."

"Yes," he said. "All we can do is get on with it."

# Out Like a Lion

## Bill Crider

---

Frank Packard, star of several sword-and-sandal epics at Gober Studios, was not wearing sandals. He wasn't carrying a sword, either. Instead he was wearing a garterbelt, nylons, cotton panties, and a bra.

He might have gotten away with it if he'd been in costume for a movie, but he wasn't. He was in his garage, about to get into his car. He'd told his wife he was tired of living a lie.

His wife was a starlet at Gober Studios, and she didn't mind living a lie at all, not as long as she kept getting parts. So of course she called Mr. Gober, and Mr. Gober called me.

"Godammit, Ferrel!" Gober said. He always begins his conversations with me that way. I've never figured out why.

"Goddammit, Ferrel! You've got to stop him! *The Roaming Roman* opens next week!"

I asked who I had to stop, and he told me. I hung up, got in my 1940 Chevy, and caught up with Packard before he managed to get more than five blocks from home. He didn't want to go back, but when I explained that he'd never get to hang around with a cast of thousands of guys wearing togas again, he decided to give the straight life another try.

A job well done, I thought as I drove to my office. I'm a licensed private detective, and I take regular cases now and then, but being on retainer to Gober Studios pretty much assures that I'll never be without work. In fact, by the time I got back to my office and sat down to wonder how much of a bonus Gober would pay me, the phone rang again.

"Goddammit, Ferrel," Mr. Gober said, "get out here! Sidney's killed Howard Steele!"

Howard Steele had been a heavily-decorated hero of the war in the Pacific, fighting his way across a series of small islands and single-handedly wiping out machine-gun nests, picking off snipers, and raising Old Glory on whatever little hill was handy.

When he came back to the States, the newspapers were full of photos of his rugged, handsome face, and Mr. Gober, who loves publicity, signed him to be Gober Studio's new star.

It turned out that Steele was rugged and handsome, all right, and he photographed even better than he looked. But he couldn't act a lick. His line readings made the kids in high school plays look like Lawrence Oliver. Mr. Gober never let a little thing like that stop him, however. The Tarzan movies were doing all right for RKO, and they had a hero who didn't have much to say, so Gober had one of his hacks create a jungle hero named Karg, who had even less to say than Johnny Weissmuller. Gober had plans for a whole series of movies with titles like *Jungle Peril*, *Jungle Flames*, *Jungle Terror*, and on and on.

As it happened, Steele looked great in a loin cloth, a lot better than Weissmuller, who'd put on a few pounds since his first Tarzan movie and these days was wearing what looked like a pair of leather boxer shorts to help cover his paunch. The Karg movies were a hit and were among the studio's biggest money-makers, not just because they attracted huge audiences but because they could be filmed in a hurry and on the cheap on the studio's back lot, with a fake jungle. Plenty of scenes of authentic jungle animals were spliced into the film, but I doubt that they fooled anyone over the age of eight.

I never knew where the authentic stuff came from. Probably some guy shot it on safari and sold it to Gober for a couple of hundred bucks. The same scenes turned up in nearly every movie—the same giraffes running across the veldt, the same crocs slithering into the river, the same elephants trumpeting—but no one ever complained. Maybe nobody cared.

The only real animal that ever appeared in the movies was Sidney, who was a lion, or so Gober claimed. It was hard to tell. Sidney was pretty much fangless and clawless, and whenever there was a big fight between him and Steele, which was just about every movie, Steele had to work hard to make it look as if there was a real struggle going on. Sidney himself never seemed to work up much interest. The technicians juiced up the soundtrack with roars and growls, and audiences never seemed disappointed, but I knew for sure that Sidney hadn't killed anybody. Sidney couldn't maul a mouse.

I pulled my wheezing crate up to the studio gatehouse and old Ray waved me through. He'd seen me often enough to know I belonged there.

I drove on back to the lot that served as the jungle. There were plenty of cars parked around, but no police yet. No reporters, either. Gober didn't believe in calling them until everybody got together and settled on the story Gober wanted told to the cops and the papers.

When I walked onto the set, one of the first people I saw was Anna Lonestar. I'd always thought she was the real reason for the success of the Karg pictures. She was as regal as a lioness, her auburn hair touched with gold highlights, and when she put on one of those skimpy jungle outfits to play Karg's wild jungle love, well, there wasn't a guy in the theater whose eyes didn't bug out just a little.

She wasn't wearing the costume at the moment, I was sorry to see. Instead she was wearing jodhpurs and a tight white shirt with a red scarf tied around her throat, but it didn't matter. She was the one you looked at, no matter what she was wearing. Whatever star quality is, she had it by the truck load.

Standing beside her was Doctor Christopher Benton, her astrologer. Everywhere that Anna Lonestar went, Dr. Benton was sure to go. I wasn't sure where the "doctor" came from. Maybe he was a doctor like Georgie Jessel was a general. Not that I cared. Everybody in Hollywood has a con going, and one more didn't much matter.

Mr. Gober wasn't there, of course. He didn't like to mingle with the talent. But his flunkies were there, running around and telling everybody to keep quiet until the word came down from the top. The crew was there, too, of course: grips and stagehands and lighting technicians. George Zenko, the director, was there, and a guy who had to be the producer. I didn't know him, but you can always spot a producer when there's trouble. He's the one who's sweating buckets.

So naturally it was the producer who buttonholed me. He was about five-six or-seven, which made him the same height as most of the stars he worked with, not counting Steele, who was a genuine six-footer.

"You're Ferrel, right?" the producer said.

I admitted that I was.

"I'm Anderson. The producer."

I said I'd figured that out.

"You gotta do something," he said. "This is going to cost us an arm and a leg. The picture was almost in the can, and now Steele's dead. It's going to be hard to finish the picture without him, but it can be done. We'll just cut in some shots from the earlier pictures. Nobody'll notice. The publicity from this could kill us, though. We can't have people thinking there's a killer lion on the set. We could get sued."

Anderson didn't seem too worried about Steele, so I said, "Something's already killed your star."

"Yeah. It was the lion. Come on. I'll show you."

I followed him into the fake jungle. A bunch of the others trailed along behind, but I didn't look to see who was there. It sounded like quite a lot of them.

The trees looked even less like jungle trees in real life than they did in the movies. They were real enough, but some of them had broad rubber leaves stuck on them to make them look more tropical, and of course there were vines everywhere. The vines weren't real. They were mostly ropes, disguised to look like vines. When it came to swinging from tree to tree, ropes were much safer than vegetation.

A lot of the plants growing by the trees needed water. There's not as much rain in Southern California as there is in the jungle.

It wasn't noisy like a real jungle. There were no birds calling, no monkeys howling. All those sounds are added to the movie later, like the scenes with the real animals.

Howard Steele was lying not far from one of the trees. Overhead in the crotch of the tree was the house where Karg and the lovely

Kiela, portrayed by Anna Lonestar, lived. The treehouse was very solid, put together with nails and screws even if everything was supposedly tied in place with vines.

But while Steele was lying under the tree, he didn't look as if he'd fallen from the treehouse.

He looked as if he'd been mauled by a lion.

"We should have warned him," Benton said, and I turned around to look at him.

"Warned who?" I asked. "About what?"

He had a cherubic face, except that cherubs don't have beards. He also had lots of curly black hair that was turning gray and didn't quite cover the bald spot in the middle of his head. He wore a black suit, white shirt, narrow black tie, and he was holding a beat-up black hat, which I suppose he'd removed out of respect for the dead. He looked more like an out-of-work rabbi than an astrologer.

"We should have warned Steele," Benton said. "About his impending doom."

"Yes," Anna Lonestar agreed. Her voice was as much a purr as anything. It sounded even better in person than it did on the screen. I felt the little hairs on the back of my neck stand up.

"How could you have known?" Anderson asked, but I already knew the answer he'd get. Anna never worked with anyone whose horoscope Benton hadn't cast.

"It was in the stars," Benton said. He really talked like that: *impending doom, in the stars.* "He was an Aries, of course, ruled by Mars, as his success in the late war would attest. Pure raw energy! But that success is long past. His natal chart shows Neptune conjunct Mars in the eighth house. And his Sun was in the twelfth house."

He looked at me as if I'd have some idea of what he meant, but of course I didn't.

Anderson probably didn't, either, but he said, "That's malarkey. Don't give me that cheap newspaper crap."

Benton looked pained, as if he had to deal with skeptics all the time, which he probably did. He said, "Horoscopes that you might see in magazines and newspapers are not entirely 'crap.' But they usually look only at the Sun sign. Real astrology, such as I practice, is much more complex. It looks at all the planets, both in the present and in the birth chart. It—"

"Yeah, yeah, yeah," Anderson said. "But what good does that do us?"

I was wondering the same thing, but I was curious. So I said, "What about Miss Lonestar's horoscope?"

"She, of course, is a Leo," Benton said.

So she not only looked like a lioness; she was one. Anna smiled as if it should have been obvious to anyone.

"Her magnetic personality," Benton went on, "is typical of the Leo. It draws people to her. People love her. She has millions of fans because her natural warmth comes through on the screen."

"OK," I said, but I wasn't convinced.

I thought she had millions of fans because of the way she looked in that skimpy jungle outfit, especially after a swim, and there was a swim in every movie. Besides, I was a Leo, too, and I'd never been accused of having a magnetic personality. The only thing that stuck to me was lint.

"What was that you were saying about Steele's Sun being in the eighth house?" I asked. "What does that have to do with anything?"

"The twelfth," Benton said. "Not the eighth. It means that Steele was killed by—"

"A lion!" someone screamed.

I looked into the trees over Benton's shoulder, and there came Sidney.

He looked pretty bedraggled, like a giant alley cat wearing a moth-eaten fur that someone had found in the attic and thrown away. His mane was as scraggly as Benton's beard, and he stared around near-sightedly with his watery old eyes.

I heard lots of pounding feet at my back as people fled from the ferocious maneater.

Not everyone was running away. Benton and Anna Lonestar stood their ground. A stagehand and a script girl were still there, along with the director, George Zenko, and a guy who looked as if he might be dressed for safari: Randall Curry, Sidney's trainer. And of course Anderson was there. Lions don't scare producers. They have to deal with actors and directors all the time.

"Get out your roscoe," Anderson told me.

"Roscoe?" I said.

"Your gat, idiot. Your heater."

He'd been watching too many of Gober's gangster pictures. I said, "My gun?"

"Yeah, your gun. Get it out."

"I don't carry a roscoe."

"You're a detective and you don't carry a gat?"

"I've never needed one," I said.

"Well, you need it now. That's a rogue beast over there."

Sidney was standing there watching us hopefully, as if he thought one of us might have a case of tuna for him. His chain was hanging from his leather collar.

"I don't think I need a gun for Sidney," I said.

"What about you, Curry?" Anderson asked. "Don't you have a whip or something?"

"I'd never use a whip on Sidney," Curry said. "He's gentle as a lamb."

"Sure he is," Anderson said. "Why don't you go over there and see how gentle he is."

"That might not be prudent," Curry said. He looked down at Steele. "Considering the circumstances."

"I'll go over," Anna said, with what I guessed must be typical Leo bravery, except that I, as the other Leo on hand, wasn't feeling particularly brave. Maybe she just didn't think Sidney was dangerous.

Anderson grabbed her arm.

"Oh, no, you don't," he said. "We can't risk it. Ferrel goes. That's what Mr. Gober pays him for."

Sidney walked over and looked down at Steele's body. He bent his head to sniff.

"For God's sake, Ferrel," Anderson said. "Stop him before he takes a bite!"

I didn't think Sidney would bite anyone, even a dead man, so I started over to him. He looked up at me quizzically, and I said, "Hey, Sidney. How's it going?"

Sidney, naturally enough, didn't answer. He just stood there until I took his chain. I looked at the end of the chain, saw a broken link, and then led the docile lion over to Curry.

"He's all yours," I told the trainer.

Curry took the chain and looked at Anderson.

"Get him out of here," Anderson said. "And be sure he doesn't get loose again."

As Curry led Sidney away, I said, "Who found the body?"

"I did," the stagehand said, his voice sad.

He was a big guy with dirty blond hair, and he wore blue denim overalls, the kind with a bib. There was even a little loop to hang a hammer in.

"Who are you?" I asked.

"Roger Ruggles. I was supposed to do a little work on the house, and when I came back here, I found Steele lying there."

"What about Sidney?"

"He was standing over the body. When I tried to check on Steele, the lion growled at me. I was afraid he'd tear me apart, so I left to find Mr. Zenko."

"That right, Zenko?" I asked.

"Is right," he said.

He was from Russia, I think, or somewhere like that. He directed westerns, jungle yarns, and detective tales with equal facility, which is to say, not much. But he worked fast, and he worked cheap. That was the kind of director Gober liked.

I went over to have a better look at Steele. No matter what anyone said, I didn't believe he'd been killed by Sidney. Sidney was just a scapegoat. Or a scapelion.

As I knelt down, I said, "Anybody on the set have a reason to kill Steele?"

I couldn't see any faces, but I could almost feel people freezing up behind me.

"You don't need to ask questions like that, Ferrel," Anderson said. "You know better than that."

"I thought you didn't want it to be the lion."

"Better the lion than somebody on the set. We don't need a scandal like that. And we won't have one, because I'm beginning to think Steele fell out of the treehouse."

"Not with these marks on him," I said.

Now that I could see them better, I could tell they'd been made with something that had ripped the skin and flesh away from the bone. No wonder Steele looked as if he'd been mauled by a lion. He'd been mauled, all right.

"He wasn't killed by the lion," Anna said, using that voice again.

I was pretty sure she was correct, but I said, "How do you know?"

"The stars," Benton said.

I remembered that he'd been interrupted before he could answer my question about the Sun and the eighth house, or maybe it was the twelfth. So I asked him again.

"You're very astute," Benton said. "I would like to cast your horoscope some day."

"Sure," I told him. "But first, what about that Sun business?"

"The eighth house is the house of death," Benton said. "And Mars and Neptune in the eighth house could indicate a violent death surrounded by mysterious circumstances. Things here are therefore not what they appear to be."

I could have told him that. But I hadn't.

"Furthermore," Benton went on, "the twelfth house is the house of self-undoing, and the Sun in the twelfth house implies that Steele may have somehow played a part in his own death."

I'd sort of figured that out, too.

"And finally," Benton said, "the Sun in the twelfth house suggests that Steele had hidden enemies. The lion was not Steele's enemy. He was killed by a human being."

I had a feeling he was right on the money. I said, "What was Steele doing out here anyway? Why wasn't he waiting in his trailer?"

I stood up and turned around as I asked. No one was looking at me. They were all looking at the script girl, who was blushing. I didn't know that there was anyone in Hollywood who could do that. It made her look very young and innocent, which was probably deceptive.

There are plenty of young people in Hollywood. I wasn't so sure about innocent.

"What's your name?" I asked her.

"Martha Varner," she said.

"You knew Mr. Steele?"

She nodded.

"How well?"

She didn't answer, but then she didn't have to. I didn't know anything about astrology, but Benton had said Steele was an Aries. I knew a little about rams. I also knew a little about Howard Steele.

"Couldn't you have had a little privacy in the trailer?" I asked. "Why meet here?"

She still didn't feel like answering, and Anderson said, "Leave her alone, Ferrel. What happened was that Steele was going to meet her in the treehouse and he climbed up and fell back down. That's the way Mr. Gober would want it, and that's the way we'll play it. I'll go call the cops and give them the story."

"I don't think so," I told him. "It's pretty clear that's not the way it happened."

"Who pays your retainer?" Anderson asked.

He knew the answer, so I didn't bother to tell him. I said, "You might be able to pay a doctor to swear to a false cause of death, but there are too many witnesses for you to keep it quiet."

"They all work for the same boss," he said. "And so do the cops if we want them to. We'll keep it quiet."

Maybe it would've worked, but I wasn't going to let it.

"I'm not keeping quiet," I said. "Not about murder."

"Murder? What are you talking about? He fell, that's all."

That wasn't all, and he knew it. We all knew it. But I was the only one who said it.

"He didn't fall. You can see that. We all can."

"You're right," Anderson said. He was getting desperate, I guess. "Sidney did it. Look at those claw marks."

Back to the lion again. There were claw marks on Steele, all right, but Sidney hadn't made them.

"Were you and Steele playing footsie?" I asked Martha Varner.

"I wouldn't call it that," she said, still blushing.

"But you were fooling around."

"Maybe just a little. He was so handsome."

She looked at Steele's mangled body, and tears ran down her cheeks.

Benton either didn't notice her grief or didn't care. He said, "Mars conjunct Neptune in the eighth house can also indicate a possible sexual scandal or confusion."

I was beginning to wonder if there was anything that Mars and Neptune *couldn't* suggest. I said to Martha, "Was there anyone on the set who thought he had a claim on you?" I asked.

She started sobbing as she tried to answer, but I could make out that she said, "No."

I wasn't sure she was telling the truth. I looked around. One of our little party was missing.

"What happened to the stagehand?" I asked.

Zenko pointed at the trees and said, "He went thataway."

I thought he'd been reading too many western scripts. I also thought I should've been watching Ruggles more closely. After all, I'd thought for the last ten minutes that he was the killer. I took off into the trees after him.

A stagehand wearing overalls with a hammer loop, but no hammer? I'd wondered from the beginning what had happened to it. They don't call them *claw hammers* for nothing. I suspected that Ruggles had used his to beat Steele and rip away his flesh, and I also thought he'd used it, along with a chisel, to break Sidney's chain and set him free, hoping to throw the blame for Steele's death on the old lion.

I pounded through the underbrush, slapping branches out of the way and trying to keep my legs from tangling in vines. I hadn't gone far when I heard someone behind me. I turned and saw Anna Lonestar.

"You don't know the jungle," she said, as if reciting a line from one of her movies. Her voice was no longer a purr.

"I can follow a trail," I said.

"Then you should be going that way," she told me, and pointed off to the right. Sure enough, there was a broken branch that I'd missed.

"Do you know something about Steele that I should know?" I asked.

"The stage hand wasn't jealous of him," she said, which surprised me.

"Roger was jealous of the girl," she continued, which should have surprised me, but didn't.

"You mean that Steele would swing on any vine that happened to be handy."

"That's one way to put it. Neptune was in the eighth house, remember? Come along."

She started off in the direction she'd pointed, and I followed. It wasn't long before we came to the fake river and pool where the swimming scenes were filmed. I was hoping Anna might dive in, the way she had in *Jungle Menace*. She wasn't wearing her skimpy jungle get-up, but I thought she'd look just swell in a wet shirt and jodhpurs.

She didn't jump in. She got a running start, grabbed a vine, and swung across. When she hit the other side, she turned around and looked over at me.

"Come along," she said, purring again.

I would have followed that voice anywhere. I spotted a vine, trotted over, and made a leap. The next thing I knew, I was sailing out over open water, and my hands were slipping on the vine.

I hoped there weren't any real crocodiles around, not that I thought there was much of a chance.

I didn't fall in the water, but I slid so far down the vine that when I hit the other side, I landed on my knees instead of my feet and skidded through the undergrowth on my stomach. I knew I'd ruined a good pair of pants, a jacket, a shirt, and a tie.

I struggled to my feet and tried to knock some of the dirt and mashed plants off my pants. Anna was already loping down a trail, so I stopped cleaning myself and followed.

It wasn't long before we came to a clearing that held a village of huts made of wood and straw. I remembered it from several of the Karg movies. In one of them, *Jungle Jeopardy*, I believe, Anna, as

Kiela, had been tied to a stake in the center of the village, her hands bound and her arms pulled above her head. The evil hunters who had taken over the village planned to burn her alive. It was a scene that had done wonders for her appearance in the scanty outfit as she writhed from the flames, and when Karg had come riding to her rescue on the back of a mighty elephant, audiences all over the country had broken into wild applause. They applauded even louder when the unbound Anna skewered the leader of the bad guys with a spear thrown from atop the same elephant.

There appeared to be no one in the village now. As Karg would have said, it was quiet. Too quiet. I found myself wishing I had a roscoe, or that Anna had a spear.

There was a rustling noise at the back of one of the huts, and I saw Ruggles break through and sprint off into the jungle again.

"He's going back to the treehouse," Anna said.

I looked down at my ruined clothes and wished we'd just waited there for him.

"This way," Anna said, and we were off in hot pursuit.

When we came to the treehouse, the others were still there, but they were no longer looking down at Steele. They were all looking up at the treehouse.

"Ruggles?" I said.

"There," Zenko said, pointing up.

Anna Lonestar started for the rope ladder, but before she could reach it, Ruggles pulled it up and out of sight.

"What now?" I asked Anderson.

"I don't suppose we could just forget the whole thing," he said, and I figured someone had filled him in on Steele's sexual proclivities, if he hadn't known already. "Or we could still claim that Steele fell."

"Not with his killer on the loose," I said. "When there's a murder, someone has to pay. And this time it's Ruggles."

"This is going to make us look really bad," Anderson said.

"We'll worry about that after we take care of Ruggles," I said, and turned to Anna to ask how I could get up in the tree.

She was already walking toward another tree, with Benton at her heels trying to stop her.

"You Leos," he said to her. "Always wanting to be the center of attention. That young man might kill you. You must let someone else catch him."

He put a hand on Anna's arm, but she shook him off. I saw that she was headed for a large tree that looked easy to climb, and of course I'd seen it in the movies. In *Jungle Terror*, Steele had eluded his pursuers (a band of greed-crazed gold hunters) by climbing it, swinging to the treehouse on a vine, and bombarding them with co-conuts. I wasn't at all sure that there were any coconuts in Africa, but that hadn't bothered the audiences. They'd loved the scene.

"Benton's right," I told Anna. "I'll go. It's what Gober pays me for."

It wasn't, really. What he paid me for was more along the line of what I'd done earlier that day, stopping scandals before they got started. But there was no use in thinking that way. Somebody had to go after Ruggles. Better me than one of the stars.

Anderson agreed. He said, "Let Ferrel do it, Anna. We can't afford to lose you."

For a second I thought she might object, but instead she moved aside. I took off my jacket and shoes and went up the tree. I felt like a kid again until I got to the branch where the vine was waiting. Ruggles wasn't going to treat me like a kid, not if he'd retrieved his hammer.

I tried not to think about that as I snatched the vine and jumped off the tree branch. As the air rushed past my face I thought about trying one of those jungle yells like Johnny Weissmuller did, but I thought better of it. Karg didn't have a yell, and I didn't want to infringe on another studio's property. Besides, I couldn't have yelled like Weissmuller, anyway.

My hands slid on the vine again, and I hit the railing of the treehouse with my stomach. By great good luck I folded in the middle and toppled onto the porch instead of falling back in the other direction.

Ruggles came rushing out and tried to make up for my good luck by kicking me off the edge. He got in a couple of solid blows to my ribcage, but at least he didn't have his hammer.

He did have a powerful leg, however, and the next thing I knew I was dangling above the jungle floor, hanging from the side of the treehouse porch by my fingertips.

I looked up at Ruggles, who smiled down at me as he raised his foot to stomp my hands.

I thought about telling him that he wouldn't get away with it, which he wouldn't have. But I didn't think he'd care.

"I'll break every finger you have," he said.

He would have done it, too, if Anna Lonestar hadn't come swinging across from the tree, her legs extended stiffly in front of her.

Her right foot took Ruggles in the nose.

Her left foot took him in the throat.

He gurgled and gasped as he stumbled back into the treehouse, clutching his face.

Anna landed lightly on the porch and looked inside to check on Ruggles. He must not have seemed to be a threat because she bent down and took my wrists. With both of us straining hard, I managed to get up onto the porch, where I lay and gulped air. It's not easy, dangling fifty feet above the ground. Or twenty feet. Whatever it was, it seemed like fifty to me.

Anna threw the rope ladder down, and by the time I'd recovered, Benton had joined us.

"I suppose it's a good thing she doesn't like to share the spotlight," he said.

"It's fine by me," I told him, and went in to have a look at Ruggles.

He wasn't doing well. His breath rasped in and out through his broken nose, and he kept pointing at his throat as if to say he couldn't talk. And he couldn't, which was just fine as far as I was concerned.

I left Anna and Benton with him while I climbed down to talk to Anderson.

Zenko was off to one side, comforting Martha Varner. I'd heard he had a talent for that sort of thing, so I left him to it and pulled Anderson aside.

"Here's the way we'll play it," I told him. "Ruggles was abusing Sidney, trying to get him excited for a scene or something. Steele, soft-hearted war hero that he was, intervened, and they got into a fight. Ruggles took out his hammer and killed him. Ruggles was captured by the heroic efforts of Anna Lonestar, who will no doubt go on to get top billing in her own series of jungle thrillers."

Anderson thought it over and said, "Not bad."

"Not bad? It's great. Steele dies a hero's death, the studio looks good, Anna Lonestar looks good, and I get a bonus. And maybe the undying gratitude of Anna Lonestar."

I smiled at the possibility.

"Benton has all her gratitude already," Anderson said. "Not to mention everything else."

"Oh," I said. "Well, there's still that bonus. And I'll get to see her in the movies. Gober really should do her series in color. And take a few more square inches off her costume."

"Why don't you tell him that," Anderson said.

"Maybe I will," I said, but of course I never did.

# Slaying the Serpent

## Jane Lindskold

I KNOW WHAT you're going to say. We should have seen the pattern sooner. It was there from the start.

You're right. That's true. It was. But let me tell you, you don't have a pattern until you have pieces. Would you have seen a pattern in this?

April 9: Young caucasian male found murdered in a seedy hotel room. Victim was tied face down to the bed frame and his head was crushed. Murder weapon right there—a tire iron. No prints. Only other items in the room were the victim's own clothes and a cheap stuffed toy—a purple bull.

Investigation shows that victim was a homosexual interested in rough sex. Hotel clerk remembers that victim himself took the room that evening. No one remembers seeing him with anyone.

Stuffed bull proves to be of a kind available at a local street carnival. Hundreds have been won at various games of chance over the past two weekends.

May 10: Three people—one caucasian female, two caucasian males— found dead in the woman's home. The woman was violently subdued, then beheaded. The two men, who turn out to be identical twins, were shot using a gun belonging to the woman.

Gun is checked for prints and proves to have been wiped, confirming what is already obvious, that a fourth person was present. Some forensic evidence suggests that the twins were killed elsewhere and their bodies brought to the woman's house.

One theory is that the twins frightened the woman in some fashion and that she shot them. Then, in a panic, she moved the bodies to her home. She herself was killed in revenge for the deaths of the twins. Alternate theory suggests that she was killed by someone she called on for help who then panicked and attacked her.

No one is happy with either theory. Extensive investigation shows no prior connection between the woman and the twins.

June 18: Hispanic female is found murdered in mid-class hotel. She had been gagged, then killed in a particularly disgusting fashion. Her arms had been cut off at the shoulder joints and she had been allowed to bleed to death. Autopsy shows large amounts of barbiturates in her system. We hope to hell she was too out of it to feel what happened to her.

Murder weapon proves to be a fine bladed knife used for filleting and boning. It's of a type available in dozens of stores. Found in room wiped clean of prints. Even so, we are encouraged to think that the murderer must have known something of anatomy. However, check of doctors, butchers, and the like turns up nothing except the discouraging information that lots of people — hunters, taxidermists, even frugal shoppers — could have had the basic skills needed for this simple cut.

Evidence shows that murderer probably showered in the victim's bathroom before departing. Chemical declogger poured down the shower drain dissolved any useful evidence. Needless to say, the place was wiped clean of prints.

Other items in the room include the victim's luggage and a large stack of newly opened packages. Investigation discovers that the day of the murder was the woman's sixtieth birthday. A former resident of the area, she had returned to celebrate with local friends. Had stayed at a hotel because all of her friends had cats and she was very allergic to cat dander.

Even with all the killer's care, we got two breaks here. First, at our request the friends with whom the victim — Martina Alvarez — had been celebrating inspected her belongings. All swore that a large ce-

ramic crab placed on top of the stack had not been among Martina's
presents.

The crab, however, was itself a dead-end. It was a type sold in about
half the tourist shops in the area. The top came off and doubled as
a cute candy dish or ash tray. Well . . . It's not my idea of cute, but
you know what I mean.

Our second break was that the proximity of Martina's death date
to her birth date rang a bell in my mind. I went and checked the
unsolved murder files. Mind, I'm being easy on you. We had more
unsolved murders than these, I'm sad to say. Anyhow, sorting through
the files I learned that in two cases, the very two listed above, one of
the victims had died within a few days of his or her birthday.

The homosexual man, Allain Fedorov, had celebrated his birthday
a week earlier. The woman who'd been beheaded — Patricia Cooper —
had celebrated hers two days earlier. The pattern broke with the
twins — Gus and Julius Howell — though. Their birthday wouldn't
come until January. None of our other recent unsolveds — there were
three — fit the pattern, so I dismissed the idea that there might be a
connection.

Turns out I was a bit hasty.

July 2: African-American male found dead in mid-class hotel room.
His throat had been cut; he was naked except for a tight nylon tank
top. Defensive bruising on his arms shows that he'd been at least
somewhat aware of his danger. Large amounts of alcohol in his blood
show why he hadn't been more successful. Autopsy also suggests that
he'd been knocked out before having his throat cut.

The victim — Samuel Morgan — was travelling on business. He was
a closet homosexual, not adverse to a casual pick-up. Like Allain Fedorov, Morgan had taken the room himself. As with Fedorov, no
one — not at the gay bar he visited or even the night manager/owner
of the hotel — had seen anyone with him. I believed the manager at
least. He was so pissed about having a new mattress blood sodden
beyond saving, he'd have turned in his own mother if he thought she
was guilty.

Placed on a chair next to the bed was a molded glass figurine of a lion. Other than the lion, the only things in the room were Morgan's clothing and personal effects.

Oh, and his birthday had been about a week and a half before. He'd just turned thirty-eight.

See the pattern yet? I bet you think you do, but then you have an advantage over me. You have a hint from my tale being included here. All I had were six dead people, unrelated to each other except by being dead and their deaths being unsolved.

Six, In the months that had passed since Fedorov's death, I'd solved one of the unsolveds—turned out to be a domestic homicide. Husband and wife. His alibi broke down under careful checking. One of my colleagues had solved the other two—drug and gang. That left us six. Far too many for a small city swollen to medium-sized by summer tourism.

Okay, so four of our six were connected by having been killed within a month of their birthdays. Big deal. Lots of people break out of their usual lifestyles around that time of year. They take a trip or decide to go some place they've never been before to celebrate their personal New Year. That makes them vulnerable, and our killer seemed very good at exploiting that particular vulnerability.

I looked for other connections between them. Professions. Fedorov had been a stockbroker. Cooper had worked at a store that sold rocks and minerals. Gus and Julius Howell had both driven taxis. Martina Alvarez had been a fortune-teller. Samuel Morgan had been a representative for a publishing company. Didn't seem to be a link there.

In the Howells' case, their profession had, indirectly at least, led to their deaths. They'd responded to a call requesting two cabs to take a large party to some restaurant. They'd never returned. When we found their cabs, evidence showed that the men had been shot in their vehicles and then their bodies driven in one of the cabs to Cooper's house. That cab was later ditched in a parking lot behind a strip mall.

Still, while the cab told us a bit more about how they died, their deaths didn't link them to any of the others—except, of course, to Patricia Cooper whose gun had been used to shoot them. Strange thing, though, if the forensic evidence was right. She was dead *before* the Howell brothers were killed.

Race and age were dead-ends, too. Four of the victims were caucasians. One Hispanic. One black. Ages ranged from sixty (Alvarez) all the way down to twenty-two (Julius and Gus Howell). Or down to twenty-five (Allain Fedorov) if you only counted those who died near their birthdays.

Sexual inclination did us no good either. Samuel Morgan and Allain Fedorov were homosexual. All the rest were heterosexual. Julius Howell and Patricia Cooper had spouses. Martina Alvarez was divorced. Gus Howell was single. (In case you're wondering, Patricia Cooper's husband was out of town when his wife died. We checked his alibi carefully, but his breakdown when told that his wife had been murdered seemed genuine).

As far as we could tell, except for the Howell twins, none of the victims knew each other. Alvarez and Cooper had a few acquaintances in common, but they didn't know each other. Morgan's job had taken him to the gem and mineral store where Cooper worked, but only after she was already dead.

By this point, I was frustrated, terrified that any time now another unsolvable murder would happen. I brought my problem to my chief. He agreed to let me call the FBI's Behavioral Science Unit and ask for a profile of our killer.

We lucked out. Turns out one of their men—Agent Josh Terrell— was in-state teaching a course and, with the Fourth of July holiday coming up, he had time off. Lousy way to spend your vacation, but I was grateful.

Terrell came to town and put up in one of the business hotels that have sprung up just about everywhere in the past few years—the type that is made up all of suites. I brought my stuff to him, rather than having him come by the station. We'd managed to keep things quiet so far, but that wouldn't last if someone realized we'd called in the FBI.

As I went up to Terrell's room, I found myself grateful that we wouldn't have to discuss these singularly nasty murders while perching on the edge of his bed.

Terrell both did and didn't look like what I'd expected. He was just under six feet tall and in good shape for his age—which I guessed to be somewhere on the hind end of forty. His brown hair was short and neatly trimmed, his clothing so unremarkable that it became remarkable. But Terrell lacked the steely gaze and the square-cut jaw I'd been subconsciously expecting. In fact, he looked like the kind of guy with whom it'd be easy to kick back, share a couple beers, and chat about the football pre-season.

We didn't though. Instead I stacked my files on the round table in the outer room, accepted Terrell's offer of coffee from the miniature pot nestling on one side of the equally diminutive sink unit, and launched into the basics of my report.

Even though Terrell didn't interrupt much, just a few times to make sure he had names and dates right, it took me nearly two hours to cover the six murders. Then, encouraged by his nod, I went over all our attempts to find a connection between the murder victims. This took a long time because I included a lot of material I've omitted here.

When I was done, we sat staring at each other for a long moment. Then Terrell said:

"Let me think for a few minutes."

He rose and started making another pot of coffee. I escaped to the tidy little bathroom to pee. There were a few touches of Terrell the human being here. He used the same antiperspirant as my father, I noticed. He obviously worried about appearances, because the toothpaste coiled in the side pocket of his shaving kit (it was unzipped) was one of those new ones with extra whiteners. No wonder, given the amount of coffee he drank.

I re-emerged feeling like the pressure was off on more than one level, easier for knowing that this silent, neatly groomed figure sweated and worried about tooth discoloration. Terrell sensed my changed mood and gave me a little smile.

"The first thing I want to remind you," he said, "is that contrary to what some movies and books want you to believe, a profile can't do magic. It can offer an idea of what kind of person you're dealing with, but it can't tell you who the killer is. If you had any suspicions . . ."

"Which I don't," I muttered, reaching for the coffee pot.

"The profile might help you narrow them down," Terrell continued, politely ignoring my interruption. "Since there are no suspects in this case, maybe the profile will help you consider where to continue your investigation. At the very least, we can brainstorm together. Sometimes a fresh point of view opens all sorts of mental doors."

I nodded stiffly. I'd known this. I am a professional, after all, but I hadn't realized how much I was hoping Terrell would give me an answer—The Answer—until he reminded me that he couldn't.

"Right," he said. He pulled a yellow legal pad over to him and referred to his notes. "I'll give you this written out all pretty, but here are my initial thoughts. First, your killer could be two killers. One of the cases might be unconnected to the others, distorting the pattern."

I nodded again, feeling a touch of a burn at the thought that Terrell might be condescending to me. I straightened my own note pad to cover my reaction.

"Go on," I said.

Terrell did.

"Your killer—assuming for the moment that we are dealing with one killer—is quite likely a white male in his mid-thirties. He is almost certainly attractive, if not actually handsome, and in excellent physical condition. He lives alone, is of at least average intelligence, but is not well-grounded in reality as you or I would define it. There will have been a shock to his version of reality sometime in the twelve months preceding the murders, perhaps the death of someone close to him. It could be a divorce, or separation, but I don't think so.

"The killer is a local resident and has lived in this area for at least five years. He was probably known by sight to one or more of his victims. He may have seen military service, but is no longer on active duty. His hobbies involve hunting, shooting, or weight-lifting. He may be a police groupie. Certainly he has more than a passing interest in criminology. Because of this, you are likely to hear from him in the course of the investigation. Perhaps I should say 'You are likely to hear *more* from him,' because I think he's been communicating with you all along."

I stared at Terrell. I couldn't decide if this was brilliant deductive reasoning or unmitigated hogwash. From Terrell's expression, I could tell that he'd met my type of reaction before.

"Let me explain how I drew these conclusions," he said.

"The white male part is almost cheating," he said. "Most serial killers in this country seem to be white males. However, there are independent reasons for my conclusion. Given the sheer amount of physical strength needed for three of the killings — Fedorov, Alvarez, and Morgan — we have evidence of a male. Cooper's throat slash was performed, according to the autopsy, in a clean stroke that went nearly through her neck. That again argues for physical strength, so does the hauling around of the bodies of the two cab drivers, both of whom were grown men."

"Go on," I said.

"As to the killer's race, the majority of the residents of this city are white, with black next in concentration, followed by a growing Hispanic population. The killer has been able to go unremarked in at least three hotels. The same is not likely to have been the case for a black or Hispanic male — especially a large, muscular one."

"We thought the same," I said a touch defensively, "though he could have been posing as a porter."

Terrell gave me a quick grin.

"I never said I wasn't going to tell you things you'd figured out on your own," he reminded me, "only that I'd be pulling those things together into a profile of the killer."

I nodded, a bit embarrassed by my pique.

"Go on."

Terrell obliged.

"As for him being attractive . . . Well, I deduce that from the fact that he was able to pick up two men, and that both Cooper and Alvarez apparently let him into some sort of proximity with them. Even the cab drivers — a notoriously cautious profession — didn't shy off. This same ease of proximity is why I think he may have been known to one or more of his victims. However, I doubt it was a close acquaintance or you would have stumbled across him in more than one of your very detailed background investigations."

I felt complimented but said nothing and gestured for Terrell to continue.

"I'm closer to guessing when I say that he lives alone, but certainly if he lives with someone it isn't a close relationship since he can go out and prowl gay bars and hotels without raising questions. However,

I do feel fairly confident that he is intelligent. These are not disorganized, impulsive killings. They took planning. The level of planning is also why I push the killer's age up into his thirties."

"I hadn't thought of that," I said, and felt better for the admission. "Now, I can understand why you say that his reality is warped—I mean, he's killing people—but why do you think he's had a shock of some sort?"

Terrell shrugged. "Part of my reasoning is based on the Behavioral Science Unit's studies. There usually is some sort of trigger event that sets the killer off—provides justification, as it were, for what he has been fantasizing about doing for years. The reason I favor a death— probably of a parent, to stick my neck out a bit—over a divorce or separation is the peculiar sexual neutrality of the killings."

"Neutrality?"

"Not one of the six victims shows any sign of molestation either before or after death—not even the men, who were clearly picked up on the promise of sex. Sexual killers fall into all sorts of categories that I won't bother with here, but, at least with the evidence we have, the nature of the killings doesn't show sexual motivation; therefore, the trigger is not likely to be sexual as, for example, rejection by a spouse or lover could be seen to be sexual."

I thought about this for a moment, then nodded.

"That seems to be reaching," I said, "but I can follow your reasoning. I don't know how whether the killings are sexually motivated or not is going to help us catch the killer, though."

Terrell shrugged. "Maybe it won't, but it might help you when he contacts you."

"Contact," I said. "That's right. You mentioned that. What are you getting at? We haven't had any contact with him."

"But you have," Terrell said calmly. "The ceramic crab left in Martina Alvarez's room was probably left by the killer."

"She could have bought it herself," I said stubbornly. "They're sold all over town, even in her own hotel's gift shop."

"Not that one though," Terrell said.

"No, not that one," I admitted, "but she could have bought it elsewhere."

"Why?" Terrell pushed. "Why, if the same item was available right in her own hotel? Why was it put on top of the stack of newly opened gifts? Alvarez returned to her room directly from the birthday party. The friend who came back without her late that night recalls the gifts being put on that chair. There was no crab then. Within the next few hours Alvarez was murdered. When did she add the crab to the pile?"

I pressed my fingers to my face, trying not to feel badgered.

"All right," I said, making an effort to keep my voice level. "Let's surmise that the murderer left the ceramic crab. I assume you're also saying he left the toy bull and glass lion."

"Why not?" Terrell replied, so reasonable I wanted to slug him. "They're odd things for grown men to have in their rooms."

"Patricia Cooper didn't have anything left at her house," I reminded Terrell. "So I guess she's the one who doesn't fit the pattern, the one you're putting off on another killer."

"I'm not," Terrell said, for once losing a bit of his own cool, "putting anything off on anyone, but you must admit that there was nothing left in her house."

But I wasn't listening. Things were falling together in my head in a way I didn't like at all.

"Unless," I said, my voice suddenly so hoarse I had to swig coffee to clear my throat. "Unless the killer left the twins."

That shocked even Terrell. The idea of a killer so ruthless that he'd murder two men simply to provide a prop for a third killing was sickening. Up until then, we'd been looking for a reason behind the killings. Now I wasn't certain there was a reason. Maybe it was just senseless bloodlust.

"No reason?" Terrell responded when I voiced my fear. "There is always a reason. Sometimes it only makes sense to the killer, but there will be a reason."

"Maybe it has something to do with the birthdays," I offered. "Maybe he was leaving a gift for the dead person."

"Warped, but possible," Terrell agreed. "And even if the items were not connected to the birthdays, almost all cultures leave gifts for the dead. Only modern cemeteries try to keep people from being buried with treasured belongings."

"To stop grave robbing," I said, nodding, "or pilfering in mortuaries. Let's leave this for a moment and go back to your profile. What was the next point?"

Terrell hurried to take my suggestion.

"Local resident. I deduce this from how the killer knew the local homosexual joints—not a thing your city advertises."

I nodded, but felt I had to protest. "Samuel Morgan found one, and this was only his first visit."

"Moreover," Terrell went on undeterred, "the Howell cab was stashed behind a strip mall that was closed, so that the vehicle wouldn't have been noticed until at least the following day."

"If then," I said. "That mall's closed on Sundays."

"Better yet," Terrell replied. "Then there are my guesses as to hobbies and possible military service."

I was learning how these profilers thought by now.

"Let me guess," I said. "The weight lifting because he moved those bodies and all that other stuff, the same reasons you were sure he was male."

Terrell nodded.

"The hunting and shooting because of how he used the gun on the Howell brothers, and because of how he cut off Martina Alvarez's arms. We'd thought of that, you know, but it didn't prove to be much of a lead. Three-quarters of the males in this area seem to hunt. The first day of hunting season's just about a state holiday."

Terrell shrugged. "I never said that everything in my profile was going to be a revelation."

"I know," I admitted. "Just wishing it would be. I don't quite get the military service, though."

"I could be wrong," Terrell admitted. "It's a long shot based on the killer's coolness around dead people and quantities of blood. It suggests that something desensitized him."

"He could just as easily work for a mortuary," I argued, but I smiled, too, so Terrell would know that I'd gotten his point.

"Maybe," Terrell said. "If he's in the military, he wouldn't be on active service now because there'd be too many people around to notice if he kept disappearing."

"Kept?" I asked skeptically. "We only have four incidents here—counting the Cooper related murders as one."

"Four that you know about," Terrell replied. "I also don't think these were impulsive. It's likely he hunted out his victims over a period of time, looking for people who wouldn't be missed immediately. It's too much to believe that he got lucky every time he went out."

That was an appalling thought. It meant the killer could be out there right now, looking for number five.

"My profile's last item," Terrell went on, "was that the murderer could be a police groupie. Oddly enough, many serial killers are, but beyond that, we have his careful wiping away of finger prints . . ."

"Which anyone who watches television would do," I protested.

"But would someone with only a television viewer's interest in criminology be so careful on other points? All the weapons were common makes—no tracing the murderer through them. He left them behind—no telltale bloody knife or crowbar to get neighbors or casual visitors curious. He poured chemicals down the drain after he showered to remove forensic evidence. That shows more than causal interest."

"I see your point," I said, "though to me it more supports your contention that he's intelligent and organized than that he's a police groupie."

"Only," and from the way Terrell stiffened slightly I could tell where he was heading, "if you dismiss the evidence that he was leaving those odd items—the lion and the bull and the crab—in the rooms. What if he was leaving them for the police?"

I felt weary and stupid, never mind that it was only midday and that my nerves were dancing the caffeine boogie.

"Right. He's been leaving us messages and we haven't been catching on. So what the hell is he saying?"

"I wish," Terrell sighed, "that I knew."

I didn't really want to admit that Terrell was right about the killer sending us messages, but a few days after our meeting the killer himself resolved the matter. Seems that we slow coach police had pissed him off, not catching onto his cleverness, and he decided to prompt us a little.

The letter came to the station, addressed to me, and, just in case someone missed the point, sub-addressed:"The officer in charge of the investigation of the murder of Samuel Morgan." After the greeting line, the text continued:

*I am slaying the Serpent and its minions. Are you so stupid that you can't see? Martina Alvarez would have recognized the signs, so would Patricia Cooper and Samuel Morgan. Allain Fedorov might not have, but then he was my first and perhaps I chose less than wisely.*

*I did. I admit it. I was new and went for ease of execution rather than perfection. It may be that I shall need to kill him again, but I have a circle to round before then. And he wasn't a bad choice, just not the best.*

*I am disappointed by your stupidity. Each time I have left you a sign as to who shall next fall. You muddle around. I wonder if you will like my next message. It will surely break your heart even as I will break the next one's heart.*

*I cannot tell you more clearly. Then the Serpent would not be destroyed as it must be destroyed, its lying perfidy would not be revealed to the listening world. They must listen. It must die so they will listen and I will slay the circle round and round again until someone stops me and at last they listen.*

*I give you this. You have some weeks grace. Use them well.*

I had the damn thing dusted, but, of course, there was nothing. Nothing to the paper, either. The text had been produced on an ink-jet printer. No worn letters to trace. I could hate computers.

I copied the letter and expressed it to Terrell. Confided in the chief. He agreed with me that it was best to keep the entire thing under wraps. We didn't need the press to get a hold of it. I hated to think of the panic, the recriminations, the . . .

I didn't have time to think. The killer said I had a few weeks grace. He might be lying. He might not. Either way, I wasn't going to risk wasting a blessed day.

Now, I wasn't such a fool as to miss that the killer had linked Cooper, Alvarez, and Morgan. I set out to find what they had in common. Our earlier investigation—questioning people from Cooper's work place and who had attended Alvarez's birthday party—had revealed that a few of the same people knew both women. We'd even checked out alibis, but no one seemed a likely suspect for even one of the murders, much less for both.

Alvarez's friends had been, like her, fortune-tellers of one sort or another. Many had been her students. I decided to phone Mr. Cooper and learn if Patricia Cooper had been at all interested in fortune-telling.

Mr. Cooper, still stunned from the violence of his loss, was really helpful. Actually, I think he was too shaken for any question to seem odd.

"Fortune-telling?" He paused. "Well, not precisely. Pat was more interested in the mystic properties of various stones. She practiced scrying in a crystal ball, you know . . ."

I didn't, but I didn't say so. This was fascinating.

". . . And had some success. I always wondered how much was what she read in her crystal ball and how much was her innate knowledge of human nature. She was very sweet and insightful, my Pat."

His voice broke then and I hastened to say soothing things.

"One more question, Mr. Cooper," I asked. Then I went on. "Did your wife ever say anything about a serpent or someone called or nicknamed 'Serpent?' "

It sounded improbable to me, but Mr. Cooper considered.

"No, I don't think she ever did."

I thanked him and got off the line, frowning. I'd established a connection of sorts between two of the victims. Both told fortunes. There was one between Cooper and Morgan, too. He'd sold books to the store where she worked, though as far as I knew his only contact had been with Mina Ross, the store's owner. I called her.

"Ms. Ross," I said after identifying myself, "I have a possible lead to the killing of Patricia Cooper."

"That's wonderful!" she said in that tone of voice which really means, "It's about time."

"Yes, ma'am," I said, feeling chided. "May I consult you in confidence?"

I heard her get up and close a door. When she returned, her voice was crisp and businesslike.

"I'm in private now. What is it?"

"You recall that Samuel Morgan, the bookseller's rep, was killed last month?"

"It's not something you easily forget," she said. "The papers said that was gay-bashing or something . . ."

"It may well be," I said, "but we're looking into his death from another angle. Was there any connection between him and Patricia Cooper—any, no matter how slim?"

"You asked me that before," she said, "and I told you, I don't think so. He was a new rep, making the rounds to get to know store owners. We visited in my office and he left directly after. Anyhow, Pat was already dead, then."

Her voice broke, just like Mr. Cooper's had. Patricia Cooper must have been a nice person.

"How about fortune-telling?" I asked. "Did Samuel Morgan have any interest in that?"

Ms. Ross recovered herself.

"I don't know about him personally. I only met him once, but the press he works for—McWeylan Press—is known for its books on New Age subjects. We carry a few—on the mystic qualities of crystals and the like—because people *will* ask about that stuff and it's just easier to point them to a book than get into all of that."

Clearly, I thought, Mina Ross was not a believer in the mystic powers of crystals.

"Thank you," I said. "One more question. Can you think of anything related to Patricia Cooper having to do with something called a 'serpent' or perhaps a person with that nickname?"

Mina Ross, disbeliever in the mystic power of crystals, surprised me.

"Oh, that . . ." She chuckled. "If you're looking at fortune-telling, the serpent is an old name for the full cycle of the zodiac—all twelve signs."

I was glad that I'd phoned rather than gone to interview her in person. This way she couldn't see the astonished expression on my face. I rang off after cautioning Mina not to say anything to anyone. Then I got the file out and made some notes.

Bull. Twins. Crab. Lion.

I frowned, went out and borrowed the appropriate section of the newspaper from the day room, made some more notes.

Aries (Ram). Taurus (Bull). Gemini (Twins). Cancer (Crab). Leo (Lion). Virgo (Virgin).

I could have stopped writing after Cancer, even after Gemini, but I forced myself to finish the list. A quick trip to the main library just across the town square got me a couple of children's books on astrology and Linda Goodman's *Sun Signs*.

I'd just finished reading and making more notes when the phone rang. It was Terrell of the FBI.

"Got your letter," he said and if he sounded a bit smug, who was going to blame him? "So, the killer got in touch."

"Like you said," I replied giving him the pat on the head he clearly wanted. "And I've figured out a hell of a lot."

"That's great," Terrell said. "Tell me."

I did, starting with my interview with Mr. Cooper, then moving to Mina Ross and surging into my recent deductions.

"You were right," I said. "He was leaving us messages. Each of those things he placed in the rooms is linked to a sign of the zodiac, but not the sign of the person he'd just killed, the next sign on the cycle."

"Telling us," Terrell said, and I liked him for that "us," "that his next victim was going to be someone with that sign, that he was continuing 'slaying the serpent,' as he said in his letter."

"Right," I said, "but he left us more than that. The location of the death wound was also linked to the victim's sign of the zodiac. Fedorov was an Aries. Aries is the first sign in the zodiac calendar. It's associated with the head."

"And Fedorov," Terrell said, "was beaten about the head."

"Right." The words spilled out of me as I explained. "He followed right down the body. Neck for Taurus. Arms for Gemini — explaining that particularly gruesome way of killing someone. Chest for Cancer. He even hinted at the Leo connection in his letter. Leo is associated with the heart and he says he'll break the next one's heart."

Terrell made encouraging noises and I kept talking.

"The thing that really bothers me is the pattern he's established. Leo is followed by Virgo—that's the virgin, sometimes termed the maiden. Given how he killed the Howell twins rather than leaving matching dolls or pictures of some famous twins, I'm afraid he's going to kill a young girl or maybe a nun or someone like that to leave as his token."

"Seems reasonable," Terrell replied, but the anger in his voice made it clear he didn't think it at all reasonable. "Ask for any and all missing person's reports to cross your desk. Maybe you can anticipate him. He must have spotted the Howell twins and figured out how he could get them without much fuss. A child or a nun he'll probably snatch earlier."

"Any ideas on how we pinpoint his Leo?"

"One," Terrell said. "All four of his previous victims—if we categorize the Howells as tokens—were in some way associated with fortune-telling."

"How do you fit Fedorov in?" I asked.

"He was a stockbroker," Terrell said with a dry laugh. "If playing the market isn't trying to foretell the future, I don't know what is. Seriously, the killer himself admits that Fedorov didn't fit his pattern as neatly as he could wish."

"Okay," I said. "I'll buy your theory. So I need to find and watch all Leos who are associated with fortune-telling."

"Nearly impossible, I know," Terrell said, "especially with a small force."

"Nearly, but not impossible," I agreed. "The hard part will be keeping this out of the papers. The chief has spoken to the mayor, and both say to keep this quiet."

"Sounds cold," Terrell said, "but that may be the best thing. Widespread publicity could feed the killer's ego. Right now he's playing to you. Let's keep him on that smaller stage."

I agreed. We'd already had evidence of the killer's growing confidence. The man who had killed Fedorov because an Aries stockbroker came close enough to fitting his pattern wasn't the same man who had killed the Howell twins just a month later or who had written me that chiding note.

The sun wouldn't enter Leo (I think that's how the books put it), until July 23. We had time. Unless something set him off sooner, that is.

I don't want to live those weeks again, not ever. The first thing I did was get my family out of town. I felt like a heel for doing it, but I couldn't concentrate with them near. I'm divorced, but my mother lives with me and takes care of my kids. They all went to California to see my mom's sister.

Then I started putting in eighteen hour days and sleeping at my desk the other six. The chief assigned me a few officers, including the one who'd broken the gang-related murders. They took the news of what we were after pretty well, sealed their lips, and worked almost as many hours as I did. I made sure they took time off, though, because I didn't want anyone asking questions about the overtime. I've a reputation as a workaholic and with my family out of town . . .

The killer's letter had come on July fifth. I'd sorted out things that day and into the sixth. Between the seventh and the twentieth, my team and I pinpointed every potential Leo we could. Happily, driver's licenses have birth dates, so do requests for business licenses. I put a couple members of my team to hunting out psychics, fortune-tellers, crystal ball readers, and all the rest. We even checked registered stockbrokers, just in case the killer had to slip back to that less than satisfactory type of prognosticator.

We rated these potential victims on a scale of one to five with those actively involved with the zodiac rated one and down from there. We gave pluses for those whose lifestyle made them tempting targets. After all, Samuel Morgan had, as far as we could tell, done nothing worse than sell books that dealt with fortune-telling, but his lifestyle had made him vulnerable.

We also gave pluses to those who frequented places dealing with fortune-telling and related matters. These occult groupies—as I couldn't help but think of them—would be easier for our killer to find and chat up. I had one of my team disguise herself and hang around these places, trying to get a line on our killer.

Sounds calm and organized, doesn't it? Sure until you realize that every day that passed was cramped guts and nervous tension. I drank nearly as much coffee as Terrell. I reviewed missing person reports like a preacher with the Bible. Every death—murder or accident— had to be reviewed, just in case it fit the killer's pattern.

Then on July twentieth, the little girl who lived next door to me was kidnapped. Her name was Sabrina, and she was as pretty a little fair-haired, blue-eyed angel as you could wish. I'd known her since she was a bump in her mom's belly and, since she was just a year younger than my own daughter, Elaine, I saw a lot of her. Sabrina and Elaine were in the same scout troop, went to the same school, played together and squabbled together.

To make matters worse, Sabrina was snatched off the swings in my yard. I felt a chill right down to the soles of my feet because I knew that the killer had meant to get Elaine. I'd preserved my daughter, but at the expense of her best friend.

I called Terrell and he calmed me down some. Now that it was a matter of kidnapping, we could bring the FBI in without raising eyebrows. In fact we'd have raised more if we hadn't brought them in.

The newspapers covered the kidnapping, of course, but they didn't tie things to the unsolved murders. We just had to hope that the killer wouldn't do it for them. It was bad enough that a few journalistic bright lights had speculated that Elaine, not Sabrina, had been the target. We didn't need for them to guess why. We let them go on about gangs and revenge, and appreciated that they didn't dig deeper.

At last, the two weeks of legwork we'd done began to pay off. We had a list of suspects. Quietly, carefully, we began to check if any of them were behaving oddly. More oddly, I should say. Lots of these folks seemed pretty strange to me.

Carrie, my undercover officer, had pinpointed a couple good possibilities. On the very day Sabrina was kidnapped, one showed signs of breaking his usual routine. His name was Floyd Fletcher and he fit our profile rather more neatly than I liked.

Floyd was a big, muscular man. While not precisely handsome, in the fairly peaceful, bookish community we were discovering, he stood out like a bull in a herd of cows. He was a local, he hunted, had done a hitch in the Army, was unattached. While not precisely a police groupie, he was the kind of rebellious personality who keeps a close eye on what he thinks of as the enemy. Finally, his mother, to whom he had been very close, had died the previous winter. Floyd, by all reports, had been devastated.

Usually on Sundays, Floyd dropped in at a rather nice coffee bar and book store called Danu's Children for lunch and to pick up a weekly periodical. On the day Sabrina was kidnapped, he didn't show. One of the store clerks who had a bit of a crush on Floyd served as Carrie's informal watchdog. She was more than pleased to have Carrie ask after the object of her affections, even admitted that she'd called his number but had only gotten the answering machine.

Carrie, who has the makings of a great cop, called in right away rather than going to check out Floyd's house by herself. Terrell and I drove by in Terrell's car. The place was a former farmhouse set on a couple of acres. It looked quiet, but Floyd's truck, a Dodge Ram pickup, was in the driveway.

My street's paved, but the FBI forensics team had lifted a partial tire print from the dust at the curb in front of Sabrina's house. It sure matched what we saw repeated over and over again in the dirt driveway.

"Justifiable?" I asked.

Terrell shrugged. "A friendly judge might give us a warrant. I wouldn't want to try without one."

I knew he was right, but I hated waiting. The thought of little Sabrina in there, scared, maybe dead, made me sick. Still, I kept my cool, phoned the station, and by the time we got back the chief had a warrant from our friendly judge.

"I love working with the locals," was all Terrell said as the warrant was run out to us.

Our contact team included Carrie. Our plan was to have her go in first since we were afraid that if Floyd realized the police were onto him, he might panic and hurt Sabrina.

Carrie's persona was what she called a gypsy goth. I took her word for it, pleased that the floaty skirts and loose blouse meant that she could both be wired and pack a weapon. The heavy cosmetics she wore—pale foundation and black around her eyes like Nefertiti or something—made certain that even someone who watched the cops wouldn't recognize her.

She drove up Floyd's driveway in a sedan painted matte black and nearly papered with bumper stickers saying things like "The Force is with Me" and "Goddess Knows." We trailed in Terrell's car, grateful for the thick summer greenery that lined both sides of the road. A couple other officers were standing by about a half mile back, ready to speed in at my signal.

Carrie sauntered up to the house's side door—the front one was clearly never used. She had Floyd's usual reading material tucked under one arm. She rapped on the door, rapped again. We listened to the sound of her heart beating far faster than anyone looking at that pert confidence would have imagined. Just as she was turning away, the door opened and she swung around.

*Carrie*: "Hi, Floyd! Misty was worried when you didn't come in. I told her I'd drop by and make sure you were okay."

Her voice was cheerful and friendly, with just the smallest hint of flirtation underlying the inflection.

*Floyd*: "That's real nice of you, Carissa."

*Carrie*: "So this is your place. Mind if I see it?"

*Floyd*: (obviously reluctant) "Well, it's a bit of a mess. I haven't exactly kept it in what Mother called apple pie order."

*Carrie* (laughing) "I always thought apple pies were kind of messy, but if you don't want me to . . ."

*Floyd*: "Well, why not the nickel tour?"

We were racing up the edge of the driveway now that Carrie had Floyd's line of sight restricted. Her "Mind if I see it?" let us know that the way was clear.

We didn't waste any time. Just as she was stepping after Floyd, we were thundering up the wooden steps. I was displaying the search warrant and reciting the routine. Terrell was just behind me, his hand near enough to his gun that I didn't doubt he'd have it out if Floyd gave us trouble.

Floyd didn't though. He just grinned, a weird grin, goofy and maybe a bit relieved.

"You found me," he said, and he was looking right at me. It was as if Terrell and Carrie weren't even there. "Don't worry, the little girl's okay. I didn't want her rotting and smelling up the place before I'd killed the Lion, you know."

He was so matter-of-fact, I nearly choked. I managed to keep my cool, though, sent Carrie to find Sabrina, and recited Floyd's Miranda rights before asking:

"Why did you do it, Floyd?"

He grinned. "The Serpent had lied. I tried to tell everyone, but they wouldn't listen to me. I needed a platform."

I didn't understand, but later, when Floyd had talked and talked, both to us and to his court-appointed lawyer, I got a glimpse into his twisted view of reality.

Mrs. Fletcher had been a complete nut about the zodiac and stuff like that. She'd had her chart cast and practically lived by the damned thing. She'd raised her son by his, too, promising him that fame and financial security were in the stars.

I guess she was right, in a way, if being convicted of kidnapping and multiple murders, then spending your life in prison is your idea of fame and financial security.

But this alone hadn't been what pushed Floyd over the edge. His mother claimed she had been promised a long life. When she died from heart disease at age fifty-seven, he felt personally betrayed.

He set out to ritually slay the zodiac by killing those who foretold the future. Moreover, he sought to make himself so notorious that his story — like the stories of Charles Manson, Ted Bundy, or John Wayne Gacy — would be told over and over again. He was caught in a bind. He wanted to be caught so he could tell the world about the zodiac's betrayal, but he wanted to keep killing, too, in order to add to his notoriety.

When Floyd was led out of the courtroom that last time he turned to me and smiled:

"I knew I'd get my way," he said, "when I learned you were on my case. You see, Mother always said a woman would be my downfall."

# THE SEA HORSE

### Edward Marston

"WELCOME ABOARD THE *Sirius*!" said Luke Sanderson, giving her a mock salute. "Your captain is at your service."

"That remains to be seen," she replied with a teasing smile.

"Is that an invitation or a challenge?"

"Who knows?"

"You're being very provocative today, Tania."

"I hope that you don't object."

"Quite the opposite."

"Good." Her smile broadened. "I have a soft spot for sailors."

They shared a laugh then Luke helped her to get the luggage aboard. When it had been stowed away in the cabin, he took a proper look at Tania Kew and signaled his approbation with a roll of his eyes. Short but shapely, she wore a red T-shirt, white trousers and a pair of navy blue deck shoes with white lacing. Luke had only ever seen her before across the table in a restaurant when Tania was immaculately dressed in one of the sober outfits she favored at work. Clients who saw her now would hardly recognize her as the efficient young lawyer with whom they did business. Dark brown hair that was brushed neatly back into a chignon now hung loosely to her shoulders. Luke, too, had undergone a complete transformation. The financial consultant from a top firm in the City was sporting a uniform that would have done justice to the skipper of cruise ship in the Caribbean. It made a pleasantly ugly man in his thirties look decidedly raffish.

"When are the others due?" asked Tania.

"Any moment," he said. "Neil will probably drive down with Kit Greeves."

"What about Faith?"

"Oh, she's coming as well."

"Isn't Neil bringing her?" wondered Tania. "I thought they were an item."

Luke sighed. "Yes, they were until last weekend. I need to warn you about that. Apparently, they had another of their explosive rows and split up."

"Yet they're still *sailing* together?"

"Neil being Neil, there was no way he'd miss out on the treat."

"It won't be much of a treat if Faith is scowling at him all the time," said Tania with a frown. "And I can't see that she'll enjoy being cooped up on a boat with her latest reject. It could make for a very nasty atmosphere."

"Not while I'm around," promised Luke with a grin. "This is a voyage of pleasure. Neil and Faith both accept that. They'll be no problem. Besides," he went on, "they'll be too busy to have a slanging match. Neil will be helping me to sail the boat and Faith will be preoccupied with her new friend."

Tania was surprised. "A new *boy*friend?"

"No," said Luke, shaking his head, "even Faith doesn't work that fast. It's an old flatmate of hers who surfaced again after ten or twelve years. They were at Cambridge together. Faith was delighted when she got in touch again and begged me to let her come along. She said it was like having a wonderful new friend."

"And who is this wonderful new friend?"

"Miranda Hart."

"Is she an academic like Faith?"

"No, Tania. She's a consultant astrologer."

"A what?"

"Miranda casts horoscopes."

"Only for the idiots who believe in such things," said Tania sceptically.

'You don't, obviously.'

'Horoscopes are a load of crap.'

"I know. Nevertheless, we all take a peep at them in the morning papers. Miranda sounds like an interesting lady," observed Luke. "She could turn out to be a lot of fun."

"Could she?"

"Yes, Tania."

"As long as she doesn't try that Madame Miranda routine on me."

"You underestimate her. Miranda doesn't sit in a tent with a crystal ball. She's much further up the food chain than that. There's serious money in astrology. She writes books, gives lectures, attends conventions."

'There must be a lot of gullible people in the world.'

'Thank heaven!' said Luke cheerfully. "Most of them are my clients. Three cheers for gullibility! It's what helped to buy this amazing boat for me."

Tania softened. "It's marvelous, Luke," she said, glancing around. "So spacious."

"She can sleep six with comfort, eight at a pinch."

"Who decides the sleeping arrangements?"

He grinned. "Mother Nature."

Luke was very proud of the craft, purchased on impulse at the Boat Show but a source of continuous pleasure for him. He loved to be able to take his friends for weekend trips in the *Sirius*. Assuming the mantle of captain gave him a sense of power and excitement. He showed Tania around the vessel and pointed out its special features. His guest was more interested in the people with whom she would be sailing.

"How old is this stargazer?" she asked.

"The same age as Faith, I suppose. Early thirties."

"Single?"

"Widowed, from what I gather."

"Does that mean she's on the prowl?"

"I hope so," said Luke with a smirk. "I like prowling females."

"Faith will be on the loose again, if she's junked Neil. The boat will be overrun with spare women. That will suit you, Luke." He laughed merrily. "Who was that other chap you mentioned?"

"Kit Greeves? He's a bookseller."

Tania was disappointed. "He works behind a counter at Waterstone's?"

"No, Tania. He specializes in rare books and cartography. Kit is an expert."

"At what?"

"Doing what we all do," said Luke complacently.

"And what's that?"

"Making a healthy profit out of our chosen professions."

"I wouldn't call astrology a profession," she observed sourly.

"Miranda makes a mint out of it."

"I'm a lawyer, remember. I'd call that fraud."

Luke beamed. "I sail pretty close to the wind at times myself," he admitted. "Much of my work is akin to a glorious confidence trick."

"That's different."

"Is it?"

"Yes, Luke," she said sharply. "I'm sorry but I have a thing about so-called astrologers. They're complete crooks. Only an imbecile would be taken in by them."

"Miranda may change your mind."

"Don't bank on it."


The men were the first to arrive. Big, bearded and relentlessly affable, Neil Ambrose was a former chef who now had his own column in a national newspaper. As well as helping to sail the boat, he was in charge of any meals eaten aboard and had brought boxes of food with him. Tania liked Neil though she wondered if she could endure his hearty laughter for a whole weekend. Kit Greeves was the oldest of the passengers. Almost forty, he had somehow managed to keep his hair, his slim body and his handsome features. Tania warmed to him immediately. Kit was an intelligent man with a dry sense of humor. He also donated four bottles of champagne to the galley. Like Neil and Luke, he was clearly determined to enjoy the trip. Tania basked in the glow of their attention.

The women arrived in a flurry of apologies. The train had been late leaving Charing Cross and they had difficulty finding a taxi at Folkestone station. They clambered aboard the *Sirius*. Faith Brigh-

twell was an intense woman of medium height and spreading girth,
her striking beauty now encroached upon by bulging cheeks and a
supplementary chin. She taught Mathematics at a London Polytech-
nic that had now been elevated to University status and it gave her a
faint air of superiority. Evidently, she and Neil had reached a prior
agreement to be excessively nice to each other because they kissed
affectionately, exchanged happy banter and went out of their way to
indicate that their estrangement would not be allowed to spoil the
weekend for the others. Luke was relieved. Tension aboard was bad
for everyone.

It was Miranda Hart who was the revelation. After the praise heaped
on her by Faith, Luke had expected a female paragon. Instead, he
was introduced to a tall, thin, angular woman who stooped badly and
who was painfully shy. Her hair was straggly, her face plain and un-
acquainted with cosmetics. In her woolly cardigan and mustard-
coloured skirt, she looked a ridiculous sailor. Luke gave her a cordial
welcome.

"I might have named the boat in your honor," he said to her.

"Might you?" she murmured.

"*Sirius*. The brightest of stars."

"Ah, yes."

"Be honest, Luke," joked Neil, giving him a nudge. "You named
her after yourself. Sirius is the dog-star. Luke Sanderson is not only a
star of the financial world, he's the most lecherous old dog, I know."

Miranda did not join in the general laughter. She seemed to be
having doubts about the wisdom of accepting the invitation to join
the party. Even when the first bottle of champagne was opened, she
did not relax. Tania began to feel sorry for the woman but she was
also relieved. Miranda Hart would pose no threat to her primacy nor
would the overweight Faith Brightwell. She had a clear field. Luke,
Neil and Kit Greeves were all hers. Tania could play the three of
them off against each other. It was the kind of game that she relished.

The crossing was remarkably calm. With Luke at the helm, the *Sirius*
glided effortlessly across the water, her powerful engine purring steadily away. Neil prepared a snack for the passengers then relieved Luke
so that he could enjoy the refreshment with the others. It was exhil-

arating to sit on deck with the sun beating down on them and the wind ruffling their hair. They were soon into the third bottle of champagne. Miranda Hart was monopolized by Faith who reminisced endlessly about their time together at Cambridge.

"I never dreamed that you'd end up in astrology," she said.

"Nor did I, Faith."

"You were a linguist."

"That was a bonus," said Miranda quietly. "I've been able to read French and German astrologers in the original. Nothing is wasted."

"That was your motto at Cambridge."

"I once sold a copy of *Zadkiel's Almanac*," said Kit Greeves, inserting himself politely into the conversation. "A rare early edition. I got an excellent price for it."

"I'm not surprised," said Miranda.

"Who was Zadkiel?" asked Faith.

"Who cares?" muttered Tania under her breath.

"His real name was Richard James Morrison," explained Miranda. "He was an naval officer who became an astrologer and founded the Almanac in 1830. As a seafaring man, he knew the value of being able to read the stars."

"I could steer by them if I had to," boasted Luke.

Miranda smiled. "I hope that it won't come to that."

"What did your husband do?" asked Tania, irritated that Miranda had now taken center-stage without even trying. "Was he in the same line of business as you or did he earn an honest penny?"

"Oh, Howard was no astrologer," said Miranda fondly.

"No?"

"He sold swimming pools." She heaved a sigh. "It was ironic, really."

"Why is that?"

"I can't swim."

Luke laughed. "You were hardly well-matched, then."

"We were," said Miranda loyally. "It was a marriage of true minds in every sense. But, unhappily, it didn't last. Howard was killed last year. It was the one time when I felt guilty about being an astrologer."

"Guilty?" repeated Faith. "Why?"

"Because I foresaw his death."

"Nobody can do that," argued Tania.

"I did," said Miranda.

"You're lying."

"No, I'm not," said Miranda solemnly. "I cast his horoscope. It was a chilling moment. I foretold both the time and manner of my husband's death."

Even Tania was silenced by the announcement. There were tears in Miranda's eyes. Faith put a comforting arm around her, Kit looked deeply sympathetic and Luke wondered if he should press for details. Neil's voice rang out across the deck.

"Any of that champagne left?"

When they reached Boulogne that afternoon, they went ashore immediately to explore the town. Tania linked arms familiarly with Neil and Luke. Determined to be the center of attention, she was peeved when Miranda once again stole her limelight. The dowdy astrologer not only spoke fluent French, she seemed to have a fascination for Kit Greeves. He plied her endlessly with titles of obscure books about astrology, trying to win her favor by a display of arcane knowledge. Faith was prompted into airing her own expertise, talking contemptuously about her students and comparing them unfavorably to the undergraduates with whom she had studied at Cambridge.

Dinner was eaten on the terrace of a restaurant that overlooked the harbor. Tania was careful to sit between Luke and Kit, flirting with both while exchanging intermittent glances with Neil Ambrose. As the acknowledged chef, he was allowed to choose from the menu though Miranda's command of the language was once again called into play during the discussion with the waiter. Wine flowed freely. It made Faith more intense, Kit more desperate to impress Miranda, and Neil more prone to bursts of incongruous laughter. Luke was in his element, hosting the party and regaling them with tales of how he had cleverly overcharged some clients to the tune of fifty thousand pounds. Tania felt his hand on her thigh. Neil was shooting even more lustful glances at her. She was beginning to enjoy the situation when the whole mood suddenly changed.

"Tania thinks that astrology is a load of crap," declared Luke.

"Most people do," said Miranda tolerantly. "I did myself at first."

"Was that before you saw the commercial potentialities?" said Tania spikily.

"No, it was before I cast my own horoscope and found it uncannily accurate."

"Sheer coincidence!"

"Is it, Tania?"

"Of course."

"Then how do you explain the fact that I foresaw that my husband would be killed in a car accident during the month of April? Was that sheer coincidence as well?"

"He should have given up driving," said Neil with a misplaced laugh.

"He did," said Miranda calmly. "He even refused to let me drive him."

"So what happened?"

"Howard went everywhere by bus or train. Unfortunately, on his way back from a client in Hereford, the train broke down. The passengers had to be ferried to the next station by a fleet of coaches and taxis. Howard was in a taxi," she recalled. "It never reached the station. He was the only person to die in the crash."

"What rotten luck!" said Kit.

Faith nodded soulfully. "It must have been a shattering blow."

"It might still have been a coincidence," said Tania.

"Don't be so cynical," reproved Luke.

"Somebody around here has to keep in touch with reality."

"Howard was killed exactly as I predicted," said Miranda. "That was my reality."

"Have you made any predictions about yourself?" asked Kit.

"Yes," she replied. "I cast my horoscope at the start of each year."

"So what does 2002 hold for you?" sneered Tania. "A meeting with a tall, dark handsome man? Or a string of incredulous clients who pay to listen to your claptrap?"

"It's not claptrap," said Faith defensively.

"Do *you* believe it?"

"Well . . . not entirely, perhaps."

"Nor me," added Neil, emitting his thunderous laugh.

"Astrology has a much more scholarly base than you imagine," insisted Kit. "Those who've plumbed its mysteries can make remarkable predictions."

Tania was unconvinced. "Is that what Miranda's done?" she teased. "Plumbed its mysteries? Or is she just lucky with her guesswork?"

The debate was shifted to another level. Luke and Kit spoke up for Miranda but Tania and Neil were openly derisive about the claims of astrologers. Faith was caught in the middle, anxious to support her friend yet having reservations about her ability to make accurate predictions. Miranda said nothing. As the arguments became more heated, she withdrew into her shell. It was Neil Ambrose who drew her out again.

"Prove it!" he taunted. "Come on, Miranda. Prove it."

"Prove what?" she said.

"That there's some truth in all that nonsense."

"Yes," goaded Tania. "Prove it."

Miranda shrugged. "It's not as easy as that." Neil and Tania jeered at her. "Is anyone around this table a practicing Christian?" she asked.

"I am," said Luke, "but no matter how hard I practice, I never get it right."

Miranda spoke over Neil's braying laughter. "It was a serious question. Kit?"

"I'm a sort of Pick and Mix Christian," he confessed.

"That would sum up my position as well," said Faith. "In spite of my name, my faith comes and goes. However, I'd insist on getting married in a church," she went on, shooting a look of hostility at Neil, "but the only person who ever proposed was a confirmed atheist."

"Guilty as charged," said Neil with a chuckle. "What about you, Tania?"

"I loathe all religions," said Tania with sudden ferocity. "And with good cause. I was born in China where my father was a Catholic missionary. It was excruciating. I think I was ten when I saw through the whole charade. I hated my parents for trying to bring me up as a good Catholic. In my view, that's a contradiction in terms."

"Right," said Miranda calmly. "We obviously don't have any potential saints around the table but all of you have had some kind of Christian upbringing. And what was the sign that marked the birth of

Jesus Christ? A star in the east. When you believed in that, as you all once did," she pointed out, "you believed in astrology."

The remark set off another barrage of complaint and accusation. Luke ordered two more bottles of wine before joining in the discussion. Stroking Tania's leg under the table with one hand, he turned to Miranda.

"I'm a Taurus," he declared. "What does that make me?"

"The bull of the herd," said Neil.

"I asked Miranda."

"The miserable cow!" said Tania to herself.

"Taurus is a fixed sign," explained Miranda. "If stressed, it will make the mind just, uncompromising, constant, firm of purpose, prudent, patient, industrious, strict, chaste, mindful of injuries, steady in pursuing its object—"

"What is this?" interrupted Tania. "Some mantra that you chant at your clients?"

"I was quoting the most famous astrologer of ancient times—Ptolemy."

"He was writing in the third century B.C," said Kit knowledgeably.

Tania was scathing. "They didn't even know that the world was round then."

"You still haven't *proved* anything, Miranda," challenged Neil.

"What's the point of offering proof to those who wouldn't recognize it?" she said.

"*I'd* recognize it," promised Faith.

"So would I," said Luke, emptying his glass as fresh wine arrived. "A moment ago, you described the salient characteristics of a Taurean. Could you do it the other way around, Miranda? When you get to know someone well enough, can you guess the sign under which they're born?"

"Usually," said Miranda. "For instance, even if I didn't already know that Faith's birthday was in December, I'd pick her out as a typical Sagittarian. She belongs to the Fire Element. She's a great optimist who thrives on challenges. Faith never does anything by halves. She pursues her interests with real vigor. Oh, and she's very honest as well. She's not given to deception."

Faith was pleased. "That sums me up perfectly."

"She missed out the fact that you have a foul temper," said Neil bitterly.

"Okay," resumed Luke, filling their glasses with a new bottle, "you've got Faith and me pegged. What about Tania, Kit and Neil? How long would it take you to work out their birth signs."

"Not too long," said Miranda. "I've plenty to go on already."

Kit was amused. "Do we give ourselves away so easily?"

"Certain characteristics always show through."

"Then find them," decided Luke. "Tell me the month in which the three of them were born and I'll never have doubts about astrologers again. Is it a deal?"

Miranda looked around the faces. The expressions on them ranged from curiosity to cold antagonism. She sipped her wine before making her announcement.

"I'll make one prediction," she said confidently. "By the end of this year, one of us will have met a premature death." She gave a knowing smile. "Who will it will be?"

By the time they got back to the boat, most of them were too drunk to do anything more than tumble into their bunks. Miranda remained on deck, wrapped in the warm blanket of night as she gazed up at the stars. It was Kit Greeves who eventually joined her.

"You certainly shut them up," he said with admiration.

'Who?'

"Neil and Tania. They were baiting you, Miranda."

"I'm used to that kind of thing," she said wearily.

"That prediction about one of us dying really shook them. It takes a lot to put Neil Ambrose in his place," he continued, sitting beside her. "Faith could never manage it. That's why she broke up with him. Neil laughs at everything."

"Yes, I know. Faith told me all about him on the journey down here."

"Deep down, I think that she still loves him. That's her weakness."

"What's yours, Kit?"

"Oh, there's no doubt about that. Books. I can't resist them."

"So I gather."

"They never let you down, Miranda. Books are always there to yield up their treasure whenever you want it. No angry moods, no squabbles, no recriminations. The printed page is the most reliable of friends."

"That depends on what's printed on it, surely."

"Of course," he said loftily. "One has to be selective."

"You sound as if you're highly selective, Kit."

"I am, believe me."

"You only choose the best."

"That's why I'm here," he said, slipping an arm rather clumsily around here. "I got fed up with listening to Neil's snores so I came up on deck. It seems a shame to waste such a beautiful night as this."

Miranda neither resisted nor encouraged him. When he kissed her gently on the cheek, she offered no reproach. Kit pulled her closer and turned her to face him. The look in her eyes made him release her at once.

"What's wrong?" he whispered.

"You chose the wrong book."

"Is it your husband? Are you still grieving over him?"

"Yes, but that's not the reason."

"Then what is? We don't want to be the odd ones out, do we?"

"What do you mean?"

"Oh, come on, Miranda," he said, taking her hand. "You're not that naïve. Luke didn't invite us on this trip to enjoy our intellectual companionship. He's got his eye on Tania. Sooner or later, they'll be sharing the same bunk. The same goes for Neil and Faith, if you ask me," he predicted. "Did you notice the way he squired her back to the boat? When he wakes up in the morning, the first thing he'll do is to reach out for her and Faith will be there for him." He leaned in closer. "That leaves you and me."

"Does it?"

"You don't need to be a mathematician of Faith's standard to work it out."

"Six minus four equals two."

"Three men, three women, three partnerships."

"I thought that you preferred books."

"Not while you're around," he said, about to kiss her on the lips.

Miranda shielded herself with a palm. "No, Kit."

"Why not?"

"Because I just wanted to enjoy a quiet night under the stars."

"That's what we *are* doing, isn't it?"

"I'm afraid not. You have a different agenda, Kit. I don't flatter myself," she said levelly. "I'm not as attractive as Faith or as sexy as Tania. If you really wanted a woman, you could have gone after one of them but you deliberately went for me—the last resort."

"That's not true," he protested.

"Yes, it is. They threaten you. I don't." She eased him away. "But I'm sorry, Kit. I simply can't do it."

"Do what?"

"Help you to prove that you're not gay. Why bother? We both know the truth."

Eyes blazing, he leapt to his feet. "Tania was right about you," he said with vehemence. "You're a bitch, Miranda. A cruel, calculating, nasty little bitch!"

And he rushed back to the cabin.

Sunday morning found them in varying stages of recovery. Neil Ambrose was in high spirits, showing no signs of a hangover and serving breakfast to each new person who emerged from the cabin to join in the *al fresco* meal. As he handed a plate to the somnolent Kit Greeves, he described some of the tricks of the trade he had used as a chef to persuade his customers that they were eating something far more exotic than they actually were. It was clear to Miranda that one prediction had been borne out. At some time during the night, Faith Brightwell had obviously succumbed to her former partner. There was an air of triumph about Neil as he flitted to and fro between the galley and the deck. Faith, by contrast, was grumpy and withdrawn, regretting her capitulation and angry at the way that Neil was, in effect, trumpeting it aloud. Tania Kew was at her most tetchy. A dawn fumble with Luke Sanderson had been deeply disappointing and she had let him know it in the most vivid language. When the skipper of the *Sirius* finally came out into the light of day, he was still suffering the effects of too much wine and brandy. His eyes never dared to stray in Tania's direction.

By mid-morning, Luke had revived enough to take the boat along the coast to a quiet little bay. Anchored well out from the shore, it became a diving board for the swimmers. Neil was the first to go in, eager to show off his physique. Luke went into the water with a spectacular dive, anxious to impress Tania and to show that he had recovered completely from the excesses of the previous night. Faith was eventually lured into the water but she kept well clear of Neil who was thrashing about wildly. Tania, too, could not resist the temptation of a swim on such a hot and sunny morning, though she posed on the edge of the boat for a long time before jumping in, allowing the men to appraise her trim body in its scanty bikini.

Kit was the last to take the plunge. Wearing a pair of neat blue swimming trunks, he was lean, muscled and tanned to a light brown. He looked across at Miranda.

"Aren't you going in?" he asked.

"I told you. I can't swim."

"Then do us all a favor and leap overboard."

Miranda ignored the gibe and the water that splashed over her when Kit dived in. She remained on deck in a blouse and a pair of slacks, glad to be alone at last. When an impromptu game of water polo started, the men became very competitive. Miranda watched them from the safety of the boat, noting how quickly they regressed into childhood. Faith was treading water lazily but Tania was striking out for the shore as if to prove her credentials as a swimmer. An hour soon passed. Having worked up an appetite, they all came back to the *Sirius*. Luke toweled himself off in the sunshine.

"We're still waiting for that proof, Miranda," he said.

"Yes," added Neil, grinning at her. "You haven't told me what I am."

"A prize idiot!" muttered Faith.

"Start with Kit," suggested Luke. "What's his birth sign?"

Miranda pondered. "I think he's a Piscean," she decided. "True or false?"

"True," conceded Kit with a scowl.

"There you are!" shouted Luke. "It *does* work."

Tania was still skeptical. "A fluke guess."

"It was more than that. Tell us how you did it, Miranda."

"By simple observation," she said. "Pisces is the last of the Water signs and the twelfth in the Zodiac. It's in a privileged position. Pisceans are extraordinary people as a rule. Compassionate and understanding. They're very high-minded. In practical terms," she went on, indicating the sea, "they're drawn to water which is why Kit is such a good swimmer."

"I'm a good swimmer," asserted Luke, "but I'm no Piscean."

"No, Luke. You're ruled by Venus."

He chuckled lecherously. "I won't argue with that."

"Kit, on the other hand, is ruled by Neptune, the planet of mystery, escapism and deception. That's the down side of being a Piscean, I'm afraid. They make excellent martyrs but they're also inclined to self-deception." She raised a quizzical eyebrow. "Is that a fair description of you, Kit?"

"Not in the slightest," he retorted.

"I'd say that it was spot on," said Luke. "What about Neil and Tania?"

"I'm still working on them," admitted Miranda.

"Count me out," snapped Tania, drying her hair. "I'm not playing this silly game."

Luke waved an admonitory finger. "It's not a game, Tania. It's a scientific experiment under controlled conditions. So far, Miranda has scored a hundred per cent."

"Nice to know that someone has scored around here," she murmured to him.

"Tania!"

"I'm going to get changed."

She flounced off into the cabin and Luke went after her, gesticulating wildly.

Neil read the situation. "Perhaps I should give him a few tips," he said.

"Be quiet, Neil!" reproached Faith.

"Sex is only a form of astrology. Celestial bodies moving in the same orbit."

She was livid. "Do you have to tell everybody?"

"The only person who doesn't seem to know that it happened is you, Faith."

It was her turn to stalk off to the cabin. Neil went after her, showering Faith with a mixture of apology and blandishment. Raised voices continued for some time. Kit finished drying himself off and moved across to Miranda. He seemed contrite.

"I'm sorry for what I said earlier," he began. "You caught me on the raw."

"Your secret is safe with me."

"It's hardly a secret, Miranda. I think that Luke rumbled me years ago."

"Faith hasn't. She told me you were an eligible bachelor."

"Technically, that's what I am."

"One eligible bachelor searching for another."

"No, Miranda. Someone who prefers his own company most of the time."

"Yet you were willing to stretch a point for me last night."

"That was a mistake," he said tartly.

"Was it?"

"An example of that self-deception you talked about."

"Self-deception?"

He was genuinely hurt. "I thought you were my friend."

Neil Ambrose cooked such a superb lunch for them all that even Faith was won over. Rich food and good wine helped to restore a happy atmosphere and they were soon chatting and joking as if there had been no trace of friction aboard. Kit was on his best behavior, Tania seemed to have forgiven Luke, and Miranda was not pestered for any more demonstrations of her astrological skills. Time rolled gently on. Neil ended up with a proprietary arm around Faith, Luke danced slowly with Tania to the music that oozed out of his CD-player and Kit conversed with Miranda on the neutral subject of books. A mood of contentment reigned. It did not last. Seated apart from the rest of them, Neil and Faith were engaged in a quiet but intense discussion. When she whispered something in his ear, he turned round to fling an accusation at Miranda.

"Is that what you said?" he demanded angrily. "Did you tell Faith that she'd be better off without me?"

"Yes," answered Miranda.

"Why?"

"Because she asked me my opinion."

"It's none of your bloody business."

"Probably not."

"You don't even know me."

"I know enough to see that my advice was sound."

He lurched towards her. "What do you mean?"

"Sagittarians rarely get on with Cancerians," she said evenly, "and I'd bet anything you were born in mid-July. All the indications are there, Neil. You're loving, sympathetic and tender when you want to be. Behind all that laughter, you're a very sensitive soul. You're a true home-lover who likes his creature comforts. You even do the cooking. Well?" she asked. "Am I right? Were you born under Cancer?"

"Get stuffed!"

"You *were*, Neil," said Faith, betraying him. "Your birthday is July 15th."

Neil glared at her as if about to strike her then his ire shifted back to Miranda.

"It's a pity you weren't in that taxi with your husband," he snarled.

Still in his shorts and T-shirt, he dived overboard in a rage.


Dinner was a muted affair. Though they returned to the same restaurant in Boulogne, they could not recapture the spirit of the previous night. Miranda could see that she was chiefly to blame. Tania had resented her from the start but, in Kit and Neil, she had made two additional enemies. As the host, Luke felt obliged to jolly everyone along but there was his amiability was half hearted. When Miranda excused herself from the table, the others were able to vent their fury.

"Why the hell did you invite that witch?" said Neil, rounding on Faith.

"Miranda isn't a witch," she countered.

"Well, she's certainly cast a spell on this trip. She's spoiled everything."

"Not necessarily," said Luke. "Try to ignore her."

"If only we could!" sighed Tania.

"She's just not used to this kind of thing," said Kit with asperity.

"While the rest of us have all mucked in, Miranda is like the specter at the feast."

Neil nodded in agreement. "Inviting her was a disaster."

"I felt sorry for her, Neil," said Faith.

"You should have felt sorry for the rest of us and kept her well away."

"Miranda's not *that* bad," opined Luke, trying to calm them down.

"She's diabolical!"

"And so fucking pleased with herself!" added Tania, turning to Faith. "Miranda is the pits. What on earth do you see in her, Faith?"

"I don't know," confessed the other. "She's changed so much. Miranda was a lot of fun at Cambridge. We had some great laughs together. But now . . ."

Neil was vicious. "The only laugh I'd get from her is if I heard that she swallowed one of her own predictions and choked to death on it."

"That's unkind!" said Faith.

"Oh, I can be much more unkind than that," offered Tania.

"So can I," said Kit softly. "I'd like to kill the bitch."

"That's enough!" ordered Luke, embarrassed by the intensity of their hatred. "We're stuck with Miranda so we've all got to make the most of it. She's not my favorite person by a long chalk but I can put up with her for one more night. So can the rest of you. Agreed?"

The nods of consent were slow and reluctant.


When they got back to the boat, Luke uncorked a couple of bottles of wine then started the engine. While the others bantered on deck, he steered them back to the little bay when they had spent the morning. It was an ideal spot for a quiet night. Dropping anchor well out from the shore, he cut the engine and joined the others. Drink had mellowed them all. Faith was pouring contempt on the Higher Education System, Neil was shaking with mirth, Tania was nurturing fresh hopes about Luke's virility and Kit was at his most expansive. When Luke told them about some of the sharp practice in which he engaged from time to time, Kit saw an opportunity to air his knowledge.

"I feel as if I'm in *Das Narrenschiff*," he said with mock disdain.

"What's that?" asked Neil.

"The Ship of Fools. It's a famous narrative poem by Sebastian Brant. Written over five hundred years ago."

"So why bring it up now?"

"Because you appear in it, Neil," said Kit. "One of the characters on the boat is a dishonest cook. Yes, Luke, there's a usurer aboard as well. He's another arrant fool. There's even an unscrupulous lawyer like Tania and a pretentious scholar like Faith."

"I'm not pretentious!" denied Faith.

"Yes, you are," said Neil, unleashing yet another laugh.

"What about Miranda?" asked Luke. "Is she is this Ship of Fools?"

"Oh, yes," said Kit. "There's a trendy theologian who sounds just like Miranda."

"You're forgetting the Buchenarr," said Miranda with asperity. "The Bookish Fool. He takes pride of place on the ship, sitting on the prow, surrounded by useless books. He might almost have been modeled on you, Kit."

Kit glared back but said nothing. The others sniggered at his expense. When his glass was empty, he was the first to peel off to bed but not because of fatigue. As he lay on his bunk, Kit Greeves was throbbing with anger. Back on deck, Tania allowed Luke to slip an arm around her and fondle a breast. Neil's hopes of any reconciliation with Faith were doomed. Whenever he tried to get close to her, she inched away. He blamed Miranda for coming between them. After a long wait, he took his hurt feelings off to bed. Luke and Tania were the only couple destined to share a bunk. As they headed for the cabin, he remembered something.

"You never told us what Tania's birth sign is, Miranda."

"And she's not going to," said Tania, dragging him off. "We've had enough of that nonsense for one day."

The two women were left alone. Their friendship had been quietly fractured.

"All things considered," said Faith ruefully, "it might have been better if you hadn't come."

"You were the one who pressed me, Faith."

"I wanted you as a buffer against Neil."

"I rather hoped that you'd invited me for my own sake."

"Well, yes," added Faith quickly, "that, too, of course. I'm sorry that it didn't work out. I thought that you'd *like* everyone."

"I did," said Miranda. "The trouble was that they didn't like me."

"Especially Tania. She didn't have a good word to say for you."

"Tania has a lot of problems. Who wouldn't have if they'd been brought up in the Far East by a family of Catholic missionaries?" She gave a hollow laugh. "That's enough to put the curse on anybody."

"Are you coming to bed?"

"No," said Miranda. "I'll stay up here and enjoy the stars. While I can."

It was hours before she finally dozed off to sleep on the deck of the *Sirius*. It was a humid night and the boat bobbed gently on the swell. Miranda Hart did not hear the footsteps that came up out of the cabin and approached her with stealth. Her dreams were suddenly invaded by something hard and metallic that struck the side of her skull. Caught between sleep and waking, she could not resist the hands that eased her over the bulwark and into the unforgiving water. When the anchor was hauled up, the *Sirius* drifted slowly out to sea on the tide. It was soon quite distant from the scene of the crime.

Just before dawn, Luke Sanderson came out of a deep sleep and realised that his boat was no longer at anchor. Climbing over the naked body of Tania beside him, he went up on deck and saw that they were now out in the Channel, being buffeted by waves. He started the engine to establish control over the craft. The noise soon woke the others. They tumbled out on deck one by one. The last to arrive was Faith Brightwell.

"Where's Miranda?" she said.

"Isn't she in her bunk?" asked Luke.

"No, she stayed up here last night. I left her gazing up at the stars."

"She must be on the boat somewhere," said Kit, wiping the sleep from his eyes.

Luke was alarmed. "Where else could she be?"

The search was brief but thorough. There was no doubt about it. Miranda had disappeared. The only explanation was that she had somehow gone overboard. Since they were several miles from their anchorage in the bay, they had no idea where and when her departure occurred. Everyone was thrown into turmoil. Luke felt a personal responsibility for the loss of a passenger. Kit wondered if they should report the missing person to the French coastguard. Tania suggested that Miranda might somehow have made her way ashore, alienated by the general antipathy towards her. Faith pointed out that her friend would not have left without her belongings and she went into the cabin to search for them. It was left to Neil Ambrose to put into words the thought that worried them most.

"Somebody pushed her overboard," he concluded. "Miranda couldn't swim."

"Who would do such a thing?" said Kit with disbelief.

Neil was honest. "There was a moment yesterday when I would cheerfully have done it," he confessed. "The woman just got up my nose."

"And mine," said Tania. "But wanting her dead and actually killing her are two different things. I mean, where's the proof?"

"Someone hauled the anchor up," said Luke. "That's our proof."

"It's only supposition," she argued. "Miranda might have done that herself."

"I agree," said Kit. "Maybe she was trying to play a trick on us all and tumbled overboard in the process."

Neil was not persuaded. "Then why didn't she cry for help?"

"Perhaps she did. We were too drunk to hear her."

"I went out like a light," said Luke. "A typhoon wouldn't have woken me. One thing is certain," he added, looking out across the water. "It's pointless to search for her. Miranda could be any-where within a radius of miles. We'll never know what happened."

"I'm not so sure," announced Faith, coming back on deck with a large diary in her hand. "I found this in Miranda's bag. It contains that personal horoscope she mentioned."

Kit shuddered. "It was too uncannily accurate. Miranda warned that one of us would meet with a premature death. She didn't know that it would be her."

Faith held up the diary. "Oh, yes, she did. She even named the killer."

"That's impossible!" exclaimed Tania.

"We can't even be sure if she *was* murdered," said Neil.

"Yes, we can," said Faith, looking around them. "You had cause to push her over the side, Neil. So did Kit. She really upset him somehow. And I don't suppose that you were overjoyed with her either, Luke."

"Me?"

"You set up this trip and along comes Miranda to ruin it."

"Not deliberately."

Tania was watchful. "What's this about her naming the killer?"

"I'm coming to that," said Faith. "I can see now why you didn't want to go along with that guessing game about birth signs, Tania. The Sun Signs don't apply to you, do they? You were born in China. They have their own astrology there."

"So?"

"My guess is that your date of birth was early in 1978. February, say."

"What if it was?"

"Then you were born in the year of the Horse. Look what it says in Miranda's diary, Tania," said Faith, thrusting it at her. "Read it. 'This year, I will be killed by a horse.' In this case, it was a sea horse but it amounts to the same thing. You pushed her over the side of the boat, didn't you, Tania? You're behind all this."

Tania tried to brazen it out but her guilt was plain for all to see. Eyes darting wildly, she backed against the bulwark. Neil and Kit looked on with disgust. Luke was horrified to realize that he had slept with a woman who left his bunk in the middle of the night in order to commit murder. Faith snapped the diary shut.

"Tell them what 2002 is, Tania," she said. "The Chinese year of the Horse."

# THE AQUARIUS MISSION

### Brendan DuBois

LIKE MOST PROBLEMS I've experienced in the past, this one originated from my parents.

My mother called right after I had gotten off-line one March day at my small apartment near the campus of the University of New Hampshire, after another depressing morning on the Internet, going through the very thin listings of graduate student positions that came with a work-study program for the fall semester in other colleges and universities in New England. My grades had been just fine, but trying to keep those grades up while working two or three part-time jobs was proving to be a challenge.

"Jason?" she called. "Have you been on the phone all morning?"

I sat back on the sagging couch, kept up on one corner by the judicious use of a cement block. "I've been on the 'Net, ma, looking for work this fall. You know what I've been up to."

"Well, if you say so," she said, a tone of disapproval coming over the hundred or so miles of phone line that separated the two of us. My mom and dad are quite the pair: they met during the heydays of the 1960's, and unlike most of their contemporaries, they haven't shaken off the mantle of a Permanent Revolution Against The System. I think the fact that I've gone to college, have gotten good grades, and want to continue my schooling has always been a major disappointment to them. I think they'd rather I run away to Mexico and join some sort of farm collective or guerrilla group. They both run a coffee shop in Maine that offers organic bean curd, oppression-free coffee beans, and a healthy dose of attitude with each order.

"How's dad?" I asked.

"He's not here," she said. "He's down at the Post Office Building."

I rubbed my forehead, closed my eyes. "He's not going to get arrested again, is he?"

"Only if the cops overreact," she replied.

"What's he protesting about today?"

"Genetically-modified tomatoes, that's what," she said.

"And the Post Office is connected to genetically-modified tomatoes by . . ."

"Never mind that," she snapped. "I didn't call you to get mocked. I called you about your Grandfather Morris."

"What about him?" I said, thinking of the older man—George Morris—that was my father's father, retired from the State Department, years ago. I've always thought that the dinner time conversations between dad and grandfather must have been interesting, back there in the Sixties, but father has never said word onc about those long-ago battles. He was living down south now, and except for an occasional birthday or Christmas card, I hadn't really heard from him in years.

"He called us last night," she said. "He wants to help you with your schooling."

I sat up so quickly that the couch fell off the supporting cement block, nearly tumbling me to the floor. But I kept the phone up to my ear and said, "Ma, you're not kidding, are you?"

"No, I'm not," she said. "Though I didn't want to call you, your father insisted. To tell you the truth, I think this is something you should get on your own."

"Gee, thanks," I said dryly.

"Never you mind," she said. "Grandfather Morris is keen on helping you. He even sent over the paperwork allowing it, since your father's name is on your grandfather's checking and savings accounts. He wants to pay for your education, as long as you want."

As long as I . . . "Say that again?"

She sighed. "You heard me. As long as you want. Graduate school, post-graduate school, if you want to get advanced degrees or doctorates or whatever. Is that what astrology students can get, a doctorate?"

"Astronomy," I said automatically, while part of me was almost drooling at the thought of being able to continue my schooling without having to worry about money. Grandfather had always been well-off, but had been tight in spreading it around. Birthday cards from him came each year with a dollar bill enclosed, right up until you were eighteen, when the dollar bill stopped appearing. After you were eighteen, he figured you could fend for yourself.

"Excuse me?" she said.

"Astronomy, ma," I said. "I'm studying astronomy, not astrology. A big difference."

"Well," she said dismissively. "It's all stars and planets, right? I don't see the difference."

If it was possible to bite one's tongue without actually using your teeth, I did it. My mother went on, and I almost missed it, when she said, "Oh. One more thing. Grandfather said there's a condition to you receiving all this funding."

Uh-oh, I thought, and it was like all the windows in my apartment were open to the cold March wind. "Go on, what kind of condition?"

"He wants you to accompany him on a trip. To Florida. All expenses paid."

"For how long?"

"Well, don't you have a spring break coming up or something?"

"Yeah . . ."

"So wouldn't a Florida trip be nice?"

Sure. Beaches, cold drinks, and young ladies wearing as little clothing as possible, trying to get a tan in less than a week. Yeah, that would be nice, except that I'd be accompanied by a forgetful old man who probably needed his hand held while going to the men's room. Still, for what he was offering, I'd accompany him almost anywhere in the world.

"What part of Florida? Did he say?"

"That cape down there, where they launch the space shuttle. That place."

Oh. Cape Canaveral. Not swinging Miami or Ft. Lauderdale. Well,

Cocoa Beach would have to do. "Okay," I said. "So what's the deal? I fly down to Charleston, and from there, we fly to Orlando?"

"Well, no," she said. "He doesn't want to fly. He wants you to drive him down to Florida."

"Drive?" The vision of long days on the sparse beaches of Cocoa Beach started to fade out. They were replaced by thoughts of long days in a rental car, driving south, with Grandfather telling me obscure tales of his diplomatic battles in the State Department, while looking for restaurants that offered early bird specials . . .

But full funding. No scurrying around for work-study jobs. Take some time, apply to some really great schools, not to worry about tuition. All paid for.

"Sure, ma, I'll do it. Even horse and carriage if he wants. Tell me, does he—"

"Hold on, there's another call," she said, and my mother promptly put me on hold. I waited for a while, staring at the cracked ceiling and cracked plaster walls, and then I couldn't stop grinning. Full tuition, for whatever I wanted. It sounded too good to be true.

"That was your father," mother's brisk voice announced. "I've got to go."

"Has he been arrested again?" I asked, but I was talking to a dead phone. She had hung up. I hung up as well and then clapped my hands together and jumped around the apartment in glee. Be a good tour guide, m'boy, I thought, and maybe the old man will pop for a healthy stipend as well, so you could afford an apartment with a couch that had four legs, instead of three.

What a deal.


A week later I was in a rental car, still unfamiliar with the functions of various knobs and switches on the dashboard, when I pulled up to an administration building for an assisted living community where grandfather lived, outside of Charleston, South Carolina. I had earlier guessed that I would have to spend a while on the grounds, trying to find him, but he surprised me by waiting outside the white cement building, sitting on a light green park bench. I parked the car and got out, and he stood up and offered me a slight wave. He was wearing a light, two-piece blue suit with white shirt and no tie. His white beard was closely trimmed, and except for a fringe of equally white hair around his scalp, he was bald. I went up to him and his blue eyes behind his wire-rimmed glasses looked moist.

"Jason, my boy, my, have you grown!" he said, shaking my hand firmly. At his feet was a small tan suitcase, and a little black case beside it that looked like a gym bag.

"Thanks, grandfather," I said, reaching by him to pick up his suitcase. "You're looking good, too. Ready to get going?"

He grinned. "This is going to be so fine, to leave the smothering embrace of this place, even if it is only for a while. No offense to the lovely people who run the show here, but they think you're ill if you don't feel like playing Scrabble, or take an arts and craft class, or—hey, don't touch that!"

I stepped back, the suitcase only in my hands. "Sorry," I said, now almost regretting I had agreed to make the trip. "I was just getting your gym bag."

"No, only I get to carry that," he said, picking it up and clasping it to his chest. Funny thing, when he had shouted at me, his face was red and mottled white with what looked like barely restrained fury. But now, he just shook his head and smiled again, and looked like the kindly old man I had always known.

"Oh," I said. "Okay. Well, are you ready?"

He kept on smiling. "Yes, Jason, let's get going."

A while later we were on Route 17, heading to I-95, and as I drove, I tried to keep an eye on the geography—growing up in New England, I had never seen such a flat place like where we were driving through, swamps and streams and marshland—and tried to maintain a conversation with grandfather. But soon the conversation became as flat as the scenery.

"Grandfather, I really appreciate what you're doing, helping me out with my schooling," I said.

"Unh-hunh."

A few miles passed, and I said, "It's going to make a huge difference, in deciding what kind of schools I can apply to, and what I can study."

"Unh-hunh."

I turned and he was just sitting there, a little smile on his face, his black gym bag in his lap, watching the miles roll past us. I cleared my throat and said, "Grandfather, anything you need? A drink? A snack? Anything?"

He looked over at me, the smile still there, but his eyes just a bit icy. "I'll tell you what, Jason. I'll tell you what I need when it becomes necessary, all right? A drink, a snack, a potty visit. In the meantime, we can just relax and listen to some music on the radio. No need to try to build some special bond between us in just a few days. We'll just travel well and arrive in Florida refreshed and rested. Does that suit you?"

"Sure."

"Oh. One more thing. I want to spend our nights in little, out-of-the-way motels. No huge chains. I want to stay at a place that has a nice dark sky."

"Why?" I asked.

"Silly boy," he said, turning back to look out the window. "So I can look at the stars."

We made good time on I-95 and managed to pass over into Georgia before night fell. I found a place a ways off the interstate, called the Welcome Place Inn. I only chose it because it was in a remote area, with just a few streetlights, and I hoped the sky would be dark enough for grandfather's wishes. It was a typical one-story motel with parking lots and rooms and a swimming pool that was closed, and after a forgettable dinner at a diner across the street, we walked back. Grandfather hooked his arm through mine and said, "A look at the night sky, Jason, and then to bed. All right?"

"Sounds fine," I said, wanting desperately to lay down and let the acid feeling in my stomach cool off. We walked around the parking lot of the motel and at the far edge, got a pretty good look off to the western sky. The eastern sky was too washed out from the lights of Savannah, and grandfather sighed as he tilted his head back some. "Beautiful, isn't it."

I had to agree with him, it was beautiful. There was no moon and the stars were as bright and hard as I could ever recall. And to the west, low in the sky, were three stars that weren't stars at all: Jupiter, Saturn and Mars.

"Yeah, grandfather. A good night sky. I hope we can keep it up, the further south we get."

We stood there, listening to the drone of traffic in the distance, and then he said, "Isn't it something, to look up there, and realize you and I are gazing upon the same objects, the same lights, that FDR saw, that Lincoln and Napoleon and Washington saw, the medieval kings, the Roman emperors, the Egyptian pharaohs, all the way back in time, all the way back in history. All those people, all those ancestors, saw exactly what we are seeing, right now. Buildings will rise and fall, rivers will change courses, even mountains will wear down, but these lights in the sky, they're immortal."

My stomach was really hurting, and I remembered some antacid I had in my own suitcase. "Yep, that's a thought, grandfather."

"The stars. Don't you think the stars govern our lives, Jason?"

I had to remember that grandfather was my father's father, not my mother's. While both were flighty, father was a bit more down to earth than mother, though grandfather was beginning to sound like he came from her side of the family. "Not really, grandfather."

"Oh? Not a believer in astrology?"

I sighed, my stomach really burbling along. "No, I'm sorry, I don't."

"But you're an astronomy student. Correct? Don't you study the stars?"

"Well, the planets," I said. "I'm more interested in planetary astronomy than stellar astronomy. Especially Mars. More room for new discoveries, with probes and satellites and new ground-based observing systems. Stellar astronomy's just too theoretical for my taste."

"Oh. But don't you know that astrology is what led into astronomy, Jason? That without astrology as your science's ancestor, that modern-day astronomy wouldn't even exist?"

"Maybe so," I said. "But that's like telling a medical student to pay homage to alchemy. It's so far in the past, it doesn't make a difference."

"Lots of people believe in astrology," he said.

"Yes," I shot back. "And lots of people believe that Elvis is still alive."

He laughed at that, and said, "What's your sign, Jason?"

"I don't know."

"Of course you do. Everybody knows their sign, even if they don't believe in astrology. You're an Aquarius, aren't you. The water giver. That's you, is it not?"

"I guess it is," I said.

He tugged on my arm. "I won't keep you. Let's get back to our room. We've got a long day ahead of us. And pretty soon, you'll see how Aquarius will make it all come together."

I was pleased that for an old man, grandfather didn't snore or talk in his sleep, or go to the bathroom about a half-dozen times during the night. I slept in shorts, he had a beige pair of pajamas, and he let me control the television and the lamps, and he was asleep after ten minutes in bed. After a breakfast that was marginally better than last night's dinner, we were again heading south, heading to Florida. We had a late start but I didn't mind. If the driving went well, we should be at our destination in just under two days. Which led me to ask him something about an hour into our trip.

"Is there anyplace in particular you want to see at Cape Canaveral?" I asked.

"Some things, everything," he said, the gym bag still in his lap. "Even a particular person."

"Who?"

He smiled, leaned back in his seat, his eyes fluttering. "You'll find out. It's someone who I was very interested in, back before I retired."

"Really?"

"Really," he said, his eyes closing. "Back at my days at Langley."

"Langley?" I asked.

But he didn't answer. He was just breathing slowly, sleeping. Langley.

We stopped for gas and lunch at a truck stop just south of Brunswick, Georgia, getting quite close to the border with Florida. While grandfather took a bathroom break, I made a call to my parents' house from a payphone in the lobby, and again, talked to mother.

"How is the trip going?" she asked.

"Fine, I guess. Look, can you—"

"Bring back some healing crystals, will you?"

"Excuse me?"

"There must be a place in your travels that sells some healing crystals," she said. "I need a specific—"

Grandfather emerged from the men's room, picked up a free shopper's newspaper. "Ma," I interrupted. "We've got to get going. Look, where did grandfather work while he was in Washington?"

She sighed. "You know where. The State Department. He was some consul official or something."

"Never the CIA?"

"The what?"

"Grandfather, did he ever work for the CIA? At Langley, in Virginia."

She laughed. "Did he say that? Look, Jason, he's getting along in years. He's beginning to feel guilty about what he did, working for the government during the Vietnam era. He's just reinventing himself, telling you a story—"

I knew she would be mad at me for days, but I had to go. I hung up the phone.

Grandfather came to me, the free newspaper under his arm. "Who were you calling?"

"My mom."

He grimaced. "Everything fine at home?"

"Sure," I said. "Things are swell."

He took the newspaper out, softly batted me on the side. "I doubt that. Let's get going, shall we?"

\*       \*       \*

After a while on the road, I couldn't stand it and said, "Grandfather, where did you work before you retired?"

"The government, you know that," he said.

"I know the government, but what branch?"

His fingers tapped on the gym bag. "The State Department, of course."

I felt foolish but went on. "Not the CIA?"

"The CIA?" he said, and then laughed. "What gave you that idea?"

You did, I thought, but aloud I said, "Oh, I think my mom did, once."

He laughed again. "No offense, Jason. But your mother . . ."
I decided to let it drop.

Another night, another motel, this one in northern Florida. Again, I
was lucky, in finding a place that met with grandfather's needs. The
area was swampy but was flat, and we had another good view to the
west. The barest sliver of the new moon was visible, hanging just near
to the three lights marking Jupiter, Saturn, and Mars. We sat on a
large boulder that marked the end of the parking lot and grandfather
asked, "Why are you so opposed to astrology?"

I sighed. "Where should I begin? There's no scientific evidence
that anything associated with astrology even exists. Thinking that
having the stars and the planets in certain positions when you were
born, can actually determine your existence, your personality, your
future . . . it's totally ridiculous. Especially since you consider that
since horoscopes were invented, thousands of years ago, the positions
of the constellations have changed."

"Even allowing you all of that, you don't think the stars and the
planets exert some sort of influence on us?"

"Grandfather, the doctor and nurses who deliver a child at birth,
they would have more gravitational influence upon the child than the
position of Saturn."

"Who says anything about gravity? Isn't there anything out there
that could have some sort of influence on what kind of a person you
are, some sort of force that science can't measure, can't even detect.
Isn't it possible?"

Conscious that it was late, and also conscious that I was depending
on his good humor, I didn't want to press the argument. "Sure, grandfather. Anything's possible."

"Look out there," he said softly. "Look at that gorgeous new moon.
Look at the stars, at those three planets. For millennia man has tried
to decipher them, tried to reach them, tried to read their secrets.
That's how astrology started. There's nothing foolish about that. Nothing at all."

We sat for a while in silence, until he stood up and I followed him
into our room.

*       *       *

I woke up at two A.M., my bladder demanding release. I tossed and turned and then gave it up, and tried to be quiet, walking into the bathroom. When I came out I saw something in the light, something I hadn't noticed before: grandfather, dressed in his beige pajamas, sleeping soundly, with a thin chain running from his wrist and down to his gym bag. I paused, looking at the scene. The chain was wrapped around the handle and through the zipper. I rubbed at my face, wondered at what was going on. That gym bag hadn't left his side since we left Charleston, not for a moment. He brought it into the restaurants and restrooms, and during our long drives, it had rested in his lap, like a pampered cat or puppy that couldn't be left out of one's sight.

He shifted some, breathed loudly through his nose. I suppose I could have snuck over, tried to undo the chain and look inside. Or think of some strategy where I could separate him from his bag, long enough where I could unzipper the top and peek in. And, of course, there was the direct strategy: just come out and ask him directly what was in the bag.

Then, for some reason, my eye drifted to the other side of the room, where a couch was sitting. It was a typical, small motel couch, probably one of thousands sprinkled up and down this part of the Atlantic Coast. Still, as small and tacky as it was, it was considerably better than the couch back home. Back home, where just a few days earlier, I had been struggling, trying to map out my future.

My own mapmaker snorted some, rolled on his side. I left him alone, as well as the thoughts of asking anything, and went back to bed.

*    *    *

The next day, we were making good progress, heading further south, going beyond Jacksonville, still on I-95, until suddenly, brake lights from vehicles in front of us started quickly lighting up. Grandfather grasped his bag tight and leaned forward. "What's wrong? What's wrong?" he demanded.

I was tempted to ask him why he thought I'd have an instant analysis of what was going on up ahead of us, but I said, "Let me scan the local radio stations, see what's what."

Which is what I did. A few minutes of moving through the AM

channels, and I came to an all-news station that said a tractor truck had jackknifed, a few miles ahead of us. Traffic was expected to be standing still for hours, at least. Grandfather swore and turned around. "No exits nearby, are there."

"Nope."

"Damn it, we were making such good time," he said. "You don't understand. We've got to get the Cape, and soon."

"Well, grandfather, we've been doing all right so far."

"That's not good enough!" he nearly shouted.

I turned to him. "If you were in such a hurry, why are we driving? You could have paid for airfare, no problem, with what you've paid for so far in room costs, gas, and food. Why didn't we fly down?"

Grandfather seemed to shrink a bit, wrapping his lanky arms around his bag. He said slowly, "I'm sorry, you're right."

"Okay."

We waited, traffic not moving. "Oh, and another thing," he said.

"Yes, grandfather?"

"You raise your voice like that one more time, and you can kiss your higher education good-bye. At least, that portion I'm prepared to pay. Understand?"

Oh, yeah, I understood all right, and I was getting so angry that I was about ready to tell him where to stuff his educational offer, when I remembered that damn three-legged couch, waiting for me, back up there in New Hampshire.

"Sure, grandfather," I said, sighing, tapping my fingers on the steering wheel. "I understand."

We spent the night about an hour's drive north of Cape Canaveral, near Daytona Beach. Grandfather wanted to push on, but I politely told him that I was falling asleep behind the wheel, and while I wasn't criticizing his judgment and his choices, I'm sure he didn't want to end up in a drainage ditch, visiting an alligator colony. Grandfather grunted and said I was making sense. My, what a victory.

Yet he still asked for a quick walk outside by the motel's parking lot, which we did, going down to a small dock that went out into a wide stream. We still had a good view to the west, and the three amigos were hanging there in all their glory: Jupiter, Saturn and Mars, and the sliver of the moon was even more visible. Grandfather sighed and asked me to help him sit at the edge of the dock, and I joined him, and the two of us sat there, our feet swinging free, and I had a nervous thought about a hungry alligator, leaping up for a snack, and pushed it aside.

"Moon's coming along nicely," he said.

"Yep." I was tired and needed a quick meal, but if he needed some conversation, fine.

"Trivia question time," he asked.

"Go ahead."

"How many men have walked on the moon?" he asked.

"Is this a trick question?"

"Nope," Grandfather said.

"Okay, twelve men have walked on the moon," I said. "Apollo Eleven, Twelve, Fourteen, Fifteen, Sixteen, and Seventeen. Satisfied?"

He chuckled. "Very, very good, Jason," he said. "You've restored at least a shred of my confidence in your generation. You know, I don't even think you father cared about the first moon landing. He was up at Woodstock or someplace, wallowing in the mud and rain, with tens of thousands of counter-culture comrades, listening to poorly amplified rock music. He didn't even care. Can you believe that? The first time men had set foot on another world, the first time men could look back at their own earth as a sphere, from another world, well . . . that's something that people will remember, thousands of years from now. Not some muddy farm like Woodstock."

Grandfather breathed and then coughed some. I yawned, making it louder than usual, trying to put the idea into him of he and I leaving the dock, but he would have none of it. He said, "Jason, why astronomy?"

"What do you mean?"

"I mean, why bother studying things from afar. Why not put your talents into putting people up there, instead of more machines?"

I said, "What's the point?"

"The point?" he replied, his voice shocked, like I had just come out in favor of puppy euthanasia. "The point is that the stars, the moon, and the planets, they've been calling to us and our souls, and our ancestors' souls, for millennia. Don't you think we belong up there, where we came from?"

"I don't understand what you mean, where we came from," I said. "You're not talking about ancient astronauts, are you? Crazy stories about Adam and Eve being stranded visitors from another planet, nonsense like that?"

"Of course not," he said. "I'm talking about what's in you and me, and everyone alive in this planet. Billions of years ago, all that existed was gas and dust, until the stars and planets formed. We came from those stars, so long ago. Don't you think we belong back there, with them?"

If only I had been a bit more forceful, I thought, he and I would be working on a piece of Key Lime Pie for dessert, and getting ready to head back to our room. So instead, here we were, discussing cosmology on the end of a dock in a swampy piece of Florida.

"I think our machines belong back there, but not us," I said.

"Why?"

"It's obvious, can't you see?"

"No, I can't," he said. "Enlighten me."

"Look," I said, warming up to an argument I've had before with other students at UNH. "Nothing against manned space exploration, but it's a waste of time, money, and resources. Satellites and probes don't need radiation protection, they don't need water, air or food, and they can travel millions of miles without worrying if a medical emergency is going to crop up. For the cost of just one space shuttle mission — just one! — you could fund two or three deep planet probes. For the cost of one year's worth of manned missions, you could have a dozen satellites, each year, exploring the surface of Mars, landing on the moons of Jupiter and Saturn, heading out to Pluto."

Grandfather murmured something and I said, "I'm sorry, I didn't hear what you were saying."

"I said, there's no poetry in machinery."

"Maybe not, but there's no deep-space knowledge to gain from having a space truck orbiting the earth."

We sat there, for just a little while longer, until Grandfather started stirring and I helped him up, still holding onto his gym bag. I could hear something moving around inside, and again I wondered what was in there, what was so important. But I tried not to look at it too long, for I didn't want to raise any suspicions.

As we headed back to the motel, Grandfather said, "Don't underestimate poetry, Jason. Sometimes, it's the only thing we can hold onto, century after century."

The next day we were back on I-95, continuing our southward journey, and my own sense of curiosity—buried all these past days—was beginning to come back. Grandfather seemed more alive, the further south we went, and he practically clapped his hands with childish glee, the first time he saw a highway sign that said KENNEDY SPACE CENTER. I figured this was as good as time as any, and said, "Who are we seeing down here, Grandfather?"

"Oh, somebody."

"I know that. But who?"

He turned to me, face somber. "A man who changed the course of history. A very famous man."

"Really? Somebody I've heard about?"

"No, not really," he said. "Though you might have heard of what he did."

"And what did he do?"

Grandfather resumed looking out the windshield. "I'll tell you later. In fact, if all goes well, I'll see him today. And then it'll make sense."

We drove for a few more miles, and then I took an exit that got us onto Route 405, heading east. More signs for the Kennedy Space Center, and I said, "What about Aquarius?"

"What about it?" he asked.

"Well, earlier you said something about Aquarius, bringing it all together. What does that mean?"

He laughed. "Jason, let's just say you're part of the equation, being Aquarius-born."

"And the other part?" I asked.

"You'll figure it out," he said.

"I will?"

"Sure," grandfather said. "Or the money I'm giving you will be wasted on your higher education, won't it."

"I sure hope not," I said.

*     *     *

The next several hours were a blur, as we finally got to Spaceport USA, the visitor's center just outside the Kennedy Space Center. Dominating the entrance as you drove in was a scale-model replica of a space shuttle, complete with orange fuel tank and two booster rockets. There were other rockets as well, smaller ones, set up in a place called the Rocket Garden, and grandfather—bag in hand— seemed to lose about sixty years of his age as we went through the exhibits. He didn't want to miss a thing, and he was patient—even more patient than me—as sometimes we had to stand in line for some of the more popular displays. Outside in the rocket garden, he caressed the side of a rocket booster, only a few stories tall. "Can you believe somebody would get strapped onto the top of this, to be catapulted out into space?"

"No, I can't," I said.

"Poetry," he said, shaking his head, and we continued our tour. There was a movie theater showing an Imax movie about the space shuttle—my stomach got queasy at some of the shots showing weightlessness—and when we walked out of the auditorium, grandfather was wiping his eyes with a handkerchief.

"I'll never go there, you know," he said.

"Where?"

"Space." We stood outside the theater, resting for a bit on a padded bench. "When I was your age, I was reading those pulp science fiction magazines. Great stuff, exciting stuff, and they were full of stories about where we'd be at the end of the twentieth century. Space stations orbiting the earth, colonies on the moon and Mars. Tourist excursions into outer space. It made sense, growing in the 1940's and '50's, that this would all come true. And now? We went to the moon and abandoned it, and now, starting a new century, we're barely working on the first real, extensive space station."

"Sometimes things just take longer than people dream about," I said.

"True, and sometimes other people take the dreams away," he said, looking out at an exhibition hall near the theater, filled with drawings and paintings of space exploration. "We had an opportunity, just for the briefest moment, during the moon landings, to build on those successful missions. To set up a moon colony. To prepare for Mars. To really be a part of the stars, Jason. To fulfill our destiny, the one that started with astrology. And we blew it. We tossed the chance away. Maybe it'll come back. Maybe before you get too old, you'll get a chance to get out there. But not me. I'll be dead."

"Well, I don't—"

He interrupted me. "The bus tour for the Apollo exhibit will be leaving soon. I can't miss it, Jason. Let's go."

And so we did.

We and a long line of other tourists filled up coach excursion buses, their diesel engines grumbling loudly under the hot Florida sun, and I smiled at seeing the excited faces of the youngsters. I hoped that a few of them would come away from this place with a thirst for science, for learning things. So many of my fellow college students—if asked—couldn't probably identify a single star in the night sky, but knew what their astrological sign was. It didn't make a lick of sense, but there it was.

We sat up front and looked out the tinted windows, and the driver gave a brief chat as we headed out to the exhibit spotlighting the Apollo moon missions. Along the way we passed a huge square building, called the Vehicle Assembly Building—one of the largest in the world—and which was used to assemble the space shuttle. Grandfather leaned into me and said proudly, "I've been in there."

"You have? When?"

He smiled. "Can't tell you. It's a secret."

And I thought: a Langley secret, or a State Department secret?

Once past the complex of buildings, the bus made a right-hand turn, and went down a newly-paved access road, to a large parking lot. Other buses were there as well, and there were a set of viewing stands, by a slow-moving and wide river. Before us was a large exhibit hall, and we filed in, seeing a presentation about the Apollo moon-landings in a mock mission-control area. From there, we were dumped into a cavernous hall, and even I couldn't help myself, by gasping at what I saw there. Laying on its side was the largest rocket in the world, the one that had propelled twelve men to walk on the face of the moon, the Saturn V. Beyond the Saturn V were large emblems, hanging from the metal rafters, displaying the mission patches for each of the Apollo missions. I walked with Grandfather slowly as he went from display to display, pausing for a moment at the area commemorating the disastrous Apollo I fire, to another display for Apollo VII, which started the Apollo journey to the moon. We took our time, Grandfather going close up to view each display, and despite what I had told grandfather the other night, there was something about the place that spooked me. It was like being in some great medieval cathedral, with areas within showing relics of the saints, and my noble talk about the uselessness of men and women in space seemed silly and childish, in this place marking where we really had gone up to the stars.

We rested for a bit, both of us eating an ice cream cone, and Grandfather said, "Don't be so hard on astrology, Jason. Maybe that was just thc logical start, a logical place to put into words and deeds our longing to go out there. Thousands and thousands of years later, we've gone and dipped our toes into the water. Maybe your generation, or your children, will get there and fulfill their destiny."

"Maybe so," I said.

He wiped his fingers on a paper napkin, picked up his gym bag and said, "One more display. Saved it for last. C'mon."

Then he walked me over to the Apollo XIII exhibit, and I remembered the movie of the same name, that I had seen during a re-release at the campus theater last year. I had gone with a couple of other astronomy students, and we had made sport of the film, especially since our professor had been rejected — again! — by NASA in getting funding for a satellite he had planned and worked on for years, to measure some exotic types of X-ray emissions. We guessed that the special-effects budget for the movie would probably have paid for two or three of those proposed satellites, but now, standing in front of the display marking the actual mission, and showcasing the three astronauts — Jim Lovell, Jack Swigert and Fred Haise — well, I felt pretty small.

Grandfather nodded and then wiped at his eyes again, as he read and re-read the display. "That's where it all went wrong, you know," he said.

"Why?" I asked. "They got back safe and sound, didn't they?"

He put his handkerchief back into his pocket. "Sure, but it ripped the heart out of NASA's confidence and the public's support. The public started asking questions about safety and the expense, and NASA got too cautious afterwards, in planning future missions, in taking risks, in going to the mat with the Congress and the President to get the necessary funding. Oh, it was a successful failure, as they like to say, but Apollo XIII . . . I think it really marked the end of an era. We were going through the motions after that mission. We never really recovered."

I looked again at the displays, and something caught my eye, just as Grandfather tugged my elbow and said, "C'mon, it's time to go."

And I turned and walked with him, and then looked back, one more time, just to be sure.

For during the Apollo missions, names had been assigned to the command module—the spacecraft ferrying the astronauts out to the moon and back—and to the lunar module, the craft actually landing on the moon. Most people remember the famous quotation from Neil Armstrong: "Houston, Tranquility Base here, the Eagle has landed." Eagle was the name for the lander, and Columbia was the name for the command module.

So names were assigned for Apollo XIII as well.

The command module was called Odyssey.

And the lunar module, which served as a lifeboat and saved the crew, but never touched down on the moon's surface, that had a name as well.

Aquarius.

It was getting late in the afternoon and we took the bus back to the visitor's center. Once there, grandfather said, "It's time."

We got into the rental car, and I winced as my back went against the hot car seat. "Time for what? An early dinner? To find a motel?"

"Nope," he said, rearranging the gym bag in his lap. "Time for me to see that man I've been talking about."

And damn it to hell, just as I started up the car and backed it out of the space, Grandfather opened up the gym bag and took out a much-folded slip of paper. If I had been more on the ball, I could have gotten a glimpse of what he had been carrying, but by the time we were heading out to the highway, the gym bag was firmly closed.

"All right," Grandfather said. "Take a left when we get to the highway. We shouldn't be more than a half hour away."

"And who are we seeing?" I asked, joining a line of cars, all of them seemingly also heading left. "This famous man, the one who changed history? Is that who we're seeing?"

"Yes," he said simply.

"And does he know you're coming?"

Grandfather looked at me, horrified. "God, I hope not."

He was true to his word, and we were to our destination almost exactly a half-hour later, in a residential area of Rockledge. The homes were all one-story ranches, set on identical looking lots, and he found the number he was looking for—119—and said, "Okay, pull over up there, at the stop sign."

I did that and he looked over and extended his hand. I shook it, wondering what in hell was going on. Grandfather said, "This is the deal, and it's not negotiable. All right? Not if you want that financial support. I'm going over there by myself. You leave me alone. You come back in a half-hour. If I'm here on the sidewalk, pick me up. If not, just keep on driving. Call your father and have him pay for a flight back home, out of my funds. Don't do anything else. Understood?"

My lips were dry. I tried to gauge what was going on behind those watery eyes and I failed. "Yes, grandfather. Understood."

"Good. You've been a good boy, these past few days. I've enjoyed looking at the stars with you, talking about astronomy and astrology. Do well in school."

I tried to think of what I could possibly say in return, when he opened the door, got out on the sidewalk, and started heading to the light pink house, the gym bag swinging in his hand.

I started up the rental car and drove off.

\*     \*     \*

And turned the corner and switched off the engine. I was going to be damned if I was going to tell dad that I had dropped off his father at some small house in Florida, and had left him behind. Lucky for me, a lot of the homes had elaborate hedgework around them, which gave me the chance to get out and walk back, and to keep an eye on the house. A half-hour. I looked at my watch. Maybe the neighbors around here kept to themselves, but I think several would be suspicious of a college student, standing on the sidewalk for thirty minutes.

I was wondering how long I could stay there in one spot, when there was a hollow-sounding boom! coming from the pink house. I stopped crouching and stood up. Another boom! and then the front door flew open, and a short, pudgy man, dressed in white shorts and nothing else, tumbled down the front steps. Grandfather was right behind him, swearing loudly, and holding the biggest damn revolver I had ever seen in my life.

Boom! came another shot, and the pudgy man ducked and ran across his tiny lawn, and I couldn't believe it was possible, but the man jumped over his neighbor's fence, cleared it no doubt through the aid of adrenaline and fear, and grandfather was running right after him, waving the revolver around.

"Grandfather!" I yelled, and I went after him, too, and another gunshot shattered the still air of the neighborhood, and even before I reached him, I could make out the sound of approaching sirens.

After a few hectic and confusing hours, I was allowed to see him in a small interview room at the local sheriff's department. He was wearing an orange jumpsuit and his hands were cuffed to a metal ring on top of the table, and the first thing he said to me was, "I told you to wait."

"I couldn't."

And the second thing he said was, "Damn my shaking hands. I missed. I can't believe how I missed. The little bastard was so fat and could hardly move at first."

"Grandfather, who was he?"

His watery eyes blinked. "The man who stole the stars from us, that's who. Who sabotaged our destiny."

"And for that, you tried to kill him?"

"Of course," he said. "Look. You were at the exhibits today, right? Tell me why the Apollo Thirteen mission failed."

"An oxygen tank exploded."

"Why?" he asked.

I couldn't believe we were having this discussion, yet I answered, almost automatically. "There was a mistake. A heating element inside one of the tanks accidentally got damaged, before the launch."

He smiled, shook his head. "A cover story, one that's lasted three decades. No, Jason, that was sabotage. Pure and simple. And only through the grace of God and whatever else is up there looking out for us. That man . . ." and he said that phrase with disgust ". . . was one Miles Grayson. More than thirty years ago, he was working for North American Aviation, the contractor that was building all of the Apollo command and service modules. But he was also working for the KGB. The Soviets were getting close to beating us to the moon, and they didn't want Apollo Eleven to get there first. So he sabotaged an oxygen tank he thought was going in the spacecraft for the first lunar landing. But some paperwork got shuffled around, that tank was set aside, Apollo Eleven made it, and right after that landing, the Soviets said—surprise!—they never had any plans for a manned landing. And so that tank eventually ended up in Apollo Thirteen. And I swore, if I ever found out who had done that, I would get my revenge. For stealing the stars away from us."

I couldn't even imagine how to respond to that, so I took a different tack. "That's why we drove down. Because you couldn't smuggle that revolver through airport security."

A smile, a nod. "Very good."

"And you really didn't work for the State Department, did you."

He moved, the chain around his wrists tinkling a bit. "Can't say anything to that, Jason. Sorry."

I shifted in the uncomfortable plastic chair. "So, why now? Why after thirty years?"

He shrugged. "My old contacts where I once worked . . . they let me know things, here and there. And thirty years later, well, some records get uncovered. We decode old messages. Old secrets get uncovered. And when this one came my way, well . . . there you go."

I looked at him. "This sounds nuts."

"I'm sure it does, and I don't care. He stole the stars from me, and from everybody else."

"The cops, the local D.A., they're going to think you're crazy," I said. "This story about Apollo Thirteen, old KGB agents, a taste for revenge that you've had—"

He leaned over the desk. "Nope. I'm not going to tell them a damn thing about why I came here and did what I did. And neither are you."

"Grandfather . . . you tried to kill a man! And you're not going to tell them why?"

He sat back in his chair, a satisfied look on his face. "Nope. And like I said, neither are you."

"Look, if you're going to threaten me with taking away my educational support, then forget it. I don't want it. Not a damn penny. All right? I'm not going to cover up things for you."

Grandfather smiled again. "Nice to see you have a little backbone, Jason. Okay, here's an offer. You keep your mouth shut for an hour. All right? Then, if I'm still here, locked up, you can say anything you want. Anything at all. I don't care. The money will be yours. But just one thing. Okay?"

I suddenly felt exhausted, like I could crawl under the table and sleep for a week. "Okay. One thing. What is it?"

He scratched one hand with the other. "You take my money, you do good things for us. That moron I missed, he took the stars away for us, for at least a couple of generations. You do your best to bring them back to us, all right? To bring us back home, where we belong."

I rubbed at my face. "All right. One hour."

"Good."


I spent the next fifty-five minutes, sitting in a dirty lobby at the sheriff's station, reading and re-reading a *Time* magazine that was a year old. I had told the representatives from the sheriff's department that I needed time to think before making phone calls, to get a lawyer, to try to arrange bail, and the truth be told, I just needed to sit and think. Though I have to admit, I didn't get much thinking done, leafing through the sticky pages. I kept on thinking of the exhibits and displays we saw, and the pure hate I saw on Grandfather's face, as he tried to kill a man he claimed had stolen the stars.

Fifty-six minutes. Or had he, that poor guy named Miles. Mom and Dad had been adamant, that Grandfather had always worked at the State Department. Maybe he was losing it. Maybe he really was making up stories.

Fifty-seven minutes. I put the magazine down and was rehearsing what I was going to say when I called Dad, when the door to the lobby opened up and three well-dressed men in suits came in. Two were in their mid-30's, it looked like, and the other was about grandfather's age. They talked to the desk clerk and they went into a back room, and eventually there was some yelling and shouting. Then one of the younger guys came out and said, "You Jason?"

I stood up. "Yes."

"Can we talk to you?"

"Sure."

But there was no "we" as I was ushered into a break room, chairs and tables and vending machines. Just the older man, dressed well in a crisp white shirt and red-tie, dark blue suit, his face tanned and his white hair closely trimmed. He was sipping a cup of coffee and didn't bother to offer me one. I wasn't insulted.

"You're Jason, George's grandson?" he asked.

"I am," I said.

"A hell of a mess he's gotten us into, hunh?"

"Who's us, if I might ask?"

He smiled, a fine little smile of a man who keeps lots of secrets, and doesn't feel like sharing any of them. "Let's just say very good friends of a former, well-respected co-worker."

"I see. And what about the guy that this well-respected co-worker tried to kill?"

"If there was such a guy—which I'm not admitting—then he'll be taken care of. Moved somewhere else. Kept hidden."

"Oh," I said.

"Tell you what," he said. "Give us a little while, we'll have your grandfather ready for you to take home."

"Really?"

Another sip from the coffee cup. "Sure. Why not?"

I folded my arms. "Who are you guys, anyway?"

He didn't answer. Just kept his cup of coffee handy. I said, "His story, about what happened. Is it true?"

A shrug. "Not mine to say, right. Come along, son. Just head out into the parking lot, take a break. He'll be out, no problem, no court date, no record, not a thing. Free and clear, and you can take him away."

I let out a breath. "You guys are good, aren't you?"

That made his smile wider. "Some days, yeah, we're the best."

So I left him and went outside.

It was muggy but the night sky was fairly clear, though the ambient light was washing out most of the stars. Underneath my arm was a tattered copy of that day's *Florida Today* newspaper, which I had picked up on the way out of the lobby. Something to look at while I waited. I hugged myself and leaned up against the rental car, right underneath a streetlight, not quite believing what kind of trip this had been. But no matter how much my head spun, no matter how many bad dreams I'd probably have, I could only think of one thing: a three-legged couch, back up in New Hampshire, and a promise. A promise that I had the very best education now available for me.

I opened up the newspaper, flipped through, and just for the hell of it, read the horoscope for today, for Aquarius, and when I read the single sentence, it was like I was back home, in New Hampshire, on a cold winter day:

"A promise made to a relative will show you the path to a new life."

I looked up at the washed out sky. I looked about until I was sure I was looking in the right direction, and on the horizon was a fuzzy glow of light. The Kennedy Space Center at Cape Canaveral. I suddenly had a feeling that one of these days, I'd be back there. And be back there for a while. One more promise. I looked to the door where I had just come out, waiting for my grandfather to emerge.

"Okay," I whispered. "Grandfather, I'll do my best. To bring us home."

# REASON TO BELIEVE

## Mat Coward

"I TAKE IT you're a thoroughgoing disbeliever in astrology?"

"Of course."

"Why of course?"

"Because," he said, "I have a penis."

She didn't look baffled, or disgusted, or annoyed, or even superior. She laughed: opened her eyes wide and laughed. Harry liked that. Laughing made her ears pink and he liked that, too. He'd quite like to lick her ears, should a suitable opportunity ever arise. Not very likely, but worth bearing in mind.

"It may surprise you to know," she said, "though I suspect it wouldn't, that I have many male clients."

Sure, he thought, but they're all homosexual, and that's different. They don't believe in astrology because they believe in astrology — they believe in astrology because *women* believe in astrology.

Emma Gillie laughed again and leant over the table and punched him lightly on the upper arm. "And I know what you're thinking," she said, "and they are—"

*Punched him lightly on the arm?*

Harry was a detective sergeant in the Metropolitan Police and he was very large. When people punched DS Harry Peacock on the arm, lightly or otherwise, it was usually their way of saying 'I wish to visit the emergency room at the local hospital. Could you arrange this for me please?'

"—*not* all gay! Plenty of men, heterosexual and otherwise, are in-

terested in having their charts prepared and interpreted by a professional astrologer. Some of them, even, are men who drink beer and
shout 'Wa-hay!' at teenage dancing girls on television."

Whereas, she had punched him on the arm in the way that a
woman punches a man: with nothing behind the knuckles except
lipstick and pheromones. Harry had been punched that way before,
because although he was very large he wasn't at all fat or ugly, but
usually it had happened when he was off duty. He didn't think he'd
ever until now, in twenty-two years on the job, been punched on the
arm in a flirtatious manner by a murder suspect.

Though he must remember not to mention to her, or to anyone
else, that she was a murder suspect, because he wasn't supposed to
know it was a murder. Not yet.

"Well of course, Miss Gillie—"

"Or Emma," she said.

Perhaps she was one of those forty-one-year-old women who wake
up one day with the belief embedded in their minds that if they don't
get married this week they'll have missed their chance. So they just
set about marrying the next man they see, whether it's a gay plumber
with a big moustache, a Franciscan friar with a past, or even a large
detective who was supposed to be suspecting them of murder.

"I know that at least one of your clients is a heterosexual man, Miss
Gillie," he said, "or at least a married man. Mr. Alex Croft."

She stopped smiling and pushed her lips hard against each other
as if she were trying to crack a nut without using her teeth. "Yes, poor
Alex. You say he's missing?"

"I don't, particularly, but his wife does. That's Mrs. Bridget Croft."

"Yes," she said. "Bridget."

"Do you know her?"

She thought about that for a moment or two, and then said: "I
haven't met her."

Emma Gillie's workplace was above a kitchen appliance shop in
West Hampstead. The room they were sitting in was reached via a
small waiting-room. A second door in the waiting-room led, Harry
supposed, to a lavatory, or possibly a storeroom. This room looked
very much like an office—there was a desk, a computer, a combined
phone, fax and answering-machine, and some bookshelves—but it

also looked a little like a psychiatrist's consulting-room, in that it was furnished with pastel curtains, wallpaper and carpet, two easy chairs, a low coffee table and a couch. Emma and Harry were drinking coffee, but they were sitting either side of the desk while they did so.

While she'd poured the coffee, Harry had made what he thought was an innocent remark — or what he'd told himself he thought was an innocent remark. He'd said, "This is a nice office, Ms. Gillie. Business must be good." She'd replied that she preferred 'Miss,' or 'Emma,' and had gone on to say *I take it you're a thoroughgoing disbeliever in astrology?* Which he was. Thoroughgoing. Harry Peacock had found little use in his life for agnosticism, although it would be fair to say he hadn't spent much time looking.

"Mrs. Croft believes her husband's last appointment on Friday was with you, at 6.30 p.m."

"Yes."

Emma Gillie seemed quite tall for an astrologer, Harry thought. Or maybe just tall for a woman. Her hair was predominantly blond, and her face was lined by too many smiles held for too long.

"And would she be right about that?"

"She would be right. Alex came here straight from work."

"He showed up for his appointment?"

"Oh yes. Harry never missed an appointment, and he was never late."

"His wife described him as a very punctual man. Very well-ordered."

Emma sipped her coffee for a while and peered through its steam at nothing. "He was very punctual, I would agree."

"And when did he—"

"You're not one of those Christians are you?"

"Which Christians?"

"You know, the ones who think astrology is evil. Like in America."

"I'm not religious, Miss Gillie. When did—"

"*Ah.* You're one of *those.*" She smiled. Her eyes were brown, but she flashed them as if they were green.

"Miss Gillie, when did Mr. Croft leave here on Friday night?"

"He was here three-quarters of an hour."

"So he left about 7.15?"

"That's when he left."

Harry finished his coffee and thought about buying a pipe. He'd never smoked a pipe, but it was something he wondered about from time to time. "And while he was here, did he seem normal to you? Was he agitated in any way, or did he say anything which gave you reason to —"

She put her coffee cup down and shook her head quite vigorously. Because the coffee cup was back in its saucer, she didn't spill a drop. "Sergeant Peacock, I can't discuss with you anything which Mr. Croft may or may not have said to me during his consultation. For obvious reasons."

Harry stared at her for seven seconds. Then he shrugged. "No, I'm sorry, nothing comes to mind."

"I'm sorry?"

"Your obvious reasons are not obvious to me."

Her lips hardly moved as she said, "Client confidentiality."

"Oh, of course. Yes, of course, I quite understand."

"Well . . . yes. Well, I'm glad you understand that, because —"

"I quite understand how someone who believes that star signs determine your love life would also believe that astrologers are protected by common law from giving vital evidence to a police officer investigating a missing person."

Her lips didn't move at all as she said, "Piss off."

Harry leant forward. "What did you say?"

"*Piss off.*"

"Oh, that's a relief. I thought you said 'piss off.' "

She said it again.

Harry got up, and thanked her for her time. As she opened the street door to let him out, she said: "Why do you think he's dead?"

"Miss Gillie —"

"Or Emma."

"I don't believe he's dead. I don't believe anything. I am merely following up a report of a missing person."

"In that case," she said, closing the door behind Harry, "I can't imagine why you think I killed him."

*     *     *

DI Wright's office was a partitioned cubicle in a corner of the CID room. Inside, there was just about room for a desk, two chairs and a hat stand. DI Wright didn't have a hat stand, so the cubicle seemed bigger than it really was.

"He's definitely missing, then?"

Harry was too large to sit in either of DI Wright's chairs, so he was standing. "He hasn't been seen at home since Friday morning, it's now Tuesday afternoon. Mr. Croft is apparently a highly punctual and organised man."

"OK, so he's missing. Voluntarily or otherwise. What does he do for a living?"

Nothing, Harry thought; he's dead. "He drives a lorry which collects full bottle banks from recycling centres and replaces them with empty bottle banks. Then he takes the full bottle banks to—"

"*Yes*, Harry, *fine*—he's a lorry driver?" DI Wright was a small man with a grey moustache, but he wasn't nearly as small as Harry Peacock was large. Harry Peacock had no moustache.

"Yes, sir."

"And he wasn't in work yesterday or today?"

"He should have been in today, but yesterday was his day off, anyway."

"Ah," said DI Wright. He scratched his moustache with his pen. "Voluntary disappearance? Girlfriend?"

"Could be, sir."

"OK. You all right to run with this for a little longer?"

Harry wondered what would happen if he said that, in fact, no, he wasn't OK to run with this; that, in fact, he rather thought he'd spend the rest of the day swimming in the lido. It *was* a hot day. He wouldn't mind a swim.

"Yes, sir," said Harry.

"Good. So, what will you do next?"

Strip down to my trunks, thought Harry, and do a belly-flop. "Have another word with the missing person's wife. Visit his workplace. So far, I've only spoken to his supervisor on the phone."

"Excellent." DI Wright got to his feet. "OK, Harry, that's fine—I won't hold you up."

Harry wondered what would happen if he said, no, don't worry, you're not holding me up. I'm in no hurry.

"Thank you, sir," said Harry, and went to have another word with the missing person's wife.

"Has your husband always been interested in astrology?"

"No," said Bridget Croft. "I wouldn't have said so."

The Croft's living-room was a little pink for Harry's taste. The furnishings seemed unnecessarily decorative; the cushions had little ruffles on them, and the curtains were heavily pleated. Still, the sofa was deep, which meant that Harry could sit on it comfortably. That made a nice change. Mrs. Croft herself, as if by contrast, was not decorative. Her face, her hair, her clothes, the way she moved—all were understated and unremarkable. It wasn't that she was unattractive; she just wasn't someone who went in for attracting.

Of course, having a missing husband showed on her face, too. She had what Harry thought of as a widow's tremor about her lips and eyelids.

"So his interest in astrology is recent?"

"It must be, I suppose."

"Does he have a taste for that sort of thing generally?"

"Sort of thing?"

"Similar to astrology. Tarot, feng shui, crystal balls, religion, reincarnation, seances. Fortune telling. Spiritual matters." Harry shrugged. "Beliefs."

"Not at all." She smiled, and pushed a fall of hair off her forehead. The gesture looked clumsy to Harry, perhaps because she didn't have any hair on her forehead. She wore a hair band. "Rather the opposite."

"For instance?"

"Well . . . My parents are Irish, OK? They're Catholic. I mean, you know—not practicing, or anything, but you know, Catholic. And when Alex and I were getting married, Mum and Dad wanted us to do it in a Catholic church. In their view, that's what a church is for, you know? You don't have to believe in the religion or anything, it's got nothing to do with God, it's just a church is where you go to get married and buried."

There was a wedding photo on the sideboard, in which Alex looked like a big-boned boy, and Bridget looked like a girl who didn't go in for attracting. The clothes in the photo dated it to around twenty years ago.

"Did you get married in a church?"

"No. Alex wouldn't hear of it. He said, neither of us believed in the Catholic faith, we didn't follow its, you know, its teachings, we didn't attend its services. He said to get married in a church would be irrational, hypocritical, and above all an insult to all the real Catholics."

"What did your parents say to that?"

"Dad said, you know, it doesn't matter whether you believe in it or not, you can still get married in church. But Alex said that if you use the clubhouse you should join the club, and if you join the club you should follow the rules."

I wish you weren't dead, Alex, thought Harry. I'd like to meet you. "He felt strongly about this?"

"I think where that came from—his union, locally, they have their own bar. You know, cheap drinks and all that. And Alex used to get very cross, because some people who wouldn't join the union, they didn't mind getting the cheap drinks."

"Past tense."

"Past tense?"

"You said Alex *used* to get very annoyed."

"Oh. Right. No, they got it sorted out. Members only, now."

"Did Alex and your parents fall out over the wedding?"

"Not at all." She laughed. It was a small, unadorned laugh, about the minimum required, Harry reckoned, to be classified as a laugh under existing legislation. "Nobody falls out with Alex. He isn't the sort you could fall out with. He made a joke of it in the end—he wound up my dad, telling him that since he—you know, Alex—was a practicing atheist, I'd have to convert to atheism before we got married! Undergo instruction and everything, you know, like the Catholics do. And the Jews, I think."

"Your father was amused?"

"Well, he was, yes—once he realised he was being had, you know. He already knew Alex liked practical jokes. Alex always says a joke can be a very powerful thing."

"I don't care for practical jokes," said Harry.

"Oh?"

"No. Never liked them. I like impractical jokes. I'd like to climb up on someone's roof on Christmas Day and leave two live elephants there."

Bridget's face said she didn't know what to say to that. "That would be impractical, sure."

Harry nodded. "Then I'd ring him up and say, *Let's see you explain that one to the wife, then!*"

"Right," said Bridget. "Well, he'd have a job."

If Harry had bought a pipe, he'd have puffed it now. Except that you might not want to smoke in such a pink room. You'd leave a stain. "You must have been surprised when you found out Alex was visiting an astrologer."

"I didn't *find out*. It wasn't a secret." Bridget's nose was red at its tip. "He wasn't keeping it from me."

"When did you find out?"

"I didn't *find out*. He told me. Last week."

"He'd been visiting the astrologer for eleven weeks."

"Yes. So?"

"He didn't tell you before he started going to the astrologer. He told you after he'd already been going for eleven weeks. So he was keeping it from you."

"He was not."

"In what sense would you say, Mrs. Croft, that he was not keeping it from you?"

"In the sense that he was not." Bridget folded her arms across her chest. Then she unfolded them and lit a cigarette.

"Can you think of any reason why your husband might wish to disappear?"

"None."

"Have there been any problems at home lately, such as—"

"None whatsoever."

"I mean, anything—an argument, just something trivial, or—"

"None whatsoever." She shook her head.

"Or do you have any reason to believe that your husband was unhappy about anything, or that he was—"

"None whatsoever."

Harry took a deep breath. He quite enjoyed it, so he took another one. "None whatsoever?"

"None whatsoever."

Harry stood. "Thank you, Mrs. Croft. I'll be in touch as soon as there's anything to report."

Although actually, he thought, he wouldn't. When they found Alex Croft's body, they'd send a uniform to break the news.

A little man in a large jacket sat in a small Portakabin. DS Harry Peacock was too large to sit down in the cabin, and too large to stand up properly in it, so he flexed his knees and bent his neck and decided that this would be a short interview. It was cold in the cabin, although it was hot outside. It wasn't cool; it was just cold.

The little man's name was Len, and he was Alex Croft's boss.

"No idea, mate. He was off yesterday, but he should be here today."

"So you're expecting him in tomorrow?"

"Definitely. I hope so. Except you're telling me he's missing?"

"His wife hasn't seen him all weekend. As far as you know, does Alex have a girlfriend?"

"Not that I know of. Never heard anything pertaining to such, at any rate."

"Pertaining to such," said Harry.

The little employer took off his glasses, spat on them, and polished them on his shirt. "Not a whisper. That's where he's gone, you reckon?"

"Is Alex interested in astrology, do you know?" Harry asked. "Or matters pertaining to such?"

"Astrology?" Len put his glasses back on. He turned his mouth down at the corners and he frowned. "No, definitely not."

"You sound very certain."

"I am, mate. He reckons it's all bollocks, all that. Says so, most vocally. Whenever the subject comes up, he says *All bollocks, that is.*"

"Pertaining to bollocks," said Harry. All the blood in his body seemed to be dammed between his knees and his neck. This, he felt sure, was an undesirably inequitable pattern of distribution.

"He won't even look at his horoscope."

"What horoscope?"

"You know, like when you're on your tea break. Someone gets the paper out, has a look what's on TV, has a look at the football scores, then he says to the rest of them, like, what's you star sign, then? Reads out the horoscope. Taurus: keep your eyes open for an unexpected opportunity this afternoon."

"What," said Harry. "Even the men do this?"

"I'm *talking* about the men. Drivers, I'm talking about. All our drivers are men."

"Alex doesn't join in with that? Doesn't want to know what his horoscope says?"

"Thinks it's all bollocks. Thing is, he's right." Len looked up at the detective and nodded. "It is bollocks."

"Bollocks," said Harry. He nodded, too.

"That stuff in the paper, that's not real astrology."

"It isn't?"

"Course it's not. How can you have a horoscope for millions of people, all exactly the same? Eh? I mean, think about it, what are the chances of one twelfth of the entire population of the world receiving an unexpected opportunity on the same afternoon?"

"Yes," said Harry. "I've often wondered the same thing."

"Well, it can't happen, can it? Statistical impossibility."

"Statistical bollocks."

"Course it is. No, see, if you want to know what the stars have in store for you, you've got to do the thing properly."

"Right."

"Get your own, personal chart made out for you. That's how you do it. Get a professional, qualified astrologer, with certificates and that."

"Certificates pertaining to astrology."

"Precisely. Which you can get. There's courses and that."

"I suppose there must be."

"There are," said Len. "Now that's a completely different matter. It's not just sun signs, you know. It's moon signs, and ascendants, and things rising and what have you. Different houses, and quadrants. All sorts. It's a science."

"So is physics," said Harry. "Or so we are told."

"Now, *that*—a proper individual, tailor-made horoscope—that's something worth having. That can be most revelatory, pertaining to the lifestyle choices facing any given person."

"Lifestyle choices," said Harry. "Yes, I can see that."

"But Alex—he reckons all that's a load of old bollocks, too. Which is where he's wrong, you see."

"Because it's a science."

Len nodded again. Or maybe he hadn't stopped nodding from before. It was hard to tell from Harry's angle. "Course it is. Maths, and everything. Logarithms, the lot. But you see, Alex—he doesn't have a very open mind about that sort of thing."

"No?"

"No. Which is a pity."

Harry waited, and when he'd finished waiting, he said: "Why?"

"Why?"

"Why is that a pity?"

"Well, it's got to be, hasn't it? I mean, come on! If you don't keep an open mind, how you going to learn anything new?"

"Right," said Harry. "Like physics. So, you've had one of these professional charts done yourself, have you?"

"I have done. Certainly I have done."

"Recently?"

"Not for a while, not for years. I mean, the thing is—I'm a married man. What do I need to know my future for? I know my bloody future all too bloody well, thank you!"

"More of the bloody same," Harry guessed.

"You've got it, son. More of the bloody same, and then death. *And* guess who pays for the bloody funeral?"

Harry was fascinated to find himself in conversation with a man who objected to paying for his own funeral, but his neck was now entirely immobile and his knees were audible, so he left.

"You have three rooms. Your waiting-room, your—"

"I'm with a client," said Emma Gillie. "If you want to speak to me, do you mind phoning first?"

"What's the third room?"

She closed the door behind her, so that she was standing next to him on the pavement. "It's a bathroom."

"Is that bathroom in the American sense, or bathroom in the correct sense?"

"Both," she said. "Neither, in fact. It's a small room containing a lavatory, a basin and a shower cubicle."

"Thank you."

"And a wastepaper basket. And a medicine cabinet. And a box of tissues."

He nodded to her, and turned to go.

"Do you want to see it?" she said. "Do you wish to search my bathroom?"

Harry stopped, and swivelled. "Not really. Thanks, anyway."

"Then why are you so bloody interested in it?"

"I'm not especially. I was just wondering, that's all. Now I know."

"You're not especially interested, but you're interested enough to disturb me while I'm with a client. Why couldn't you ring first? Wouldn't that have been basic courtesy?"

"Sorry." Harry patted his left suit coat pocket. "Battery's run down." Harry's left suit coat pocket rang. "It does that sometimes when you pat it," he explained. "Faulty connections."

Emma Gillie pushed at the street door, found she'd locked herself out, and pressed the buzzer, long and hard. "I might well report you to your superiors."

"I have no superiors," said Harry. "They're all small men with moustaches."

The door to Emma's suite buzzed and clicked and she pushed through it. Harry answered his phone. It was a wrong number. He noticed something on his mobile that he'd never noticed before. A feature. He pressed some buttons, and discovered that his lucky number for today was 77.

He turned left into the high street, and walked into a betting shop. He went up to the counter and told the elderly woman behind the glass: "I'd like to put one thousand pounds on a horse named Seventy-Seven, please."

The woman frowned. "Seventy-Seven?"

"To win, please."

"Where's it running?"

"I don't know. Sorry."

The woman sucked her teeth and checked her lists. "I don't think there *is* a horse called Seventy-Seven," she said.

"Just as I thought," said Harry. "Thank you for your help." He gave the clerk a friendly nod, and left the shop.

In a cafe, Harry ate a cheese and pickle roll and a doughnut, and drank seven cups of tea. He made a list in his notebook of things he needed to think about.

1. Where is the body?
2. Why does a man with no interest in astrology visit an astrologist?
3. Buy a pipe — yes or no?

Between the fourth and fifth cups of tea, he came up with an answer of sorts to the second question: Alex Croft was *not* a man with no interest in astrology. Quite the opposite, in fact.

When he went up to pay his bill, Harry asked the Greek man who ran the cafe whether he allowed smoking.

The Greek man looked suspicious. He knew what Harry did for a living. "What sort of smoking?"

"Pipes."

"Pipes, no. Cigarettes, OK, only not French. But pipes and cigars — no. Too much."

"Right," said Harry. "Well, that seems to settle that, then. Thanks."

"You smoke a pipe?"

Harry shook his head. "Never have."

The Greek man gave him his change, looking at his face all the time. "Well, at least the weather's brightened up, then."

"True," said Harry. "Not the weather you'd want to leave a corpse lying around in."

The Greek man pressed a final pound coin into Harry's palm with a firm finger, and said: "Well, it takes all sorts."

"I've changed my mind."

"What about?" Emma Gillie stood aside, to let Harry go up the stairs before her. "Astrology? The poll tax? White men singing the blues?"

"I would like to have a look at your bathroom, after all."

"I see you haven't changed your mind about turning up without phoning." They stood in her waiting-room, and both looked at the door to the bathroom. It was closed. "You wouldn't answer me yesterday when I asked you why you thought Alex was dead. So, I'll answer myself. It's because you have a feeling. A hunch. Intuition."

"No, not intuition. Instinct."

She shrugged. "Whichever—"

"No, it's not the same thing. Intuition is magic. What I have is instinct, shaped and sharpened by experience. Including, it may be assumed, *unconscious* experience. Nothing mystical about it."

"Yeah. Well. OK. Do you want a cup of tea?"

"No thank you, I've had one."

Emma laughed. "It's the kind of thing you're allowed to do more than once."

"Frankly, I've had seven," he said. "Within the last hour."

"Oh, right. Is that why you need to visit my bathroom?"

Harry smiled. "No. That has to do with the murder of Alex Croft."

She sat down on a two-seat sofa. Harry stayed where he was. "Instinct or whatever, that's all you're going on, isn't it? There's no actual evidence that Alex is dead, right? I mean, you haven't found his body, or anything?"

"No body. Not yet."

Emma relaxed into the cushions of the sofa. "Thought so. And this is how you decide whether someone's been murdered or not: you use your *instinct*. Hey, Sergeant Peacock—no wonder you hate astrology! Like a dog hates a wolf."

Harry put his hand on the bathroom door-handle. "May I?"

"You need my permission?"

"At the moment, yes."

She got up. Very elegantly, Harry thought, considering how low the sofa was. "You may. But it's locked."

Harry didn't try the door to see if it was locked. He took his hand off the handle. "Do you always keep your bathroom door locked?"

Emma shook her head. Her hair danced to a rumba beat. "That's not really how locks work, Harry. You know? Always locked or always open. That would be a waste of a good lock."

"Will you open it for me?"

"You still need my permission?"

"At the moment, yes."

Emma took a small bunch of keys out of her pocket. "May I come in with you, or do you prefer privacy?"

Harry slid a hand through the air, to suggest that she should enter first. The narrow room was as she had described it; at the far end, facing the door, a lavatory; to the right, a basin; to the left, a shower cubicle which would serve someone of Harry's size as a footbath or perhaps, at an undignified angle, as a bidet. Beneath the basin there was a wicker wastepaper basket. It was empty. Above the basin was a medicine cabinet, above the shower an extractor fan, and above the lavatory a window.

"I don't see a box of tissues," said Harry.

"I made that up," said Emma, sitting on the lid of the lavatory seat. "It was a *touch*. I thought you'd appreciate it."

"Well," said Harry, "as long as you knew what you were doing. Lying to the police is always dangerous. Always and irrespective."

"Shall I fetch a screwdriver?"

"If you like. What for?"

She jabbed an elbow into the turquoise plastic behind her. "So you can unscrew the cistern. See if I chopped Alex up and put him in there after I killed him in the shower."

Harry wasn't interested in the cistern. "May I look at the window, please?"

"The window?"

"The one behind you. I'm interested in the view."

There was barely room for them to pass, sideways on, as she moved towards the door and he moved towards the lavatory. He could smell her shampoo.

It was a clean, single-glazed window, chin-height on Harry. He opened it, and looked out onto an alleyway devoted to dustbins and lockups and piles of rubbish. The drop was only about five foot, the building being taller at the front than at the back.

"You should have a word with our crime prevention people about this," he said. "Anyone with a ladder could break in through here."

"Right. Maybe that's what happened to my tissues." She walked out of the bathroom and into the waiting-room and Harry followed her. She sat on the sofa, and he leaned against a wall.

Harry said, "My lucky number today is seventy-seven."

"You're a great man for the non-sequiturs, aren't you? Did you know that otters have permanent erections?"

"I didn't know," said Harry. "But that does explain why they don't play croquet."

"So, seventy-seven. How do you know?"

Harry held up his mobile phone. "Says so on here."

Emma's nose and chin performed a ballet of contempt. "Oh, that stuff's just crap."

"That stuff is crap, but your stuff isn't crap?"

She put her elbows on her knees and her face in her hands. "Look, Harry, in all fields there are people who know what they're talking about, and people who don't. If you had a pain in the chest you could either take it to a quack who'd tell you that your lucky number is seventy-seven, or you could go to a proper doctor who'd tell you whether you were experiencing indigestion or a heart attack."

"Or both," said Harry. "I've often wondered how they know when it's both. It must be both sometimes. Just because you're having a heart attack is no reason why you shouldn't have indigestion as well, is it?"

She ran her hair through her fingers and breathed out loudly. "That would be enough to turn a man sceptic, wouldn't it?"

"Who let you in earlier on?"

"What are you onto *now*?"

"You locked yourself out. You pressed the buzzer and the door opened. Who opened it?"

She sat back against the sofa at speed, as if punched there by sheer astonishment. "That only applies to *male* otters, obviously. My client. My client let me in. Why do you care?"

"I thought perhaps it was your accomplice. Obviously, I was wrong."

"You see, that's where you've been a detective for too long. Sergeant, people only need accomplices when they're up to no good.
The rest of the time, we make do with friends and acquaintances."

"Why did Alex need so many sessions with you? Once you've had
the chart done that's it, isn't it?"

"Not necessarily."

"Tell me about astrology."

"What, tell you everything about astrology? OK, but you'd better
loosen your tie. This is going to take two or three years."

"Fair enough. Tell me this: how long does it take to become a
professional astrologer?"

"*Two or three years*. And that's only to become competent. To know
everything about it would take several lifetimes. Literally."

"You haven't tried to guess my star sign."

Emma slapped her hands on her knees. "I'm a *professional*! Do
professional policemen *guess* who's committed a crime? Oops, sorry,
no offence intended."

"I like it when women at parties try to guess my star sign."

"You go to parties? That must be fun."

"What I do is I get them to write down their guess on a piece of
paper. And then, without looking at what they've written, I tell them
they're wrong."

"That," said Emma, "sounds suspiciously like a practical joke."

Harry looked at her for a long moment, and then said: "So?"

"So? So nothing. So what?"

Harry sorted through in his memory the various conversations he'd
had over the last couple of days. Then he said, "Excuse me," and
stepped outside onto the landing to make a phone call.

When he re-entered the waiting-room, Emma said: "I've never
waited so long for a punch-line in my life."

"The punch-line is that, due to the particular circumstances of my
infancy, my birthdate is unknown."

"I see. I take it you had an interesting infancy."

"I don't remember. I was young at the time. I like your ears."

"Anyway," said Emma, "if you don't know when you were born,
the guesses could be right, couldn't they?"

"I suppose so. Thanks, you've just ruined my only party trick."

"Presumably, you have an official birthday. Like the Queen?"

"Yes," he said. He waited for her to ask when it was, and was glad when she didn't. "Perhaps you could do me a chart for my randomly-assigned birthdate. It'd be interesting if it turned out to be eerily accurate, wouldn't it?"

"Have you ever asked yourself why it is that you so strongly don't believe in astrology?"

Harry shook his head. "No. You can't have reasons for not believing in things. Only for believing in things. People seem to have forgotten that obvious fact, and that is largely what's wrong with the world today." He took out a red handkerchief and blew his nose. "That was one policeman's opinion and should not be interpreted in any way as being the formal policy of the Metropolitan Police nor of its allied contractors."

Emma stood up. "Do you want a cup of tea yet?"

"No thanks."

"You won't have a cup of tea, and yet you think I killed Alex Croft in my shower and then—with my mighty muscles—heaved him out of the bathroom window, right? But—ah-ha!—*but* what was he doing in my shower in the first place? Sergeant Peacock, I don't do horoscopes in the shower. Such a service may, for all I know, be available in some parts of London, but not here, it isn't."

"He was your lover," said Harry. "He must've been. Why else did he keep coming to see you when he didn't believe in astrology? Especially once he knew you were a fake."

"I'm a *what*?"

"You're a quack. A lucky number merchant. You're not a properly qualified astrologer. And Alex, being the kind of hardcore sceptic he was, would have seen that straight away. He'd have seen that he knew more about astrology than you did."

She raised her arms in the air, and then let them flop to her sides. She let her mouth fall open. "Wow! Even given that you're guessing, that is an amazingly crazy idea! Even for *you*."

"May I see your certificates?"

"No, you may not. Not without a warrant. They're none of your business. What brought this on?"

Coincidentally, Harry was wondering the same thing. "You just don't sound right. Or act right. You just don't—"

"Ha-ha!" She pointed at him with the index fingers of both hands. "Intuition, Harry—I told you!"

"You could prove me wrong, I suppose, by showing me Alex's chart."

"I don't have it. The client keeps . . ." She stopped, and bit her lip.

"Only, I don't remember seeing the chart when I was round at Alex and Bridget's house." *Why is it*, Harry wondered, *that telling the truth dishonestly is always so much more satisfying than telling a lie?*

Emma folded her arms across her chest. "All right, Mr. Intuition, very clever. The reason Alex came to see me was that he wanted me to prepare a fake chart for a friend of his, a workmate."

"Name of Len?"

She nodded. "Nothing nasty, you know, just a bit of a piss-take between pals."

"Not the sort of thing a professional astrologer would countenance doing."

"That would depend, I suggest, upon the degree of difference between her rent and her income. Astrology is not as hot as it was when I started up. The public is fickle."

Harry gave a sympathetic nod. "Those feng shui bastards, eh? Coming over here and stealing our jobs."

"Look, Sergeant, it was just a joke. Nothing sinister."

DC Ali pressed the door-buzzer and was admitted. Harry introduced him to Emma Gillie, and then asked him to examine the scene in the alleyway beneath the bathroom window. "It may be that a corpse has been dropped from the window onto the ground below."

When Ali had gone, Emma said: "He doesn't carry much gear for a forensics guy. Maybe your superiors don't like to commit too many resources on a detective sergeant's instinct."

Harry liked the way she kept rallying. Obviously, he wished she wouldn't do it, but he liked it. "DC Ali is just the advance guard, Miss Gillie. And he has sufficient equipment to tell if a body has indeed fallen in that spot, I can assure you. Even if it fell onto a cushioning pile of rubbish which has since been assiduously cleaned up, splashes of Alex will remain."

She shrugged.

Harry said: "And making up this bogus chart—that took eleven weeks, did it?"

The shrug was still in place, so she didn't need to repeat it. "Alex and I enjoyed each other's company. And I will *thank* you not to raise your eyebrows at me in that immature manner!"

"I'm sorry. I didn't know I was doing it."

"Then I will thank you not to raise your eyebrows at me involuntarily. We enjoyed each other's company in the office, and here in the waiting-room, but we did not do so in the shower."

"If Alex has been in that shower recently, it will yield traces of him, no matter how well you've cleaned it."

She sat on the sofa again, her hands under her thighs. "Maybe he had a shower there once. He did work at a pretty sweaty job. I don't remember. The point is, he didn't have one with *me*."

Harry went downstairs and spoke to DC Ali, who was busy making meaningless measurements of the space immediately beneath the bathroom window, while trying not to contaminate what might, after all, turn out to be a crime scene.

"I want you to take her back to the station, and—"

"You haven't arrested her?"

"No, I'm going to tell her we think maybe the missing man was abducted, and we want her to look at mug shots in case she's seen the abductor hanging around the area. She can hardly refuse. I just want you to sit her in a spare interview room and keep her there for at least an hour."

"What mug shots?"

"Doesn't matter. Muggers, rapists, bank robbers. Your holiday in Tuscany. Just keep her there."

"So I've finished being a forensics expert for the day?"

"Thank you, yes."

DC Ali shoved his equipment back into his holdall. "Sarge, I have a degree in criminology."

"Nonetheless, I have confidence in you." Harry set off for his car, then stopped and called back to Ali: "Be sure to show her mug shot number seventy-seven."

"Seventy-seven? Whose photo is that?"

"I don't know," said Harry. "How could I be expected to know something like that?"

During the drive over to Bridget Croft's place, Harry decided on a motive: fear of exposure. Alex was a man who did his homework. He would have spotted Emma as a fake. To stop him exposing her, she killed him.

While he was parking the car outside Bridget Croft's place, Harry decided on another motive: rage. Alex and Emma were having an affair. Bridget found out. She killed him.

As he walked up Bridget Croft's drive, Harry was sure of one thing: any one woman could have killed Alex Croft, but one woman on her own could not have disposed of the corpse. Alex weighed too much for that.

The delay between Harry's ringing of the doorbell and Bridget's answering of it gave him enough time to think: the body's not going to be here or at Emma's. Neither of them are that stupid.

"Mrs. Croft, I think it only fair to tell you that Emma Gillie is at the police station as we speak, helping us with our inquiries."

"Would you like a cup of tea?" said Bridget.

"In all honesty, Mrs. Croft, I think your hands are shaking too much to make me a cup of tea. I think you should talk to a lawyer."

"I don't need a lawyer. I haven't been arrested."

"All right." Harry took out his mobile phone. "Do you mind if I make a phone call?"

"Help yourself. Shall I . . . ?"

"No, that's fine, no need for you to leave the room."

Harry dialled Alex Croft's workplace and asked to speak to Len. "I'm calling Alex's boss," he told Bridget.

"All right," said Bridget, tucking her shaking hands into her armpits.

"Len, this is DS Peacock. Pertaining to your missing colleague. I just wanted to check, does your place work twenty-four hours?"

Len told him that the recycling centre closed at eight, due to local by-laws. Harry repeated this information out loud, for the benefit of his audience.

"And Len, what sort of security do you have there?"

Good security, Len told him, in the form of high fences and gates. Once the recyclable materials had been sorted, they had commercial value. Harry nodded as he repeated Len's words.

"You also have a dump, though, for the rejected stuff? Outside the fence. Could someone get in there? No, I'm not thinking of someone stealing the rubbish — more of someone adding to it."

Yeah, that happened a bit, Len admitted. There was a proper council dump only just down the road, but some people were too bloody lazy to drive the extra half mile.

"OK, just one more question. Are you a Leo? No? Just as I thought. Thanks, Len."

Harry put the phone away. "Bridget, what I'm going to do next is to send a search team to look through Len's dump. If we find your husband's body there, forensic teams will then study your car, and any other vehicle you have access to. Why don't you ring a lawyer now, and arrange for him to meet you at the station?"

Bridget stared at the floor for a while, then she said: "Alex was Aquarius."

The two women were interviewed separately, first one, then the other, then the first one again, and so on.

"I found out by chance he wasn't at a union meeting. I rang him at the union club to tell him my mother had been taken ill, and he wasn't there. When he got home, he said, that's right, he had an appointment with an astrologer. He was doing some research. He said it like it was nothing, you know?" Bridget Croft took a sip of water. "Like it was none of my business, anyway. So, next time he had a union meeting, I followed him. He went up to her place—"

"Emma Gillie's office?"

"Her place. So I waited outside. Then I buzzed the door, gave her a false name, told her I wanted to make an appointment. A series of appointments. I wanted to find out who I was, and where I was going. She sat me in the waiting-room, said she wouldn't be a minute, she just had to tidy something away in the office. Confidential papers. I don't know what she was doing in there — putting her knickers on, probably."

*     *     *

"Was he threatening you with exposure?" said Harry. "One thing a sceptic can't stand, it's a fake. Maybe that's why you killed him."

"We were having an affair," said Emma Gillie.

"You seduced him, to *prevent* him exposing you. I'm disappointed in Alex, I must admit. I might have thought he was more self-possessed than that."

Emma made a scoffing noise at the back of her nose which was not, Harry decided after due consideration, actually all that attractive. "It doesn't matter how sceptical a man might think he is; a mammal is only ever a mammal." She took a sip of water, leaving lipstick on the rim of the glass. "Harry, when a woman who looks like me decides to have sex with a man who's been married since he was twenty, it's going to happen. You've heard of gravity, haven't you?"

"He was in the shower," said Bridget Croft. "I'd heard the water running, and him whistling. I'd heard it as soon as I came up the stairs."

"I closed the office door behind me," said Emma, "and did a quick tidy of the office. Tights under the couch, condoms in the desk drawer, that sort of thing. Spent a couple of minutes repairing my face. When I'd finished, the waiting-room was empty. I thought she'd just buggered off at first, but then I saw that the door to the bathroom was open. I went in, and there was Alex, dead in the shower, with a kitchen knife sticking out of him. And there was the woman—"

"Who you now know to be Bridget Croft?" said DI Wright.

"—there was the woman—"

"For the benefit of the tape," said DI Wright, "the suspect nodded in the affirmative."

"I did *not* nod. Stop making things up."

"I am *not* making things up," said DI Wright. "For the benefit of the tape—"

"Do you *want* me to nod?"

"For the benefit—"

"Emma," said Harry. "Was it Bridget?"

"Of course it bloody was. And she was kicking him. She was wearing pink slippers, and she was kicking him."

"But not very hard," said Bridget, "because it was slippery in there and I didn't want to fall over."

She stopped, and gave DI Wright an uncertain smile as if she thought perhaps the fact that she hadn't kicked her dead husband *very hard* might be worth mentioning to the judge.

"What did Emma say to you when she saw what you were doing?"

"She said, 'It's all right, don't panic, I'm not going to tell anyone.' "

Harry thought: I'll bet she wasn't. From a business point of view, having a client murdered in your own shower was pretty bad. On the other hand, if they could get away with it, it was a good enough solution to the problem of Alex.

\*     \*     \*

"I suppose that's true, in a horrible way," said Emma. "Though I wasn't thinking like that—I was just sorry for his poor little wife in her pink slippers."

"Alex might have tired of you eventually. And then exposed you."

"Anything's possible, I suppose. Certainly, death is more permanent than sex."

"It is," Harry agreed. "Even amongst otters."

DC Ali brought the news that the corpse found buried amid a mound of decomposing rubbish at the recycling center had been positively identified by Alex Croft's in-laws as that of their son-in-law.

Bridget Croft was formally charged with the murder of her husband. She cried, and said nothing.

Ten minutes later, Emma Gillie was formally charged under various Acts, in connection with the murder of Alex Croft. She decided not to cry, a decision which caused her, too, to remain silent. It was only when she was being led away, to be returned to her cell, that she said: "What do you mean, you like my ears?"

"I don't know," said Harry, thinking *I wish you weren't a murderer*

*and I wish Alex wasn't dead, because I'd have liked to have had a drink
with both of you. Separately, I think.*

She shrugged. "Oh well, Happy Birthday, anyway."

"Happy Birthday?"

"Hey, who knows?" said Emma. "It could be."

# TO CATCH A FISH

## Marcia Talley

I DON'T WANT anyone to think that just because I'm sitting at the Pisces Bar & Grill every day with goddam Saturn—rings and all— dangling over my head from a string that I believe any of that astrology crap. Sure, I read my horoscope in *The Island Packet* every day, but I read the obituaries, too, and I don't hear anybody saying I must be harboring some sort of death wish. The reason I'm sitting here, day after day, is because Mary Beth makes the best damn coffee in the Bahamas, and that's no lie.

Of course, she serves advice with her cappuccino. "When you gonna get a real job, Hon?" (She calls me "Hon," although my real name's Stuart.) "You know you'll never make any real money with that old boat of yours."

Mary Beth is right. All I want to do is write, but until I sell my novel to the movies—*ha, ha, ha,* pardon me while I laugh—I gotta take it as I can get it, which means sitting in the Pisces Bar & Grill most days at noon and dinner time, nursing a sandwich and a coffee, and scribbling in my yellow, college-ruled, three-subject notebook.

Mary Beth's place started life as a conch shack, growing higgledy-piggledy over the years until it morphed into an open-air restaurant, sprawling untidily over the Swiss-cheese limestone that makes up the island of Bonefish Cay. There's a hand-painted sign swinging from a wrought-iron rod out front—two fish chasing each other's tails—and inside, exposed pipes and electrical wires snake around the ceiling, connecting all the lights and overhead fans, but everything's painted

156

black so you aren't supposed to notice. She's got a menu written on a blackboard in colored chalk, except I hardly ever look at it any more. Grouper, mahi-mahi or conch, served with peas and rice and the best damn slaw—nothing changes. And Mary Beth has that new age music playing—singing whales and that rain forest crap—but it doesn't dry up the creative juices like some I can think of. Whitney Houston, for example. The way she yowls, if a dog sounded that miserable, they'd put it down. But most days, when she sees me coming, Mary Beth switches off the CD so I can get some writing done.

This one day, I'm sitting there as usual, listening to the waves slosh against the shells piled outside the window, munching on a pretzel and trying to write my heroine out of some perilous corner she'd painted herself into when in she walks. Really. Patience Bledsoe, my heroine. Same hair, same eyes, same dimpled chin and tip-tilted nose. She was standing at the bar, studying the menu, so I knew she'd never been to the Pisces Bar & Grill before.

"A skinny latte," she says to Mary Beth behind the bar, just like Patience would have done.

I leafed back to the beginning of my notebook. It was like Patience had walked right off the page. I half expected to find a blank spot on page twenty-seven, but, no, she was standing right there at the bar, no doubt about it at all. I couldn't take my eyes off her, Patience, I mean. She had long hair the color of caramel syrup, and she'd braided skinny strands of it at each temple and fastened the braids at the back of her head with a silver barrette. Then she turned her eyes on me, gas blue and about as hot, and I had to thump my chest to get my heart beating again.

"New on the island?" Mary Beth asked.

Patience shrugged. "Just passing through." She picked up her latte, moved sideways to the fixings table and tapped a packet of sugar—the brown stuff—into it.

"Thanks for stopping in," Mary Beth said with a note of disappointment in her voice. I could see Mary Beth sizing her up. Hell, Mary Beth could probably tell by the way Patience stirred her latte, little finger sticking out like that, that she was a Capricorn ruled by Saturn with her moon in the tenth house. Give Mary Beth two days and she'd have your whole life mapped out—zodiacologically speaking.

I'm a Pisces, for example, although what the hell difference that has ever made in my life I couldn't say. I was married to a Capricorn once, which was supposed to be perfectly compatible — like beans and franks or rum and Coke — but she ran off with a day trader from Boca Raton, a Sagittarius, not a compatible sign at all, so go figure. Mary Beth says it's because Saturn was in my seventh house, but that's bologna. The day trader had money, and my ex always liked men with money because they had bigger, uh, toys.

But, I got over that a long time ago.

So, that's why I was sitting there in the Pisces Bar & Grill, sending telepathic messages to Mary Beth — *find out her name* — hoping she was tuned into the cosmos that morning, particularly since her dishwasher still hadn't shown up.

"Come back and see us," said Mary Beth.

Patience sipped at her latte, testing it. "Oh, I'll be back," she drawled, then pointed with her cup to The Blue Dolphin across the street, one of our island's few B&Bs. She strolled over to the window with her latte and sat down under a picture of the Maharishi Mahesh Yogi. Mary Beth liked to hedge her bets.

Patience unfolded a copy of *The Island Packet*, our local fish wrapper, spread it out on the table in front of her and began to read. I tried to get back to my writing, but now that the girl had stepped off the page, what could I do? I fantasized that huge chunks of my novel had disappeared — the cop would be arguing with dead air and Patience's boyfriend would wake up in a big, empty four-poster bed. Mama taught me it wasn't polite to stare, so I turned in my notebook to the courtroom scene and worked on Todd Blackburn's cross-examination for a while, looking up every now and then to make sure Patience — the real one — hadn't vanished. She hadn't. One time she caught me looking at her and her eyes smiled at me over her cup. When I could breathe again, I smiled back. *Say something. Tell me your name.* But there must have been static in the ether that morning because Patience finished her coffee in silence. I watched as she tossed away her empty cup then strolled out the door and across the street. She disappeared into the Blue Dolphin, stayed inside about ten minutes, then left again, walking east along Queen Street toward the market. *Good. No luggage.*

I paid for my breakfast, waved to Mary Beth and took off for the Blue Dolphin. I stood at the desk and banged my palm on the bell until Mrs. Brozman waddled out. "That girl," I said, "the one that just left, with hair like honey. I think I went to school with her. Patience somebody?"

Mrs. Brozman's white curls trembled. "Nope. Her name's Lily. Lily Farmer."

*Lily.* I stood on the Blue Dolphin's porch and rolled the name around on my tongue like fine wine. *Lily.* It suited her. Better than Patience, if you want to know the truth. I pointed my big, flat feet down the dock to my boat, powered up my laptop and did a Find and Replace — *Patience* replace with *Lily.*

*Lily scowled at the officer.* Sounded OK.

*With her heart pounding in her ears, Lily crouched behind the tree.* That worked.

But I'd forgotten and set the blasted software to Replace All, so *Captain Faraday showed remarkable Lily with the D.A.* I leaned back in my chair and laughed until I got a stitch in my side.

I had dinner with Lily that night, so to speak. She was already there when I arrived, sitting at my table under Saturn, eating a veggie club sandwich.

"Hi, Stu," Mary Beth called when I walked in. "What will it be? The usual?"

"No," I said, feeling reckless. Lily was doing that to me, pulling my chain in some cosmic way. "What about the portobello burger?"

"Sure thing, Hon." She plopped a bottle of Kalik on a paper coaster and slid the icy brew across the bar. I took a grateful swig and was just trying to figure out where to sit when Lily drawled, the voice of a goddess, "Stu? Why don't you join me?"

"How . . . ?" I stammered, wondering for a mad moment if I were wearing my bowling shirt with my name embroidered on the pocket, when I remembered that Mary Beth had just shouted it out for everybody and his brother to hear. "Uh, sure," I bumbled — oh so suave. I slipped my notebook from under my arm, threw it on the chair opposite Lily and sat down on it. "Thanks. Thought I'd have to sit at the bar."

"No problem." She took a bite of her sandwich and chewed thought-fully. "Mary Beth says it's because I'm a Virgo. Always trying to manage others."

"She's gotten to you already, huh?" I laughed out loud. "Usually takes a couple of days. She must like you."

Lily shrugged and sipped an iced tea, her plump lips forming a deli-cious "O" around the straw as she drew the amber liquid, slowly, into her mouth. I imagined the tea sliding over her rough, pink tongue and slipping down her gorgeous throat. My fingers itched for a pen, but it was tucked into the spiral notebook now digging uncomfortably into my butt like the princess and the pea. "Watch it," I said, my forehead feeling suddenly hot. "If she gets out the tarot cards, run like hell. It means she wants to adopt you."

Lily smiled around the straw. "I'll try to remember that, but I don't think I'll be on the island long enough for the adoption to go through."

Even the arrival of my portobello burger, plump and juicy with melted mozzarella oozing over the sides of the bun, the whole delicious mess sitting on a bed of fat, hand-cut fries, did little to cheer me up after that news.

"Are you a vegetarian, too?" she asked suddenly.

"Huh? Oh, the burger. No, I just like it is all. I'm not into sprouts and bean curd, if that's what you mean." I laid down a fry. "Where are you from?" I asked her.

"Pittsburgh."

"What brings you to Bonefish Cay?"

"I needed a break."

"When do you leave?"

"In a week or two."

I munched on a fry, trying to look blasé, hoping disappointment wasn't written large all over my face. I had this insane feeling that if I followed Lily around, my novel would write itself.

"I'm Lily, by the way."

"Huh?" I must have sounded a pretty dim bulb, then I remembered she didn't know I knew her name. "Nice name, Lily," I said, thinking it suited her much better than Patience.

"What do you do, Stu?" she asked.

I stared into the trap of her bottomless eyes. I felt the muscles in my tongue go slack. "Manage investments," I lied.

Lily jerked her head toward Mary Beth who was washing glasses behind the bar. "I have more confidence in astrology than I do in the stock market," she said, her blue eyes seriously boring into mine.

"If you could get the two of them in synch," I offered, stunned by the thought, "it could be dangerous."

"Uh huh," Lily said. "Dream on."

Mary Beth suddenly materialized at my elbow with a fresh pot of coffee. "Stu also runs a charter fishing business," she said. I was grateful that she didn't add that business was in a deep slump. Hurricane Floyd had wreaked havoc with the island and tourists were staying away in droves.

I pointed down the long pier to a thirty-two foot cabin cruiser tied up in a slip. "That's my boat." *Reel Life* was also my home, but I didn't tell her that. Or the fact I was fishing mostly for myself lately, trading my catch of mahi-mahi, grouper and snapper with local restaurants in exchange for meals like this. I sank my teeth into my burger.

"Mary Beth tells me you're a writer."

I nodded, my mouth full of cheese. She sat there, one eyebrow raised, waiting politely for me to swallow.

"Stu's writing a murder mystery," Mary Beth called out helpfully.

Lily smiled a slow, seductive smile. "If John D. MacDonald can do it, so can you, Stu," she said. "There's a memorial to the *Busted Flush* in Ft. Lauderdale, you know."

At that precise moment I fell hopelessly in love with Miss Lily Farmer.

While I stared at her with a goofy expression on my face, Lily finished her sandwich, polished off her chips, laid a ten dollar bill on the table and slipped past me and out the door like a lavender-scented breath of spring. After she left, Mary Beth sauntered over with the coffee pot again. "What's the *Busted Flush*?" she wanted to know, refilling my cup.

"A boat. MacDonald's detective, Travis McGee, lived on it."

"Oh," she said.

"Of all the gin joints in all the towns in all the world, she had to walk into mine," I growled.

"Stu? Earth to Stu?" Mary Beth poked my arm. "Your eyes have glazed over."

"Sorry. I was busy channeling Bogart. Been receiving movie dialogue through my back fillings lately. Might be sun spots."

Mary Beth opened the *Island Packet* to the inside back page where the cartoons and crossword puzzle always appeared. With a stubby finger, she tapped the horoscope column. "Check out what Madame Zara has to say today."

"As if you didn't know," I chuckled. Mary Beth *was* Madame Zara. Wrote the silly column every day. It was probably the worst kept secret on the island.

Mary Beth ignored me. "Sudden romantic encounters are quite likely," she read. "Get out and mingle. You may find an ideal partner." She pushed the paper across the table until it rested against my cup.

I grinned up at her. "Maybe there's something to this horoscope business after all," I said.

The next morning, I got to The Pisces early. Lily hadn't come in yet and I was feeling unaccountably bereft. Mary Beth refilled my coffee, looking over my shoulder as I read my horoscope: *Don't be shy. Turn on your seductive charm and make a play for that passionate partner you've been dreaming about.*

"Go for it, Hon," she said.

I don't need to be hit over the head with a two-by-four. Over the next couple of weeks, I put Patience Bledsoe on the back burner and spent every waking minute with Lily Farmer, that bewitching lady from Pittsburgh, Pennsylvania. I showed her the Cays. We snorkled along the north shore of Man-o-War, got tipsy on rum punch slushies at Nipper's Beach Bar on Guana, and at the top of the red-and-white striped lighthouse in Hopetown, with the Sea of Abaco framing her lovely face, I tipped up her chin and kissed her lips for the first time.

We were looking forward to a romantic weekend in Port Lucaya when an old customer from Miami Beach called to book a week-long charter. At five hundred dollars per day, I could hardly turn the man down. So I picked him up at Marsh Harbor airport, packed him and his buddies aboard *Reel Life* and spent the next week with four beer-guzzling, cigar-smoking guys, each deliriously insane at being away from his bride. I was fishing, back-slapping, telling dirty jokes and peeing off the rail with the best of 'em, hopping from island bar to island bar and thinking that this male-bonding stuff is all well and good—especially with somebody else picking up the tab—but I'd trade it all in an island minute for one hour back home with Lily Farmer.

When I finally ditched my clients and hustled *Reel Life* back to her slip at the Pisces Bar & Grill, Mary Beth told me she hadn't seen Lily since I left. I called in at the Blue Dolphin and learned she'd checked out, leaving no forwarding address. Low as a dead man's blood pressure, I wandered the streets of Bonefish Cay looking for her, but Lily was so thoroughly gone that I almost convinced myself that I had made her up.

Except I hadn't, of course. As Mary Beth reminded me as she shoved a second cold one across the bar. "She wasn't for you, Stu. She's a Virgo."

"Virgo, schmirgo," I said.

"Let her go."

Easy for Mary Beth to say. She had a wife at home—good-looking, too—and before you start beating me about the head and shoulders for political insensitivity, it's Mary Beth who calls Kathy "the little woman," not me. I thought it'd be easier to fill up the big, black hole in my notebook than it would the big, black hole in my life.

Then I got the letter. Dropped through the hatch one day, *plop* on the galley table, envelope covered with stamps like seashells and written in her familiar backhand.

"Stu," she wrote. "Please understand. I like you, I really do, but I've met this guy, Jack Browning, and we clicked right away. I hope you and I can still be friends. Love, Lily.

What else could I do? I dragged myself to the Pisces Bar & Grill and tried to fill myself up with the spirit of understanding.

By the third margarita, I came clean. "She's left me, Mary Beth. Run off with some bozo named Jack Browning."

Mary Beth swiped a damp rag across the bar. "God, Stu. Browning's twice your age and worth millions. Has a place over on Egg Island. Hell, he *owns* the whole island."

Holding my glass in both hands, I stared at her over the salted rim. "That's supposed to make me feel better? That's she's ditched me for some rich S.O.B.?"

"Better to find out now, rather than later," said Mary Beth philosophically.

"Yeah," I said and I thought about the way Lily's hair fell like a waterfall over her left eye and how small and soft her hand felt in mine and I wanted to put my head down on the bar and bawl.

Mary Beth pointed out that my horoscope said: *Sudden romantic connections may be short-lived. Keep alert for deceptive statements. Just walk away.* So I walked. I got over it. So much so, that a month or so later, when Lily hailed me on Channel 68 inviting me to Egg Island for dinner, I heard myself coolly accepting.

I put on clean chinos and my finest t-shirt, fired up the engine, cast off and pointed *Reel Life* down the channel and into the bay, curious as hell about the competition. At Egg Island, I expected to see Lily waiting for me at the pier, but two dockhands stood there instead, identically clad in tan shorts and blue polo shirts, waiting to help me slide *Reel Life* into a slip next to Browning's boat, one-hundred pretentious feet of gleaming wood and chrome, a yacht that made *Reel Life* look like something you sail around the pond in Central Park. His lifeboat, hanging from davits over the stern, was bigger than my boat. It was embarrassing.

"Thanks," I grunted to one of the guys as he caught my line and looped it in a neat figure-eight over a cleat. Browning's boat had *Liquid Asset* painted in large, gold letters on the stern. In smaller letters underneath the name it said Georgetown, C.I. A Cayman Islands registration. Why was I not surprised?

I grabbed a six-pack of cold brews and a fresh-caught, ten pound grouper—never let it be said that Stuart Anderson, model guest, had arrived empty-handed—stepped gingerly out onto the dock and hustled up the stone steps that led to Browning's villa.

Lily met me at the door, a fantasy in a crisp white cotton sundress. A red flower was tucked behind her ear, and her feet were bare. While I stood there like a dummy, clutching the beer and worrying that the fish might drip on the carpet, a maid appeared to relieve me of it. Lily kissed the air next to my cheek, grabbed my hand, and dragged me into the garden to meet her friend.

Jack Browning was old. Way old. Must have hauled him out of his wheelchair and propped him up with pillows just for the dinner. I managed to make it through the evening somehow, with Lily fetching and toting for the old fart between bites of her pasta primavera even though there was a houseful of servants to do it for her. Then I high-tailed it home and poured half a six-pack of Bud Lite over the Kansas City steaks, salad and red wine the old guy and I had eaten, not to mention the cognac. Next morning I had a hangover the size of a satellite map of Hurricane Floyd. Can't say I felt much like writing.

Two days later, my radio crackled to life.

*"Reel Life, Reel Life, Reel Life. This is Liquid Asset. Over."*

I was up on deck cutting new dock lines and melting the ends with my dad's old Zippo lighter so they wouldn't fray. I jammed my big toe painfully against a cleat as I hurried below deck to answer the call. "This is *Reel Life*," I panted into the microphone. "Over."

"Stu!" Lily's voice was high-pitched and hysterical. "Jack's sick. Real sick. We're taking him to the hospital in Marsh Harbor. Can you meet me there? Please?"

"Sure," I said, grateful that my services were being required.

I powered up the engines and screamed across the bay, but by the time I got to the hospital it was too late for Jack Browning. I found Lily in the waiting room, tears streaking her face. "He's gone," she wept. "I can't believe it."

I handed her a napkin I had folded up in my pocket and she blew her nose into it, hard. "The nurse said the doctor would be out to talk to me soon."

We sat in silence for a while, knees touching, my hands cradling hers. "He took sick after dinner last night," she sobbed. "Nausea, vomiting, stomach cramps, diarrhea. I gave him some water, but he complained that the ice burned his lips. Oh, Stu, I'm so afraid they'll think I poisoned him or something." She looked up at me, her pale lashes beaded with tears. "He rewrote his will, Stu," she whispered. "And it's in my favor."

"Jeeze . . ." I began, but the doctor straight-armed his way through the swinging door just then. When Lily saw him, she leapt to her feet. I did, too. We stood there together, my arm wrapped protectively around her shoulder. "Ciguatera," the doctor told us. "Common in these parts."

"What's ciguatera?" Lily asked, tiny lines attractively furrowing her forehead.

"Fish poisoning," he explained. "Ordinarily, it's not fatal, but in someone so old and frail . . . " He shrugged.

"But, how?" she asked, dabbing at the corner of each eye with the napkin. "The grouper was fresh." She glanced at me sideways. "My husband said it was the most delicious . . ." She choked back a sob.

"You get it from eating certain kinds of reef-feeding fish," the doctor explained. "Especially big ones at the top of the food chain like grouper, or amberjack and red snapper."

Lily squinted, clearly puzzled. "But restaurants serve those kind of fish every day! You can buy them in the market. How can you tell what fish is safe to eat and what isn't?"

"It's difficult," the doctor said, "because there's no effective test for ciguatera. But to be sure, ask any local fisherman. He'll know."

Lily's shoulder stiffened under my hand. Then relaxed. She leaned against me, curving her body slightly to fit mine. "I'll remember that," she snuffled.

Like I said, I'm not much into horoscopes, but when Madame Zara tells you *plans may not go as you wish, so prepare for delays and make adjustments if you want to succeed* — well, why take any chances?

# SHARING

## Jon L. Breen

"So, how was *your* day?"

"What are we now, an old married couple? How was my day!"

"Okay, okay, I know I tend to be clinging, you need your space, et cetera, et cetera. I have a long history of driving people away, pushing too hard. It's a fault of mine I'm very sensitive to, and I'm working on it. But consider what a natural, reasonable question I've asked, how was your day?"

"Fine."

"No, you can't just answer fine. Start again. How was your day?"

"When I'm with you, I like to forget my day, all right?"

"No, that's a very nice sentiment, but it won't fly. In a real relationship, we have to share these things. I told you about my day, didn't I?"

"Well, sure, but I get a kick out of your days. What I mean is, your days are funny. I mean, don't get me wrong, I know you take your work seriously and you're damn good at it, but all those people you meet in a beauty parlor—"

"We prefer hair salon."

"Whatever. The different weird stuff they want done to their hair and their problems with their kids and their boyfriends and girlfriends and husband and wives, how vain they are, the crazy fashions they follow, the tattoos and the piercings, that's funny stuff, entertaining, a relief from my work, so I love to hear about it. I mean, they're not usually killing each other, are they?"

"Only with words and the occasional glare. As a rule. Well, now, let me see. I deduce you caught a murder today. Am I right?"

"I caught a murder. You're picking up the jargon, aren't you?"

"I guess so. Do you mind?"

"I don't know. I mean, no, why would I mind?"

"So who got killed?"

"A psychiatrist."

"Where?"

"In his home."

"And do you know who killed him?"

"Ah, no, not yet."

"So, it's a whodunit, huh? Like *Murder, She Wrote* or Agatha Christie."

"Baby, in real life police work, I've told you before and you have to trust me, there are no whodunits like *Murder, She Wrote* or Agatha Christie. Don't get me wrong. I don't have anything against mysteries as entertainment, not at all. I used to love *Columbo*, even if no real cop I ever knew operated like that."

"Mysteries may not be the most realistic things in the world, but when they're about people you can believe in, they have insights to offer. They're more than just games."

"Yeah, right, sure they are. Who was that writer you read all the time where you couldn't tell if the detective was male or female?"

"Sarah Caudwell. She died."

"I never bought that whole premise, you know? How could you write about a person and not tell the reader if they're male or female?"

"Have you ever read one of her books?"

"No."

"Well, try one before you generalize. Think about all the people you know. If you had a transcript of what they said, would you be able to tell if they were male or female?"

"Most of the time."

"I think most of the time you couldn't."

"So, ah, what are we having for dinner?"

"You just come here for the food, don't you? Admit it."

"Come on, you know I come here for lots more than the food. Are you doing the rosemary chicken? With the cinnamon squash? Or am I just imagining that smell?"

"Sit down, and stay out of my kitchen, if you please."

"This wine would go great with the rosemary chicken."

"A Gewürztraminer goes with anything, so you may be surprised. Now quit changing the subject. You don't know who killed this psychiatrist, right?"

"Ah, no."

"Well, tell me about it. Share. I want to know more about your work. I might even be able to help. In my job, I have to understand people, all kinds of people, male, female, gay, straight. I get to, you know, observe a lot of things. I have to be a sort of psychologist in my way. It's an intimate profession, hairstyling, sort of like tattooing or bartending or dental hygiene. Give me a chance, huh?"

"Look, it's bad enough we have to deal with that kind of stuff all day. I don't want to subject a private citizen to it, especially a private citizen I am very fond of, okay?"

"Look, that's very endearing, but I don't gross out that easily, and I'm not asking to study the autopsy photos, okay? You can tell me about it and leave out the close-your-eyes parts, can't you? This is important to me. I want to share every part of your life."

"What is that smell? Smells like pineapple. Or is it your hair I'm smelling?"

"Cut it out. No more food references till you tell me about this murder."

"All right, all right. If it doesn't give you nightmares, you'll probably just find it boring, but okay, here goes. The psychiatrist is a guy named Dr. Sanford Klingman. He has an office in a high rise downtown, but he also sees patients at home sometimes. He lives alone, has a nice place out in Windy Acres. I guess the shrinks really haul down the heavy bread. I hope that doesn't count as a food reference. Anyway, this morning his housekeeper arrives for work, lets herself in with her key, and finds him dead in his study, stabbed about a dozen times with a letter-opener he kept on his desk. It was still on the desk, covered with blood but wiped clean of prints, unfortunately."

"You should check the blood for DNA, in case the assailant cut himself. Or herself. It could happen in a frenzied attack like that."

"Uh, yeah, I think we'll be doing that. This story isn't going to spoil your dinner, is it?"

"No, and if you get on with the story, it won't spoil yours either."

"Right. The medical examiner says Klingman died some time last night, which we could have figured out for ourselves. We went to his office this morning and talked to his secretary. She said yesterday he told her he was seeing a patient at home that evening, but not the name of the patient."

"Didn't he write it down somewhere, his desk calendar maybe? Or one of those little hand-held computers?"

"Not that we could find. We had one break, though. Turns out, he kept his patient files on floppy disks, which he thought was safer and more convenient than keeping them on his hard disk or old-fashioned paper. When he left the office yesterday, he took a floppy with him from the office files that had the records of four patients on it. The secretary told us the only reason he'd take it home was if he was going to see one of those patients last night."

"And you're telling me this isn't a whodunit?"

"It's sort of a whodunit, I guess."

"So you checked 'em all out for alibis?"

"Ah, no, we couldn't. He had their case histories on the floppy, some details about them, but not their real names. The secretary said he did that with all his patients. He was very security conscious. He had some prominent patients and was terrified of confidential information leaking out."

"And where do their real names appear? In the billing files?"

"Sure, I guess. But he had a lot of patients. It'll take a while to check them all out, match them up with the information on the floppy. That's if some lawyer doesn't get a liberal judge to stop us on the grounds of breaching doctor-patient confidentiality."

"If you had probable cause to suspect one of them of murder—"

"It would help to know which one, though, wouldn't it?"

"I assume Dr. Klingman had a computer on his desk?"

"Yes."

"When he was found, was it turned on?"

"No. And the floppy wasn't in it; it was tucked in a corner of the blotter on his desk."

"I'll bet he'd have reviewed the patient's record before he or she came, though, wouldn't he? When I have an appointment with a client, I always look up their file before they come, see what their quirks and preferences are. If it's important for a hairdresser, it'd be even more important for a shrink. And if his computer works like mine, you could bring up his files and see what he'd been looking at most recently. Then you'd have one patient to identify instead of four and less civil liberties issues."

"Yeah, we thought of that. We are marginally computer literate, us bulls down at the station house. No dice."

"So you really do have a whodunit. A closed circle of four unidentified suspects."

"Don't get too excited. We don't even know for sure one of them killed him."

"But it certainly seems the most likely scenario, doesn't it? Any other clues?"

"God, clues. Why are we talking about this?"

"Come on, I want to help. Don't push me away, please. This is important to our relationship."

"It's important to your ghoulish curiosity, you mean."

"Okay, okay, my ghoulish curiosity then. Was there a clue?"

"Well, actually, yes, there was a sort of a clue. A sort of a dmgmg. . . ."

"What? You're mumbling. Say that louder."

"Okay, okay. A dying message. Sort of."

"Hey, Ellery Queen lives! This gets better and better. But wait a minute, the guy was stabbed a dozen times, and he had time for a dying message? I mean, was it between stabs or after all the stabs or what?"

"He didn't actually do it while he was dying. It's not a message in blood. That's why I said sort of. There was a pad of paper on his desk, and he'd written one note on it, we assume on the basis of something his patient said to him. 'Depressed. Planet downgraded.' Whatever the hell that means. Maybe the patient was kidnapped by space aliens, I don't know. I'll bet you're doing some sea bass, right? Would that go with this wine?"

"Sure, it would, but at the rate you're guzzling it, we'll be on a bottle of something else by the time we eat."

"Will that be my fault?"

"I'm not criticizing. I know you have to unwind. Here, let me fill that up, and tell me about the suspects. What were the names Klingman called them on his floppy disk?"

"Okay, I can see I'm not getting off the hook. The four patients were two men and two women. The two men he referred to as Sylvester and Louis B. The two women were Doris and Buster."

"Buster is a woman?"

"Yeah. Cute, huh?"

"Why Buster, I wonder."

"Judging by her case history, it could stand for Ballbuster."

"Do you see a pattern in those four names?"

"Not really what you could call a pattern, no. Do you?"

"Maybe. It's too soon to tell. Tell me about Doris first. Just a quick rundown of what you can remember. But then you're a trained professional. You remember everything."

"Yeah, it's my curse. I remember every detail of every case I ever worked on, even the stuff I'd rather forget. Of course, sometimes a good memory is a blessing. I also remember each bite of every meal I ever ate here, and every time we—"

"You were going to tell me about Doris."

"Okay, here goes. Doris is a twenty-five-year-old paralegal, unmarried, lives alone. According to Klingman's notes, she was outwardly very calm and self-possessed but inwardly in turmoil, obsessed with health and her personal appearance, always wanting to solve everybody's problems. One of her own problems seemed to be that she was too efficient, was always pointing out everybody else's mistakes, and it made her unpopular at work."

"Sounds like somebody who might erupt in violence, doesn't it?"

"She'd have to be a big, strong woman to have done that to Klingman. There's nothing in the file about her size."

"There are some strong women around, though, and an adrenaline rush can make them stronger. You should know that as well as anybody. Don't remember her date of birth by any chance, do you?"

"Her date of birth? No, I don't. Why?"

"Just an idea I have. Now tell me about, ah, Sylvester next."

"Right. Sylvester is a forty-year-old unemployed accountant, divorced. Klingman's notes say he was depressed over losing a job, thought he got fired for blowing the whistle on a cheating client, had a lawsuit in the works. Sylvester used to spend his weekends in various daredevil activities: skydiving and rock-climbing were among the tamer ones. When Sylvester got unemployed, he seemed to court danger even more furiously, every day of the week, and Klingman feared he might have an unconscious death wish. He was also stalking his ex-wife; she had a restraining order against him."

"Sounds like a real beauty. Good fit for a homicidal maniac, huh?"

"You want his birth date, too?"

"Do you have it?"

"No."

"Thought not. I may need it later, for confirmation."

"You may need it later, huh? For confirmation. What am I doing discussing police business with a civilian? Hey, is there anything to eat around here or not?"

"We'll eat, we'll eat. But first tell me about Louis B."

"Louis B., right. Sixty-five years old, married thirty-five years, wealthy, a business executive, the business not specified in Klingman's notes. The guy's been a leader all his life and now he's worried about being pushed into retirement. Active in community theatre for years but got kicked out because of a run-in with the director of his last show. Used to running things."

"Okay, got it. And now what about Buster?"

"Thirty-eight-year-old woman, married for the third time, works in real estate sales. From Klingman's notes, this woman sounds like the most neurotic of the bunch."

"Crazier than Sylvester?"

"Maybe not, but everyday neurotic. Quick to take offense, never forgets a slight, always playing angles, claims to have loved all her husbands dearly but Klingman thought she smothered them until they had to get out. Klingman had a really funny note on her: she found out more about him in their sessions than he was able to find out about her."

"Oh, that is so typical."

"Typical of what?"

"I'll tell you in a minute. Did you check out Klingman's library?"

"His library?"

"Yeah, what kind of books did he have on his shelves? Apart from the psychiatric texts, I mean? I specifically wondered if he had a lot of movie books."

"I don't remember any. But he owned more videos and DVD's than I've ever seen outside of a video store."

"Sure, a big movie buff, I could see that. Those tags he used for his patients, they all have Hollywood associations."

"Oh, come on. Most names do if you want to look for them."

"Doris, for example. Suggests Doris Day, doesn't it?"

"Not to me. How many people have you known named Doris? My mother was named Doris. That checker on the express lane at Safeway is named Doris. Maybe Klingman shopped at the same Safeway we do."

"Not likely if he had a mansion in Windy Acres. But I get your point. We have a manicurist named Doris at the salon. But how many Louis B.'s have you heard of? Only one I can think of is Louis B. Mayer."

"Yeah, okay."

"And how about Sylvester?"

"That's the cat that goes after Tweety Bird, right?"

"Maybe."

"His name was Sylvester, wasn't it?"

"Sure, it was. I just mean maybe that was the Sylvester Klingman was thinking of."

"He stalked that canary the way this Sylvester stalked his wife, so that could be a connection. Sylvester never got to have Tweety for dinner, and I know how he felt, because I really am hungry. I know you don't care about food the way I do, but—"

"No, not the way you do, no. Not in the same quantity anyway, but I'm considered a gourmet chef in some circles. As I will soon prove to you once again, but not until we're finished here. How about Buster?"

"Buster Keaton, right?"

"Maybe."

"So what does all that prove?"

"Nothing. By itself. But you have to combine it with another interest that Klingman and his patient apparently had."

"And what, pray tell, is that?"

"Astrology."

"Astrology? I don't believe in that crap."

"What you believe in doesn't matter. Klingman's patient believed in it, and Klingman himself may not have believed in it, but he sure knew a hell of a lot about it."

"How do you know that?"

"I'll get to that in a minute. Let's look at the patient's belief first. Why would a psychiatric patient be seeing the doctor at night? A crisis. And what might bring on a crisis in a patient who believed devoutly in astrology?"

"I don't know. An unfavorable horoscope in the morning paper, maybe?"

"They're rarely unfavorable, and anyway that comes with the territory. Tomorrow's horoscope might be a winner. But if I'm a psychiatric patient in precarious mental balance who believes in astrology, I could be laid really low by bad news about my ruling planet."

"Your ruling planet."

"Yes. Every sign of the zodiac has what's called a ruling planet, sometimes more than one. And which planet in our solar system has recently been threatened with downgrading from a planet to a big overblown asteroid?"

"You got me."

"Pluto, that's which one. Some big astronomer said maybe Pluto wasn't really a planet at all, but an asteroid or an inactive comet. It seems it has a lot in common with objects in what's called the Kuiper belt. Pluto is a lot bigger, but it's icy like they are and it has a similar orbit. The Kuiper belt is where most of the comets come from. So this astronomer thought maybe we should demote Pluto. It that's my ruling planet, I could be in a sweat. I mean, who wants a disgraced and thereby weakened ruling planet? It could spell disaster."

"You talk about this stuff at the beauty parlor?"

"Hair salon, and don't sneer. No, we don't talk much about astronomy, not as much as we do astrology, but I read about it in the paper between clients. Now I guess your cop's instinct will lead you to the next obvious question."

"What question is that?"

"Honestly! Your question is, for what signs of the Zodiac is Pluto the ruling planet? And I have the answer. Pluto, it turns out, is one of two ruling planets for both Aries and Scorpio. So if one of your four suspects was born under one of those signs, there's your murderer."

"I don't see the motive."

"Maybe Klingman blundered the treatment, said the wrong thing. The thing to do, or anyway the thing I'd do if one of my clients was worried about their planet getting downgraded, would be to remind them that Mars was still there as a ruling planet, even if Pluto was no longer an official planet. And anyway the moon, which isn't even a planet at all, is the ruling planet for Cancer, so maybe you don't really need an official planet to be your ruling planet. Now, if you're a Leo, the sun is your ruling planet. That should be even better than an official planet, don't you think?"

"Slow down. You're giving me a headache. I didn't think you believed in this crap any more than I do."

"Did I say I did? But some of my clients do, and I've picked up quite a bit. Now if Dr. Klingman was a skeptic, if he ridiculed his patient's beliefs, that could have brought on the murderous attack. If the patient used the doctor's own letter-opener, the attack obviously couldn't have been premeditated, could it? Clearly it was a crime of passion. Not sexual passion, religious passion. Astrology is almost a religion to some people. I wouldn't ridicule one of my clients' belief in astrology any more than I'd ridicule their belief in Christianity or Buddhism."

"You know, I wasn't kidding, this really has given me a headache. Maybe having something to eat would help. Don't get me wrong, I really appreciate your help."

"God, but you're patronizing! Why don't you just pat me on the head?"

"No, no, I really do. We'll be sure to check it out."

"Check what out? I haven't even told you who did it yet."

"And you know?"

"Well, I know which patient's ruling planet got downgraded. Look, I know I'm just a hairdresser, I'm not a detective like you, okay? But I do know who Klingman's note had to refer to. And he did know something about astrology, because the nicknames he gave his patients were keyed to the signs of the Zodiac. Start with an easy one, Louis B., who we agree he must have named for Louis B. Mayer. Now which sign of the Zodiac would Louis B. Mayer represent?"

"How the hell should I know?"

"Think! Work with me here! Louis B. Mayer was the head of MGM studios. MGM's mascot is a roaring lion. So he obviously represents Leo. Get it?"

"Okay."

"And it just so happens the characteristics of the patient called Louis B. you got from Klingman's notes were classic Leo characteristics. The leadership ability, the need to have his own way."

"I thought you didn't believe in this stuff."

"I don't really, but sometimes I wonder if there might be something to it."

"Okay, now I'm curious, I admit it. What sign is Buster Keaton supposed to represent?"

"I don't think it's that Buster."

"Then who is it? Buster Brown who lived in a shoe?"

"No, these are all movie references, remember. Think of another famous movie Buster."

"Uh . . . got one! The guy that played Flash Gordon in the old serials? Buster Crabbe?"

"Very good. So he represents the sign of the crab, Cancer. And the characteristics of the female Buster—the sensitivity, the grudge-bearing, the sneakiness—are classic Cancer characteristics. Now, moving on to Doris, not the grocery checker or the manicurist. In the latter part of her career, Doris Day was kiddingly known as a professional virgin. Virgo, get it? And the characteristics of Klingman's Doris—"

"All right. Classic Virgo characteristics. I catch on fast. So what sign of the Zodiac does Sylvester the cat represent?"

"Not the cat. Another Sylvester."

"Stallone?"

"Right. And what was Sly Stallone's most famous part?"

"Rocky."

"Okay, what was his second most famous part?"

"Rambo?"

"The sign of the Ram! Aries! And didn't I tell you, Aries is one of the signs ruled by Pluto? Sylvester's a typical Aries—risk-taking, obsessive. And he's also your murderer."

"Terrific. Thanks. You've had your fun. Now can we eat?"

"Sure, we can. You'll love it, and we've both earned it. But first you have to promise me one thing."

"I'm hungry enough to promise you anything. Almost."

"I know this has all been for laughs, okay? An intellectual exercise, at best, right? I'm not kidding myself, not really. I know real life crimesolving isn't about dying messages or locked rooms or anything like that. I do understand that. I really do. So what we've been doing here is just a sort of a parlor game, and my conclusions are probably all wrong. You'll check them out, of course, because you're a thorough professional who won't leave any stone unturned."

"That's me. I said I'd check it out and I will."

"But if by some quirk I should turn out to be right, you will come back, won't you?"

"What?"

"You have to promise me. You'll still come back if it turns out I'm right."

"Why wouldn't I? I love you. Of course, I'll come back."

" 'Cause it would be just an accident if I was right. A form of beginner's luck. And I wouldn't say I told you so. I really wouldn't."

"I'll come back. I'll always come back. Can we eat now?"

# NOT IN THE STARS

## Catherine Dain

"WELL, IF THERE'S anyone who would think the fault is not in ourselves but in the stars, it's you, Bobby," Faith said, annoyed at having to turn her head and talk over her shoulder. She didn't like having conversations with people in the back seat of the car unless she was driving and didn't have an obligation to look at them. The need to keep her eyes on the road was deeply ingrained.

"That's not it at all, Faith, and you know it," Bobby answered. "I just want to know what's coming so that I can prepare for it, like having an earthquake kit in the closet. And learning more about astrology can only help."

"Besides," Michael said, "you'll be able to amaze your friends with insightful comments about their personalities, just from knowing their birthdates. Think how in demand you'll be at parties."

Michael was driving, and the need to focus on the dimly lit canyon road spared him from having to look at either of them.

Faith turned back to Michael, relieved that he had stepped in. "I don't think my sun sign says anything about me."

"You're a Leo," Bobby said, "and you like to be the center of attention. How can you argue with that?"

"What? You're reducing me to one trait? One superficial trait? A trait that doesn't begin to describe who I am?" This time Faith turned all the way around, clutching the side of the seat.

"Now, now, kiddies, this is all for fun," Michael said. "It was nice of Bobby to invite you, Faith, and you didn't have to come."

"And you're a Libra," Bobby said, "so you're trying to strike a balance between us."

Faith stifled the impulse to tell Bobby what she thought he was. Instead she eased back in her seat, facing the road again. This was a wealthy neighborhood, and she didn't understand why someone hadn't insisted that more streetlights be installed.

"Besides," Bobby continued, "it isn't all sun signs. There are rising signs, and moon signs, and where your planets are, and all kind of aspects."

"Please," Faith said. "Please tell me Michael's right, that this is all for fun, that you don't really believe that the orbit of Pluto, which may just be a chunk of ice, not even really a planet, affects your life."

"It is for fun," Bobby said. "Nevertheless, it works. Whether Pluto is a planet or not. Where Pluto is in your natal chart says something about you, but I don't remember what it is. I can look up where it is in my ephemeris, and somebody tonight will be able to tell you the meaning."

"Your ephemeris is that fat blue book you're waving?" Faith asked.

"Yes. You can find out what signs the planets are in at any moment of the first fifty years of the twenty-first century. I'm carrying it everywhere these days. It's a great way to start conversations," Bobby replied.

"You know," Michael said, "this may be an example of Neils Bohr's famous dictum, that the opposite of a profound truth is another profound truth. The orbit of Pluto can't possibly affect your life. Nevertheless, astrology works."

"What? 'Famous dictum'? When did you start reading Neils Bohr?" Faith asked.

"Never read him. But a friend of a friend is writing a relationship book for the self-help market, and I was looking at the manuscript, and he used the Neils Bohr thing to talk about men and women. Our differences are more important than our similarities, and our similarities are more important than our differences," Michael said. "So I've been trying to think of other examples."

" 'It was the best of times, it was the worst of times,' " Faith said.

"Exactly."

"Turn right here," Bobby said. "And look for a parking place."

Michael turned right as directed. They had been traveling up one of the more tortuous canyon roads into the Hollywood Hills, and the right turn took them onto a narrow, twisting street with parking on one side only, the other side, with no open spaces in sight. Michael inched along slowly, looking for a driveway without a gate so that he could make a u-turn.

"We should have parked a block back," he said.

"Bobby, how can you tell where we're going?" Faith asked. "You can't see the houses for the walls and the shrubs, and you can't see any numbers because the streetlights don't illuminate."

"I have directions. There's a cul-de-sac somewhere up here where we can turn around, and the numbers are on the curb, so we'll be able to see them when we're outside the car, and anyway, we're going where everybody else is going," Bobby said.

What Bobby called "everybody else" was actually two couples slipping single file between the parked cars and the dark walls and walking through the gates of one of the driveways.

"They don't look like professional astrologers," Faith said.

"And what do professional astrologers look like?" Bobby said with a sigh.

"I don't know. But not that normal."

"If you want normal, Faith, that lets us out," Michael said.

They were something of an odd threesome, she would have to admit, although both Michael and Bobby had a West Hollywood hip-at-forty smoothness, and she thought she herself could fade into a crowd better than most TV personalities who had been forced into second careers. Not that being a therapist felt like second choice, not any longer. Besides, she had always been interested in people.

Michael found the cul-de-sac, turned the car around, and started slowly back down the hill.

"There's a space," Faith said.

"It's a driveway," Michael countered.

"Yes, but there's enough room between the edge of the driveway and the car parked ahead of it that you could argue it's a space."

"We'd block half the driveway," Michael said, not slowing further.

They were almost back down to the main canyon road by the time Michael found a space he was comfortable with. He maneuvered in, and Faith sighed with relief.

Bobby led them up the narrow path that passed for a sidewalk and through the same driveway gate they had seen the four others enter.

Once past the wall, they discovered an estate that had been carved out of the hillside. A circular drive swept up to a two-story, brightly lit, white stucco house that Faith vaguely recalled having seen in a *Los Angeles Times Magazine* spread. Some favored cars were blocking the path to the arched front doorway, which had been left open.

Faith stopped just before they reached the lights.

"We aren't going to be the only nonastrologers here, are we?"

"It's too late to ask that," Michael said.

"Of course we won't be," Bobby answered. "It's mostly a meeting for members, who are all professionals, but anybody who's interested, and who can get an invitation, can come. Like the Magic Castle. I told you. Avery Whitlock set it up that way in his will."

"Who would have thought someone could make this kind of money writing an astrology column?" Faith asked.

"Avery Whitlock didn't just write a daily column," Bobby said. "He was the astrologer to the stars—the movie stars—for decades. Nancy Reagan is supposed to have consulted with him on soul mate advice before she met Ronnie. Come on."

Bobby led the way inside, to a foyer where a table had been set up to block further entry. A gray-haired, middle-aged man whose paunch pushed against a green polo shirt smiled at them. The younger woman sitting next to him, who was dressed in a tailored pantsuit as if she had come straight from an office, looked too earnest to smile.

"Do you have an invitation?" she asked.

Bobby gave their names and explained that a friend of his, a member, had called to okay their presence. While the woman was checking her notes, Faith peered through the doorway into the room to the left, which was large and sparsely furnished, as if guests were expected to remain standing. There were a few groups of chatting people, but not as many as she had expected. They were also more ordinary looking than she had expected, with many of them dressed as if they had come from day jobs having nothing to do with New Age oracles. Her attention was caught by a painting over the fireplace on the far wall, a portrait of a thin, old man in a blue suit, white shirt, and red tie. Avery Whitlock, to be sure, done when he must have been in his eighties.

"Okay," the woman said. "You're on the list."

The man held out three sheets of paper, one for each of them.

"Here's a list of the discussion groups and the rooms they're being held in. Decide where you want to go, and come back if you need help finding something. Refreshments are out by the pool," he said, pointing down a hall toward the back of the house.

Faith started to look at her sheet, but Michael grabbed her hand to get her out of the way of the people coming in behind them. Bobby was already heading along the hall, and they followed him to another open door, this one taking them to a patio and a broad expanse of lawn with an Olympic-sized pool.

More small groups were scattered around the yard. A much larger group of people had gathered around a long table near the door with three large silver urns, plates of cookies, and cups and napkins on it, and an ice bucket resting on the cement at either end.

"Do you want anything?" Michael asked.

Faith shook her head. She pulled her glasses out of her purse to read the small print on the sheet of paper.

"Astrological psychology," she said. "There's actually a discussion group that meets on astrological psychology."

"And one on karmic astrology, one on special cases in horary astrology, one on the transits of Pluto, just in case you want to find out how that orbiting hunk of ice affects you. Here's one on sidereal astrology as the true interpretative tool for the New Age, whatever that means," Michael said, reading his own sheet.

"Did you think it was all fortune telling?" Bobby asked.

"Well, sort of," Faith said.

"You were wrong," Bobby said triumphantly. "You might even learn something at the discussion group on astrological psychology."

"Maybe," Faith said.

She stared at the paper, wondering exactly what astrological psychology was. Bobby tucked his ephemeris under his arm and fished around in the nearest ice bucket for two small plastic bottles of spring water. He handed one to Michael.

"I'm going to the one on compatibility charts," he said. "Sun signs just don't do it, I've learned that much."

Faith stifled a retort, and then forgot what she was going to say anyway.

An argument between two men on the other side of the pool became loud enough to catch her attention. One of the men was short and gnomish, with a dark goatee. He was wearing a well-tailored, silky jacket over a black turtleneck shirt. A purple beret was perched rakishly on a head slightly too large for his body. The other was a heavy-set, gray-haired man in a green polo shirt who could have been the twin of the one at the front desk. People all around them became quiet as well, listening as the heat rose.

"Avery Whitlock would throw you out on your ear," the larger man shouted. "He wouldn't have put up with this kind of heresy in his house."

"Whitlock was a gentleman," the gnome shouted in return. "He was gracious to everyone. And he must be spinning in his grave at the thought that narrow-minded, reactionary boors are running his foundation."

"Actually, Avery was cremated," a woman standing near Faith muttered. "His ashes are in an urn on the mantel, under his portrait."

Faith glanced over at the woman and was relieved to note that she was talking to someone else. The woman and her male companion met the appearance standard that Faith had expected to find in astrologers. The woman, a slender blonde with the kind of heavy makeup that doesn't really hide lines around the eyes, was dressed in several layers of leopard print gauze. Sheena, queen of the jungle, twenty years past her prime, Faith thought. The man, bald and bearded, sported an Hawaiian floral shirt and a bright green feathered earring that dangled from his left ear almost to his shoulder.

"The astrology that was good enough for Ptolemy was good enough for Avery Whitlock." The heavy-set man was turning purple.

"Are you suggesting that Ptolemy knew the sun was the center of the solar system? And he secretly discovered the outer planets? Avery's astrology was heliocentric, he incorporated Pluto into his charts, and he would have been open-minded where the influence of Chiron, Ceres, and the other asteroids is concerned. And you know it." The gnomish man wasn't giving ground.

"But not the Beatles! Saying that the cluster of four asteroids named after the Beatles can influence the development of musical talent is making a mockery of everything we do, everything Avery Whitlock stood for." The large man's voice was full of agony.

"Avery embraced Jung. He believed that synchronicities happen because everything in a time period is connected with everything else in that time period. Thus, the four asteroids were named for the four Beatles because they emanate cosmic rays that influence the development of musical talent, whether the naming scientists knew it or not," the gnomish man replied. "And Avery would have understood that. If you hadn't connived with the attorneys when he was old and tired, he would have made me the trustee, not you, and you know it!"

The gray-haired man stepped back, gasping, speechless.

The smaller man raised both fists in a gesture of triumph.

A few people laughed, and one woman applauded.

"Right on, Carlo!" she called.

The small man bowed in her direction. The heavy-set one turned and walked away from the pool, beyond the lighted area, still struggling for breath.

"I guess I can skip the discussion group on the influence of the asteroids," Michael said.

Faith nodded, but she was more interested in the couple next to her.

"How could you have married him?" the man with the earring asked.

"Carlo is brilliant, really. And I knew as soon as I saw his chart, with the conjunction of his Mars, my Venus, that we had been destined to meet, and that something significant would happen as a result," the Sheena-woman answered. "He was so difficult, though, that I made sure we got married when Mercury was retrograde. I knew I'd want out sooner or later."

"Seven years is a long later," the man said. "Although I guess it was a lucrative seven years."

The Sheena-woman glared. "I earned my money, Kevin."

Kevin leaned over and kissed her cheek. "Yes, dear. Anyone married to an astrologer who stakes his reputation on a comet hitting Rome, without bothering to consult Avery Whitlock first, has earned her money."

The woman jerked her cheek away.

"Avery adored Carlo," she said. "He was amused at Carlo's error over the comet and took the opportunity to point out that Aquarius was the sign of geniuses and fools, and Carlo was simply being both at the same time. And he did give us reason to believe that we would be the trustees of his estate."

"We? You and Carlo?"

"Avery saw us as married on the level of spirit, no matter what we were doing on the mundane level," the woman replied.

"Is that why you didn't feel the need to save any of your earned money? You thought you'd have Avery's trust to loot?" Kevin sounded almost amused. "You were way down on the list, my dear."

Faith didn't hear what the Sheena-woman said next, but it wiped the smile off Kevin's face.

"All right, everybody," a man's voice called from the doorway to the house. "I hope you've all decided which group you're going to, because it's time to get started."

The Sheena-woman started toward the house, Kevin following.

"Where are you going?" Michael asked.

"Oh, the psychology one, of course," Faith said. "What about you?"

"That's the only one I have a prayer of understanding," Michael replied.

"I'll meet you back here afterward, then," Bobby said. "And I'll take notes on compatibility charts so that I can tell you about them on the way home."

The three of them held back, not wanting to push past the people who clearly knew their destinations. They moved to the doorway only when there was space to do so comfortably.

The man who had called out was the same one who had checked them in, the apparent twin of the man who had been arguing with

Carlo. Faith held out her sheet of paper to him, pointing to the astrological psychology discussion group. He glanced at the paper, then back at her.

"Up the stairs, all the way to the front of the house, door to the right," he said.

More people had come into the house while the poolside argument was going on, and now everyone from house and yard had converged on the stairs at the same time. Faith and Michael pulled back again to avoid the bottleneck.

"Do you remember something about an astrologer predicting a comet would hit Rome?" she asked.

"The fashion designer, Carlo Firenza," Michael said. "I heard he went bankrupt, too. Not exactly Nostradamus. Is that the same Carlo as the little man by the pool?"

"I think so. I wonder who the twins are."

"They're not really twins, but they are brothers," a man interjected. "Larry and Ed Martin. The one who acts as gatekeeper is Ed. They're the trustees of Whitlock's estate."

Faith flushed when she realized that Kevin was standing next to her. He was smiling to let her know that he hadn't taken offense at her eavesdropping, and was merely replying in kind.

"Thank you," she said. "It's our first time here, and we don't know who anyone is. I'm Faith Cassidy, this is Michael Haver."

"Kevin Solis," he said, holding out his hand to each. "I believe I heard you say something about going to the astrological psychology discussion."

"Yes, we did," Faith said, returning his smile.

"You will have an interesting evening. Sophia leads that group." Kevin's feathered earring bobbed against his neck. It looked a little less festive than it had earlier.

"Sophia?"

"The former Signore Firenza. She was a student of astrology long before she met Carlo."

"And psychology?" Faith asked.

"That, too," Kevin answered. "She knew one of Jung's mistresses quite well, in fact."

"I can hardly wait," Michael said.

"Then you'd best move along," Kevin said. "She'll want to start on time."

Faith nodded her thanks to Kevin and moved away. The bottleneck had begun to clear, and she and Michael were able to start the ascent to the second floor.

They hadn't quite reached the landing when a piercing scream from the pool area stopped the entire group on the spot.

A second scream followed the first.

The stream of people stopped moving. Faith and Michael were stuck.

"Somebody call the paramedics!" a man's voice cried.

Murmurs of distress began to ripple up and down the stairs.

"Does anyone know CPR?"

"What happened?"

"It's Larry. He fell and hit his head. They found him in the hot tub."

"Is he all right?"

"Well, no."

The woman in the tailored suit who had been at the front desk threaded her way to the foot of the stairs.

"Please go ahead to your discussion groups," she said, her voice loud and tense. "We'll send someone around to let you know about Larry after the paramedics have seen him."

"And Larry was . . . ?" Michael whispered to Faith.

"The one in the argument with Carlo," she whispered back.

The line began to move upstairs, and Faith and Michael were pushed up to the second floor.

A siren wailed briefly outside, ending in abrupt silence.

"I've changed my mind about the discussion group," Faith said. "I really want to know what's going on."

Michael shook his head. "Probably nothing, and it's none of our business."

"You're right. But suppose they were really arguing about the trust, not the asteroids? Suppose neither one was willing to let it go? I'll just feel better if I know it was really an accident," Faith said.

She turned sideways to squeeze past the people who were still coming up the stairs, and Michael followed.

Once she reached the back door, Faith felt a momentary lurch, as if she had gone back in time. The gnome and the large man were again arguing on the far side of the pool. But this time Carlo was arguing with Ed.

"You pushed him!" Ed shouted. "Larry didn't slip—you pushed him!"

"Larry was fat and clumsy," Carlo shouted in return. "Like you! Oafs! Both of you! I was nowhere near him! He fell!"

Faith looked around to see where the hot tub might be. There were steps leading up to a deck at the end of the house, and three people with worried expressions stood watching some activity.

"Ed wouldn't have gone anywhere near the hot tub on his own," Larry shouted. "You lured him up there and pushed him in! You hate us both!"

"Yes! I hate you both! And Ed wouldn't have done anything I asked him to do," Carlo shouted. "And he's bigger than I am! He would have pushed me in the hot tub!"

"Carlo! Ed! Stop it right now!" Sophia was suddenly in the doorway next to Faith. She paused until everyone's attention was on her, then proceeded toward the two men. "We don't know that anyone pushed Larry. How is he doing?"

"Not good," said one of the people near the deck. "The paramedics haven't been able to revive him."

"Murderer!" Ed screamed. "Police! Someone call the police!"

"Someone already has," the man near the deck said.

"Not me!" Carlo shouted. "I am not a murderer! Sophia! Sophia has Pluto conjuncting Mars in her twelfth house! Sophia is capable of murder!"

"And I was upstairs ready to begin the meeting," Sophia said calmly. "Whoever pushed Larry into the tub—if anyone pushed Larry into the tub—I didn't. You are the one with the most to gain from Larry's death, Ed, and you have Pluto squaring Mars, so stop the accusations right now!"

Faith edged her way toward the deck.

Michael grabbed her arm, but she shook his hand off.

"There's still one other person who has a stake in this," she whispered. "The other person who wanted to be trustee."

"And the police will find him," Michael whispered back.

"But the evidence may be gone by then."

"What evidence?" Michael said it a little too loud, and Faith shushed him.

The deck was raised about three feet off the ground, so that inhabitants of the master bedroom could walk out through a pair of French doors to the hot tub. Larry Martin's body was on the polished wood. One paramedic was on top of him, still performing CPR, the other one knelt beside. Several people were on the stairs, blocking access.

Faith stayed on the lawn and walked around to the spot nearest the hot tub. She bent over slightly so that her eyes were almost level with the deck. Although she needed glasses for reading, her distance vision was good, and she almost immediately spotted what she was looking for.

"There!" she whispered. "Caught on the edge of the tub!"

"What?"

"The green feather." She straightened up and backed away from the deck to make certain that only Michael heard her. "Kevin went into the house ahead of us, but he somehow ended up behind us when we were getting ready to go up the stairs. He's the one who confronted Larry Martin by the hot tub."

"And thank you for finding the one thing that connected me." Kevin had been part of the group on the stairs, hidden by the others. Now he was beside them. "I have a gun. Please walk slowly around the side of the house."

"You have a gun? At an astrology meeting?" Even as Faith asked the question, she felt the barrel jam into her back.

"I'm a reserve sheriff's deputy," Kevin replied. "I always have a gun. And I know how to use it, although I'd rather not."

"Why didn't you just shoot Larry?" Michael asked. He was trying to edge away from Faith, hoping to attract the attention of someone on the deck.

"Get back over here," Kevin said quietly. Michael did as he was ordered. "I only wanted to talk to Larry about the terms of the trust. But he turned on me, just as he turned on Carlo. He lunged at me. I was only defending myself."

"Then why are you attacking me?" Faith asked.

"Because I don't want to be connected with any of this. With Larry out of the way, I'll be named trustee, as long as there's no sign of foul play. I'm sorry to threaten you, and if you'll agree to keep your mouth shut, maybe we can work something out," Kevin said.

"I don't think I can promise that," Faith said.

"Of course we will," Michael said at the same moment.

"Around the corner," Kevin said, prodding Faith with his gun.

She had barely taken a step when something thunked into Kevin's head, knocking him to the ground.

"Good shot!" Michael called.

A fat blue book was splayed on the ground not far from Kevin, who was already beginning to sit up. The gun had fallen from his hand, and Faith kicked it away from him. Then she looked up to see Bobby waving at her from the second floor window.

"I'm a witness!" Bobby shouted. "He threatened you with a gun! I'm a witness!"

The crowd surged around Faith and Kevin, only stepping back when a man with a badge flashed his way through.

"I'll need statements from everybody," he said.

The statements took much of the night.

By the time the detective told Faith, Michael, and Bobby that they could leave, they were exhausted. They rode in silence to Faith's apartment.

Michael let the car engine idle while Faith gathered her energy for the short walk.

"I'll buy you a new ephemeris," Faith said. "And thank you for your help."

"You're welcome," Bobby answered.

"I still don't understand how you managed that throw."

"I played high school football, Faith, and I still play in an occasional pick-up game on Saturdays. And I was lucky."

"Lucky," Faith said. "Yes. All those astrologers were arguing about what was in whose chart, and stopping Kevin came down to a lucky throw."

"Actually, Sophia explained it from Kevin's chart while you were talking to the detective," Bobby said. "It didn't have anything to do with Pluto. It was something about Neptune."

"Well, knock me over with an ephemeris," Michael said.

"Don't ever say that again," Faith told him.

"Good night."

# KELLER'S HOROSCOPE

## Lawrence Block

KELLER GOT OUT of the taxi at Bleecker and Broadway because that was easier than trying to tell the Haitian cab driver how to find Crosby Street. He walked to Maggie's building, a former warehouse with a forbidding exterior, and rode up to her fifth-floor loft. She was waiting for him, wearing a black canvas coat of the sort you saw in Western movies. It was called a duster, probably because it was cut long to keep the dust off. Maggie was a small woman—*elfin*, he had decided, was a good word for her—and this particular duster reached clear to the floor.

"Surprise," she said, and flung it open, and there was nothing under it but her.

Keller, who'd met Maggie Griscomb at an art gallery, had been keeping infrequent company with her for a while now. Just the other day a chance remark of his had led Dot to ask if he was seeing anybody, and he'd been stuck for an answer. Was he? It was hard to say.

"It's a superficial relationship," he'd explained.

"Keller, what other kind is there?"

"The thing is," he said, "she wants it that way. We get together once a week, if that. And we go to bed."

"Don't you at least go out for dinner first?"

"I've given up suggesting it. She's tiny, she probably doesn't eat much. Maybe eating is something she can only do in private."

"You'd be surprised how many people feel that way about sex," Dot

193

said. "But I'd have to say she sounds like the proverbial sailor's dream. Does she own a liquor store?"

She was a failed painter who'd reinvented herself as a jewelry maker. "You bought earrings for the last woman in your life," Dot reminded him. "This one makes her own. What are you going to buy for her?"

"Nothing."

"That's economical. Between not giving her gifts and not taking her out to dinner, I can't see this one putting much of a strain on your budget. Can you at least send the woman flowers?"

"I already did."

"Well, it's something you can do more than once, Keller. That's one of the nice things about flowers. The little buggers die, so you get to throw them out and make room for fresh ones."

"She liked the flowers," he said, "but she told me once was enough. Don't do it again, she said."

"Because she wants to keep things superficial."

"That's the idea."

"Keller," she said, "I've got to hand it to you. You don't find that many of them, but you sure pick the strange ones."

"Now that was intense," Maggie said. "Was it just my imagination, or was that a major earth-shaking experience?"

"High up there on the Richter scale," he said.

"I thought tonight would be special. Full moon tomorrow."

"Does that mean we should have waited?"

"In my experience," she said, "it's the day *before* the full moon that I feel it the strongest."

"Feel what?"

"The moon."

"But what is it you feel? What effect does it have on you?"

"Makes me restless. Heightens my moods. Sort of intensifies things. Same as everybody else, I guess. What about you, Keller? What does the moon do for you?"

As far as Keller could tell, all the moon did for him was light up the sky a little. Living in the city, where there were plenty of streetlights to take up the slack, he paid little attention to the moon, and might not have noticed if someone took it away. New moon, half moon, full moon—only when he caught an occasional glimpse of it between the buildings did he know what phase it was in.

Maggie evidently paid more attention to the moon, and attached more significance to it. Well, if the moon had had anything to do with the pleasure they'd just shared, he was grateful to it, and glad to have it around.

"Besides," she was saying, "my horoscope says I'm going through a very sexy time."

"Your horoscope."

"Uh-huh."

"What do you do, read it every morning?"

"You mean in the newspaper? Well, I'm not saying I never look, but I wouldn't rely on a newspaper horoscope for advice and counsel anymore than I'd need Ann Landers to tell me if I have to pet to be popular."

"On that subject," he said, "I'd say you don't absolutely have to, but what could it hurt?"

"And who knows," she said, reaching out for him. "I might even enjoy it."

A while later she said, "Newspaper astrology columns are fun, like *Peanuts* and *Doonesbury*, but they're not very accurate. But I got my chart done, and I go in once a year for a tune-up. So I'll have an idea what to expect over the coming twelve months."

"You believe in all that?"

"Astrology? Well, it's like gravity, isn't it?"

"It keeps things from flying off in space?"

"It works whether I believe in it or not," she said. "So I might as well. Besides, I believe in everything."

"Like Santa Claus?"

"And the Tooth Fairy. No, all the occult stuff, like tarot and numerology and palmistry and phrenology and—"

"What's that?"

"Head bumps," she said, and capped his skull with her hand. "You've got some."

"I've got head bumps?"

"Uh-huh, but don't ask me what they mean. I've never even been to a phrenologist."

"Would you?"

"Go to one? Sure, if somebody steered me to a good one. In all of these areas, some practitioners are better than others. There are the storefront gypsies who are really just running a scam, but after that you've still got different levels of proficiency. Some people have a knack and some just hack away at it. But that's true in every line of work, isn't it?"

It was certainly true in his.

"What I don't get," he said, "is how any of it works. What difference does it make where the stars are when you're born? What has that got to do with anything?"

"I don't know how anything works," she said, "or why it should. Why does the light go on when I throw the switch? Why do I get wet when you touch me? It's all a mystery."

"But head bumps, for Christ's sake. Tarot cards."

"Sometimes it's just a way for a person to access her intuition," she said. "I used to know a woman who could read shoes."

"The labels? I don't follow you."

"She'd look at a pair of shoes that you'd owned for a while, and she could tell you things about yourself."

" 'You need half-soles.' "

"No, like you eat too much starchy food, and you need to express the feminine side of your personality, and the relationship you're in is stifling your creativity. Things like that."

"All by looking at your shoes. And that makes sense to you?"

"Does sense make sense? Look, do you know what holism is?"

"Like eating brown rice?"

"No, that's whole foods. Holism is like with holograms, the principle's that any cell in the body represents the entire life in microcosm. That's why I can rub your feet and make your headache go away."

"You can?"

"Well, not me personally, but a foot reflexologist could. That's why a palmist can look at your hand and see evidence of physical conditions that have nothing to do with your hands. They show up there, and in the irises of your eyes, and the bumps on your head."

"And the heels of your shoes," Keller said. "I had my palm read once."

"Oh?"

"A year or two ago. I was at this party, and they had a palmist for entertainment."

"Probably not a very good one, if she was hiring out for parties. How good a reading did she give you?"

"She didn't."

"I thought you said you had your palm read."

"I was willing. She wasn't. I sat down at the table with her and gave her my hand, and she took a good look and gave it back to me."

"That's awful. You must have been terrified."

"Of what?"

"That she saw imminent death in your hand."

"It crossed my mind," he admitted. "But I figured she was just a performer, and this was part of the performance. I was a little edgy the next time I got on a plane—"

"I'll bet."

"—but it was a routine flight, and time passed and nothing happened, and I forgot about it. I couldn't tell you the last time I even thought about it."

She reached out a hand. "Gimme."

"Huh?"

"Give me your hand. Let's see what got the bitch in a tizzy."

"You can read palms?"

"Not quite, but I can claim a smattering of ignorance on the subject. Let's see now, I don't want to know too much, because it might jeopardize the superficiality of our relationship. There's your head line, there's your heart line, there's your life line. And no marriage lines. Well, you said you've never been married, and your hand says you were telling the truth. I can't say I can see anything here that would make me tell you not to buy any long-playing records."

"That's a relief."

"So I bet I know what spooked her. You've got a murderer's thumb."

\*    \*    \*

Keller, working on his stamp collection, kept interrupting himself to look at his thumb. There it was, teaming up with his forefinger to grip a pair of tongues, to pick up a glassine envelope, to hold a magnifying glass. There it was, his own personal mark of Cain. His murderer's thumb.

"It's the particular way your thumb is configured," Maggie had told him. "See how it goes here? And look at my thumb, or your left thumb, as far as that goes. See the difference?"

She was able to recognize the murderer's thumb, he learned, because a childhood friend of hers, a perfectly gentle and non-violent person, had one just like it. A palmist had told her friend it was a murderer's thumb, and the two of them had looked it up in a book on the subject. And there it was, pictured lifesize and in color, the Murderer's Thumb, and it was just like her friend Jacqui's thumb, and, now, just like Keller's.

"But she never should have given you your hand back the way she did," Maggie had assured him. "I don't know if anybody's keeping statistics, but I'm sure most of the murderers walking around have two perfectly normal thumbs, while most people who do happen to have a murderer's thumb have never killed anybody in their life, and never will."

"That's a comfort."

"How many people have you killed, Keller?"

"None, for God's sake."

"And do you sense a burst of homicidal rage in your future?"

"Not really."

"Then I'd say you can relax. You may have a murderer's thumb, but I don't think you have to worry about it."

He wasn't worried, not exactly. But he would have to say he was puzzled. How could a man have a murderer's thumb all his life and be unaware of it? And, when all was said and done, what did it mean?

He had certainly never paid any particular attention to his thumb. He had been aware that his two thumbs were not identical, that there was something slightly atypical about his right thumb, but it was not eye-catchingly idiosyncratic, not the sort of thing other kids would notice, much less taunt you about. He'd given it about as much thought over the years as he gave to the nail on the big toe of his left foot, which was marked with ridges.

Hit man's toe, he thought.

He was poring over a price list, France & Colonies, wrestling with some of the little decisions a stamp collector was called upon to make, when the phone rang. He picked it up, and it was Dot.

He made the usual round trip by train, Grand Central to White Plains and back again, He packed a bag before he went to bed that night, and in the morning he caught a cab to JFK and a plane to Tampa. He rented a Ford Escort and drove to Indian Rocks Beach, which sounded more like a headline in *Variety* than a place to live. But that's what it was, and, though he didn't see any Indians or rocks, it would have been hard to miss the beach. It was a beauty, and he could see why they had all these condos on it, and vacation time shares.

The man Keller was looking for, an Ohioan named Stillman, had just moved in for a week's stay in a beachfront apartment on the fourth floor of Gulf Water Towers. There was an attendant in the lobby, Keller noticed, but he didn't figure to be as hard to get past as the Maginot Line.

But would he even need to find out? Stillman had just arrived from sunless Cincinnati, and how much time was he going to spend inside? No more than he had to, Keller figured. He'd want to get out there and soak up some rays, maybe splash in the Gulf a little, then zone out some more in the sun.

Keller's packing had included swim trunks, and he found a men's room and put them on. He didn't have a towel to lie on—he hadn't taken a room yet—but he could always lie on the sand.

It turned out he didn't have to. As he was walking along the public beach, he saw a woman approach a man, her hands cupped. She was holding water, and she threw it on the man, who sprang to his feet. They laughed joyously as he chased her into the surf. There they frolicked, perfect examples of young hormone-driven energy, and Keller figured they'd be frolicking for a while. They'd left two towels on the sand, anonymous unidentifiable white beach towels, and Keller decided one was all they needed. It would easily accommodate the two of them when they tired of splashing and ducking one another.

He picked up the other towel and walked off with it. He spread it out on the sand at the private beach for Gulf Water Towers residents. A glance left and right revealed no one who in any way resembled George Stillman, so Keller stretched out on his back and closed his eyes. The sun, a real stranger to New York of late, was evidently wholly at home in Florida, and felt wonderful on his skin. If it took a while to find Stillman, that was okay with him.

But it didn't.

Keller opened his eyes after half an hour or so. He sat up and looked around, feeling a little like Punxutawny Phil on Groundhog's Day. When he failed to see either Stillman or his own shadow, he lay down and closed his eyes again.

The next time he opened them was when he heard a man cursing. He sat up, and not twenty yards away was a barrel-chested man, balding and jowly, calling his right hand every name in the book.

How could the fellow be that mad at his own hand? Of course he might have a murderer's thumb, but what if he did? Keller had one himself, and had never felt the need to talk to it in those terms.

Oh, hell, of course. The man was on a cell phone. And, by God, he was Stillman. The face had barely registered on Keller at first, his attention held by the angry voice and the keg-shaped torso thickly pelted with black hair. None of that had been visible in the head-and-shoulders shot Dot had shown him, and it was what you noticed, but it was the same face, and here he was, and wasn't that handy?

While Stillman took the sun, Keller did the same. When Stillman got up and walked to the water's edge, so did Keller. When Stillman waded in, to test his mettle in the surf, Keller followed in his wake.

When Keller came ashore, Stillman stayed behind. And, by the time Keller left the beach, carrying two towels and a cellular phone, Stillman had still not emerged from the water.

Why a thumb?

Keller, back in New York, pondered the question. He couldn't see what a thumb had to do with murder. When you used a gun, it was your index finger that gave the trigger a squeeze. When you used a knife, you held it in your palm with your fingers curled around the handle. Your thumb might press the hilt, as a sort of guide, but a man could have no thumbs at all and still get the business end of a knife to go where he wanted it.

Did you use your thumbs when you garroted somebody? He mimed the motion, letting his hands remember, and he didn't see where the thumbs had much of a part to play. Manual strangulation, now that was different, and you did use your thumbs, you used all of both hands, and would have a hard time otherwise.

Still, why a murderer's *thumb*?

"Here's what I don't get," Dot said. "You go off to some half-a-horse town at the ass end of nowhere special and you poke around for a week or two. Then you go to a vacation paradise in the middle of a New York winter and you're back the same day. The same day!"

"I had an opening and I took it," he said. "I wait and maybe I never get that good a shot at him again."

"I realize that, Keller, and God knows I'm not complaining. It just seems like a shame, that's all. Here you are, the two of you, fresh off a couple of planes from the frozen North, and before either one of you gets the chill out of your bones, you're on a flight to New York and he's rapidly approaching room temperature."

"Water temperature."

"I stand corrected."

"And it was like a bathtub."

"That's nice," she said. "He could have opened his veins in it, but after you held his head underwater for a few minutes he no longer felt the need to. But couldn't you have waited a few days? You'd have come home with a tan and he'd have gone into the ground with one. You meet your Maker, you want to look your best."

"Sure," he said. "Dot, have you ever noticed anything odd about my thumb?"

"Your thumb?"

"This one. Does it look strange to you?"

"You know," she said, "I've got to hand it to you, Keller. That's the most complete change of subject I've ever encountered in my life. I'd be hard put to remember what we were talking about before we started talking about your thumb."

"Well?"

"Don't tell me you're serious? Let me see. I'd have to say it looks like a plain old thumb to me, but you know what they say. You've seen one thumb . . ."

"But look, Dot. That's the whole point, that they're not identical. See how this one goes?"

"Oh, right. It's got that little . . ."

"Uh-huh."

"Are mine both the same? Like two peas in a pod, as far as I can make out. This one's got a little scar at the base, but don't ask me how I got it because I can't remember. Keller, you made your point. You've got an unusual thumb."

"Do you believe in destiny, Dot?"

"Whoa! Keller, you just switched channels again. I thought we were discussing thumbs."

"I was thinking about Louisville."

"I'm going to take the remote control away from you, Keller. It's not safe in your hands. Louisville?"

"You remember when I went there."

"Vividly. Kids playing basketball, guy in a garage, and, if I remember correctly, the subtle magic of carbon monoxide."

"Right."

"So?"

"Remember how I had a bad feeling about it, and then a couple got killed in my old room, and—"

"I remember the whole business, Keller. What about it?"

"I guess I've just been wondering how much of life is destined and preordained. How much choice do people really have?"

"If we had a choice," she said, "we could be having some other conversation."

"I never set out to be what I've become. It's not like I took an aptitude test in high school and my guidance counselor took me aside and recommended a career as a killer for hire."

"You drifted into it, didn't you?"

"That's what I always thought. That's certainly what it felt like. But suppose I was just fulfilling my destiny?"

"I don't know," she said, cocking her head. "Shouldn't there be music playing in the background? There always is when they have conversations like this in one of my soap operas."

"Dot, I've got a murderer's thumb."

"Oh, for the love of God, we're back to your thumb. How did you manage that, and what in the hell are you talking about?"

"Palmistry," he said. "In palmistry, a thumb like mine is called a murderer's thumb."

"In palmistry."

"Right."

"I grant you it's an unusual-looking thumb," she said, "although I never noticed it in all the years I've known you, and never would have noticed it if you hadn't pointed it out. But where does the murderer part come in? What do you do, kill people by running your thumb across their lifeline?"

"I don't think you actually do anything with your thumb."

"I don't see what you *could* do, aside from hitching a ride. Or making a rude gesture."

"All I know," he said, "is I had a murderer's thumb and I grew up to be a murderer."

" 'His Thumb Made Him Do It.' "

"Or was it the other way around? Maybe my thumb was normal at birth, and it changed as my character changed."

"That sounds crazy," she said, "but you ought to be able to clear it up, because you've been carrying that thumb around all your life. *Was* it always like that?"

"How do I know? I never paid much attention to it."

"Keller, it's your thumb."

"But did I notice it was different from other thumbs? I don't know, Dot. Maybe I should see somebody."

"That's not necessarily a bad idea," she said, "but I'd think twice before I let them put me on any medication."

"That's not what I mean," he said.

The astrologer was not what he'd expected.

Hard to say just what he'd been expecting. Someone with a lot of eye makeup, say, and long hair bound up in a scarf, and big hoop earrings—some sort of cross between a Gypsy fortune-teller and a hippie chick. What he got in Louise Carpenter was a pleasant woman in her forties who had thrown in the towel in the long battle to retain a girlish figure. She had big blue-green eyes and a low-maintenance haircut, and she lived in an apartment on West End Avenue full of comfortable furniture, and she wore loose clothing and read romance novels and ate chocolate, all of which seemed to agree with her.

"It would help," she told Keller, "if we knew the precise time of your birth."

"I don't think there's any way to find out."

"Your mother has passed?"

Passed. It might be more accurate, he thought, to say that she'd failed. He said, "She died a long time ago."

"And your father . . ."

"Died before I was born," Keller said, wondering if it was true. "You asked me over the phone if there was anyone who might remember. I'm the only one who's still around, and I don't remember a thing."

"There are ways to recover a lot of early memory," she said, and popped a chocolate into her mouth. "All the way back to birth, in some instances, and I've known people who claim they can remember their own conception. But I don't know how much to credit all of that. Is it memory or is it Memorex? Besides, you probably weren't wearing a watch at the time."

"I've been thinking," he said. "I don't know the doctor's name, and he might be dead himself by this time, but I've got a copy of my birth certificate. It doesn't have the time of birth, just the date, but do you suppose the Bureau of Vital Statistics would have the information on file somewhere?"

"Possibly," she said, "but don't worry about it. I can check it."

"On the Internet? Something like that?"

She laughed. "No, not that. You said your mother mentioned getting up early in the morning to go to the hospital."

"That's what she said."

"And you were a fairly easy birth."

"Once her labor started, I came right out."

"You wanted to be here. Now you happen to be a Gemini, John, and . . . shall I call you John?"

"If you want."

"Well, what do people generally call you?"

"Keller."

"Very well, Mr. Keller. I'm comfortable keeping it formal if you prefer it that way, and—"

"Not Mr. Keller," he said. "Just plain Keller."

"Oh."

"That's what people generally call me."

"I see. Well, Keller . . . no, I don't think that's going to work. I'm going to have to call you John."

"Okay."

"In high school kids used to call each other by their last names. It was a way to feel grown up. 'Hey, Carpenter, you finish the algebra homework?' I can't call you Keller."

"Don't worry about it."

"I'm being neurotic, I realize that, but—"

"John is fine."

"Well then," she said, and rearranged herself in the chair. "You're a Gemini, John, as I'm sure you know. A late Gemini, June 19, which puts you right on the cusp of Cancer."

"Is that good?"

"Nothing's necessarily good or bad in astrology, John. But it's good in that I enjoy working with Geminis. I find it to be an extremely interesting sign."

"How so?"

"The duality. Gemini is the sign of the twins, you see." She went on talking about the properties of the sign, and he nodded, agreeing but not really taking it all in. And then she was saying, "I suppose the most interesting thing about Geminis is their relationship to the truth. Geminis are naturally duplicitous, yet they have an inner reverence for the truth that echoes their opposite number across the Zodiac. That's Sagittarius, of course, and your typical Sadge couldn't tell a lie to save his soul. Gemini can lie without a second thought, while being occasionally capable of this startling Sagittarean candor."

"I see."

He was influenced as well by Cancer, she continued, having his sun on its cusp, along with a couple of planets in that sign. And he had a Taurus moon, she told him, and that was the best possible place for the moon to be. "The moon is exalted in Taurus," she said. "Have you noticed in the course of your life how things generally turn out all right for you, even when they don't? And don't you have an inner core, a sort of bedrock stability that lets you always know who you are?"

"I don't know about that last part," he said. "I'm here, aren't I?"

"Maybe it's your Taurus moon that got you here." she reached for another chocolate. "Your time of birth determines your rising sign, and that's important in any number of ways, but in the absence of available information I'm willing to make the determination intuitively. My discipline is astrology, John, but it's not the only tool I use. I'm psychic, I sense things. My intuition tells me you have Cancer rising."

"If you say so."

"And I prepared a chart for you on that basis. I could tell you a lot of technical things about your chart, but I can't believe you're interested in all that, are you?"

"You're psychic, all right."

"So instead of nattering on about trines and squares and oppositions, let me just say it's an interesting chart. You're an extremely gentle person, John."

"Oh?"

"But there's so much violence in your life."

"Oh."

"That's the famous Gemini duality," she was saying. "On the one hand, you're thoughtful and sensitive and calm, exceedingly calm. John, do you ever get angry?"

"Not very often."

"No, and I don't think you stifle your anger, either. I get that it's just not a part of the equation. But there's violence all around you, isn't there?"

"It's a violent world we live in."

"There's been violence swirling around you all your life. You're very much a part of it, and yet you're somehow untouched by it." She tapped the sheet of paper, with his stars and planets all marked out. "You don't have an easy chart," she said.

"I don't?"

"Actually, that's something to be grateful for. I've seen charts of people who came into the world with no serious oppositions, no difficult aspects. And they wind up with lives where nothing much happens. They're never challenged, they never have to draw upon inner resources, and so they wind up leading reasonably comfortable lives and holding secure jobs and raising their kids in a nice safe clean suburb. And they never make anything terribly interesting of themselves."

"I haven't made much of myself," he said. "I've never married or fathered a child. Or started a business, or run for office, or planted a garden, or written a play, or . . . or . . ."

"Yes?"

"I'm sorry," he said. "I never expected to get . . ."

"Emotional?"

"Yes."

"It happens all the time."

"Oh."

"Just the other day I told a woman she's got Jupiter squaring her sun, but that her Jupiter and Mars are trined, and she burst into tears."

"I don't even know what that means."

"Neither did she."

"Oh."

"I see so much in your chart, John. This is a difficult time for you, isn't it?"

"I guess it must be."

"Not financially. Your Jupiter—well, you're not rich, and you're never going to be rich, but the money always seems to be there when you need it, doesn't it?"

"It's never been a problem."

"No, and it won't be. You've found ways to spend it in the past couple of years—" Stamps, he thought "—and that's good, because now you're getting some pleasure out of your money. But you won't overspend, and you'll always be able to get more."

"That's good."

"But you didn't come here because you were concerned about money."

"No."

"You don't care that much about it. You always liked to get it and now you like to spend it, but you never cared deeply about it."

"No."

"I've prepared a solar return," she said, "to give you an idea what to expect in the next twelve months. Some astrologers are very specific — 'July seventeenth is the perfect time to start a new project, and don't even think about being on water on the fifth of September.' My approach is more general, and . . . John? Why are you holding your right hand like that?"

"I beg your pardon?"

"With the thumb tucked inside. Is there something about your thumb that bothers you?"

"Not really."

"I've already seen your thumb, John."

"Oh."

"Did someone once tell you something about your thumb?"

"Yes."

"That it's a murderer's thumb?" She rolled her eyes. "Palmistry," she said heavily.

"You don't believe in it?"

"Of course I believe in it, but it does lend itself to some gross oversimplification." She reached out and took his hand in both of hers. Hers were soft, he noted, and pudgy, but not unpleasantly so. She ran a fingertip over his thumb, his homicidal thumb.

"To take a single anatomical characteristic," she said, "and fasten such a dramatic name to it. No one's thumb ever made him kill a fellow human being."

"Then why do they call it that?"

"I'm afraid I haven't studied the history of palmistry. I suppose someone spotted the peculiarity in a few notorious murderers and spread the word. I'm not even certain it's statistically more common among murderers than the general population. I doubt anyone really knows. John, it's an insignificant phenomenon and not worth noticing."

"But you noticed it," he said.

"I happened to see it."

"And you recognized it. You didn't say anything until you noticed me hiding it in my fist. That was unconscious, I didn't even know I was doing it."

"I see."

"So it must mean something," he said, "or why would it stay in your mind?"

She was still holding his hand. Keller had noticed that this was one of the ways a woman let you know she was interested in you. Women touched you a lot in completely innocent ways, on the hand or the arm or the shoulder, or held your hand longer than they had to. If a man did that it was sexual harassment, but it was a woman's way of letting you know she wouldn't mind being harassed herself.

But this was different. There was no sexual charge with this woman. If he'd been made of chocolate he might have had something to worry about, but mere flesh and blood was safe in her presence.

"John," she said, "I was looking for it."

"for . . ."

"The thumb. Or anything else that might confirm what I already knew about you."

She was gazing into his eyes as she spoke, and he wondered how much shock registered in them. He tried not to react, but how did you keep what you felt from showing up in your eyes?

"And what's that, Louise?"

"That I know about you?"

He nodded.

"That your life has been filled with violence, but I think I already mentioned that."

"You said I was gentle and not full of anger."

"But you've had to kill people, John."

"Who told you that?" She was no longer holding his hand. Had she released it? Or had he taken it away from her?

"Who told me?"

Maggie, he thought. Who else could it have been? Maggie was the only person they knew in common. But how did Maggie know? In her eyes he was a corporate suburbanite, even if he lived alone in the heart of the city.

"Actually," she was saying, "I had several informants."

His heart was hammering. What was she saying? How could it be true?

"Let me see, John. There was Saturn, and Mars, and we don't want to forget Mercury." Her tone was soft, her gaze so gentle. "John," she said, "it's in your chart."

"My chart."

"I picked up on it right away. I got a very strong hit while I was working on your chart, and when you rang the bell I knew I would be opening the door to a man who had done a great deal of killing."

"I'm surprised you didn't cancel the appointment."

"I considered it. Something told me not to."

"A little bird?"

"An inner prompting. Or maybe it was curiosity. I wanted to see what you looked like."

"And?"

"Well, I knew right away I hadn't made a mistake with your chart."

"Because of my thumb?"

"No, though it was interesting to have that extra bit of conformation. And the most revealing thing about your thumb was the effort you made to conceal it. But the vibration I picked up from you was far more revealing than anything about your thumb."

"The vibration."

"I don't know a better way to put it. Sometimes the intuitive part of the mind picks up things the five senses are blind and deaf to. Sometimes a person just knows something."

"Yes."

"I knew you were . . ."

"A killer," he supplied.

"Well, a man who has killed. And in a very dispassionate way, too. It's not personal for you, is it, John?"

"Sometimes a personal element comes into it."

"But not often."

"No."

"It's business."

"Yes."

"John? You don't have to be afraid of me."

Could she read his mind? He hoped not. Because what came to him now was that he was not afraid of her, but of what he might have to do to her.

And he didn't want to. She was a nice woman, and he sensed she would be able to tell him things it would be good for him to hear.

"You don't have to fear that I'll do anything, or say anything to anyone. You don't even need to fear my disapproval."

"Oh?"

"I don't make many moral judgments, John. The more I see, the less I'm sure I know what's right and what's wrong. Once I accepted myself—" she reached, grinning, for a chocolate "—I found it easier to accept other people. Thumbs and all."

He looked at his thumb, then raised his eyes to meet hers.

"Besides," she said, very gently, "I think you've done wonderfully in life, John."

She tapped his chart. "I know what you started with. I think you've turned out just fine."

He tried to say something, but the words got stuck in his throat.

"It's all right," she said. "Go right ahead and cry. Never be ashamed to cry, John. It's all right."

And she drew his head to her breast and held him while, astonished, he sobbed his heart out.

"Well, that's a first," he said. "I don't know what I expected from astrology, but it wasn't tears."

"They wanted to come out. You've had them stored up for a while, haven't you?"

"Forever. I was in therapy for a while and never even got choked up."

"That would have been when? Three years ago?"

"How did you . . . It's in my chart?"

"Not therapy per se, but I saw there was a period when you were ready for self-exploration. But I don't believe you stayed with it for very long."

"A few months I got a lot of insight out of it, but in the end I felt I had to put an end to it."

Dr. Breen, the therapist, had had his own agenda, and it had conflicted seriously with Keller's. The therapy had come to an abrupt end, and so, not coincidentally, had the doctor.

He wouldn't let that happen with Louise Carpenter.

"This isn't therapy," she told him now, "but it can be a powerful experience. As you just found out."

"I'll say. But we must have used up our fifty minutes." He looked at his watch. "We went way over. I'm sorry. I didn't realize."

"I told you it's not therapy, John. We don't worry about the clock. And I never book more than two clients a day, one in the morning and one in the afternoon. We have all the time we need."

"Oh."

"And we need to talk about what you're going through. This is a difficult time for you, isn't it?"

Was it?

"I'm afraid the coming twelve months will continue to be difficult," she went on, "as long as Saturn's where it is. Difficult and dangerous. But I suppose danger is something you've learned to live with."

"It's not that dangerous," he said. "What I do."

"Really?"

Dangerous to others, he thought. "Not to me," he said. "Not particularly. There's always a risk, and you have to keep your guard up, but it's not as though you have to be on edge all the time."

"What, John?"

"I beg your pardon?"

"You had a thought, it just flashed across your face."

"I'm surprised you can't tell me what it was."

"If I had to guess," she said, "I'd say you thought of something that contradicted the sentence you just spoke. About not having to be on edge all the time."

"That's what it was, all right."

"This would have been fairly recent."

"You can really tell all that? I'm sorry, I keep doing that. Yes, it was recent. A few months ago."

"Because the period of danger would have begun during the fall."

"That's when it was." And, without getting into specifics at all, he talked about his trip to Louisville, and how everything had seemed to be going wrong. "And there was a knock on the door of my room," he said, "and I panicked, which is not like me at all."

"No."

"I grabbed something—" a gun "—and stood next to the door, and my heart was hammering, and it was nothing but some drunk who couldn't find his friend. I was all set to kill him in self-defense, and all he did was knock on the wrong door."

"It must have been upsetting."

"The most upsetting part was seeing how upset I got. That didn't get my pulse racing like the knock on the door did, but the effects lasted longer. It still bothers me, to tell the truth."

"Because the reaction was unwarranted. But maybe you really were in danger, John. Not from the drunk, but from something invisible."

"Like what, anthrax spores?"

"Invisible to you, but not necessarily to the naked eye. Some unknown adversary, some secret enemy."

"That's how it felt. But it doesn't make any sense."

"Do you want to tell me about it?"

Did he?

"I changed my room," he said.

"Because of the drunk who knocked on your door?"

"No, why would I do that? But a couple of nights later I couldn't sleep because of noise from the people upstairs. I had to keep my room that night, the place was full, but I let them put me in a new room first thing the next morning. And that night . . ."

"Yes?"

"Two people checked into my old room. A man and a woman. They were murdered."

"In the room you'd just moved out of."

"It was her husband. She was there with somebody else, and the husband must have followed them. Shot them both. But I couldn't get past the fact that it was my room. Like if I hadn't changed my room, her husband would have come after me."

"But he wasn't anyone you knew."

"No, far from it."

"And yet you felt as though you'd had a narrow escape."

"But of course that's ridiculous."

She shook her head. "You could have been killed, John."

"How? I kept thinking the same thing myself, but it's just not true. The only reason the killer came to the room was because of the two people who were in it. They were what drew him, not the room itself. So how could he have ever been a danger to me?"

"There was a danger, though."

"The chart tells you that?"

She nodded solemnly, holding up one hand with the thumb and forefinger half an inch apart. "You and Death," she said, "came this close to one another."

"That's how it *felt*! But—"

"Forget the husband, forget what happened in that room. The woman's husband was never a threat to you, but someone else was. You were out there where the ice was very thin, John, and that's a good metaphor, because a skater never realizes the ice is thin until it cracks."

"But—"

"But it didn't," she said. "Whatever endangered you, the danger passed. Then those two people were killed, and that got your attention."

"Like ice cracking," he said, "but on another pond. I'll have to think about this."

"I'm sure you will."

He cleared his throat. "Louise? Is it all written in the stars, and do we just walk through it down here on earth?"

"No."

"You can look at that piece of paper," he said, "and you can say, 'Well, you'll come very close to death on such and such a day, but you'll get through it safe and sound.'"

"Only the first part. 'You'll come very close to death'—I could have looked at this and told you that much. But I wouldn't have been able to tell you that you'd survive. The stars show propensities and dictate probabilities, but the future is never entirely predictable. And we do have free will."

"If those people hadn't been killed, and if I'd just gone on home—"

"Yes?"

"Well, I'd be here having this conversation, and you'd tell me what a close shave I'd had, and I'd figure it for just so much starshine. I'd had a feeling, but I would have forgotten all about it. So I'd look at you and say, 'Yeah, right,' and turn the page."

"You can be grateful to the man and woman."

"And to the guy who shot them, as far as that goes. And to the bikers who made all the noise in the first place. And to Ralph."

"Who was Ralph?"

"The drunk's friend, the one he was looking for in all the wrong places. I can be grateful to the drunk, too, except I don't know his name. But then I don't know any of their names, except for Ralph."

"Maybe the names aren't important."

"I used to know the name of the man and woman, and of the man who shot them, the husband. I can't remember them now. You're right, the names aren't important."

"No."

He looked at her. "The next year . . ."

"Will be dangerous."

"What do I have to worry about? Should I think twice before I get on an airplane? Put on an extra sweater on windy days? can you tell me where the threat's coming from."

She hesitated, then said, "You have an enemy, John."

"An enemy?"

"An enemy. There's someone out there who wants to kill you."

"I don't know," he told Dot.

"You don't know? Keller, what's to know? What could be simpler? It's in Boston, for God's sake, not on the dark side of the moon. You take a cab to La Guardia, you hop on the Delta shuttle, you don't even need a reservation, and half an hour later you're on the ground at Logan. You take a cab into the city, you do the thing you do best, and you're on the shuttle again before the day is over, and back in your own apartment in plenty of time for Jay Leno. The money's right, the client's strictly blue chip, and the job's a piece of cake."

"I understand all that, Dot."

"But?"

"I don't know."

"Keller," she said, "clearly I'm missing something. Help me out here. What part of 'I don't know' don't I understand?"

*I don't know*, he very nearly answered, but caught himself in time. In high school, a teacher had taken the class to task for those very words. "The way you use it," she said, " 'I don't know' is a lie. It's not what you mean at all. What you mean is 'I don't want to say' or 'I'm afraid to tell you.' "

"Hey, Keller," one of the other boys had called out. "What's the capital of South Dakota?"

"I'm afraid to tell you," he'd replied.

And what was he afraid to tell Dot? That the Boston job just wasn't in the stars? That the day the client had selected as ideal, this coming Wednesday, was a day specifically noted by his astrologer—his astrologer!—as a day fraught with danger, a day when he would be at extreme risk.

("So what do I do on those days?" he'd asked her. "Stay in bed with the door locked? Order all my meals delivered?" "The first part's not a terrible idea," she'd advised him, "but I'd be careful who was on the other side of the door before I opened it. And I'd be careful what I ate, too." The kid from the Chinese restaurant could be a Ninja assassin, he thought. The beef with oyster sauce could be laced with cyanide.)

"Keller?"

"The thing is, Wednesday's not the best day for me. There was something I'd planned on doing."

"What have you got, tickets to a matinee?"

"No."

"No, of course not. It's a stamp auction, isn't it? The thing is, Wednesday's the day the subject goes to his girlfriend's apartment in Back Bay, and he has to sneak over there, so he leaves his security people behind. Which makes it far and away the easiest time to get next to him."

"And she's part of the package, the girlfriend?"

"Your call, whatever you want. She's in or she's out, whatever works."

"And it doesn't matter how? Doesn't have to be an accident, doesn't have to look like an execution?"

"Anything you want. You can plunge the son of a bitch into a vat of lanolin and soften him to death. Anything at all, just so he doesn't have a pulse when you're through with him."

Hard job to say no to, he thought. Hard job to say *I don't know* to.

"I suppose the following Wednesday might work," Dot said. "The client would rather not wait, but my guess is he will if he has to. He said I was the first person he called, but I don't believe it. He's the type of guy's not that comfortable doing business with a woman. Our kind of business, anyway. So I think I was more like the third or fourth person he called, and I think he'll wait a week if I tell him he has to. Do you want me to see?"

Was he really going to lie in bed waiting for the bogey man to get him?

"No, don't do that," he said. "This Wednesday's fine."

"Are you sure?"

"I'm sure," he said. He wasn't sure, he was miles short of sure, but it had a much better ring to it than *I don't know*.

Tuesday, the day before he was supposed to go to Boston, Keller had a strong urge to call Louise Carpenter. It had been a couple of weeks since she'd gone over his chart with him, and he wouldn't be seeing her again for a year. He'd thought it might turn out to be like therapy, with weekly appointments, and he gathered that there were some clients who dropped in frequently for an astrological tune-up and oil change, but he gathered that astrology was a sort of hobby for them. He already had a hobby, and Louise seemed to think an annual check-up was sufficient, and that was fine with him.

So he'd see her in a year's time. If he was still alive.

The forecast for Wednesday was rain and more rain, and when he woke up he saw they weren't kidding. It was a bleak, gray day, and the rain was coming down hard. An apologetic announcer on New York One said the downpour was expected to continue throughout the day and evening, accompanied by high winds and low temperatures. The way he was carrying on, you'd have thought it was his fault.

Keller put on a suit and tie, good protective coloration in a formal kind of city like Boston, and the standard uniform on the air shuttle. He got his trench coat out of the closet, put it on, and wasn't crazy about what he saw in the mirror. The salesman had called it olive, and maybe it was, at least in the store under their fluorescent lights. In the cold damp light of a rainy morning, however, the damn thing looked green.

Not shamrock green, not Kelly green, not even putting green. But it was green, all right. You could slip into it on St. Patrick's Day and march up Fifth Avenue, and no one would mistake you for an Orangeman. No question about it, the sucker was green.

In the ordinary course of things, the coat's color wouldn't have bothered him. It wasn't so green as to bring on stares and catcalls, just green enough to draw the occasional appreciative glance. And there was a certain convenience in having a coat that didn't look like every other coat on the rack. You knew it on sight, and you could point it out to the cloakroom attendant when you couldn't find the check. "Right there, a little to your left," you'd say. "The green one."

But when you were flying up to Boston to kill a man, you didn't want to stand out in a crowd. You wanted to blend right in, to look like everybody else. Keller, in his unremarkable suit and tie, looked pretty much like everybody else.

In his coat, no question, he stood out.

Could he skip the coat? No, it was cold outside, and it would be colder in Boston. Wear his other topcoat, unobtrusively beige? No, it was porous, and he'd get soaked. He'd take an umbrella, but that wouldn't help much, not with a strong wind driving the rain.

What if he bought another coat?

But that was ridiculous. He'd have to wait for the stores to open, and then he'd spend an hour picking out the new coat and dropping off the old one at his apartment. And for what? There weren't going to be any witnesses in Boston, and anyone who did happen to see him go into the building would only remember the coat.

And maybe that was a plus. Like putting on a postman's uniform or a priest's collar, or dressing up as Santa Claus. People remembered what you were wearing, but that was all they remembered. Nobody noticed anything else about you that might be distinctive. Your thumb, for instance. And, once you took off the uniform or the collar or the red suit and the beard, you became invisible.

Ordinarily he wouldn't have had to think twice. But this was an ominous day, one of the days his motherly astrologer had warned him about, and that made every little detail something to worry about.

And wasn't that silly? He had an enemy, and this enemy was trying to kill him, and on this particular day he was particularly at risk. And he had an assignment to kill a man, and that task inevitably carried risks of its own.

And, with all that going on, he was worrying about the coat he was wearing? That it was too discernibly green, for God's sake?

Get over it, he told himself.

A cab took in to La Guardia and a plane took him to Logan, where another cab dropped him in front of the Ritz-Carlton Hotel. He walked through the lobby, came out on Newbury street, and walked along looking for a sporting goods store. He walked a while without seeing one, and wasn't sure Newbury Street was the place for it. Antiques, leather goods, designer clothes, Limoges boxes—that was what you bought here, not Polartec sweats and climbing gear.

Or hunting knives. If you could find such an article on here in Back Bay, it would probably have an ivory handle and a sterling silver blade, along with a three-figure price tag. He was sure it would be a beautiful object, and worth every penny, but how would he feel about tossing it down a storm drain when he was done with it?

Anyway, was it a good idea to buy a hunting knife in the middle of a big city on a rainy spring day in the middle of the week? Deer season was, what, seven or eight months off? How many hunting knives would be sold in Boston today? How many of them would be bought by men in green trenchcoats?

In a stationery store he browsed among the desk accessories and picked out a letter opener with a sturdy chrome-plated steel blade and an inlaid onyx handle. The sales girl put it in a gift box without asking. It evidently didn't occur to her that anyone might buy an item like that for himself.

And in a sense Keller hadn't. He'd bought it for Alvin Thurnauer, and now it was time to deliver it.

*        *        *

That was the subject's name, Alvin Thurnauer, and Keller had seen
a photograph of a big, outdoorsy guy with a full head of light brown
hair. Along with the photo, the client had supplied an address on
Emerson Street and a set of keys, one for the front door and one for
the second-floor apartment where Thurnauer and his girlfriend would
be playing Thank God It's Wednesday.

Thurnauer generally showed up around two, Dot had told him,
and Keller was planted in a doorway across the street by half past one.
The air was a little colder in Boston, and the wind a little stiffer, but
the rain was about the same as it had been in New York. Keller's coat
was waterproof, and his umbrella had not yet been blown inside-out,
but he still didn't stay a hundred percent dry. You couldn't, not when
the rain came at you like God was pitching sidearm.

Maybe that was the risk. On a fateful day, you stood in the rain in
Boston and caught your death of cold.

He toughed it out, and shortly before two a cab pulled up and a
man got out, bundled up anonymously enough in a hat and coat,
neither of them green. Keller's heart quickened. It could have been
Thurnauer—it could have been anybody—and the fellow did stand
looking across at the right house for a long moment before turning
and heading off down the street. Keller gave up watching him when
he got a couple of houses away. He retreated into the shadows, waiting
for Thurnauer.

Who showed up right on time. Two on the button on Keller's
watch, and there was the man himself, easy to spot as he got out of
his cab because he wasn't wearing a hat. The mop of brown hair was
a perfect field mark, identifiable at a glance.

Do it now?

It was doable. Just because he had keys didn't mean he had to use
them. He could dart across the street and catch up with Thurnauer
before the man had the front door open. Do him on the spot, shove
him into the vestibule where the whole world wouldn't see him, and
be out of sight himself in seconds.

That way he wouldn't have to worry about the girlfriend. But there
might be other witnesses, people passing on the street, some moody
citizen staring out the window at the rain. And he'd be awfully visible

racing across the street in his green coat. And the letter opener was still in its box, so he'd have to use his hands.

And by the time he'd weighed all these considerations the moment had passed and Thurnauer was inside the house.

Just as well. If a roll in the hay was going to cost Thurnauer his life, let him at least have a chance to enjoy it. That was better than rushing in and doing a slapdash job. Thurnauer could have an extra thirty or forty minutes of life, and Keller could get out of the goddam rain and have a cup of coffee.

At the lunch counter, feeling only a little like one of the lonely guys in his Edward Hopper poster, Keller remembered that he hadn't eaten all day. He'd somehow missed breakfast, which was unusual for him.

Well, it was a high-risk day, wasn't it? Pneumonia, starvation—there were a lot of hazards out there.

Eating would have to wait. He didn't have the time, and he never liked to work on a full stomach. It made you sluggish, slowed your reflexes, spoiled your judgment. Better to wait and have a proper meal afterward.

While his coffee was cooling he went to the men's room and took the letter opener out of its gift box, which he discarded. He put the letter opener in his jacket pocket where he could reach it in a hurry. You couldn't cut with it, the blade's edge was rounded, but it came to a good sharp point. But was it sharp enough to penetrate several layers of cloth? Just as well he hadn't acted on the spur of the moment. Wait for Thurnauer to get out of his coat and jacket and shirt, and then the letter opener would have an easier time of it.

He drank his coffee, donned his green coat, picked up his umbrella, and went back to finish the job.

Nothing to it, really.

The keys worked. He didn't run into anybody in the entryway or on the stairs. He listened at the door of the second-floor apartment, heard music playing and water running, and let himself in.

He closed his umbrella, took off his coat, slipped off his shoes, and made his way in silence through the living room and along a hallway to the bedroom door. That was where the music was coming from, and it was where the woman, a slender dishwater blonde with almost translucent white skin, was sitting cross-legged on the edge of an unmade bed, smoking a cigarette.

She looked frighteningly vulnerable, and Keller hoped he wouldn't have to hurt her. If he could get Thurnauer alone, if he could do the man and get out without being seen, then he could let her live. If she saw him, well, then all bets were off.

The shower stopped running, and a moment later the bathroom door opened. A man emerged with a dark green towel around his waist. The guy was completely bald, and Keller wondered how the hell he'd managed to wind up in the wrong apartment. Then he realized it was Thurnauer after all. The guy had taken off his hair before he got in the shower.

Thurnauer walked over to the bed, made a face, and reached to take the cigarette away from the girl, stubbing it out in an ashtray. "I wish to God you'd quit," he said.

"And I wish you'd quit wishing I would quit," she said. "I've tried. I can't quit, all right? Not everybody's got your goddam willpower."

"There's the gum," he said.

"I started smoking to get out of the habit of chewing gum. I hate how it looks, grown women chewing gum, like a herd of cows."

"Or the patch," he said. "Why can't you wear a patch?"

"That was my last cigarette," she said.

"You know, you've said that before, and much as I'd like to believe it—"

"No, you moron," she snapped. "It was the last one I've got with me, not the last one I'm ever going to smoke. If you had to play the stern daddy and take a cigarette away from me, did it have to be my last one?"

"You can buy more."

"No kidding," she said. "You're damn right I can buy more."

"Go take a shower," Thurnauer said.

"I don't want to take a shower."

"You'll cool off and feel better."

"You mean I'll cool off and *you'll* feel better. Anyway, you just took a shower and you came out grumpy as a bear with a sore foot. The hell with taking a shower."

"Take one."

"Why? What's the matter, do I stink? Or do you just want to get me out of the room so you can make a phone call?"

"Mavis, for Christ's sake . . ."

"You can call some other girl who doesn't smoke and doesn't sweat and—"

"Mavis—"

"Oh, go to hell," Mavis said. "I'm gonna go take a shower. And put your hair on, will you? You look like a damn cue ball."

The shower was running and Thurnauer was hunched over her makeup mirror, adjusting his hairpiece, when Keller got a hand over his mouth and plunged the letter opener into his back, fitting it deftly between two ribs and driving it home into his heart. The big man had no time to struggle; by the time he knew what was happening, it had already happened. His body convulsed once, then went slack, and Keller lowered him to the floor.

The shower was still running. Keller could be out the door before she was out of the shower. But as soon as she did come out she would see Thurnauer, and she'd know at a glance that he was dead, and she'd scream and yell and carry on and call 911, and who needed that?

Besides, the pity he'd felt for her had dried up during her argument with her lover. He'd responded to a sense of her vulnerability, a fragile quality that he'd since decided was conveyed by that see-through skin of hers. She was actually a whining, sniping, carping nag of a woman, and about as fragile as an army boot.

So, when she stepped out of the bathroom, he took her from behind and broke her neck. He left her where she fell, just as he'd left Thurnauer on the bedroom floor. You could try to set a scene, make it look as though she had stabbed him and then broke her neck in a fall, but it would never fool anybody, so why bother? The client had merely stipulated that the man be dead, and that's what Keller had delivered.

It was sort of a shame about the girl, but it wasn't all that much of a shame. She was no Mother Teresa. And you couldn't let sentiment get in the way. That was always a bad idea, and especially on a high-risk day.

                              *    *    *

There were good restaurants in Boston, and Keller thought about
going to Locke-Ober's, say, and treating himself to a really good meal.
But the timing was wrong. It was just after three, too late for lunch
and too early for dinner. If he went someplace decent they would just
stare at him.

He could kill a couple of hours. He hadn't brought his catalog, so
there was no point making the rounds of the stamp shops, but he
could see a movie, or go to a museum. It couldn't be that hard to
find a way to get through an afternoon, not in a city like Boston, for
God's sake.

On a nicer day he'd have been happy enough just walking around
Back Bay or Beacon Hill. Boston was a good city for walking, not as
good as New York, but better than most cities. With the rain still
coming down, though, walking was no pleasure, and cabs were hard
to come by.

Keller, back on Newbury Street, walked until he found an upscale
coffee shop that looked okay. It wasn't going to remind anybody of
Locke-Ober, but it was here and they would serve him now, and he
was too hungry to wait.

The waitress wanted to know what the problem was. "It's my coat,"
Keller told her.

"What happened to your coat?"

"Well, that's the problem," he said. "I hung it on the hook over
there, and it's gone."

"You sure it's not there?"

"Positive."

"Because coats tend to look alike, and there's coats hanging there,
and—"

"Mine is green."

"Green green? Or more like an olive green?"

What difference did it make? There were three coats over there,
all of them shades of beige, none at all like his. "The salesman called
it olive," he said, "but it was pretty green. And it's not here."

"Are you sure you had it when you came in?"

Keller pointed at the window. "It's been like that all day," he said. "What kind of an idiot would go out without a coat?"

"Maybe you left it somewhere else."

Was it possible? He'd shucked the coat in the Emerson Street living room. Could he have left it there?

No, not a chance. He remembered putting it on, remembered opening his umbrella when he hit the street, remembered hanging both coat and umbrella on the peg before he slid into the booth and reached for the menu. And where was the umbrella? Gone, just like the coat.

"I didn't leave it anywhere else," he said firmly. "I was wearing the coat when I came in, and I hung it up right there, and it's not there now. And neither is my umbrella."

"Somebody must of taken it by mistake."

"How? It's green."

"Maybe they're colorblind," she suggested. "Or they have a green coat at home, and they forgot they were wearing the tan one today, so they took yours by mistake. When they bring it back—"

"Nobody's going to bring it back. Somebody stole my coat."

"Why would anybody steal a coat?"

"Probably because he didn't have a coat of his own," Keller said patiently, "and it's pouring out there, and he didn't want to get wet any more than I do. The three coats on the wall belong to your three other customers, and I'm not going to steal a coat from one of them, and the guy who stole my coat's not going to bring it back, so what am I supposed to do?"

"We're not responsible," she said, and pointed to a sign that agreed with her. Keller wasn't convinced the sign was enough to get the restaurant off the hook, but it didn't matter. He wasn't about to sue them.

"If you want me to call the police so you can report it . . ."

"I just want to get out of here," he said. "I need a cab, but I could drown out there waiting for an empty one to come along."

She brightened, able at last to suggest something. "Right over there," she said. "The hotel? There's a canopy'll keep you dry, and there's cabs pulling up and dropping people off all day long. And you know what? I'll bet Angela at the register's got an umbrella you can take. People leave them here all the time, and unless it's raining they never think to come back for them."

The girl at the cash register supplied a black folding umbrella, flimsy but serviceable. "I remember that coat," she said. "Green. I saw it come in and I saw it go out, but I never realized it was two different people coming and going. It was what you would call a very distinctive garment. Do you think you'll be able to replace it?"

"It won't be easy," he said.

"You didn't want to do this one," Dot said, "and I couldn't figure out why. It looked like a walk in the park, and it turns out that's exactly what it was."

"A walk in the rain," he said. "I had my coat stolen."

"And your umbrella. Well, there are some unscrupulous people out there, Keller, even in a decent town like Boston. You can buy a new coat."

"I never should have bought that one in the first place."

"It was green, you said."

"Too green."

"What were you doing, waiting for it to ripen?"

"It's somebody else's problem now," he said. "The next one's going to be beige."

"You can't go wrong with beige," she said. "Not too light, though, or it shows everything. My advice would be to lean toward the tan end of the spectrum."

"Whatever." He looked at her television set. "I wonder what they're talking about."

"Nothing as interesting as raincoats, would be my guess. I could unmute the thing, but I think we're better off wondering."

"You're probably right. I wonder if that was it. Losing the raincoat, I mean."

"You wonder if it was what?"

"The feeling I had."

"You did have a feeling about Boston, didn't you? It wasn't a stamp auction. You didn't want to take the job."

"I took it, didn't I?"

"But you didn't want to. Tell me more about this feeling, Keller."

"It was just a feeling," he said. He wasn't ready to tell her about his horoscope. He could imagine how she'd react, and he didn't want to hear it.

"You had a feeling another time," she said. "In Louisville."

"That was a little different."

"And both times the jobs went fine."

"That's true."

"So where do you suppose these feelings are coming from? Any idea?"

"Not really. It wasn't that strong a feeling this time, anyway. And I took the job, and I did it."

"And it went smooth as silk."

"More or less," he said.

"More or less?"

"I used a letter opener."

"What for? Sorry, dumb question. What did you do, pick it up off his desk?"

"Bought it on the way there."

"In Boston?"

"Well, I didn't want to take it through the metals detector. I bought it in Boston, and I took it with me when I left."

"Naturally. And chucked it in a Dumpster or down a sewer. Except you didn't or you wouldn't have brought up the subject. Oh, for Christ's sake, Keller. The coat pocket?"

"Along with the keys."

"What keys? Oh, hell, the keys to the apartment. A set of keys and a murder weapon and you're carrying them around in your coat pocket."

"They were going down a storm drain before I went to the airport," he said, "but first I wanted to get something to eat, and the next thing I knew my coat was gone."

"And the thief got more than just a coat."

"And an umbrella."

"Forget the umbrella, will you? Besides the coat he got keys and a letter opener. There's no little tag on the keys, tells the address, or is there?"

"Just two keys on a plain wire ring."

"And I hope you didn't let them engrave your initials on the letter opener."

"No, and I wiped it clean," he said. "But still."

"Nothing to lead to you."

"No."

"But still," she said.

"That's what I said. 'But still.' "

---

Back in the city, Keller picked up the Boston papers. Both covered the murder in detail. Alvin Thurnauer, it turned out, was a prominent local businessman with connections to local political interests and, the papers hinted, to less savory elements as well. That he'd died violently in a Back Bay love nest, along with a blonde to whom he was not married, did nothing to diminish the news value of his death.

Both papers assured him that the police were pursuing various leads. Keller, reading between the lines, concluded that they didn't have a clue. They might guess that someone had contracted to have Thurnauer hit, and they might be able to guess who that someone was, but they wouldn't be able to go anywhere with it. There were no witnesses, no useful physical evidence.

He almost missed the second murder.

The *Globe* didn't have it. But there it was in the *Herald*, a small story on a back page, a man found dead on Boston Common, shot twice in the head with a small-caliber weapon.

Keller could picture the poor bastard, lying face-down on the grass, the rain washing relentlessly down on him. He could picture the dead man's coat, too. The Herald didn't say anything about a coat, but that didn't matter. Keller could picture it all the same.

Green as the grass.

He stared hard at his thumb, then looked in a drawer for the copy of his chart Louise had given him. It looked even more impressive now, if no less incomprehensible. He put it back in the drawer.

Later, when the sky was dark, he went outside and looked up at the stars.

# STAR STRUCK

## Peter Lovesey

ON THAT SEPTEMBER evening the sun was a crimson skull cap, and a glittering cope was draped across the sea. I was leaning on the rail at the end of the pier where the fishermen liked to cast. By this time they had all packed up and gone. A few unashamed romantics like me stood in contemplation, awed by the spectacle.

I wasn't aware of the woman beside me until she spoke. Her voice was low-pitched, instantly attractive. She was wearing what looked like a cloak.

"I can already see a star," she said.

"Jupiter," I answered.

"For sure?"

"Certainly."

"Couldn't it be Venus? Venus can be very bright."

"Not this month. Venus is in superior conjunction with the sun, so we won't see it at all this month."

"You obviously know," she said.

"Only enough to take an interest." This was true. I'm no expert on the solar system.

"This is an ideal place to stand," she said. "It's my first time here."

Up to now I hadn't looked at her fully. All my attention had been on the sky. Turning, I saw a fine, narrow face suffused with the strange crimson light. Dark, straight hair worn long and loose. She could have modelled for Modigliani. "I thought I hadn't seen you here before. Did someone recommend it?"

Her eyes widened. "How did you know?"

"A guess."

"I don't think so. You must be intuitive. I always read my horoscope in the local paper, the Argus. This week, it said Friday was an evening to go somewhere different that gives a sense of space. I couldn't think of anywhere that fitted better than this."

"Nor I." The polite response. Privately I haven't much time for people who take astrology seriously.

As if she sensed I was a sceptic, she said, "It's a science, you know."

"Interesting claim."

"The zodiac doesn't lie. If mistaken readings are made, it's human error. Anyone can call himself an astrologer, and some are charlatans, but the best are extremely accurate. I've had it proved again and again."

You don't cast doubt on statements like that—not when they're made by a beautiful woman you've only just met. "Right. If it has a good result, who cares? You came here and saw this wonderful sunset."

Only later, hours later, still thinking about her, did I realise what I should have said: *Did the horoscope tell you what to do next?* The perfect cue to invite her out for a meal. I always think of the lines too late.

She'd made a profound impression on me—and I hadn't even asked what her name was.

Idiot.

I played the pier scene over many times in the next few days. She'd spoken first. I should have made the next move. Now it was too late unless I happened to meet her again. I went back to the pier and watched the next three sunsets. Well, to be truthful I spent most of the time looking over my shoulder. She didn't come.

I couldn't concentrate on my job. I'm a sub-editor on the Argus—yes, the paper she mentioned. My subbing was so bad that week that Mr. Peel, the editor, called me in and pointed out three typos in a single paragraph. "What's the matter with you, Rob? Get your mind on the job, or you won't have a job."

Still I kept thinking about the woman in the cloak. I can't explain the effect she had on me. I'd heard of love at first sight, but this was more like infatuation. I'm thirty-two and I ought to be over adolescent crushes.

It took a week of mental turmoil before I came to my senses and saw that I was perfectly placed to arrange another meeting. The one thing I knew about her was that she read—and acted on—her horoscope in the Argus. My paper.

The horoscopes were written by a freelance, some old darling in Tunbridge Wells. The copy always arrived on Monday, banged out on her old typewriter with the worn-out ribbon. Vacuous stuff, in my opinion, but as a writer she was a pro. The word-count was always spot on. Not a word was mis-spelt. Each week I transferred the text to my screen almost without thought.

This week I would do what I was paid to do—some sub-editing.

First, I looked at last week's horoscopes for the phrase my mysterious woman had mentioned. One entry had it almost word for word. *Go somewhere different on Friday. A sense of space will have a liberating effect.* She was an Aquarian. Finally I knew something else about her. She had a birthday in late January or the first half of February.

I picked up the piece of thin paper that had just come in from Tunbridge Wells with this week's nonsense. Aquarians had a dull old week in store. *A good time for turning out cupboards and catching up with odd jobs.* I can improve on that, I thought.

"Saturday," I wrote, "*is the ideal time for single Aquarians to make a rendezvous with romance. Instead of eating at home in the evening, treat yourself to a meal out and you may be treated to much more.*"

One word in my text had a significance only a local would understand. There is a French restaurant called Rendezvous on one of the corners of the Parade, above the promenade. I was confident my lady of the sunset would pick up the signal.

The day after the paper appeared, I wasn't too surprised to read a huffy letter from The Diviner—as our astrological expert in Tunbridge Wells liked to be known to readers. It was addressed to the Editor. Fortunately Mr. Peel's secretary Linda—who is wonderfully discreet—opened it and put it in my tray before the boss saw it. Was the newspaper not aware, The Diviner asked in her letter, that each horoscope she wrote was the result of many hours of study of the dispositions and influences of the planets? In seventeen years no one had tampered with her copy. The mutilation of last week's piece was a monstrous act of sabotage, the most appalling vandalism, calculated to undermine the confidence of her thousands of loyal readers. She demanded a full investigation, so that the person responsible was identified and "dealt with accordingly." If she was not given a complete reassurance within a week she would speak to the proprietor, Sir Montagu Willingdale, a personal friend, who she knew would be "incandescent with fury."

Rather over the top, I thought. However, I valued my job enough to concoct an abject letter from Mr. Peel stating that he was shocked beyond belief and had investigated the matter fully and found the perpetrator—who it turned out was a schoolboy on a work experience scheme. This hapless boy had mistakenly deleted part of the text on the computer and in some panic improvised a couple of sentences. The copy had gone to press before anyone noticed. *"Needless to say,"* I added, *"the boy on work experience will not be experiencing any more work at the Argus office."* And I added more grovelling words before forging Mr. Peel's signature.

After that inspired piece of fiction, I just hoped the risk I'd taken would produce the desired result.

You have to be confident, don't you? I booked a table for two on Saturday evening at the Rendezvous, a decent place with French cuisine at reasonable prices and a good wine list.

They opened at seven and I was the first in. The manager consulted his reservations book and I stood close enough to see he had plenty of names as well as mine.

"I expect you're busy on Saturdays," I said.

"Not usually so busy as this, sir. It's a bit of a mystery. We're popular, of course, but this week we were fully booked by Thursday lunchtime. It's like Valentine's Day all over again."

I hoped so.

Before I was shown to my seat, others started arriving, men and women, mostly unaccompanied, and nervous. I knew why. I was amused to see how their eyes darted left and right to see who was at the other tables. I would have taken a bet that they all had the same birth-sign.

Never under-estimate the power of the press.

In the next twenty minutes, the restaurant filled steadily. One or two bold souls at adjacent tables started talking to each other. In my quiet way, I was quite a matchmaker.

Unfortunately none of the women resembled the one I most hoped to see. I sat sipping a glass of Chablis, having told the waiter I would wait for my companion before ordering.

After another twenty minutes I ordered a second glass. The waiter gave me a look that said it was about time I faced the truth—I'd been stood up.

Some of the people around me were already on their main course. A pretty red-head alone at a table across the room smiled shyly and then looked away. She was a charmer. Maybe I should cut my losses and go across, I thought.

Then my heart pumped faster. Standing just inside the door handing her cloak to the waiter was the one person all this was set up for. In a long-sleeved blue velvet dress with glitter on the bodice, she looked stunningly beautiful.

I practically walked on air across the room, but at a fair speed, before anyone else made a move.

"You again?" I said. "We met at the end of the pier a few days ago. Do you remember?"

"Why, yes! What a coincidence." Her blue eyes shone with recognition—or was it joy that her star sign had worked its magic?

I said I was alone and suggested she joined me and she said nothing would please her more. Brilliant.

At the table we went through the preliminaries of getting to know each other. Her name was Helena and she worked as a research chemist at Plaxton's, the agricultural suppliers. She'd moved down from Norfolk three years ago, when she got the job.

"Helena—that's nice," I said.

"Actually I wish it was plain Helen. I have to keep telling people about the 'a' at the end."

I told her I've lived in the area all my life. "As a matter of fact, I'm a journalist."

"How exciting. Is that with a magazine?"

"Newspaper."

"Which one?"

"Which Sunday paper do you take?"

"The Independent."

"You've probably read some of my stuff, then. I'm a freelance." A departure from the truth, but I didn't want to mention the Argus in case she got suspicious.

"Should I know your name?" she asked.

"From my by-line in the papers, you mean? I don't suppose so," I answered with modesty. "It's Rob—Rob Newton."

"It sounds familiar."

"There was a film star. Called himself Robert. Dead now."

"I know! Bill Sikes in *Oliver Twist*."

"Right. And Long John Silver in *Treasure Island*. He cornered the market in rogues."

"But you're no rogue, I hope?"

"No film star, either." Actually I'm rather proud of my looks.

"What brought you here tonight? Do you come regularly?"

This innocent-sounding question was not to be answered lightly. I knew she was serious about this astrology nonsense.

"No," I answered, trying my best to summon up an other-worldly look. "It was quite strange. Something mysterious, almost like an inner voice, seemed to be urging me to make a reservation. And I'm so pleased I acted on it. After we spoke at the pier, I really wanted to meet you again."

She made no comment. Her eyes told me I'd got it right.

The waiter came over, and, flushed with the success of my stratagem, I ordered champagne before we looked at the menu. Helena said something about dividing the bill, but I thanked her in a lordly fashion and dismissed the idea. After all, I had my own words to live up to: *you may be treated to much more*. The champagne was just the beginning.

"How about you?" I asked after we'd ordered. "What made you come here tonight?"

"It was in the stars." She could look other-worldly, too.

"Do you really believe they have an influence?"

She said, her eyes shining with conviction, "I'm certain of it." But she didn't mention the Argus horoscope directly.

After the meal, we walked by the beach and looked at the stars. It was one of those magic late summer nights when they look like diamonds scattered across a black velvet cloth. Helena pointed to the group of ten that formed Aquarius, her own constellation, the water bearer. Personally, I have a real difficulty seeing any of the constellations as shapes, but I pretended I could make it out.

"Let me guess," she said. "Are you an Aquarian also?"

I shook my head. "Capricorn — the goat."

She giggled a little at that.

"I know," I said. "Goats get a bad press. But I'm well behaved, really."

"Pity," she said, and curled her hand around my neck and kissed me. Just like that, without a move from me.

I had to be true to the stars, didn't I? I took her back to my flat and treated her to much more. She was a passionate lover. And I am a bit of a goat.

We went out each night for the next week, clubbing, skating, the cinema and the theatre. We always ended at my place. It should have been perfect and it would have been if I'd been made of money. Aquarians are supposed to associate with water, but it was champagne all the way for Helena. She had expensive tastes, and since that first evening she didn't once offer to go halves. It was very clear she expected to be treated to much more — indefinitely.

On the Friday it all turned sour.

We'd been to London because Helena wanted a meal at the Ivy, and the Royal Ballet after. I should never have agreed. I was already overdrawn at the bank and paying for everything with plastic, trying not to think what next month's statement would amount to. Even so, I was horrified at how much it all cost. She didn't even offer to pay her train fare.

"Another day over," she said with a sigh, in the train at the end of the evening. Nothing about the ballet.

"Enjoyed it?"

"So where shall we go tomorrow?"

I said in as reasonable a tone as I could manage, "How about a night in for a change?"

"*Saturday night?* We can't stay in."

"Why not? I've got pizzas in the freezer and plenty of beer."

"You're joking, I hope."

"We can rent a video."

"Come off it, Rob."

"I've got no choice," I admitted. "After tonight I'm cleaned out." Which should have been her cue to treat *me* for a change.

"You mean you can't afford to take me out?"

"It's been an expensive week, Helena."

"You don't think I'm worth it? Is that what you're saying?"

"That doesn't come into it. I think you're terrific. But I can't go on spending what I haven't got."

"You're a freelance journalist. You told me. The national papers pay huge money just for one article."

At this stage I should have told her I was only a lowly sub-editor on the Argus. Stupidly I didn't. I tried bluffing it out. "Yes, but to earn a fat fee I have to have a top story to sell. That can mean months of research, travel, interviewing people. It's the old problem of cash flow."

"Get away," she said. "You're a typical Capricorn, money-minded, with the heart and soul of an accountant. I bet you keep a cashbook and enter it all in."

"That isn't fair, Helena."

She was silent for a time, staring out of the train window at the darkness. Then she said, "You've been stringing me along, haven't you? I really thought you and I were destined to spend the rest of our lives together. I gave myself to you, body and soul. I don't throw myself at any man who comes along, you know. And now you make me feel cheap, keeping tabs on every penny you spend on me. It puts a blight on all the nice things that happened."

"What a load of horseshit."

"Pig!"

When we reached the station she went straight to the taxi rank and got into a waiting cab. I didn't see her again. I walked home, more angry with myself than her. All my ingenuity had gone for nothing.

I'd really believed I was making all the running when in reality I was being fleeced. A fleeced goat is not a pretty sight.

At least I didn't have to fork out for her taxi fare.

I forgot about Helena when I started going out with Denise. Do you remember the red-head who smiled at me in the Rendezvous? She was Denise. I saw her in a bus queue one afternoon and there was that double-take when each of us looked at the other and tried to remember where we'd met. Then I clicked my fingers and said, "The restaurant."

We got on well from the start. I was completely open with her about my bit of improvised astrology-writing in the Argus, and she thought it was a good laugh. Denise laughed a lot, which was a nice change. She admitted she always read her horoscope and had gone along that Saturday evening—"just for a laugh"—in the hope of meeting someone nice. Such openness would have been impossible with Helena, who was so much more intense. I told Denise all about Helena, and she didn't mind at all. She said any woman who expected the guy to pay for everything wasn't living in the real world. To me, that was a pretty good summing-up of Helena.

"Was she out of a job, or something?" Denise asked.

"No. She has a good income, as far as I know. She's a scientist, a research chemist, with Plaxton's, the agricultural people."

"You wouldn't think a scientist would believe in star signs."

"Believe me, she takes it very seriously. She said astrology was a science."

Denise giggled. I don't think we discussed Helena again for some time. We had better things to do.

At work, I'd been keeping a look-out for letters postmarked Tunbridge Wells, just in case The Diviner decided to write back to Mr. Peel, but nothing came in except her weekly column—which of course I set in type without adding so much as a comma. My brown-nosing apology had done the trick. I continued with my boring subbing, looking forward to Friday evening, when I had another date with Denise. So when a package in a manila envelope arrived for The Diviner, care of the Argus, I did what I routinely do with all the other stuff that is sent to us by people wanting personal horoscopes, or advice about their futures—readdressed it to Tunbridge Wells and tossed it into the mailbag.

On our date, Denise told me she'd had an ugly scene with Helena. "It was last Monday lunch-time, in the sandwich stop in King Street. I go there every day. I was waiting in line and felt a tap on on my arm. She said, 'You're Rob Newton's latest pickup, aren't you?'—and made it sound really cheap. I shrugged and looked away and then she told me who she was and started telling me you were—well, things I don't want to repeat. I tried to ignore her, but she kept on and on, even after I'd bought my baguette and drink and left the shop. She was in a real state. In the end I told her there was nothing she could tell me I didn't know already. I said I had no complaints about the way you'd treated me."

"Thanks."

"Ah, but I only made it worse. Talking about you *treating* me was like a trigger. She wanted to know what my birth-sign is. I didn't say I was Aquarius, but she said I must be, and started telling me about the astrology piece she'd read in the Argus. I said, 'Listen, Helena, before you say any more, there's something you should know. Rob works for the Argus. He wrote that piece himself because he fancied you and knew you were dumb enough to believe in astrology.' That really stopped her in her tracks."

"I can believe it."

"Well, it's time she knew, isn't it? She's a damaged personality, Rob."

"What did she say?"

"Nothing after that. She went as pale as death and just walked away. Did I do wrong?"

"No, it's my fault. I ought to have told her the truth at the time. It's a good thing she knows. Her opinion of me can't get any lower."

I woke on Saturday to the sound of my mobile. Denise, beside me, groaned a little at the interruption. "Sorry," I said as I reached across her for it. "Can't think who the hell this is."

It was my boss, Mr. Peel. "Job for you, Rob," he said. "Have you heard the news?"

I said, "I've only just woken up."

"There's been a letter-bomb attack. A woman in Tunbridge Wells. She's dead."

"Tunbridge Wells isn't local," I said, still half asleep.

"Yes, but it's a story for the Argus. The dead woman is The Diviner, our astrology writer. Get there fast, Rob. Find out who had anything against the old dear."

I could have told him without going to Tunbridge Wells.

The police arrested me last Monday morning and charged me with murder. I've told them everything I know and they refuse to believe me. They say I had a clear motive for killing the old lady. Among her papers they found a copy of the letter to Mr. Peel complaining about her column being tampered with and demanding that the person responsible was "dealt with accordingly." They spoke to Linda, Mr. Peel's secretary, and she confirmed she'd passed the letter to me. Also in the house at Tunbridge Wells they found my reply with my poor forgery of Mr. Peel's signature. They say I was desperate to keep my job and sent the letter and must have sent the letter-bomb as well. Worst of all, a fingerprint was found on a fragment of the packaging. It was mine.

I told them why I handled the package when it arrived at the Argus office addressed to The Diviner. I said I now believe the bomb was meant for me, sent by Helena under the mistaken impression that I was the writer of the astrology column. I said I'd gone out with her for a short time and she was a head-case. I also told them she's a scientist with access to agricultural fertilisers, which any journalist would tell you can be used to make explosives. She's perfectly capable of constructing a letter-bomb.

To my horror, they refuse to believe me. They've interviewed Helena and of course she denies any knowledge of the letter bomb. She says she stopped going out with me because I'm a pathological liar with fantasies of being a top London freelance. Do you know, they believe her! They keep telling me I'm the head-case, and I'm going to be remanded for a psychological assessment. My alteration to the astrology column proves that I'm a control freak. Apparently it's a power thing. I get my kicks from ordering people to do pointless things—and from sending letter-bombs to old ladies.

Will nobody believe I'm innocent? I swear everything I've just written is true.

# BOSS MAN

## P. N. Elrod

CAITLIN READ FROM a new paperback with a gaudy cover. "It says you're headstrong, you like challenge, conquest, and pursuit, but you bore easily once your objective is achieved. That sounds about right."

"Only because it means I've finished my drink," said Nick Tarrant, suiting action to word. He polished off his Guinness with relish. "Let's boogie, chickadee."

She shoved the book in her coat pocket and scooped up her shoulder bag. Tarrant led the way from the restaurant, holding the door for her. The Texas sun was bright with the promise of a brutal summer to come, but the early spring air tempered things for the present.

"We're still in the lion part of March, dammit," Caitlin grumbled, shrinking into her coat against the chill wind.

They got into Tarrant's car, a non-descript American product, neutral in color. He drove fast, the pint of beer he'd had with his burger and fries not showing in his reflexes.

"What's this job you're on?" she asked, struggling with her seat belt, trying to get it around her bag.

"I'm not on it yet, but it's a Highland Park address, so I can probably charge more."

Caitlin snorted. "Rich people don't get rich when they spend it like the rest of us think they do."

"We'll size her up first."

"You'll size her up. I'm not sure what my job is."

"You're along to provide reassurance in case she's skittish. She's also into astrology."

"So?"

"You are, too."

"Not that much. I just read what's in the paper or on the 'Net when I bother to remember."

"That's why I got you the book." He referred to the one in her pocket. The cover featured a stylized moon and sun combination favored by New Age shops and garden centers.

"I'd wondered. If this client is really into astrology she'll know a ringer. I only believe when it's flattering or funny. Casting horoscopes is too damn complicated for me. Tarot cards are *much* better, more focused."

Tarrant nodded once, respecting her eccentricity, which wasn't as annoying as some he'd dealt with. "Doesn't matter," he said. "If the topic comes up all you do is look interested. The book's just background research. Half the work for landing a commission is knowing what makes the client tick. Before she set the appointment she wanted to know my sign. I think the answer was important to her."

"But all that stuff on the stars has pretty much been debunked." Caitlin had won the fight with her seat belt and pulled out the book again. "Most of the rules were set down back in ancient times; they're all about a month out of sync these days."

"What do you mean?"

"I read somewhere that they're a month late or early, I forget which. So instead of me being an Aquarius, I'm really either a Capricorn or a Pisces. Instead of being Aries, you're either a Pisces or a Taurus."

"Now that's funny."

"The problem is . . ." Caitlin peered at the pages. "You *act* like an Aries, and I seem to act like an Aquarian. Most of the time. Some of the personality traits for the signs are so general as to apply to anyone, though. On the other hand, maybe we grow into what's described for us. The problem with that is people like you who aren't into this kind of stuff still seem to run to type. You've got this leadership thing going for you, and as for your love life, you like to chase and catch, but sooner or later the heat fizzles out of the affair."

"Not all of them. One or two have exploded quite spectacularly. I was lucky to make it clear with my life."

"True, but was that because you're an Aries, a son-of-a-bitch or overloaded with testosterone?"

Tarrant smirked. "Probably all three."

She chuckled, putting the book away. "You don't need me on this."

"Sure I do. While I interview the client, you pretend to take notes like a secretary."

"I won't be pretending."

"Good, then I won't have to pretend to pay you."

Tarrant consulted scribbled directions he'd stuffed into the dash clipboard, negotiating turns and counting off house numbers. The houses and grounds in this section of Highland Park were very large, the low end of the real estate scale starting at a million and a half. When he pulled into the right driveway, he estimated the place as being easily in the two million range. "Wow," said Caitlin. "People really live like this, it's not just something made up for movies?"

"Yup."

"How'd you come to know them?"

"I didn't, she had my pager number. Said I'd been recommended." It was the only way he worked on a blind commission. Safer.

"By whom?"

Tarrant had an idea, but wasn't certain. "If I told you I'd have to kill you."

"You terrify me, did you know that?" she deadpanned, half-serious.

The house was southern-mansion style, post-World-War II, but pre-central air-conditioning era with its long windows. To his eyes it looked like an overgrown version of a small-town Texas funeral home.

Caitlin said *wow* again, under her breath, then shut up and squared herself, assuming a cool, friendly face. He could trust her to stay in professional mode until they were finished. Her awe was understandable; he felt its tug himself here on the threshold of a place that represented Real Money. He also understood what it took to obtain that kind of wonderfully filthy lucre.

"Sure we're supposed to use the front door?" Caitlin muttered. "I delivered flowers to get through college. A joint half this size got snotty when I knocked with my basket of posies. They made me go around to the side. It didn't sit well with my ego."

Tarrant grunted and rang the bell, assuming his own game face. He wore one of his better suits, a quietly expensive tie, his Rolex peeking discreetly from beneath a linen cuff. He would make a reasonably good impression to anyone used to GQ-style wealth. Caitlin had on new designer jeans, boots, and an oversized olive-colored sweater that played nicely off her red-head's pale complexion. Her leather coat added the right kind of flair for this job; she'd invested well in that. His instinct to ask her along had been right once again; like a really good nurse she radiated cheerful competence.

Caitlin stood up straighter at the sound of approaching footsteps within. "It's show time," she whispered.

The door was opened by a Hispanic maid who apparently knew to expect them. She smiled and led them into expensively decorated depths.

Tarrant made an accurate gauge of the surroundings, concluding it was old money, at least three generation's worth. The woman who'd set the appointment gave no name, only an address which he'd checked using a reverse directory on the Internet. He'd turned up the name of Pangford as the property owner. The family had something to do with textile manufacturing. That was all he'd managed to get by the time Caitlin arrived at his condo for a short briefing over lunch. Normally he'd be more cautious over new business, but the bills were piling up. If this interview went well he could score enough to float for a considerable period without having to dip into savings.

The indoor hike ended at a lavish home office with a wall of French windows opening onto a garden. Clumps of gold daffodils dominated the perfectly kept beds. The room was also colorful, with phalanxes of books, paintings, and appropriately matched furnishings. There were too many pillows and doilies scattered around for it to be a man's office, though it might have been one once. He saw no horoscope signs lurking in the décor.

A small woman in her young forties came in from a side door and dismissed the maid. "I'm Mrs. Dolly Pangford," she said, extending a delicate hand. A peach blond, she wore a simple dress that was nearly the same color as her creamy skin.

"Nick Tarrant," he responded. "My associate, Caitlin McGill."

Caitlin shook hands, murmuring a soft greeting in a mid-Atlantic accent she'd picked up in her drama major days. She wouldn't revert to her Texas drawl until they were back in the car.

Mrs. Pangford went through the usual social ritual of getting them seated and offering refreshments. With a tray of coffee on order from a distant kitchen — she'd used the house intercom to call for it — Tarrant thought she'd be ready to settle down and talk.

"What seems to be the problem, Mrs. Pangford?" he asked.

She glanced at Caitlin, who pulled out a small note pad and pen. "I shall want absolute privacy about this."

"You'll get it."

Caitlin nodded, smiling brightly, projecting more confidence with her silence than if she'd seconded his assurance vocally.

"Very well." Pangford took a deep breath, lifting her chin. "This is about my stepdaughter. She doesn't know that I'm interfering in her life, and she's *not* to find out. I'm sure you'll have heard this before: she's taken up with the wrong sort of man."

"Go on."

"Amanda met him at one of those clubs she's been sneaking out to since she was sixteen and got her first fake ID. She's nearly twenty-one now and not past her wild oats yet. I've not been the best mother for her; we don't get along, especially since her father died and left the bulk of the estate to me. We have horrible fights, but I don't want her walking off a cliff . . . or being pushed off."

"How so?"

"She ran away to Las Vegas a few months ago with a loser named Kyle Deacon and married him. I made sure that her trust money was tied up in such a way so he couldn't get to it even after she turns twenty-one, which endeared me to them both. Since then I've discovered he's put several insurance policies on her life. You don't have to be a rocket scientist to figure out where that might lead."

"You think he's planning to kill her?"

"I do. He's garbage, but clever. He'll have to do it in such a way as to make it seem like natural causes or an accident. I think he's just smart enough to succeed. He runs with a rough crowd. I'm sure he knows people who can arrange such things."

"Your stepdaughter suspects nothing?"

"She's in love and it's made her stupid. He's her ally against her wicked stepmother, after all. The more I disapprove, the more she clings to him. I know his type and how they work their game. When I was her age I had a similar parasite turning my head with his charm and offer of shelter from a family that didn't understand me. I emerged with only a bruised ego once I figured out the truth. I don't think Amanda will be so lucky. She's a Gemini, but not one of the smart ones. He's a Scorpio with a mean streak of rat's cunning. Their marriage will never work anyway, but I doubt he'll let it go on much longer."

"What is it you want me to do for you?"

Dolly Pangford's well-preserved pale face went still, her gray eyes hardening. "I want you to do whatever it takes to keep Amanda alive."

"That could involve any number of possibilities, ma'am."

"I will leave the means and manner to your choice, then. You've more expertise than I, though in my opinion it's best to keep things simple. I was told by Doc Jessup that you were very good at your job."

At the mention of that name Tarrant's own face went still. "May I ask how you know him?"

"Through my late husband's business dealings. Henry had a wide range of acquaintances, with many, shall we say, forceful sorts. I thought Doc might take care of this, but he's retired. He said he had every confidence in your abilities, though, and gave me your beeper number."

"Did you discuss this on a phone or by E-mail with him?"

"No, face-to-face over dinner in a noisy restaurant. He said you should see this." She drew forth a business card from her sleeve and handed it over.

Tarrant recognized the embossed lettering and phone number. Those could be faked, but on the flip side, in Doc's distinct scrawl, was a short note, addressed to him. *Syko, this one's ok. Come over and buy me a beer later.* Tarrant's mouth twitched. Only a handful of his old fight-kill-and-die-for-you cronies were alive to call him Syko these days. The job would be safe enough to take with this seal of approval. Of course, Doc would want to meet afterward and hear all the details. He loved post-game quarterbacking.

Tarrant smiled, not showing his teeth. "All right, Mrs. Pangford. I think I can come up with some kind of agreeable solution to your problem."

"Without Amanda finding out my involvement?"

"Not if I have anything to do with it. I'll have to get some basic information from you, quite a lot of it."

"Whatever you need."

The coffee arrived just then, fragrant and perfectly brewed. He drank it to be sociable, wishing for a Pepsi instead. As soon as the maid left Tarrant began asking questions. Caitlin wrote down all the replies. He got the names, numbers and addresses he'd need, a general idea of schedules, and photos.

Neither Amanda or Kyle Deacon worked; Amanda received enough from her trust fund each month to afford a loft in Deep Ellum, utility bills, and groceries. If either or both of them had a regular job they could live very well indeed. Deacon called himself as a musician, Amanda was an artist.

*God save me from liberal art degrees,* Tarrant thought, wondering what academic idiot ever thought those to be a good idea.

According to an earlier investigation Dolly Pangford had initiated, the young and carefree couple each had five credit cards, all ten hovering dangerously near their maximum limit. Amanda frequently demanded loans against her trust to pay them off. Dolly just as frequently refused, suggesting a job search and using scissors on the cards as the obvious solution to debt.

"I am then called a lot of foul names and treated to the sound of the phone slamming down," she told Tarrant. "After a week, or until the next collection agency calls, she starts all over again. Sometimes it's tears, other times she's honey-sweet and apologetic. It worked on Henry, but not on me. I don't know why her father didn't teach her how to be responsible about life and money. By the time I came into the picture she was spoiled rotten and out of control. I was the first person who ever said no to her, and it was an ugly shock for her to find out she was no longer at the center of the universe. Perhaps I should have brought in some professional help for our family. Too late now. All I want is for her to survive this and live to grow some brains."

Tarrant's own keep-it-simple solution for spoiled kids began with a good spanking followed by a lengthy stay at a boot camp. Perhaps after this was settled, he'd suggest it to Mrs. Pangford. Maybe if she got Amanda declared mentally incompetent . . . there was probably enough cash lying around lost in the mansion's sofas to buy off all kinds of doctors.

*Not my problem today.*

"I think that should do it," he said. Caitlin had filled several pages. He'd memorize it all, then destroy the notes. He had no worry about Caitlin; hers was a selective memory with a convenient ability for forgetting data when it was no longer needed or too dangerous to recall.

"What about your fee?" asked Mrs. Pangford.

Tarrant quoted her an estimate based on what he'd learned in the last hour, factoring in anticipated difficulties. It was fair, the average rate in the more rarified circles of his trade.

Mrs. Pangford didn't blink. Either she deemed it a good price for what she wanted or Doc had warned her what to expect. "You'll want that in cash?"

"If you don't mind. Small bills, nothing over a hundred. I'll need half as a retainer, and we can arrange later to pay over the balance when the job is done. All incidental expenses are included, by the way." He'd learned in the course of business that clients didn't mind forking over a flat fee even if it was huge, but most balked when presented with the chicken-change of an itemized expense account.

"I can manage that today," she said. "It will take me about a week to get the rest together."

"I trust you," he said, and almost meant it. He'd dealt with occasional hold-outs who thought they could get away with not paying the balance. Fortunately those were an infrequent annoyance. Most people were smarter.

"If you need any other information, just phone," she added.

Her hand was cool and dry when he took it. That was good. The lady was no wimp. He thought he could trust her to see things through.

"You're absolutely sure about this?" he asked. "Doc mentioned all the possibilities?"

Her gray eyes reminded him of polished granite. "I am absolutely certain, Mr. Tarrant. Doc told me everything. I will be comfortable with whatever measures you judge necessary to keep Amanda safe from harm."

"So long as we're clear on that."

She smiled. "Crystalline."

"Jeeze-Louise," said Caitlin, once they'd left the driveway. She heaved a huge sigh of relief. "That was one hell of a learning experience. Are they all like that?"

"Every job's different." For instance he'd not expected Mrs. Pangford to have the first half of his fee ready and in the house. The usual thing was to wait however long it took for a client to get hold of the required funds, then make a drop. Doc Jessup must have given her one hell of an earful.

"You didn't really need me along to take notes." Caitlin tapped the bag on her lap, which held the pad and its possibly incriminating information. It also held the money and was now quite heavy. He would work out her percentage when they got back to his condo.

"Yes, I did. You put her at ease. She glanced at you a few times."

"I noticed. I tried to look intelligent and poised."

"It worked. It helped having another woman there so I wouldn't scare her so much. She's the old-school sorority-sister type."

"As in never wears white shoes before Easter?"

"Bulls-eye."

"She didn't look scared."

"No, but it was there. She covered it well, I'll hand her that. The lady's also got plenty on the ball in the brains department, so I wonder why she goes in for astrology. You're a smart chick, why do you go in for Tarot cards?"

"I use them as psychological tools. Their images spark a response in my sub-conscious that eventually allows me to make decisions or draw conclusions to my own best advantage. Though once in a while they've predicted a few events that I never saw coming. Or maybe I just fit the events to the cards, but that doesn't always work. Like that guy I went nuts over last summer? No matter how many times I shuffled and asked about my future with him the results were all dismal. *Not* the answer I wanted to see, so I tried to make things turn out different, but they never did. You remember?"

"Yup." He'd kept his mouth diplomatically shut while Caitlin had been in the throes of her brief romance, though he could have told her it was doomed. You didn't need a deck of cards to see that. He was glad when she'd finally smarted up and broke things off. He'd been ready to kill them both on the distraction factor alone.

Caitlin shrugged, cocking her head in thought. "Maybe astrology works for Mrs. Pangford in the same way on a psychological level. I think it allows people to place order and structure into an otherwise chaotic world. It offers a weird sense of security knowing that some life events and personality traits are beyond our best efforts at control or that we're at the mercy of our stellar destiny. If it's in the stars that something nasty will happen, then we have to shrug and accept it, for what can we do about it? Mrs. Pangford can then excuse her faults and those of others by blaming them on outside forces over which she has no command."

"Or maybe it's a lot of horse hockey."

"There's that," Caitlin agreed, amiably. "So—what's your next move on the case?"

"Tonight I do a little checking up on Mr. and Mrs. Deacon in their stately Deep Ellum manor. Won't need you along, it's scut-work."

"And you think slaving over a computer chasing down obscure data for you ain't?"

"You'll be in a nice, warm indoor environment, free to use the toilet any time you feel the urge. I shall probably be confined to this mobile prison for an indeterminate time as I check out the field."

"Okay, you win. You'll change clothes, of course?"

"Of course." He made a start, loosening his tie and undoing the collar button. Once home, he retreated to his bedroom to complete the operation, while Caitlin fired up his computer. He emerged wearing a faded black polo shirt with dark cargo pants stuffed into boots. With a baseball hat and a loose pocket vest to finish things, he expected to go unnoticed in the eclectic atmosphere of Deep Ellum.

"You need an earring," said Caitlin, peering at her screen, comparing search engine results with her notes.

Sometime ago he'd had one ear pierced. "You think?"

"Oh, yeah. Anyone without metal hanging off them is the exception there, not the rule. That's why I don't fit into those artsy-fartsy circles so well." Caitlin was so squeamish she'd been known to faint when taking her pets in for their shots. Her earlobes were quite virginal.

He went back, dug around on his dresser, and found a plain silver earring, fitting it into place.

"That's better," she said, giving him a brief once-over. "You look nice and rakish."

"I need to be nice and anonymous."

"Okay, rakish in Highland Park, but Mr. Ordinary in Deep Ellum."

He looked over her shoulder while she did magic with the computer and its wide range of special search programs. Everything she found confirmed Dolly Pangford's story and then some. Kyle Deacon had a police record, only minor skirmishes for being drunk. His juvenile files were sealed, but that was no hindrance to Caitlin's hacker talents.

"My, but wasn't he Peck's Bad Boy way back when?" she muttered. "We got us a little joy-riding vandal, some assault, some shop-lifting, some drug dealing, now didn't he have fun? But it's still a long jump from murder."

"That's what I'm checking out later." He wished he'd not had the coffee or stared at the computer screen for so long; he felt a headache coming on. Of all the lousy times to get a migraine. "I need to rest until it's dark. Tell the kids to keep hush."

One of his five cats *meowed* at him, looking innocent.

Tarrant got a bottle of Stoli from the freezer to wash down a couple prescription pills. An unwise combination, but it would put him out right away and maybe halt the headache before it took too firm a hold. He gave Caitlin a wake-up time and after removing his boots, rolled into bed. As a distraction he flipped through the astrology book, reading up on his own sign, finding amusement at what it got right and wrong about him. It did seem to have nailed it square about his craving for challenge and boredom with achievement.

Just as he drifted off, he remembered that they'd not divided the money up yet.

*Later.*

*       *       *

He had a good three-hour nap, waking when it was full dark, about five minutes before Caitlin was due to come in. His mouth tasted bad, but the pain that had threatened to squeeze his skull in two was thankfully gone. He was set for the evening, no matter how long it might prove.

Caitlin was still at the computer. "I was about to give a yell. Didn't you sleep?"

"Yup. I just got an accurate body clock. What's this?" On what had been a clear coffee table newspaper pages were now spread wide over something lumpy. One of the cats sprawled on top. He scooped the animal out of the way. The payment money was underneath, neatly stacked and sorted. There was a lot of it.

"I raided my purse for a candy bar and had to remove the cash first," Caitlin explained. "Then once started I couldn't stop. Counting all that was almost as good as sex. It's all there. She didn't short you."

"No one does and lives," he intoned, dropping the papers back. He went to the fridge and pulled out a big bottle of Pepsi, taking hits off it to fully wake up. The cold carbonation made him wince, but it felt great. Tarrant did a quick calculation, returned to the money, and set aside a portion. "There's your percentage, chickadee."

"Thanks. I think I earned it." She slowly stood and stretched, audible popping noises coming from her neck and spine. "My butt's gone dead. Why don't you invest in a more comfortable chair?"

He peeled five hundred from his side and put it on her pile. "Go pick out one you like, but no leather or vinyl. Make sure it fits my color scheme." That wouldn't be difficult. His condo was dominated by blacks and whites. "What else did you find out?"

"Exactly how much those two owe on their cards and the last time they made payments. But something odd's going on. Last month they brought in enough to catch them up on all ten. I couldn't find a source for the windfall. Maybe Kyle's band got a good gig or Amanda sold a painting to the Met and they paid in cash."

Tarrant frowned. "Or he's dealing again."

"I can believe that. I also cracked into a very forbidden file and found out little Amanda has a will. She leaves everything she's got—including her trust fund—to her beloved husband. He'll have to wait until she's twenty-one to get it, though, or it reverts to the estate. That's less than four months away. It's like the poor bimbo has a death wish."

"Does he have a will?"

"Yeah. He leaves her all his worldly goods, which at present includes four guitars, an electronic keyboard, and a 1986 Ford Escort."

"Good God, and she thinks he loves her?"

"It's grounds for divorce for me," Caitlin sniffed.

"I'm gonna boogie. Put that away?" He gestured at the money. He knew it would all be there when he got back. Despite her prediliction for Tarot cards, Caitlin was extremely sensible and prudent on practical matters, like never cheating the boss man.

"Don't worry, I'll lock everything up. Have fun, but don't get caught."

"Never."

The drive to Kyle and Amanda's Deep Ellum loft, which was on the east side of downtown Dallas, took about an hour. Being Saturday night, the streets there were jammed with a mixed crowd determined to have fun. Some of the wilder clubs were overflowing, but still trying to attract more inside. One place had several new Harleys out front, each draped with a shapely young thing in leather posing for anyone with a camera. Tarrant considered the pros and cons of making the choice between having the motorcycle or one of the girls. He concluded that the machine would draw the attention of any number of females to it and in short order to himself. If he chose one of the girls, the encounter would probably last only a weekend, if that long.

He liked women just fine, but enjoyed their company more when they didn't talk much. He'd long grown bored with the no-win "Do I look fat?" discussion and the disastrous "Why were you looking at *her?*" salvo. Caitlin was one of the few with whom he could hold a decent conversation, but she was off the menu. His policy was to never shop at the company store. Too many complications. Women he could get easily enough, but good hackers for his line of work were hard to find.

The exterior of the Deacon's loft was not as depressed as he expected, but far from the level of Bohemian sophistication as seen in countless films and TV shows. The Arctic-cool heroes who lived in those fantasies never had trouble finding a parking space, either. Tarrant was a full three blocks from the main action and the curbs were still clogged. At least he was getting paid nearly enough for the annoyance.

Four blocks down he found a spot and gratefully pried out of the driver's seat. Without hurry, he locked up and strolled back, eyes raking the dim areas between streetlights. He located one parked cop car and counted three more cruising past, each with two officers inside. That was a lot of muscle even for a party night, but Ellum was long-infamous for problems. The patrol car occupants gave him the hairy eyeball, but he just smiled and sent them a friendly wave. Cops were his friends, after all, there to keep him safe from the dregs of society.

He went up the metal exterior stairs and knocked on the Deacon's door. No reply, but he'd expected that. Kyle usually played with a club band on weekends and Amanda went with him. That detail seen to, Tarrant pulled on surgical gloves and got out his collection of lockpicks and skeleton keys, entering the loft about thirty seconds later.

The place smelled heavily of incense and mildew; the housekeeping exceeded his most pessimistic prediction. Without a maid to look after things, little Amanda was quite the slob. Flipping on a light was unnecessary; they'd left several burning, indication of an after-dark departure.

He made a quick search in some of the more obvious hiding holes, turning up a wad of fifties and twenties under the futon and fine variety of pharmaceuticals: pot, some possible Ecstasy, and plenty of oblong blue pills that might be Xanax. A party-hearty paradise. His roughest estimate put them at a street value close to seven grand, and these were just what he'd turned up on a surface search. It would be easy enough to make a phone call to have a couple of DEA types waiting there for the Deacons to return, but that would land Amanda in jail. Mrs. Pangford would not be pleased, though time in a lockup might do her step-brat some good.

How had Kyle gotten the seed money for this kind of stash? Suppliers only sold in bulk, leaving the piss-ant sales to the small fry dealers. He'd need at least a grand to start with, then keep buying more stock with the profit money to build up the trade to this size. Maybe he'd borrowed against his wife's insurance or trust fund without mentioning the down side to the mob creditors, like the wife still being alive and unable to touch the money. They might get mad at him if they learned the truth. Or they might not care and off the girl for Kyle if anything went wrong.

Tarrant had an idea about how to turn that to his advantage, but first he had to close down the store and dump the inventory.

He now made a truly thorough search of the place, finding more illegal chemicals. Strips of LSD blotters lay in plain sight in the freezer. Kyle Deacon might possess a rat's instinctive cunning, but he was dumb as a brick.

Tarrant found a metal wastebasket and, after removing the battery from the fire alarm, made a little blaze of the blotters. The pot and pills he ground to oblivion in the kitchen garbage disposal, using lots of hot water to dissolve everything. After putting the alarm battery back, he left, politely relocking the front door.

The outside air was sweet and cool. He breathed deep to clear his lungs of the upstairs stuffiness and checked his watch. He'd been at work for over an hour. Not bad. He walked down the street like he owned it, until he reached the Iguana's Cave Club. On Saturday nights after ten it changed its name to The Temple, and all the Goths in the area converged there to see who was the most groveling fashion slave. A slim girl walked past him as he checked the area. She wore a transparent black body suit, only just legal in public by the use of a G-string beneath and a few strips of electrician's tape criss-crossed over her nipples.

He grinned. *And I'm getting paid to do this.*

He followed her toward the entrance. Though he was obviously of an age to drink, the bouncers asked for ID. He good-naturedly presented one that looked real and was passed in quick so he could pay the cover charge and get his hand stamped. He smiled at the girl ahead of him and wondered where the hell she kept her money.

Techno music boomed loud in the lobby and grew deafening once he found his way inside. The main dance floor was an oblong pit with platforms at each end for the more extroverted types to show off their physical coordination skills. Both sexes and a few genders in between filled the place. Nearly all of them were head-to-toe in black with matching dyed hair, lipstick, nail polish, and bits of silver-plated hardware piercing various parts of their bodies. More often than not some of them sported fangs. A round-faced girl flashed hers at him in a teasing way, flicking her studded tongue, trying to look both dangerous and seductive. All he saw was jail-bait. Tattoos, once a male's rite of passage to prove his toughness or to advertise a military affiliation, were now regulated to being a cliché fashion statement.

Girls who wanted to be noticed as such were in paint-tight outfits, breasts pushed prominently high by lace corseting; the boys were either in equally tight jeans or pants so baggy and low on the hips as to make walking difficult and underwear wedgies easy. One male walked by in a black skirt and combat boots, obviously from the peculiar end of the gene pool.

Drugs were present. Tarrant didn't have to see them, as a matter of course he simply noticed their effect on the crowd. There was an artificial quality to their body movements, like actors who'd played the same part too often. What a shame to be so young and world-weary.

He looked for Kyle Deacon, but the platform where a live band should have been was thick with dancers, not instruments. He'd be difficult to spot in this mix of darkness and flashing lights. By the time Tarrant's night vision adjusted the light show would change or a muffled faux explosion would take place. Then special effects smoke roiled across the flailing dancers and curled up to the ceiling. He'd seen real hell before in combat once upon a time; this was the urban fantasy version, dramatic enough for the inexperienced, just plain annoying to one who knew.

The music changed to a slower tempo, the driving base vanishing for an extended phrase of electronic whooshing, like jets taking off. It made a change from the techno beat, which sounded like a breathing exercise for women in the last stages of labor. Amazingly, the kids were still dancing to it, if one could call it that. A tall girl with a too-black curtain of hair in the middle of the pit looked more like she was making an invisible pizza the way she swayed and waved her arms over her head. It did show off her lack of a bra. Nice figure. She might make for a good weekend, providing she didn't talk.

Then with gratification he realized that under the dead white make-up she was Amanda Deacon, nèe Pangford. Now that was convenient. So where was husband Kyle? She didn't seem to be dancing with anyone. None of them did.

Time to gain a little altitude. Tarrant found stairs that took him to the upper level where a long balcony overlooked the pit. It was lined with tables, the patrons drinking, watching the dancers, or attempting to converse by means of shouting directly into one anothers' ears. The lighting was a little better. He found a free space next to the rail and searched the shifting faces below. Amanda remained in place, her patience sometimes rewarded when the center spotlight picked her out. He wasn't sure if she was on drugs or not, but decided it was safer to assume she'd indulged for the evening.

He didn't spot Kyle on the floor. The place was big, with a whole second dance area and a deck outside for people to catch fresh air and talk. Tarrant was glad of his nap; this could take all night.

He made a casual cruise of the upper floor, his gaze not resting too long on any one person. He wanted to look like a man trying to hook up with misplaced friends, not someone on the hunt.

Toward the back, seated at a table for two, was Kyle. Finally. Tarrant didn't miss a step as he passed close on his way to the bar. They served Coke, not Pepsi, overfilled the short plastic airline cup with ice, and wanted two dollars plus a tip.

*God, I hate these joints.*

At the table, Kyle faced an older, white-bearded man who was very out-of-place in this determinedly funereal setting. He wore a red Fedora hat, a well-fitted light brown suit with a shiny yellow brocade vest, polished wing-tips, and had a cane under one hand. His beard was carefully trimmed; reflections off his wire-rimmed glasses hid his eyes. Too classy to be a pimp, he looked like he'd been hired to sit and lend quaint atmosphere to a place already flooded with it. He might have been part of the music business or a misplaced queen who'd wandered in from the Oak Lawn area by mistake.

Kyle spoke earnestly with him; his body language trying too hard to show self-assurance and presenting exactly the opposite. He was nervous, possibly afraid, but attempting to put himself on an equal footing with the fancy-pants. The man in the Fedora held to a calm face, a bored sovereign hearing yet another a plea for favor form a supplicant peasant. That was interesting, and considering all the junk Kyle had had stashed in the loft, highly suggestive. Whatever was going on was important. Maybe this was the seed-money source. Tarrant shifted his focus to the hat-man.

Was he confident enough to hide in plain sight, or a gaudy front for the real entrepreneur? Conspicuously posing was not a healthy way to run a drug business. It could be meant to impress the natives. It seemed to work on Kyle.

They took their time. The music noise made talking difficult and evesdropping attempts impossible. Tarrant went back to interpreting body language.

The man had two guards, big and little. One for raw physical intimidation, the other for martial arts. They looked alert, and were smart enough not to hover too close. They noticed Tarrant. A couple of predators recognizing one of their own. He didn't want to be mistaken for a cop or a rival supplier; he finished his watery Coke and moved on. No one followed.

Tarrant found the other dance area. He sat at a table with a view of the front door, pulled out a pen, and wrote some lines on a cocktail napkin. They didn't serve Guinness here, so he settled for an overpriced Shiner and sat back to wait.

About an hour later Kyle and Amanda walked past. He looked nervously smug; she looked half asleep and staggered against him every other step. Tarrant gave them a five-minute start, then rolled a twenty around his note and went up to one of the door bouncers.

"Hey, bud, you know that old guy who sits in the back by the upstairs balcony? The one with the red hat?"

The bouncer only shrugged. "I see 'em, I don't know 'em."

*I just bet you don't.* Tarrant held up the bill and the note. "Do me a favor and see that he gets this. I got a fire to put out or I'd go myself."

"Must be some fire." But he took the money. He'd probably read the note, but there was nothing on it that would mean anything to him.

Tarrant escaped from the noise and smoke. Kyle and Amanda were well ahead of him, but walking slow. Amanda was in a giggling, playful mood, bumping her hip against Kyle and pretending to trip so he had to catch her. He visibly snarled, not in the mood. Tarrant went one block over to the next street, going at a brisk walk until he was way in the lead, then cutting back again.

His car was unscathed where he'd left it, but alone. Most of the fun seekers had had their fill and departed, freeing up parking spaces. He drove back toward the loft and found a spot close in. Before getting out, he slipped a semi-auto from its concealed bracket under the dash into one of his pockets, hoping he wouldn't need it. He left the doors unlocked, but that was okay as he'd be within sight.

Going behind the loft building he went up metal stairs to a fire exit that served as the Deacon's back door. He picked the lock and left the door ajar. Just in case.

Back on the street, Tarrant located an alcove between buildings and melded into its shadow. From here he commanded a view of the loft and the parking lot next to it.

Things were much quieter now. The bars would be closing soon, their patrons either going home or seeking an after-hours club to round off the rest of the night. Only one patrol car crept past. As soon as it was gone a tan Cadillac rolled up not thirty feet away and parked, dousing its lights. His mouth tightened when the smaller of the bodyguards emerged and went up to the loft, entering without trouble. He returned soon after, walking fast, limbs stiff with anger. It looked like Tarrant's note, helpfully suggesting that Kyle Deacon's inventory had gone missing, had been taken seriously.

What the fancy-pants boss's reaction was remained a mystery, but Tarrant felt the satisfaction that comes from having made the right call. The larger guy came out of the car next. Both bruisers stood ready by the loft building, waiting. Anyone within fifty yards could see they were loaded for bear; Tarrant was considerably closer.

Neither of the Deacons noticed any of the gathered company until it was too late. Big grabbed Kyle; Little grabbed Amanda. The men knew their job, making sure it was done with a minimum of noise and movement. It helped that their victims were too flatfooted with surprise to make a fuss. Kyle knew better than to try and Amanda was still stoned.

Both were dragged toward the car, and the front passenger window slid down. Tarrant got a glimpse of a red Fedora. Kyle shook his head a lot, firmly denying whatever he heard from within. He gestured toward the loft, being insistent.

This was the tricky part, waiting for what Fedora would do next. Take both kids in the car and drive off or settle things here and now? Tarrant's hand drifted toward his pistol.

The bruisers took the couple toward the loft. Tarrant faded from his shadow and sprinted across behind the building. He was up the fire escape and through back door lock while the unsteady foursome negotiated the stairs. Pulling on his surgeon's gloves, he doused lights, scanning for a decent weapon. He lucked out by finding a nearly full bottle of vodka. It pleased him that it was a brand he hated.

Tarrant was in time to get behind the front door just as it swung inward for Little and Amanda. She was whining and cursing and crying all at once, demanding to know what was going on, trying to shake off Little's grip.

Kyle was shoved in so hard he skidded and tripped. He didn't have time to curse as he fell. Neither did Big once he was past the door. Tarrant smashed the heavy bottle in just the right spot on the temple. The man may have been of a size, but damn few were tough enough to ignore that kind of greeting. He went sprawling with a grunt.

Before Little could react, Tarrant gave him a double punch in the back under the ribcage, one for each kidney. He also ceased to be an immediate problem.

Amanda was just beginning to realize there was another player in the game. She got a clout in the jaw, just enough to ring her bells, but not so hard that Tarrant couldn't use his hand. She dropped. He pulled a small bottle and a fist-sized wad of cotton from another pocket. In moments she was out completely, chloroformed into dreamland. She might be sick later, but better that than dead. Tarrant hoisted her over one shoulder and left by the back door.

With her belted into his car's passenger seat, he shifted into reverse and backed down the empty block, then cut a U-turn. He headed south until reaching I-30, then north on I-35 until he found a suitable cheap chain motel. There he checked in using his false ID and paying ahead in cash. The night clerk noted down his car tag numbers anyway, but those were false as well.

Tarrant carried Amanda into their allotted room, easing her down on the bed. She looked better unconscious, and cleaning off all the white makeup would have made her pretty, but that wasn't in his job description. She'd been removed from the line of fire for the time being, and that's what mattered. He took off her shoes, tucked her still-dressed under the covers, and adjusted the room's air unit to circulate in some fresh from outside.

He block-printed a note to her on motel paper.

*Don't go back to the loft. If you want help, just call.*

He then wrote out a pager number that damn few people ever saw. He made sure she had enough cab fare in her purse, dropped the room key on the nightstand, and left.

Tarrant returned to Deep Ellum, but there was no sign of Kyle, the bruisers, or the Cadillac. The loft door was wide open, the interior even more of a wreck than before, which he'd thought impossible. He departed, not touching anything.

He felt a little gut-sick on the long drive back to his condo, but it was a only a reaction to the lengthy adrenaline high. It was good to have cleared the job away in such short order, but Kyle had been of great help there; he'd done everything but paint a target on his chest.

For the luckless Kyle Tarrant had no pity. Some people were fish and others were sharks; that's just the way it was in the big food chain. Bad luck when you're born a minnow and don't know it.

Every job was different, he had told Caitlin. Especially so for this one. For once he'd completed a hit and not had to pull the trigger himself. It made a nice change. They should all be so easy.

But that would take the fun out of the game.

Challenge versus achievement.

He knew what he liked best.

# THE LIBRARIAN

## Simon Brett

THE FACT THAT the astrologer hadn't seen his own death coming cast doubt on the credibility of his whole career. But then Lionel Cooper had never been much of an astrologer, anyway. Nor had he been one for very long.

Don Gordon had always had a shrewd eye for economy and, when he took over as Editor of the *Daily Views*, he'd instantly decided that astrological prediction was an area where he could save money. So he'd sacked the high-profile television celebrity who had long and expensively run the column, replacing the man's photograph with a cartoon of a benign old wise woman called "Miss Tick," whose anonymity he knew would come a lot cheaper. The new Editor then offered the job to former Newsroom Supervisor Lionel Cooper for some pin money in his premature retirement.

Don Gordon had no belief in astrology. All he knew was that people did read their stars in newspapers, and his only prediction for the future was that people would continue to read their stars in newspapers. So the Signs of the Zodiac column was an ingredient he was determined not to lose from the *Daily Views*. Miss Tick's predictions, he decreed, must appear every week Monday through Saturday, though in their actual content he had no interest at all.

The only briefing he had given Lionel Cooper when they agreed terms — or rather when the older man instantly accepted the terms he was offered — went as follows. "Keep it vague. Remember, some of your readers are looking at your column after a night of the best sex they've ever had; others are on their way to the funeral of a close relative. Some of them are young, some of them are old. Very few of them have ever had any luck in their lives, and even fewer of them are ever likely to. Basically, what they want from reading their stars in the *Daily Views* is a warm glow, and they will get that from one simple message, which is: 'Things have been tough for you recently, but they're about to get better.' Your job is to find out how many different ways you can write that."

And it was exactly the same briefing he gave to Mary O'Connor, when he called her in to ask if she'd consider taking over the mantle of Miss Tick.

Mary was now in her late thirties. There were a few glints of grey in the dark brown hair, and her face had thinned down to emphasise the beakiness of her nose. But she was still an attractive woman, Don Gordon couldn't help noticing with some disquiet, as he spelled out his proposal.

There was a kind of history between them. They'd started at the *Daily Views* on the same day, both keen reporters who'd served their time on provincial dailies. Both had specialised in crime, and both had been determined to make their mark in the national press.

There, however, the similarities between them had ended. Don Gordon had been educated through school and university and started his working life in Manchester. He was good-looking in a beaten-up way, loud and tough. Sometimes brash, he hated—therefore never admitted to—being in the wrong. When he walked into a room, he made himself the focus of attention. His approach to journalism was equally confrontational. He was as tenacious as a Rottweiler, and he bullied the truth out of people. The method worked. His continuing scoops raised his profile high enough at the *Daily Views* for him to be appointed Editor in his early thirties.

There couldn't have been more contrast in Mary O'Connor's journalistic approach. A product of the Home Counties, educated at a genteel ladies' college and Cambridge, she could extract information from people so subtly they didn't even know they'd given it away. She was a great believer in homework; she would research exhaustively before ever approaching a witness. Whereas Don Gordon would act on an impulse which was very often right, Mary O'Connor would not act at all until she was absolutely certain she was right.

Her method was no less effective than his. Indeed, for the time both of them were working as the *Daily Views'* star crime reporters, Mary's strike-rate was marginally the better.

Though her quiet, studious manner might give the impression she had no sense of humour, that was entirely misleading. Her wit was as subtle as other aspects of her character, though it could, if required, become cutting. In a pub at the end of their first frenetic week at the *Daily Views*, Don had come on to her with the crass line, "I'm a Sagittarian, you know, just wondering where to aim my next arrow . . . what sign are you?"

And Mary had replied, "I'm a Libran. I suppose if a Sagittarian and a Libran had children, they'd be Librarians, wouldn't they?"

Don didn't like being outsmarted by anyone, least of all a woman, so her response had put him off. On that occasion. But not for good.

Given the subject matter of their current discussion—her taking over the Miss Tick column—Mary wondered whether Don might also be recalling that early exchange. Seeing him in the splendour of his office, dominating London from the top of Canary Wharf, she doubted that he was. Don had aged considerably in the three years since they'd last met. He had thickened, particularly round the neck, his hair was receding, and his face bore record to every deadline crisis, cigarette and bottle of whisky it had undergone. But, as usual, Mary O'Connor thought ruefully, a man can get away with it.

She tried to remember, from what she'd read in the tabloids, his current marital status. There had been a lot of high-profile liaisons in the early days after she'd left full-time work; and then an even-higher profile wedding to one of Britain's new crop of film actresses. Maybe that was still ongoing. Mary hadn't seen anything in the Press to the contrary, but she somehow doubted the relationship's long-term survival. Don Gordon, as she knew well, could be totally obsessive about a woman in short bursts, but his stamina was suspect. And, as with so many journalists, for him no woman's seductive power could match up to that of a good news story.

I don't envy any woman who ends up with Don Gordon. But, even as Mary O'Connor had the thought, she recognized that it wasn't one hundred per cent true.

The reason for the divergence of their career paths had not been the ending of their affair, though the timing had brought the advantage that they didn't have to be constantly in each other's company at such a sensitive juncture. What had taken Mary out of front-line journalism had been the onset of cancer in her father, George O'Connor. Her mother long dead, when the crisis arose Mary did not have a moment's hesitation about what she should do.

She wasn't motivated solely by duty. She had always adored her father and wanted to spend as much of the remaining time with him as possible. George O'Connor had been a moderately successful humorous columnist for a variety of publications, and it was to him that Mary owed her passion for journalism. Also her passion for the English language. As a humorist, George O'Connor had loved the potential and flexibility of words. He loved anagrammatising them, playing with their range of meanings, breaking them down into their components. One of his favourite quotations came from the Clown in Shakespeare's *Twelfth Night*:

"A sentence is but a cheveril glove to a good wit: how quickly the wrong side may be turned outward."

His daughter couldn't remember the first of the many times he'd explained to her, " 'Cheveril' is a kind of leather from a goat, Mary, so it's a kid glove he's talking about, a kid glove."

A crossword addict, George O'Connor had spent his last years, as the cancer whittled away at his body and his mind seemed to be sharpened by suffering, in solving puzzles of ever more fiendish complexity.

Of the time Mary had shared with him over these word-games, she could not regret a single minute. During his last days in hospital, when George O'Connor could not even see the grid, she had spoken out the clues of *The Times* crossword to him, and, drifting in and out of consciousness, he had still managed to produce some answers. One clue in particular she remembered from that painful time. "Almost silent part." And it had been one of those annoying four-letter ones which she knew to be simple, but whose solution just wouldn't come. Blank — U — blank — T she'd got, and she'd agonised over it for hours, trying to fill her mind with anything other than the inevitability of her loss.

And then her father, in a moment of coherence, had smiled, and hoarsely murmured, "Never forget 'Q'. When you've got an unattached 'U'. It's 'QUIT', Mary, 'QUIT'."

Those had been the last clear words he had said to her.

When Mary O'Connor had announced the decision to put her career on hold, the *Daily Views'* former Editor had tried strenuously to make her change her mind. She was good, he said, really good. She was just at the point when her career was about to take off. It'd be madness to stop now.

But she had remained adamant, and grudgingly he'd had to accept her resignation. Because he liked her, and because he wanted to stay in touch at some level, he'd offered her a part-time job, way below her capabilities. The *Daily Views'* Librarian, the woman who managed the paper's archives two days a week, was retiring. Would Mary consider taking over the job?

She'd agreed, partly because the money would help, but also because advances in computerisation made it possible for her to do more and more of the job from home, without disruption to her father's dwindling life. So she maintained a connection with the *Daily Views*, without being in the Canary Wharf office on a daily basis. And the constant hazard of running into Don Gordon was not added to her sufferings.

When his secretary Judy did finally call her, after three and a half years, Mary felt strong enough to cope without overt embarrassment. George O'Connor had finally died some six weeks before and, though she missed her father like mad, the long period during which they had faced the inevitable together had left her strengthened and grateful for his life. Because she was also at the stage of thinking what to do next with her own, the timing of Don Gordon's offer for her to take over the Miss Tick role was apposite. Mary O'Connor had no long-term ambitions to be an astrologer, but at that moment the job felt right.

So when she went to see Don, she agreed to his proposal, saying she would fill in for three months, and then assess how they both felt about the arrangement. He told her the terms he was offering were exactly the same as those agreed with her predecessor, not generous, but adequate as a stopgap until the *Daily Views'* Librarian decided what she really wanted to do with her life.

"I suppose I'd better look through Lionel Cooper's files," said Mary, as she rose to leave. "Where was his office?"

"He worked from home," replied Don, rising to see her out. "Hardly ever left the house, I gather. Certainly very rarely came in here. Had fixed a meeting with me for last Thursday, but . . ." He shrugged. 'That wasn't to be. He was dead by then. Judy's got his address and things. I think Lionel's wife's back now, so you can call her."

"Back?"

"She was apparently in Majorca when he died."

"And how did he die?"

Don Gordon's craggy face broke into a smile of surprise and amusement. "Oh, didn't you know? He was murdered."

"What?"

"Looked like a burglary that went wrong, apparently. There'd been a break-in and a lot of stuff was missing. Lionel Cooper was found in his dressing gown, stabbed through the heart."

"Poor man."

"Yes." Don Gordon let out a burst of the abrasive laughter Mary remembered so well. "And his stars had said he was going to have a good day!"

The house was surprisingly lavish for an ex-journalist. Large, three-storey, off West End Lane in Hampstead. Lionel Cooper's wife must have money, Mary thought as she rang the doorbell.

But Dilys Cooper quickly disabused her of that idea. "Going to sell this place soon as possible," she announced almost before her guest was through the door. "Worth a few bob. Nice to have a bit of dosh when you've never had none."

Lionel Cooper's widow was brash, almost what Mary's genteel mother would have called "common." She was probably early sixties, like her late husband, but no expense had been spared to make her look younger. She wore a purple trouser suit, over-fussy with gold detail. Heavy gold jewellery clunked against her Majorcan tan.

With the minimum of civility and no offer of refreshment, Mary
O'Connor was gestured to a garishly-printed armchair. The widow
was unbothered by social niceties.

And she made no attempt to pretend that her husband's death was
anything other than a merciful relief. "I wanted to buy an apartment
in Majorca when we got this place, but Lionel was against the idea."
She beamed with satisfaction. "Still, now he's dead, I can live exactly
where I want to live. Saw some lovely properties round Pollença, you
know. My sort of people out in Majorca—and this country's so dismal
nowadays. No, Lionel's death couldn't have come at a better time, as
far as I was concerned."

So overt was the satisfaction that Mary immediately ruled out the
possibility of Dilys Cooper having had anything to do with her
husband's murder. Unless she was presenting some kind of double
bluff . . . But the woman didn't appear bright enough to manage even
a single bluff.

"I'm sorry to trouble you, Mrs. Cooper, at such a painful time . . ."
The woman shrugged; if Mary wanted to call it painful, that was up
to her. "But I'm going to be taking over the Miss Tick stars column . . ."

"Lucky you."

"I'm sorry?"

Dilys Cooper gestured around her lavish, if tasteless, sitting room.
"What do you think bought all this?"

Mary decided to delay the obvious follow-up question till later. "I
gather your late husband used to do most of the work for the column
here . . ."

"That's right. He hardly ever left the house. Unlike me, Lionel had
no wanderlust—or any other kind of lust, come to that."

"Ah. Well, I was just wondering if I could go through the files on
his computer to check—"

The widow let out a harsh laugh. "No, I'm afraid you couldn't.
That was one of the things that was stolen."

"Oh?"

"By the guy who broke in. The guy who murdered my husband,"
she added without sentiment. "He went off with virtually all Lionel's
office equipment-computer, fax, photocopier . . ."

Mary O'Connor looked at the large state-of-the-art television and video in the sitting room. "But he left these?"

"Police's theory is that he started his thieving in the office, because he broke in through the window there . . . got up over the roof of the kitchen extension . . . Then it was while he was getting the office equipment together that Lionel must've heard him and gone into the room. The guy panicked and lashed out with his knife."

The explanation struck a wrong note for Mary. After panicking and committing murder, would the average burglar then calmly pack up a collection of heavy office equipment and take it out to the vehicle he must have parked in readiness? And, if he was cool enough to do that, why wouldn't he have come back into the house to remove the television and other valuables?

But she kept her doubts to herself. "So, Mrs. Cooper, none of your husband's records were left—hard copy printouts, floppies, CDs . . . ?"

Another shrug. The widow seemed to find everything about her late husband infinitely tedious, and Mary O'Connor got the feeling that had been the case even before he became "late." "I don't know what went. The office looked like a bomb had hit it, I do know that. Lionel's work was his work; I didn't interfere."

Or show any interest, so long as the money kept coming in.

"When we speak of your husband's computer, are we talking about a desktop or a laptop?"

"Both. He'd had this one on his desk for a couple of years, then just bought this new laptop with all the latest bells and whistles."

"And both machines were stolen?"

Dilys Cooper nodded, then looked at her watch, suggesting it was about time that Mary's wasted journey ended.

The Librarian rose ruefully from her seat, but a thought stopped her. "You say he'd bought a *new* laptop . . . ?"

"Yes."

"Does that imply that he had one before, that he simply upgraded to the latest model?"

Dilys Cooper nodded curtly. Her minimal supply of interest in the subject had been long exhausted.

"Did he trade in the old one?"

"No. No, he didn't want to do that. I told him he was daft, because it must be worth something." Mary saw a shadow in the woman's face of an earlier, less affluent Dilys Cooper, constantly worrying about making ends meet. "But Lionel said he'd keep the old laptop as a backup."

"So," asked Mary, as if it didn't matter, "did that get stolen too?"

"I haven't looked. Lionel kept it in the cupboard under the stairs."

Which seems an odd place, thought Mary, when all the rest of your work equipment's kept in your office.

Sure enough, the old laptop was still in the cupboard under the stairs. Probably bought only a couple of years before, but swift advances in technology already made it look dated.

Dilys Cooper was grudging, but eventually agreed to let Mary take the machine away. Only for twenty-four hours, though. The penny-pinching side of the widow's character still reckoned she could get something for it.

Aware of the woman's urgency to get rid of her, Mary O'Connor lingered on the doorstep for one last question. "Mrs. Cooper, I hope you don't mind my asking, but the Editor of the *Daily Views* has offered me financial terms for taking over the Miss Tick column which, while adequate, would certainly not enable me to . . ." She gestured to the large house " . . . live in this kind of style."

Mary commanded attention now. Money would always be interesting to Dilys Cooper.

"So I was just wondering if the Editor was pulling a fast one on me . . . ?"

"No," said the widow. "Lionel's basic fee for the column in the *Daily Views* wasn't a lot. But he spent a lot of time on the websites. That's where the money came from."

"Astrological websites?"

"I assume so. As I said, Lionel got on with his work and I didn't interfere. All I know is . . ." Dilys Cooper beamed with renewed satisfaction " . . . whatever he did it brought in a lot of dosh."

Judy, Don Gordon's secretary, put the Librarian's call through with encouraging ease.

"No," he said. "I know I'm a tight bastard, but I wouldn't do that to you, Mary. The money I offered's exactly the same as I was paying Lionel Cooper."

"But do I also get the rights to clean up on the Miss Tick website?"

"What?"

"It seems there's a lot of money in these astrological websites."

"Mary, there is no Miss Tick website. Or if there is, it has no authorisation from the *Daily Views*. I made a policy decision on this. I don't mind meaningless predictions by a non-existent crone going out in a paper that people have already paid for, but I'm not going to rip them off on the Internet."

Not for the first time, Mary was struck by the quirkiness of Don Gordon's ethical standards. But she never failed to be impressed by the passion with which he stood by them.

"So, if Lionel Cooper was running a Miss Tick website," she asked, "it was without your permission?"

"Certainly. But he wasn't. If he had tried that on, there's no way I wouldn't have heard about it, and I'd have had my lawyers down on him like lava from a volcano. Take my word for it, Mary—Lionel Cooper was not running an astrological website that had anything to do with the *Daily Views*."

Remembering how deeply Don hated appearing to be in the wrong—and how satisfying it could be to prove him so—when she got back to her flat Mary O'Connor went straight to her computer and got online.

To her annoyance, Don Gordon was proved right. She couldn't find any site featuring the name "Miss Tick." Nor did many frustrating—and occasionally mind-boggling—hours of accessing astrological websites reveal any which had any connection with the *Daily Views*.

Mary O'Connor sat back in her chair, her back tight from relentless mouse-clicking, and rubbed her long nose reflectively.

Because there was one big question her abortive research had raised. If Lionel Cooper hadn't been profiting from an astrological website, as his widow seemed to assume, then where had his money come from?

Mary O'Connor went into the *Daily Views* archives to find and print out the Miss Tick predictions for the last full week before her predecessor's death. They looked pretty bland and meaningless, but no doubt, following Don Gordon's instructions, they had given a warm early-morning glow to many readers with their simple, recurrent message: 'Things have been tough for you recently, but they're about to get better.'

Mary started to read, with ever-decreasing respect for Lionel Cooper's prose style. Because it was her own birth sign, first she followed through the predictions for Libra.

MONDAY: *Check out long overdue social shortcomings until Saturn's powerful aspect to your sign on Thursday makes you realize it was worth taking the trouble to contact long-lost friends.*

TUESDAY: *A powerful, really exciting surprise turns into great entertainment for you. You've been a bit down in the dumps recently, but today's events are just the pick-me-up you need.*

WEDNESDAY: *You will be altogether really nice and completely lovely everywhere today. Negative thoughts and all the niggling worries of the last few weeks can be put behind you.*

THURSDAY: *Today will bring whatever in life Dame Fortune is ready eventually to grant you. You are welcome everywhere and friends will appreciate your consideration and kindness.*

FRIDAY: *Lucky you, because your sign has opened even happier aspects round now. Something that happens today will restore your confidence that the future's looking really bright.*

SATURDAY — YOUR STARS FOR THE WEEKEND: *Today's benign aspect of the planets indicates treasures that are now coming early, long-lasting periods of health, happiness and prosperity. So really let your hair down and have a good time.*

*And for tomorrow too your fortune can only create knockout times and inspirational luck, which you very richly deserve. Enjoy, this is a very special time in your life.*

After she'd done Libra, Mary O'Connor subjected the other Signs of the Zodiac to the same meticulous scrutiny.

At the end of her reading, her only certainty was that, when she became Miss Tick, the old woman's predictions would at least be in better English.

* * *

Next she turned her attention to Lionel Cooper's laptop. The batteries had run down, but there was a mains lead in the carrying bag, so she soon had the machine up and running. He'd only created two directories for his personal documents; they were named "Text" and "Pix."

There was no password to access the files. Presumably, given his wife's lack of interest in any part of him except for his money, and the fact that he hardly ever left the house, Lionel Cooper had not felt any need for passwords.

Which, given the content of the first file Mary O'Connor opened in the "Pix" directory, was surprising.

Dilys Cooper had described her husband as lacking wanderlust— "or any other kind of lust, come to that." But she had been wrong.

In her crime-reporting days Mary O'Connor had seen a great deal of child pornography. But it never failed to prompt in her a visceral stab of disgust.

She didn't have to open many more to reach the conclusion that all of the "Pix" files were similar in content. So she turned her attention to the 'Text' directory.

The contents here were less obviously explained. Some files were clearly outlines or drafts of daily predictions for the Miss Tick column. But some seemed to be just random lists of words.

Mary puzzled over them for a long time, before finally coming to the conclusion that she wasn't getting anywhere.

But what about Lionel Cooper's use of the Internet? Given his lax attitude to security, there was a chance that he might have saved his connection password and she'd be able to get online.

Her surmise proved correct. He'd used Internet Explorer and through that she quickly got on to the MSN homepage. There was no chance of her accessing Lionel Cooper's Hotmail account without a password, but she could check out his most-frequently-used websites. That might tell her something. She clicked on the "Favourites" icon.

Some of the choices were predictable enough for someone who'd once worked in a newsroom . . . websites of various daily papers, the BBC, and so on. But the name of the favourite at the top of the list meant nothing to Mary O'Connor. It wasn't even a proper word, just a jumble of letters. She focused her crossword brain in search of an anagram, but came up with nothing.

When she tried to access the website, she was shut out by the demand for a password. The cursor in the dialog box blinked frustratingly at her. She didn't even know whether four letters were required, or six, or eight. But she did have an idea of her chance of coming up with the right combination by trial or error, and that figure was in many millions.

Mary O'Connor left the laptop and made herself a cup of tea. Then she sat down in what had once been her father's favourite armchair, where he had so often and so quickly completed *The Times* crossword, and she once again scrutinized the printout she'd made of Miss Tick's predictions.

There were various striking anomalies, both of phrasing and syntax. There was also some basic bad writing. Surely, thought Mary, nobody could rise to the status of Newsroom Supervisor on a national daily without having a better grasp of the English language. (But, even as she had the thought, she realised that they could—indeed, she could summon up a distressingly large number of examples of those who had.)

Methodical as ever, and remembering the painstaking detail in which George O'Connor had approached complex puzzles, she started to make a list of the moments of clumsiness in Miss Tick's predictions.

After only an hour, one thing was clear. The errors clustered in her own sign. In the horoscopes for the others, the Taureans, the Pisceans and so on, there were occasional verbal infelicities, but generally their messages of hope were much better written. There was a very definite pattern to this.

So Mary O'Connor copied the Libran predictions in a separate file and printed them out. She made some more tea, realizing it was after midnight and that she hadn't eaten since breakfast, but she still went straight back to her scrutiny of Lionel Cooper's words.

She knew the answer must be there. Her father would have worked it out in no time. She redoubled her concentration, feeling reconnected in friendly competition with the late George O'Connor.

As he would have done, she started again with the Libran stars for the Monday.

*Check out long overdue social shortcomings until Saturn's powerful aspect to your sign on Thursday makes you realise it was worth taking the trouble to contact long-lost friends.*

The first inconsistency she noticed was one of punctuation. Why should someone who wrote "long-lost" with a hyphen deny the same honour to "long overdue?" And in the column for Saturday 'long-lasting' was also hyphenated.

It was odd, but it wasn't proof of anything. Mary O'Connor had worked long enough in newspapers to know all about the fallibility of copy-editors.

Then she examined the actual choice of words. Whichever way she read the text, there was one that stuck out like a sore thumb. "Short-comings." Getting in touch with long-lost friends might be regarded as social "obligations," "duties," "commitments" perhaps. But surely in that context "shortcomings" was the wrong word.

If it was the wrong word, then why had Lionel Cooper used it? Though not the greatest prose stylist in history, he wasn't illiterate.

"Never forget 'Q.' " That piece of advice from George O'Connor wouldn't be a lot of use in the current situation. Nor would cheveril gloves have much relevance. But, his daughter realised with mounting excitement, another of her father's sayings did fit the bill.

"In a good puzzle nothing is wrong without a reason."

She looked again at the Monday prediction for Libra and she saw the reason.

Very calm now she had cracked the problem, Mary O'Connor went meticulously through the other days of the week, once again homing in on unusual word choices. At first her new-found logic seemed not to work, but she didn't panic. Carefully, she thought through the problem and managed to work out its variations. George O'Connor would have been proud of her.

When she had finished all seven predictions, she returned to Lionel Cooper's laptop and opened files in the "Text" directory, which confirmed that she was on the right track. Then she went online, tested her theory and found it worked.

It was after four o'clock when she completed her task. Before falling into bed, she left a message on Don Gordon's voice-mail, saying it was very important that they should have a meeting at the *Daily Views* that morning.

"Look," said Mary O'Connor, pointing at the printouts spread over the Editor's desk. "It's the first letter of each of the first eight words. So, from '*Check out long overdue social shortcomings until Saturn's,*' we get 'COLOSSUS.'"

"But that doesn't work for Tuesday." As ever, Don was trying to get ahead of her. "From 'A *powerful, really exciting surprise turns into great entertainment for you today*' we get 'après,' which I suppose would be fine if it was followed by ski. But it isn't. It's followed by 'tig,' and 'après-tig' is not a word that I'm familiar with. So I'm afraid, Mary, your theory falls at the first hurdle. Just coincidence that those letters worked."

Patiently, she shook her head and wiped the smug smile off his face. "It's because it's Tuesday."

"I'm sorry?"

"Tuesday is the second day of the week, so you start on the second letter. Forget the 'A' and '*powerful, really exciting surprise turns into great entertainment*' gives us . . . ?"

"'PRESTIGE!'"

"Exactly. So we start Wednesday on word three, and '*be altogether really nice and completely lovely everywhere*' gives us 'BARNACLE.' Word four on Thursday—'*whatever in life Dame Fortune is ready eventually*' . . . ?"

"'WILDLIFE!'"

"Very good, Don. You're catching on."

He grabbed the printout from her. "Then Thursday it's word five to start. So . . . '*sign has opened even happier aspects round now*' produces . . . 'SHOEHORN!'"

"Then the double whammy at the weekend . . . Word six for Saturday's, so from '*planets indicates treasures that are now coming early*'—whatever that may mean—we get 'PITTANCE.' Then, starting on word seven for Sunday . . . '*can only create knockout times and inspirational luck*' . . . ?"

" 'COCKTAIL!' " Don Gordon announced, and then sank triumphantly down into his chair. There was a sparkle in his eyes that Mary O'Connor hadn't seen for a long time, and she knew there was a matching sparkle in hers.

"So," he said, "what is this? Some kind of quiz game?"

The mood changed. "No," Mary replied. "I'm afraid it's rather more serious than that. May I use your computer?"

"Be my guest."

She went online, searched for the website whose address she had noted down only a few hours earlier, and was once again denied access for lack of a password. She consulted another printout she'd made from Lionel Cooper's laptop, and found the sequence of eight-letter words, "COLOSSUS, PRESTIGE, BARNACLE, WILDLIFE, SHOEHORN, PITTANCE, COCKTAIL."

Counting down the days since that Sunday, she found the word "JUGOSLAV."

She keyed it into the dialog box.

The website was accessed. There was a sharp intake of breath from Don Gordon. "God," he said. "I hate the bastards who do that! I'd like to nail them and get them sent down for a long, long time!"

"You can," said Mary O'Connor.

The police were delighted with the information. They had been trying for some time to track down the paedophile ring to which Lionel Cooper had belonged, but they could never get enough evidence, and never discovered how the daily passwords were disseminated amongst the members.

Mary O'Connor's research gave them just the lead they needed. Now they could access the site at will, they quickly built up a list of participants, who were rounded up in a series of dawn raids. Frightened, inadequate men, the members had been quick to betray each other, and Lionel Cooper's murderer was soon shopped.

The former Miss Tick had been getting greedy, asking for more money, and that threatened the security of the whole network. Previously very little contact with Lionel Cooper had been required. When the deal was struck, he'd been issued with five years' worth of passwords. Payments were made anonymously into his bank.

But recently he'd threatened to blow the whole thing open if he wasn't paid more. He threatened to spill all to the *Daily Views*, and even made an appointment to see the Editor.

Anyone not in a state of panic would have realised Lionel Cooper was having them on. Spilling the beans would not only put an end to his current nice little earner, it was also likely to implicate him in criminal proceedings. He must have been using the threat as a bargaining counter. He was bluffing.

But it was a bluff that cost him his life.

The success of Mary O'Connor's investigation was not an unmixed blessing to Don Gordon. While the identification of the paedophile ring had undoubtedly been a scoop for the *Daily Views*, the coverage could not hide the way in which its own pages had been unwittingly used to help the gang.

Nor could the fact be hidden that Don Gordon had . . . to put it at the mildest . . . a somewhat cavalier attitude to his paper's astrological column.

The Editor was left with no alternative but to publish an apology. And, if there was one thing Don Gordon hated more than anything else, it was admitting that he was in the wrong.

Miss Tick had to go, of course, and her place was taken by an expensive astrologer with respectable credentials — "if that's not a contradiction in terms," as the Editor had said rather balefully when appointing him.

Since her new job had proved to be a non-starter, and since she had once again proved her skills in that area, Mary O'Connor became the chief crime correspondent of the *Daily Views*. In this role, she was extremely successful for two and a half years, at which point she left on maternity leave.

The Libran had married her Sagittarian, you see, and gone off to produce what turned out to be the first of three bonny, bouncing Librarians.

# GHOSTS

## Kristine Kathryn Rusch

IT GOES LIKE this:

Fifteen layers between him and the client. His people mostly, from the front that gets the order to the hacker who checks it out. Not everyone who wants to hire a hitman should be to find him. That's why there's redundancy upon redundancy—for every hacker, there's another who double-and triple-checks. After all, he's not going to risk his life, his freedom, on the word of some nobody with a computer, a nobody he's never met.

The order comes through the system—or systems if he wants to be more accurate—and if all the information matches, he considers the job. The timetable is necessarily flexible: anyone who wants a quickie goes somewhere else. Quickies get a man in trouble. Check the evening news. Any time a pro gets caught, it's someone who specializes in quickies. Sure, they get top dollar, but they also take maximum risk.

He tries to eliminate risk. He's Aries with Virgo Rising, Moon in Libra. Born for his job, at least according to his chart. Perceived as detail-oriented, almost fussy, a painstaking perfectionist, he is at heart a warrior, brave, impetuous and independent. His true self, his emotional self, is a judge, coldly calculating, always striving for balance.

He has a superstitious side as well, and isn't sure where it comes from. In the past, he tried to bury it, but he finally gave in ten years ago and his business improved.

That was when he discovered Glenna. She had a New Age

bookstore in Sedona, Arizona, and an uncanny knack of seeing his future. The first time he entered her store, intrigued by a book in the window, she'd said from her table in the back, "Should I be afraid for myself, old friend?"

The question had both startled and intrigued him, and when he answered no, she smiled and said, "My chart was uncertain. It told me that today would introduce me to Death."

He hadn't heard of a chart, knew nothing about astrology except for the goofy write-ups in the newspapers, write-ups which never seemed to be about him. But she had encouraged him to have his chart done and after careful consideration, he'd given her his birth-date, time, and location. She promised to have a reading for him in three days.

It was that reading which changed his life, and added one more layer between him and a job.

Now he compares his client's chart, the chart of his intended victim, and his own chart, searching for the optimum day, the appropriate venue, and of course, any hint of failure. If he's not compatible with a client, he passes the work to someone else. If his read of the victim's chart makes the victim seem personally powerful, dominant over him, or just plain lucky, he passes on that job as well.

He has learned, through trial and error, that he is not right for every job, nor is every job right for him. His perfectionism serves him well, and protects him from his impetuous nature.

He has achieved balance which, for him, makes everything right with the world.

The balance starts to crumble on the fourth of May. He is in Los Angeles, using the name Carlisle because it intrigues him. He uses it as a first name because he has learned that people cannot remember an unusual first name. They remember what it sounds like—"I think it was Carl." "No, honey. He called himself Lyle."—not what it is. By the time the police are talking to them, he's long gone, vanished like smoke in a strong wind.

He has his network of astrologers, mostly because he believes in back-ups, but he never has the network handle all three things—the client's chart, his chart, and the victim's chart. Only Glenna gets all three. She is his double-check, partly because she is so very accurate, and partly because he trusts her as much as he can trust anyone.

She has never worried about who he is or what he does. When she realized what he did for a living, she did not call the police as some would have nor did she suddenly fear him. Her manner toward him did not seem to change.

The afternoon he came for his reading, she greeted him with a smile. "My chart had been right," she said. "I did meet Death yesterday, just not in the way I thought."

It had been his first lesson about horoscopes and charts. When they were done by a true professional, like Glenna, they were incredibly accurate, although, at times, useless. Sometimes the language was too cryptic, too given to misinterpretation.

He learned, through trial and error, to plan his jobs based solely on things he understood—good days, bad days, luck, and the possibility of a future.

The victim's charts were always the easiest to read. If they did not predict a major calamity within a year of the reading, then he did not take the job. He usually appeared in a person's chart as a defining event or a crisis or as Glenna would say, "A possible ending."

The first time she saw one of those in a victim's chart, she made him swear he would not tell the victim.

"I can't promise that," he had said. "But I can promise that I will not give that person false hope."

She had shaken her head at him, but had said nothing. That was when he had asked her why his work didn't bother her.

"I never said that." She folded her hands gravely over the victim's chart. "I vowed, when I went into this business, that I would not judge."

He did not tell her—indeed, he has never told her—that she made his work easier. He feels that is too much information. She probably knows it anyway, since she seems to know everything. But he does not want to take the risk of losing her. She is one of the few sure things in his life.

But he has never been long on trust, which is why he finds himself in a shop that smells of hairspray and plastic, just off Hollywood Boulevard, in the low-rent section of town. The shop has a giant hand in the window—the place is best known for its palm reader who is, in his opinion, a charlatan.

He comes for the astrologer, a pot-smoking eighteen-year-old who calls herself Elli May. She does a weekly or monthly chart for him whenever he comes to Los Angeles. The first time she saw his natal chart, she asked him if he was a cop or a private detective. She clearly lacked the life experience that Glenna had.

"I do work in enforcement," he had said, and left it at that. From that point on, Elli May never questioned him. She also stopped offering him joints.

Her charts are deceptively simple. She uses a computer program which her younger sister designed. She has not customized a chart for him because he hasn't asked her to. He wants to seem as normal as possible, given that he's a hit man visiting a teenage astrologer to find out the best date for his next job.

The shop's hairspray and plastic smell comes from the room deodorizer she uses to cover up the sickly sweet stench of pot. She hasn't yet learned the value of incense. The palm reader should know— she's old enough to be the girl's grandmother—but she doesn't seem to care. Or maybe she recognizes what the girl does not: that the only law he follows is the one he makes up himself.

"Hey ya," Elli May says when she sees him. She pops a stick of Juicy Fruit and chomps, mouth open. "Didn't think I'd see you today."

Instantly his guard is up. She knew she would see him today. They have an appointment.

"Why's that?" he asks, heading toward her tiny velvet covered table in the back.

Elli May shrugs. She's not a very good liar either. "I'm not really ready for you today, Mr. Carlson."

Here he's Carlson, on the street he's Carlisle. An easy mistake, he'll tell someone if they ever ask. The names sound alike and he's never bothered to correct her—no sense letting the girl know she's wrong.

He slips into the chair, stretching his long legs and resting his hands on his stomach, pretending at an ease he no longer feels. "I think you're ready. I think the chart shows something you don't want to mention."

She flushes a blotchy red. "I don't—"

"You may as well tell me," he says. "You gotta get used to telling clients good news as well as bad."

The palm reader harrumphs behind him, then gets up and grabs her purse. "Want some coffee or something?" she asks Elli May.

"No," Elli May says, her eyes big and pleading. He can read them, probably better than the palm reader can read palms: *Stay. Please stay. He's a scary man and I have bad news.*

"Be back soon," the palm reader says, and heads out. The door bangs behind her.

Elli May looks at him, and swallows, then coughs. He'd bet all the money in his wallet that she has just swallowed her gum.

"It can't be that bad, kid," he says, mostly because he wants out of here, but not without knowing what she knows. "Let's get it over with and you can get back to your smoke."

She squints at him, measuring him in an entirely different way. This is their last time together and she has just begun to understand that he knows it too.

As she slides around the table, she slips a hand in the pocket of her jeans and pulls out another piece of gum. She doesn't offer him any. She takes the stick from the foil, and shoves the gum in her mouth.

Then she sits down, pulls open a drawer, and his chart comes out. It looks like all the others—a wheel with meaningless notations in the outer rim, more symbols between the spokes, and numbers in the inner rim. The numbers are attached by lines that all seem to bunch up in one area. Glenna once told him that this part of his natal chart shows all his strengths. He supposes it also shows his weaknesses.

Elle May sets the chart in front of him.

"Doll," he says because he knows it'll annoy her, "you've already read my natal chart. I asked you for this week."

She wears rings on all of her fingers, including her thumbs, big cheap rings that hid her skin. She toys with one of them now, as if considering what to do next, then she reaches in the drawer and pulls out another chart.

Elli May calls this an action table, and in it are little boxes for inane things like "The Best Time to Take a Vacation" and "The Best Time to Obtain a Loan."

He slides his hand under the new sheet and grabs the natal chart. He sets it on top of the action table and taps it. "Look at all that focus on the Eighth House. What is that again?"

"Finances," she mutters.

"And secrets, mysteries, power, death, and transformation, right?" She nods.

"Don't fuck with me," he says in a very flat voice. "You give me what I asked for and I'll remember you're just a kid who's learning her job."

Her eyes widen. She folds those ringed hands together. "I, um, threw it away."

"I'm sure you did," he says. "But you remember it."

She bites her chapped lower lip. "Mr. Carlson, please, my aunt—" Apparently that was the palm reader "—she says not to tell everything. It's not smart."

"Usually it's not," he says. "But I'm not your average customer. Did you know that President Reagan, he had an astrologer?"

The girl swallows again, but as she does, she pushes the gum into her cheek where it becomes a bulging, unattractive lump. She's too young to remember Reagan. She was born during his second term. He's just a name from a dusty textbook to her.

"I'll bet that astrologer told him he was gonna get elected the first time. But you think the astrologer tells him that something cataclysmic is gonna happen on March 30, 1981? Probably not. Afraid, you know, that he'll get upset at the reading. So he don't know he's in any danger, any more than usual. That day, he gets out of his car, and wham! shot through the lung by a kid barely outta college. Lives, no thanks to his astrologer. And I'm sure that chart disappeared like nobody's business, and the astrologer says 'No one can anticipate such random events, Mr. President.'"

The girl's blotchy flush gets deeper. He knows he's got her. He had her with the word "cataclysmic," but he went on because she was young and needed to hear the point. Not for him. He's not coming here again—he doesn't like working this hard, not with one of his people—but maybe for someone else.

Occasionally, he can be altruistic, although it always surprises him. He thinks it may come from his Rising Sign. Virgos are known to be helpful at times.

She reaches into the drawer a third time, and pulls out a computer-generated sheet filled with squiggles and symbols he does not understand. The week's dates are running along the side, May 4–11. That's the only part he recognizes.

He hides his surprise; he was so convinced she had destroyed this that he almost doesn't believe it's before him.

"Okay," he says, leaning forward. "Explain it to me."

"It's called a termination event." Her voice is shaking. "But it doesn't necessarily mean you're going to die. It means that something significant in your life will end, change, terminate, you know."

"Significant how?" he asks. He knows these charts can pick out various aspects — relationships, home life, business. He needs specifics.

"It threads through everything," she says. "Work, relationships, finances. I've never seen anything like it."

Of course not. She's a baby. She's never seen anything like anything.

"It started this morning, or maybe even a couple of days ago. You didn't have me run that, so I don't know."

And wasn't bright enough to check. He's glad he's not one of the careless types, the kind who uses his power easily. He can just imagine pulling his gun from its shoulder holster beneath his suit jacket, ending this session with a bullet. But he won't, no matter how annoyed he is. He's more of a planner than that.

Besides, he has a hunch this isn't the kind of termination event she's talking about.

"It builds until the sixth, when everything comes to a head, and then, I don't know. The chart flips, and to be honest with you, sir, I haven't seen anything like this."

"Like what?"

"Nothing."

At first he thinks she's being evasive, then he realizes that she means literally nothing.

"How can that be?" he asks.

She shrugs. "I tried calling the guy who trained me, but he's at some retreat in Michigan until the 15th."

He sighs, slaps a fifty on the table, and takes all three charts, even though they're not worth that much.

"Anything else?" he asks as he stands.

"Yeah," she says, standing too, and pointing at the top sheet. "Right now, your energy is at odds with itself. A lot of things will be revealed, secrets will be uncovered. There's so much darkness here that it scares me."

"I suppose it would," he says.

"No." She straightens her shoulders, apparently thinking it makes her look stronger and taller. It actually makes her look scared. "You don't understand. All these things, they're very bad. I've never seen such a horrible chart. If I were you, I'd go to bed and not leave for a week."

"I suppose you would," he says.

Her lips narrow and anger flashes through her eyes. "I'm trying to warn you."

"Of what?" he asks, hoping this time she'll be specific.

"This week," she says, "you may lose everything."

He studies her for a moment. She seems so sincere, so worried about him, even though she doesn't really know him.

"It wouldn't be the first time," he says, and walks out the door.

The first time had been twenty years ago. He'd been working as a bouncer at a major New York nightclub, and he'd gotten friendly with the owner, a balding man who wore too much jewelry and liked a little too much blow. He supplied it to his friends, too, and used Ben, as he'd been known then, to deliver it.

Young Ben proved his honesty—he always returned the money, every dime of it, to the club's owner—and his street smarts. He'd thwarted more than one robbery attempt, and he'd beaten a handful of men much larger than himself to a bloody pulp.

After one incident, which Ben won but which left him with a broken rib, split knuckles and two black eyes, the owner gave him a gun and paid for time at a range so that he could learn how to use it.

Ben had an affinity for guns. Great aim, which improved with practice, an eye that seemed perfect even if the scope was off. He knew the damage a gun could do—saw it up close and personal one night—and vowed never to use one except in self-defense.

Of course, self-defense isn't always what the cops make it out to be.

Ben had been on a delivery when the owner's supplier went to the club and took it down. Ben may have been passing on the funds, but the owner hadn't been. The club burned with only employees inside, the result, the cops said, of free-basing, matches and too much alcohol. Everyone died. The warning was sent—and the only person left to get it was Ben.

As he saw it, he had three choices: run for the rest of his life, beg for the supplier's (nonexistent) mercy, or defend himself. He defended himself with a coldness he hadn't realized he had. He planned the attack as calmly as he planned anything, knowing that he could simply be firing the first volley in a war that would never end.

But warnings could be sent both ways, and he wanted the community to know that no one fucked with him. He cashed everything out, moved out of his apartment, and became a ghost.

Six months of work, tracking connections, finding people who specialized in being lost, and then taking care of them, quickly, efficiently, and with a minimum of fuss.

He was nearly done when they caught him. Lost five guys taking him down, wounding him badly enough that he could no longer defend himself.

That was when he learned he hadn't prepared enough. The club owner had been a small fish, the supplier another small fish, the people he took out more small fish. The man who talked to him was probably a medium fish, one who claimed to represent a larger fish.

He offered Ben training for a job, a high-paying one that he'd have to work only a few times a year.

"You have an affinity for it," the medium fish said. "Shame to let such talent go to waste."

He never wasted it. Somewhere, he lost Ben, the boy bouncer, and became the ghost, the man who could go from place to place and never be recognized, the man who had fifteen layers between himself and the world.

＊　　＊　　＊

Years later, when Glenna saw that incident in his chart, she said, "You lost everything and it stripped you down to your warrior nature. Since then, you've never looked back."

He sees no point in looking back. He learns his lesson and moves forward, in the world and not a part of it.

Losing everything means only one thing now: losing himself.

The afternoon sun is pale through the smog. Cars honk, tourists gawk at the poverty that is Hollywood Boulevard, and he remembers why he hates Los Angeles.

He didn't expect such news. He has been careless in recent months—having his own chart done only when he had a job. May was, literally, uncharted territory.

Until now.

He pulls the cell phone out of its pouch on his belt. This phone is one he cloned in Detroit a week ago. He hasn't used it yet, so it's as clean as the phone in his rental and the five he stashed at the airport.

As he walks, he dials. Glenna will be able to explain this chart. She'll run it herself and tell him what the darkness is, what the nothing is. She isn't afraid of him, and she has the experience to understand every nuance a chart can make.

He listens to the rings as he passes a diner filled with transvestites, hookers, and wanna-be stars. His rental is parked halfway up the next road, around a curve, up a hill, impossible to see from the main thoroughfare.

Even when he hasn't agreed to a job, he's cautious.

"Cosmos," says an unfamiliar male voice, loud through the earpiece.

No "May I Help You?," no "Leading the Way in Harmony," which is the store's tagline, something Glenna always insists her employees say. In fact, this man's voice is so flat he sounds disinterested, like a cop who is answering the phone to see who is on the other end.

Still, he decides to play it, just to see. "Glenna, please."

"Who's calling?"

"I need a name, sir," and he knows his hunch is right. Glenna has never screened her calls. Not in the ten years he's known her.

*A person has to take what comes,* she says, *however it comes.*

She is, if he remembers right, some combination of Pisces, Cancer and Aquarius, all intuition and emotion, sensitive, psychic and unique. Certainly not someone who would respond well to a voice as cold as this one.

He decides to push one last time. "Glenna has never asked for my name before. Just put her on."

"No can do, sir," the voice says. "I need a name."

He hangs up, then shuts off the phone, slipping it into his pocket. He'll toss it when he gets onto the freeway, somewhere near a bridge or an off-ramp near gang territory. After he wipes it down, of course.

It isn't until he gets to his rental that he realizes he's shaken. It's such an unfamiliar emotion, he's forgotten how it feels—the chill down the back, the twisting in the stomach, the unsteady nerves in the hand.

For he was wrong when he thought the only thing he had left was himself. He has Glenna, his seer, his touchstone, and the only person he's trusted since he started down this road twenty years before.

The Web is an anonymous man's best friend. On it, he has found sites that have told him how to pick hotel keycard locks, how to buy illegal and untraceable weapons, how to steal identities.

Now, in the privacy of his touristy hotel near Universal Studios, he uses the Web to learn something he does not want to know.

Glenna is dead.

Not just dead. Murdered. Two days before, in what the Flagstaff newspaper is calling a gangland style hit. In other words, a professional job.

He gets more information from the local radio news sites and a Phoenix newspaper that feels an obligation to cover the entire state. The details are familiar. He recognizes the method. The job was a quickie, gun left on the scene registered to a New Orleans police detective who had it stolen (or in New Orleans, with its corrupt department, who sold it) at a take-down five years ago. Hit happened late at night, in a private corner near a vegan restaurant she frequented. One shot, taken no more than three feet away, and not heard by the locals. Silencer, probably, or pillow or purse to muffle the sound.

There were probably other details the cops were keeping to themselves, things like a stranger seen near the store that day or that night, an abandoned rental car, wiped clean, or evidence pointing to a local, evidence that didn't pan out.

The thing that disturbs him the most is that the local police don't handle it themselves. They don't even call Phoenix for help. They assume it is a hit, which means the gunman has organized connections, and they call in the FBI.

He's glad now that the cloned phone is gone. He needs to be gone too. No time to delay. There's probably someone tracking his steps in Hollywood as he's closing his laptop.

Check out is easy. Tourist hotels, gotta love 'em. The staff doesn't care why he's leaving early. They figure they know. Too much fun in the sun. Too many rides. Too much alcohol, not enough money.

He slips out as quietly as he slipped in, drops the rental at LAX, and hops the next Southwest flight to Vegas.

For the first time in years, he needs real help, and there's only one place he can get it.

He flies Southwest because they let customers pick their own seats. If you don't like who you sit next to, you can move, no questions asked. He takes a window toward the back, grabs an airsick bag, and makes himself look queasy.

No one sits next to him.

The short flight is uneventful, but his mind is racing. Glenna may have mob connections, but he doubts it. She may have an ex-husband with access, but he doesn't believe that. Hell, she may be the mother of a high school cheerleader whose jealous rival hires a hit man, but he never believed that story in the first place. He certainly doesn't believe it now.

He has a hunch he's her only connection to the dark world he lives in.

*Should I be afraid for myself, old friend? My chart was uncertain. It told me that today would introduce me to Death.*

He leans against the tiny window, staring at the tops of clouds. She had told him at that first reading that charts weren't easily predictable. She'd looked at his and thought that he was a stand-in for Death because of his job.

*I did meet Death yesterday, just not in the way I thought.*

She had been wrong twice. Her chart had said that day would introduce her to Death. Without him, Death would never have found her, at least not in this way.

He doesn't need actual proof. He has more important things to worry about.

He needs to figure out if she's a warning or if she's a tool. Or both. The shooter had to know the cops would find her long before he did. If the shooter were after him and knew about Glenna, all the shooter had to do was wait.

So he's not an obvious target. He's something else, but what he doesn't know.

She had his charts for the next job. His chart, the client's chart, and the victim's chart. No names, only reference numbers. Numbers she promised—and he checked (late one night, easily breaking into that silly little store)—that never had names attached to them.

She never had his real name anyway or his address. He always contacted her, and she didn't seem to mind.

All she had was birthdates, times, and locations.

That was plenty.

His right hand crumples the air-sick bag. He is still shaken, and beneath that feeling is something else, something even more unsettling.

He does not want to examine what that feeling is.


Angel Bridges has an astrology palace near one of the Elvis chapels on the strip. The astrology palace is as garish as anything else in Vegas: six stories high with turrets and neon astrological symbols that flash on and off depending on the time of year and the fluctuations in the cosmos.

Angel makes her money telling gamblers how to bet based on the stars, but she runs a side business for true believers. She makes no money on that one—she does it strictly for love. And she never asks questions because she values her life and her position in a town that where people do anything to guarantee luck.

It's five o'clock when he walks in, the beginning of her evening rush. One of the little waifs who works as an assistant approaches him, but he ignores it. The waif bleats, but he continues to walk toward Angel, cutting ahead of a long and patient line.

She sits on a thick couch, a caftan spread around her ample frame. Diamonds glitter on her ears and fingers—she can't lead other people to wealth if it doesn't look like she has some of her own.

She sees him, smiles at her current customer, and excuses herself, as if she's going to get more research material. She disappears behind a gold leaf door. He takes a side hallway that seems to go in the opposite direction, but doesn't.

They end up in her office, a ergonomically correct room with no windows and a skylight that, at night, sends patterns of neon across the darkened floor. He learned that at one a.m. on a Christmas Eve as he checked her files, making sure her connections were clean ones.

As she closes the metal door, he hands her the natal chart. She's never seen it before. She's only done client charts for him. She has no idea it's his.

"I need two months," he says, "starting with April 20th of this year. And I'm going to wait for it."

He's never done that before. He's always come back. She peers at him, then adjusts her red wig. He doesn't like it. She looks better with her natural black.

"It's gonna cost," she says. "I'll lose about a quarter of the suckers out there."

"I'll pay," he says.

She nods, presses a button, and tells an assistant to inform the clients she's received news of a change in the stars. Then she focuses on the chart and punches up something on her computer.

He takes an upholstered chair designed for a frame shorter and heavier than his. It's the most uncomfortable chair he's ever sat in. But he doesn't move. Instead, he ponders.

A hit like that always draws the FBI, later rather than sooner in small towns, although he probably should expect sophistication in a strange little town like Sedona. What will the FBI learn from his files?

Too much, actually, if they plug the dates, place names, and birth times into their unsolved data base. One half of the birth information will tie to hits all over the country. It won't take a rocket scientist to figure out that the other half belong to the folks who paid good money to get the first half out of the way.

And then there's his, of course, and its repeated monthly or weekly charts. Not that it'll do the Feds much good. Ben disappeared twenty years ago. A ghost took his place, a ghost no one has been able to trace for a very long time.

They will get his patterns though and, if they put someone smart on the case, a pretty good analysis of his m.o., damn his perfectionist Virgo side. They'll also get an excellent description of him from neighboring shopkeepers and former employees because they'll know what questions to ask.

And from the client list, they'll probably track down a few of his hackers or maybe the fronts who took the order. His carefully formed fifteen will crumble to six or seven or four.

One piece of information and his operation shatters. Was that the goal? Or is he being neutralized because the big fish is finally gone or because someone has finally caught up with him?

They'd caught up with him before, but always failed in hand-to-hand. It took some planning to make him ineffective. Some planning and some unwitting compliance from himself and his superstitions.

He'd gotten complacent, a bad thing in his business.

"This is a piece of shit chart," Angel says.

"Inaccurate?" he asks.

"No, just incomplete, like they were using one of those computer downloads done by someone who only gives half a crap." She runs a bejeweled hand over her eyes. What is it about these astrologers that makes them wear too much jewelry on their fingers?

"So whatever this person told me is incomplete?"

"Dunno," Angel says. "What'd you get told?"

He slips the other chart to her, the one with the week ahead.

Angel frowns at it. "Why're you going to a crap artist when you got me?"

"You're not always with me, babe," he says, folding his hands together and leaning back.

She shakes her head, then she pushes the weekly sheet to him. "Look at this. It doesn't tie. It's as if this astrologer's forgotten the natal chart. We got a birthdate in Eastern Standard Time, and we got an analysis done for someone born in Western Daylight. Doesn't work. This is so basic."

"So it's wrong," he says.

"This weekly thing is a piece of garbage." She tosses it with a flourish into the nearby wastebasket . "But this natal chart, I gotta tell you, is the nastiest thing I've ever seen."

"Because of how it's done?"

"Because of what it means." She frowns at him, shoves the wig back so far he can see the pink of her scalp. "This is another client?"

He nods, not trusting himself to answer.

"This is one mean s.o.b. Dangerous. He thinks he's clean, but he's not. He kills for a living, and even though charts can be figurative, I don't think this one is. He sees himself as a warrior, but he's an assassin, plain and simple. Not the kind of person nice folks should hang with."

He hasn't moved, his hands still across his stomach, his feet stretched out, his body trapped in the world's most uncomfortable chair. But his muscles have all gone tense. He can feel the gun beneath his suitcoat. He hopes his expression hasn't changed, then he wonders if it should have changed. After all, she's just told him one of his clients is a killer.

"What're you supposed to do for this guy?" she asks, and he mentally curses her, wishing that she would remember she's not supposed to ask questions. "A job, like the others?"

He nods.

"I hope it's a legal job. You don't want to mess with this guy in any real way."

"What else does the natal chart tell you?" he asks. Somehow his voice remains calm.

"That he's got more secrets than God. That he's unpredictable and charming and could turn on you in a second. I won't do anything for him, no matter how much he paid me."

She's trying to be nice to him. She doesn't know. His muscles are freezing up. He's holding back the truth, that she has worked for him for five years, thinks he's a friend, thinks he's someone she can trust.

"Well," he says, "let's see what the two-month chart says."

"You don't seem shocked by this."

"I thought he was shady. You're not surprising me."

She nods, focuses on the computer screen. For a long time, all he hears is the tap-tap of keys. He resists the urge to stand and pace.

They had to have already found some of his people. The only way to get to Glenna was to find out about the blind box in Flagstaff. In the past, he used to go there, pick up the stuff and drive it down. Three years ago, he decided she could open the box on occasion. He brought her a key, and sometimes he would call, asking her to pick up the various charts. She would.

A few of his hackers and a couple of his fronts have that address. Others have a blind box in Vegas and another in L.A. If the cops triangulated that cell phone call, they know he was in L.A. Or maybe someone else knows.

He gets up so abruptly the chair bangs against the floor. Angel starts. "You okay?"

"Need to make a private call," he says. "I'll be right back."

"Take your time," she says. "This is one confusing mass of planets."

He doesn't like that sound either. He heads to the door, takes the corridor outside and goes in the Elvis chapel. There's a line here too, mostly of drunks. He congratulates one of the champagne drinking men, lifts his cell as he pats him on the side, and then goes onto the strip.

It's changed over the years. Big buildings loom over him, pretending to be something they aren't—the Eiffel Tower, the Empire State Building, a complete European City State. The neon lights make it as bright as day. Cars pass, people stumble by, many of them holding buckets with tokens in them or nickels. A few have newspapers and others clutch cash as if it isn't real.

He dials the store in L.A., hoping it's open late. On the fifth ring, a woman answers. He recognizes the voice. The palm reader.

"You get Elli May out of there," he says.

"So it's you." The reader curses him in some romance language—probably Italian. "You could have warned her."

"I had no idea."

"She comes here looking for adventure, not a gun in the face."

A gun in the face? He hadn't expected that. He expected something a few days away, maybe an FBI visit or a discreet contact. Not a direct attack. "Is she all right?"

"Scared. She gave him all her charts. He didn't want money. A good thing, eh? So now she can go back to those parents of hers, the ones who didn't even care that she was gone." The reader curses him again.

He lets her. "Who put the gun in her face?"

"I don't know his name."

"Have you seen him before?"

"No," she says.

"What can you tell me about him?"

"Why should I tell you anything?"

"Because I may be able to prevent him from coming back."

She pauses. He can feel her brain whirling. He wonders if he's making a mistake, calling her, if the attacker is still there. Then he decides it doesn't matter. Most folks can't track a cell phone call. Even if she has Caller I.D., all she can find out is what the cell phone number is, not where the call originates.

"He came in about three hours ago," she says. "He was young, white, has money—or at least thinks he does. Hand-tailored suit, but dirty shoes, like he's been traveling or forgets to shine them."

He listens, body tense.

"He points the gun at me first, and I shrug. I've seen guns before, but not eyes like his. Big and brown and spinning, almost. Crazy. He thinks he's smart, but he's only smart like a fox. This kind does not survive long."

Is she talking to the attacker now? Or is this the kind of way she always speaks? He wishes he had paid more attention to her, instead of dismissing her out of hand.

"He wants the charts. He gets angry when he finds out they're all the same birthdate. He wants the other ones, the client charts. She says she has no idea what he means, but she gives him everything.

He slaps the gun across her face and she falls. I've got my own gun and I pull it out. He turns, laughs at me, says, 'Grandma, you're no match for me,' and then he leaves, as if the fact we seen him don't matter, as if his visit is normal."

"Then what?" he asks.

"A call to the police, of course. No one's come yet. This part of town, who cares? But you care. You know this man."

"No," he says. "I don't."

"He knows you. He says you're getting old and tired and you don't even realize it. A relic, he calls you. A superstitious relic." She pauses. "You will not come back here."

"That's right."

"I am telling you, you will not come back here. My niece, she thinks he will murder you. She thinks it is her fault."

"Tell her that her chart is off. She forgot to adjust for time zones." And he hangs up.

He wipes the phone off and then tosses it on the sidewalk outside the Elvis chapel. The drunk will think it has fallen from its perch in his pocket. It won't be until he gets his bill that he realizes something has gone wrong.

He goes back into the astrology palace. The line is shorter. The person who was having his chart done still waiting near the couch, only now he is checking his watch.

He slips into the back, goes to the office. She has swiveled her chair so that she's working on a back desk, using protractors and paper charts and colored pencils. It takes him a moment to realize she's redoing her work by hand.

"What's the problem?" he asks.

"It comes out the same," she says and she sounds completely surprised. "Even with the proper adjustments, this weekly chart comes out exactly the same. Something started a week ago, something very serious, which led to a great loss a few days ago, one which had an impact today."

At that, she looks up at him, as if he can give her the information she seeks. He can, of course, but he won't.

When it becomes clear that he'll say nothing, she continues. "It builds and then there is nothing."

"Nothing?" he asks, beginning to hate that word. "What the hell is nothing?"

She shrugs. "I've never seen anything like it. There is no more chart."

"So it means death."

She shakes her head. "I've seen death in charts before, often charts you give me, sometimes in the gamblers' charts. But it usually appears as a transformation. A person's life continues even if he does not."

"What the hell does that mean?"

She smiles. This is clearly a conversation she's familiar with. "Let's say you die tomorrow. Your financial affairs will continue. Your relationships will continue, at least for a little while. You may still have an impact on the world, long after you're gone. I suppose eventually the chart will come to nothing, but I have never seen one do that. Usually the person who dies does not come back for another reading."

That last she says wryly, as if humor might help her unease. It doesn't help his.

If he stops, if he ends, nothing will continue. He has no relationships, not like she is talking about. He has no friends and family (well, he has a family, but they are not people he has thought of in decades. He left them when he stopped being Ben, maybe even before, when he went to work in the City), and his finance affairs will become untended accounts that banks all over the world will have to deal with some day.

He has no will, no legacy, no real life. When he goes, he will leave nothing behind. He will evaporate, like a spirit in the wind.

"I don't understand," he says.

"Neither do I," she says and frowns. "All we have is a cataclysmic event and then nothing. Perhaps I should run my own chart. Perhaps the world is going to end."

She does not say this with humor. He stares at her, then he flings five times her usual payment on the desk. "Thanks."

"Come back tomorrow," she says. "I'll research this, see if anyone else knows what it means."

"I think you might just want to let this go," he says. "I am."

"I can't let it go. It may have great meaning."

"I doubt it," he says, and lets himself out the door.

The line is even shorter. The man waiting for his reading is talking angrily to one of the waifs.

He goes outside, looks at the fake towns, the people pretending they're having a good time. The cell phone is gone from the sidewalk in front of the Elvis chapel. He wonders if the drunk found it or if someone else picked it up.

It is time to disappear. To become a true ghost, never thought or heard of again. Over the years, he has made a hundred escape plans, and he has liked none of them. Nothing sounds duller than sitting on a tropical beach sipping Mai Tais for the rest of his life.

No matter what Angel said, or how much contempt she said it with, he *is* a warrior. And he wants to die a warrior's death. If he cannot work, he cannot enjoy his life.

Maybe he should cut all his tics with the past, the fifteen layers (some of which are gone, some of which have betrayed him), move to a different country, and set up again. Someday, perhaps, he can come back here as an independent and start again.

But he is too old to start again. He only has ten more good years, twenty if he keeps himself in perfect condition and chooses targets as old or older than he is.

Perhaps the nothing on his chart reflects his ghost status. Perhaps it means that he will chose a new identity, with a new birthdate, and start again.

Perhaps. But he does not believe it. He has reached the end, and he is not sure what that means.

But he knows what he will do.

He will wait.


What he figures is this:

The young man is after him for his client list, which means he has not found the fronts, only the hackers. In fact, he may have only found one hacker—any one with the Flagstaff PO Box would do.

What disturbs him is the connection to astrology. The guy knew about the superstition somehow—and he thinks he knows how. Sometimes hitmen become legends in their own business, especially if they've been around a while, like he has. They get monikers, usually based on something unusual.

He hasn't been tied into the network in years—too much risk, risk he doesn't like. But the network is still tied to him, clearly, or to his reputation. They can't call him the Zodiac Killer—that had been taken by some psycho who wouldn't know a pro hit if he were instructed in how to do one—so they probably gave him a different name: the Horoscope Man, the Astrology Hits, something. And from there, this guy searched until he found something unusual.

What doesn't fit, what bothers him, is that the guy's research makes him seem cautious, but his encounters—both with Glenna and Elli May—make him seem like a quickie.

The guy's also arrogant, so he doesn't cover his tracks. The fact that he has the charts is both exhilarating and disturbing. Disturbing because the guy's going to get caught and he's going to give up what he knows. Exhilarating, because the FBI, even though they're involved, don't have the charts and can't tie Glenna's clients to anything.

If the guy is as smart as he seems, he's going to find out about Vegas. Once he finds Vegas, he'll find Angel. Once he finds Angel, his spree will end, one way or another.

There's even a timetable, according to the weekly chart. By the sixth of May, the guy'll be in Vegas—and there'll be a confrontation. Better to know that in advance. No surprises.

No surprises, the better the chance of winning.

If there is something to win.

What he doesn't admit to himself as he waits is how disturbed he is. Deep down. He's never been anyone's focus, never been the source of anyone's search—not him, not his ghostly self. Sure, he's probably in a bunch of police and FBI databases, but for his various crimes.

Right now, he's being tailed for who he is, targeted for what he knows, and the people he's surrounded himself with are being punished.

He hates that.

He hasn't realized how much he hates that until he sits in Angel's office for the second night in a row, trying to find a comfortable chair. The lights are out, but the skylight lets in so much neon ambiance that everything is well lit.

The computer is off, but he has helped himself to her files, realizes she has some connections that make him nervous. He wonders if they know who he is, if they know about his previous break-in, and if they care.

Probably not. If they cared, they'd take care of him. They're probably watching now, just to see what he's doing, just to find out what he knows.

What he knows is that he's having a hard time staying calm. And that's not like him. But he keeps thinking of Glenna, her easy manner, her smile when she saw him after a long absence, the way she believed whatever she did was for the best.

He led the guy right to her, and she had died, violently, because of him.

Strangely enough, that disturbs him. When he gets paid to take a life, that's different. It isn't about him. It's what he does. It's not personal.

This is. This loss had a direct connection to him, more direct than pulling the trigger.

This loss pisses him off. And the fact that it pisses him off pisses him off even more. He isn't supposed to have attachments. He's outgrown them. They're useless in his business. He needs to be a complete loner, and somehow he's failed to do that.

Part of him worried about Angel until he saw who she was dealing with. If the guy offs her, he'll have an entire family of people to answer to. She'll be protected.

It's his remaining astrologers who are in trouble. Them, and his hackers—the ones who haven't encountered the guy—and the fronts, and all the others associated with this little operation. He's struggled to keep them as clean as possible. He doesn't want anything to happen to them because of him.

At least, that's what he's telling himself as he sits in the shadows, watching the blue neon Scorpio signal—an M with a pointed tail—flash on and off against the cherry colored carpet. He's also thinking he may have overestimated this guy when he hears the security lock click open.

Finally.

He pulls out the semi he got at a militia convention outside of

Denver and aims it at the door. He has to wait until he's sure because he doesn't want to nail Angel by mistake.

Someone slips inside, as thin as one of the waifs. The neon is off for the moment, dammit, and the room is darker than usual. Then the gold Taurus ignites—a circle with horns—and he sees the leather jacket, the slicked-back hair, the cruel curve to the mouth.

"You could've just asked for my client list," he says.

The guy swivels, surprised. But he covers well. "I had to find you first."

His answer is a spray of bullets that rip the guy up and make him dance before slumping against the wall, lifeless and empty.

Now he's got to move quick. He suspects the palace has walls thick enough to hide the noise, but suspecting is not the same as knowing. He approaches the body, gaping and bloody where the torso should be, and stares at the face.

Unfamiliar, not that he should know who the guy was. And young, arrogant. A quickie, just like he thought. He slips on his gloves and pats the pockets, finding a Hilton room key and a receipt with the room number, and a wallet with I.D. poorly faked, from some computer site.

Not even a quickie then. An amateur, a wanna-be. No wonder he needed the client list. He didn't have connections to get jobs on his own. Glenna had been practice, proof that he could do it.

And maybe he couldn't. A real pro would've shot Elli May and the palm reader. A real pro wouldn't've left such an obvious trail.

A tiny red light is blinking on the back of the computer. He looks for the source—thinking maybe someone has a laser scope on him. How can that be? There's no way to focus the scope on him from that angle. There should be shadows from the skylight above. He's been checking. The astrological signs are sending the proper light to the carpet.

Some kind of warning light. Some kind of security trigger. He pockets the room key, but destroys the receipt. Then he peels off his gloves, and folds them over his shoes like a cheap pair of rubbers. There'll be bloody footprints. He can't help that. But that's the only clue they'll have, and with Angel's unsavory connections, the cops'll probably look somewhere else.

He reaches for the door, turns the knob, hears a second click. Not a security lock this time. Something flat and ominous, something he should have expected, but didn't because this, for him, was a quickie too.

He pulls on the door, but it doesn't open. Programmed to lock after violence like that. He's seen security like this before. He's not going to be able to shoot through the metal door, at least not in time.

"Damn," he says as he turns, hoping he has time to get up to the skylight, to break through it. The red light on the computer is blinking so fast that it seems almost constant.

He stands on one of the uncomfortable chairs, the semi pointed at the skylight. He's pulling the trigger when the computer explodes.

He has time to analyze it.

It's not really a white light. It's more like sunlight, broad and glistening, incorporating many colors, but so brightly that all he can see is white.

He's afraid to look at it, afraid he'll see that no one is waiting for him, or that the folks who are waiting are really, really, really pissed off.

He hides his eyes, but the light comes through the lids, just like it would do if he were really there. He doesn't look at it, pretends he can't feel its warm glow, and gradually, it fades away as if it never existed.

As if he never existed.

Which, he supposes, he hasn't, not for a very long time.

"Ben?"

He opens his eyes. The old lady standing over him has thin gray hair and a broad face. Her features are familiar.

"Ben?" She sounds like she's witnessing a miracle. Behind her head, a TV screen blares the news. A woman is reading headlines, and below her is a sports ticker. It gives the score of the All-Star game.

He frowns. The old lady is calling for nurses, and he realizes that he's in a bed, immobile, and very, very tired.

"You're back, Ben. Thank God. I've been here every day."

Finally he recognizes the voice. The old lady is Angel. He was wrong. Her hair's natural color isn't black. The tips are, but she's stopped dying it. A scarf lays on an endtable, along with a book about destiny. She's been waiting for him, and reading.

"You saved my life. That serial killer—"

She doesn't get a chance to finish. His room is invaded by scores of health care professionals in white coats. They surround him, stick him with things, ask him questions he doesn't know the answer to, tell him he's lucky, lucky, lucky to be alive.

He has lost more than two months. It's mid-July. He has been immobile in a Vegas hospital bed for two months—not alive, not dead.

Living in limbo. Existing. He was, he realizes, during that span, nothing at all.

They take Angel out, afraid she'll tire him, but she promises to come back.

He has to cope with many realizations—that his rehabilitation will take months, maybe years. He may not walk again. His left arm has been destroyed. He's afraid to look at his face.

They found out his real identity from his fingerprints, sent for his family, and found out he has none left. His fingerprints are on file, he remembers, because of a drug bust twenty years ago, one the club owner paid their way out of. He had forgotten that. He has forgotten more than he knows.

What he does learn from Angel over the next few days is that, in her eyes, he's a hero. Somehow, she thinks, he got the guy's chart. They're calling the guy—Dante Evans—a serial killer who specialized in astrologers.

Evans wasn't as careful as he thought. He left clues at the scene of Glenna's murder and Elli May was able to I.D. him from a photo as the guy who beat her the afternoon of May fourth.

Angel believes that "Ben" knew something was wrong, and when he figured it out, guarded her. She has no clue who he really is, and if she has no clue, then neither do her contacts—the ones who booby-trapped her office.

She is embarrassed as she explains this. "They made me promise that I'd keep their information secure," she says. "They set up this trap. At first it was supposed to go off if there was unofficial activity in the room, but I was afraid for my assistants, so they set it up to go off if there was other factors. I never asked what those factors were. They promised it would never happen."

He knows. It could have been any number of things: a response to the cordite, to the sound of gunfire, to the spray of warm liquid—like blood. Or merely a remote device, set off by someone who kept an eye on the place, whenever he believed there was trouble.

Gunfire counted as trouble.

But he says nothing to her, and he also says nothing when she offers to pay for his room. His tracks are covered, so deep that he knows he's facing an opportunity.

Angel sits beside his bed. She's still apologizing to him, feeling guilty for misreading the chart. She doesn't understand that it's not Evans' chart, that it's his chart, but he won't tell her that.

"I still have trouble believing death registers as nothing. But they can't find anything about him. We're the only ones affected," she says.

He listens. He doesn't tell her what he believes. Can't. He's afraid she'll run his chart or the serial killer's chart, which is what she believes it is. If she runs it past May 11, she'll find the nothing ended on the day he woke up. The nothing was the coma.

Even though it wasn't really nothing, not like the chart said. After all, Angel's here and she thinks he's a hero. He has had some impact on her life.

Maybe the nothing was a misinterpretation—or a non-interpretation. Maybe everything was in such flux that no one could predict what would happen.

"Angel," he says, when she finally pauses for breath, "do you believe in second chances?"

"Of course, honey," she says and pats his good hand. "The religions, they all deal with that. It's even in a person's chart, in the nodes. Past lives always have an impact on present ones."

"No, no," he says. "I'm talking about this life. What if there's a clear line, a break between what you were before and now. Can you be something else?"

She studies him for a moment. He wonders how clearly she's seeing him. Does she think he's talking about his old drug arrest, his wandering lifestyle? Or does she think something deeper is going on, maybe even suspect the darkness he let take over his soul?

"I think a person gets a second chance like that for a reason," she says, "and only a fool would pass it by."

He nods. He's been thinking that too.

"You want me to do your chart, so we can see what path you should walk?"

"No," he says. He's done with that. Charts are too accurate. He's not going to plan his life like that any more. Besides, he wants to forget that he's a warrior with a judge's soul. He wants to think he's been reborn in July. A Cancer. Sensitive, nurturing, protective. Someone else entirely.

"How come you never told me who you really are, Ben?" she asks, looking down. This question matters to her.

He gives it due consideration. "I guess," he says, "because I never knew myself."

Protected by fifteen layers, a soldier in a war he didn't believe in or understand, searching for meaning where there was none, meaning that got the wrong people killed.

He's not a hero, not even close. Doubts he ever can be. He's still superstitious, maybe more so than he was before. He's hanging up his weapons and finding a new path — one that might make him worthy of the light.

Maybe, the next time it surrounds him, he can look at it and through it, to the world beyond. Maybe the next time, he'll have enough courage to go there, and face himself, what he's been and what he's done.

The thought disturbs him and he closes his eyes, for the first time in his own memory not trying to repress feeling, but to acknowledge it.

To feel something where there was once nothing.

To be a person instead of a ghost.

# THE BLUE SCORPION

## Anne Perry

NOVEMBER 11TH, 1919. It was the birthday of two sisters, Alice and Dori Taylor. There were three years between them, exactly. But far above the celebration of any one person was the weeping and the joy of a nation that the greatest war in Europe's history was over. Every village, every household, remembered its dead: family, friends, neighbours. There was not anyone unscathed, nobody who had not loved, and lost someone. For many it was more than one, perhaps a father, a husband and a brother were gone. There were women who mourned all their sons, families who were decimated.

For Dori, twenty-two tonight, it was the end of a long, dreary nightmare, and more than time to start having fun at last. The dead should be left to rest, and the living look to the future. After the long, grey years, there was laughter again, and music . . . such music! Full of life and rhythm and promise of excitement. Fashion had changed beyond anyone's wildest dreams. No more suffocating corsets, no more skirts to the ground. One could walk freely, move, breathe, bend. And from now on it would only get better! With the end of fighting, all the soldiers back from France, no more endless waiting and dreading news, had come a sublime new freedom. Anything seemed possible. The old, rigid manners were swept away, everything that seemed stuffy and self important.

Except it seemed as if half the young men she had known before would never come home. Only God knew how many lay dead in France or Belgium, or somewhere else. She could have recited a list

of them, but she had no wish to. She wanted to be happy, to dance
the new crazes from America which were such fun, and to laugh,
and to find someone wonderful, and seize every moment of life and
live it.

In another bedroom, only a few yards away, Alice's thoughts were
very different. She had been twenty when the war began, in the first
year of her medical studies. She had fought hard for her place at
university, but she had not thought twice about giving it up and going
into the army as a nurse. This was her birthday too, but compared
with Armistice Day, that hardly counted at all. There were too many
memories crowding her mind, too many people she had known and
cared about, who were not here, and never would be except in her
thoughts.

And too many others who would never be whole again, who had lost
limbs or eyes, who were scarred or crippled, who woke in the night
sobbing.

She too would be happy this evening, the dead would not be well
served by misery. She would dance and smile. Above all she would
be with Matthew whom she had loved since he had been brought
into the field surgery where she was working. He had been wounded,
white-faced, his uniform soaked in blood, but more concerned for his
men than for himself.

Dori surveyed herself in the mirror, and was well satisfied with the
reflection that smiled back at her. Her fair hair was soft and pretty,
full of natural curl. She was slim but shapely, her ankles were excellent. Above all, she radiated gaiety, the love of life. After the long,
grey years of the war, it was more powerful than beauty or virtue, and
she knew it. Too many people had grieved too much. Now they
wanted to forget pain for a while, and she understood that very clearly.
There was a hectic, glittering need for vividness, sensation, proof of
being fully alive.

The only thing that clouded her horizon at all was that there were
so few men not suffering some affliction. It would be a lucky girl who
found one, and she intended to give luck a helping hand. Matthew
was certainly the best of them, the only surviving son of a wealthy
family with land in Berkshire and a fine London house. His war rec-

ord was excellent, twice decorated for courage. When he was ready he could take his pick of positions in the City. He was her first choice: he was handsomer than Freddie, gentler than Robert, and her parents would be delighted with him, which would make life much easier.

She pushed her fingers through her hair a last time, smoothed her slim skirts over her hips, and opened the door.

The party was a great success. The older generation had chosen to spend their evening quietly, leaving the floor to youth, laughter and the new music. Everyone danced to the flying, syncopated beat.

Matthew had not thought he would enjoy the evening, apart from the fact that Alice would be there. Too many lost friends crowded his memory, on this of all days. A year ago exactly the guns had at last fallen silent. At the service the vicar had read the names of the dead, a list that seemed to go on and on, every family he knew. In Berkshire it would probably be worse.

He stood in the entrance of the big hall, carpets taken up, the band, elegant, even foppish, playing till the sweat sheened their faces. He saw Alice across the room and felt a sweet familiarity, remembering her courage, her endless compassion during those terrible nights and days. He knew as their eyes met that she was thinking the same.

Then out of the crowd Dori came towards him, laughing, her skirt swinging as she walked, in time with the music. She had been too young to know what the fighting was really like. She had experienced the hardships here in London, of course, and she had lost many friends, but she had no conception of what it had been in France, in the trenches, of the noise and the blood, the rats, death everywhere around them, the cold of winter, and the incessant fear.

He saw the happiness in her face, the excitement. She was full of the vigour and the hope of today.

"Matthew!" she said cheerfully, holding out her slender arms. "Come and dance with me! Did you ever hear such a band? Marge told me a wonderful joke today, about Teddy Armstrong and two frogs. Let me tell you. You'll laugh till you cry. I did!" She seized hold of his hands and pulled him onto the floor.

He was happy to go with her, feeling the rhythm take hold of him. She danced well. The joke about the frogs was silly and funny, and he did laugh. It was a wonderful feeling, innocent and completely pointless, and free of all sorrow and guilt for still being alive.

The evening flew by. It was midnight before he realised he had not danced with Alice. He had spoken with her, of course, but among a crowd of others. She was a little distant. He caught sight of her once or twice and had the feeling she half disapproved of the light-heartedness of the evening, as if they somehow betrayed the fallen by laughing so hard, dancing, swinging frantically around the floor in each others' arms to such frivolous music.

At midnight they stood together at the edge of the floor, glad to stop for a few moments and take a drink of iced champagne.

"She can't help it!" Dori said with a shrug and a smile. "It's just the way she is. She's happier being miserable. She didn't really want to have this party at all, but Mother made her." Her expression was sharp and amused. "She thinks we should all be wearing black. Being a heroine were the best years of Alice's life. She's going to dwell on it for ever, one way or another." She looked up at him with shining blue eyes. "We can't change yesterday. How about today—and to-morrow? That's ours." She put her empty glass down. "Come on, can you do this step? It's new from America—it's a whizz! I'll show you. It's marvellous!"

And so it was. She taught him well and he was a willing pupil. By three in the morning he was exhausted, and went home to sleep more soundly than he had done in years, with dreams of music, and Dori's smiling face and the warmth of her body in his arms.

By Christmas he had seen both sisters again many times. He would never cease to admire Alice's courage, or the dedication she had shown endlessly, without thought to how tired or how frightened she was herself. But it was Dori's company that lifted his heart, her wit which entertained him, barbed as it often was, and made him laugh in spite of the continuing hardship of the new peace. She was so often happy. The things that angered her were the trivial irritations of ordinary life, and he could dismiss those without wasting emotion. He could even joke her out of them, something he could never have done with Alice. They knew each other too well and shared the same burdens of experience.

He had toyed with the idea of giving Alice the gift of an aquamarine brooch in the shape of a scorpion, her birth sign. He had had it made, a beautiful, sparkling thing, like light on clear water, and Scorpio was one of the water signs, apparently. It had seemed appropriate.

Now, impulsively, but beyond doubt, he knew he would give it to Dori instead. It would suit her perfectly, bright, beautiful, a thing to draw the eye. And Scorpio was just as much her sign.

He chose an evening of one of the new cocktail parties, typical of the many inventions from across the Atlantic which had become the craze. There was music playing in the background, sweet and haunting with a rhythm that stayed in the mind. The lights were bright, the fashion of the room clean and elegant.

He held the black velvet case out to her.

She opened it and her eyes brimmed with joy.

"Matthew! It's wonderful! Did you have it specially made for me?"

There was only one thing he could possibly say. "Yes, of course I did." He was surprised how happy it made him feel to see her response. He realised now how often she lifted his spirits. Every time he had seen her since that Armistice Day party she had had something cheerful to say, some hope or plan to discuss, a joke to share or a piece of gossip which made him laugh.

Loyalty was one of the supreme virtues, God knew, the last five years had proved that. He had seen men live and die for it. But he needed a space for healing, gentleness, freedom from any kind of responsibility, and above all from the overbearing guilt of having survived where so many of his friends had not. He was whole, he had sight where others were blind, and lungs uncorroded by the fearful mustard gas that had choked uncounted men. He had nightmares of course, but they were fading, and he was not haunted, numb inside, unable to stop weeping.

Dori was like a light after long darkness.

"Thank you," she breathed softly, eyes shining, turning the bright gems over in her hand. "I think you are the best person I ever knew . . . I don't think I could have borne it if we'd been as close during the war as we are now." She reached up and touched his cheek in a curiously intimate gesture which set his pulse racing. "I just want to know you are safe and happy for ever . . . and I can look after you, make you laugh, smooth out some of the difficulties for you."

"Would you do that?" he answered, half in jest, but underneath knowing as soon as the words were out that he meant it.

Her eyes widened, seriousness behind the teasing. "Is that what you want? Surely you know I would . . ." Then her voice dropped to a whisper. "I will." And she kissed him, at first softly, almost as if she were afraid, then with more hunger, holding him tightly in her arms, startlingly strong.

It was not exactly what he had meant, quite so soon . . . or was it? Perhaps it was? Someone to care for him, someone to belong to, with all her wit, gaiety and light. And she was lovely, no doubt about that. What could be better? What else did he imagine he was waiting for? Alice was a good friend, but that was not love. She was more like a comrade in arms, and he was tired of war and its grief, weary and heartsick of it. He needed laughter as he needed air.

He closed his arms around her and returned her sweet kiss.

Actually she did not wear the blue scorpion. Although he said he had had it made especially for her, she could never get it entirely out of her mind that he had thought of Alice first. After all, she too was a Scorpio. She had even taken their birthday before Dori.

She and Matthew were married in February. There was no reason to wait. Surely everyone had learned how precious time was, how fleeting. Seize the moment, never waste it.

Alice wished them well, at least she tried to. She believed she hid the crushing pain inside her. No one else must know that her younger, prettier sister had won from her the only man she had ever truly loved.

And she could not blame Matthew. Dori was like sunlight on a landscape after the long night of war. He was certainly not the only man to admire her, even to want her, he was simply the best of them, the bravest and the kindest. If Alice could not make him happy, then she forced herself to be glad that someone else could.

The spring and summer passed and the brilliance faded into autumn. Other friends married. Wounds began to heal, at least some of them, there were others which never would.

By Armistice Day 1920, different and darker shadows were on the horizon. Matthew had seen little of Alice since his marriage, and he felt vaguely guilty about it, as if he had let her down in some undefined way. He missed her friendship. There was an honesty in her, a generosity of spirit Dori never quite managed.

A couple of times he spoke of it, suggesting they invite Alice to visit for a little while. The third time he mentioned it Dori snapped back at him with a peevishness he had noticed more and more often in her lately.

"If you're so desperate to see Alice, go and visit her yourself!" she said tartly, her lips thin. "I presume you know where to find her? I'm sure I don't! She's about somewhere, like a cross between a nun and a lap dog, showing everyone what a good woman she is, ministering to the desperate and holding hands with the bereaved." She lifted one elegant shoulder in a disdainful shrug. He thought with surprise how ugly the gesture was. "I don't know what you think she'll want with you!" she went on. "She's only interested in the halt and the maimed she can be sorry for, and exercise her virtue on. She wouldn't know what to do with a whole man even if she had one!"

He was stung by the unkindness in her. Until this moment he had refused to see the shallowness of her laughter, the impatience to grasp at everything she wanted, however fleetingly, or the hurt behind her wit. Now suddenly the brightness of her was cold, like morning light on ice, and he felt more alone than he could ever have imagined, even in the worst moments in France. This was nothing to do with the fortune of war, there was no common cause. This was entirely his own fault. He had wanted warmth and ease after the misery, and he had grasped at a mirage. Now he was left with only the burning sand of possession without love, gaiety without joy, and laughter without kindness. Worst of all was the endless closeness devoid of understanding.

There was no answer to what she had said. It was not born of reason.

"It would be much more fun to go to Brighton with Teddy and Mabel," she filled in the answer for herself. "There's a new band at the Royal Hotel. Teddy says they're absolutely the rage."

"Was he sober when he said it?" he asked acidly, Teddy's inane face sharp in his mind's eye, his braying laughter grating even days afterwards.

"Who cares?" she snapped. "You're getting very waspish, Matthew. You never used to be so critical. What does it matter if Teddy drinks a little more than you do? He's a good sort, and he dances divinely."

He did not bother to argue. Teddy was a drunk and a bore, but perhaps no worse than a lot of young men with ugly memories, no particular purpose in life and no need to earn a living. The world Teddy had known before the war, the world he understood and in which his place was certain, had been destroyed forever. He was doing nothing useful with the new one that had taken its place, but perhaps he did not know how to.

"And he admires you immensely, you know," she added, looking at him critically. "You should be kinder to him."

"It's Armistice Day," he replied, turning away. "I don't feel like dancing."

"God! You're a po-faced bore sometimes!" her voice rose in explosive fury. "The war's over! You're not a hero any more, you're just an ordinary man, like anyone else! Look towards the future, not the past! I'm going to Brighton! You can do as you please!" And she went out of the room and he heard her feet light and swift up the stairs.

Dori did go to Brighton, alone. She had fully expected Matthew to follow her, and she behaved accordingly. A group of their friends, possibly more hers than his, were staying at the same hotel. She saw four of them through the archway into the bar as she was checking in, Maude Campbell in cherry red silk, slim and exaggerated, skirts well above the ankle. She was gesturing with her hands and talking animatedly to Gillian Walsh. She caught sight of Dori and called out a loud, cheerful greeting. In the background a band was playing, something jazzy, a swift, subtle beat, contagiously happy.

But three hours later when Matthew had still not arrived, Dori found it increasingly difficult to sound bright, and by midnight she no longer denied to herself that she had miscalculated her power over him, at least this time. It was a drag, but she would have to change tactics, work a little harder.

But November came and went and she had not really rectified the matter. If anything, it was worse. Matthew asked Alice to come and stay with them over Christmas, and was insistent enough that she actually did come. She seemed shy at first, as if they were strangers and must learn to know each other all over again.

"For heaven's sake don't spend the time reminiscing!" Dori said sharply. "This is a season of joy. Merry Christmas . . . remember? Happy New Year! Armistice Day is over. We all know you were a great heroine and we admire you for it. It doesn't need saying."

"Of course it doesn't," Alice agreed, making herself smile, although there was a tightness about her lips, as if the remark had hurt her. "I mean to be happy. I'd love a really good walk in the snow, even a little sledding. That would be fun."

"Sledding?" Dori said incredulously. "That's for children!"

"Then we'll find some children," Alice responded. "I'll bet there'll be lots of them out in the park, if the weather gets any better."

"You mean worse!"

"I mean more Christmassy." Alice glanced out of the window at the leaden sky. "And it looks promising."

And indeed the promise was fulfilled. The next day they awoke to a crisp, dazzling layer of snow over rooftops and pavements, even branches of the naked trees were dusted with white and the evergreens in the garden sagged beneath the additional weight.

"Wonderful!" Alice said with delight. "Let's go straight after breakfast."

It was the last thing Dori wanted. She would much rather have stayed in by the fire and read the newspaper gossip columns, or wound up the phonograph and played some music. But she was not going to be left behind. She had already seen how Matthew laughed with Alice now, not talked to her earnestly as he used to, as if consciousness of guns and warfare, injury were only a sentence away. She knew Alice worked in a veteran's hospital, but she never mentioned it, except briefly when she was asked, and then changed the subject. It was as if she too were ready to move on from the horror and try to rebuild.

Perhaps that was the worst of it. Alice was no longer the predictable, self-sacrificing misery that she used to be. If she had been anybody

else, Dori might even have found her quite fun, except that she knew
no one who mattered, never swapped gossip because no doubt she
had none, and her sense of humour was a bit odd.

But the real trouble was that underneath the lightness, Dori could
read her well enough to see that she was still in love with Matthew.
It was there in her eyes when he did not know she was looking at
him, the softening of her voice when she spoke his name, the way
she always remembered what he had said.

The three of them went out into the park and joined the children
sledding down the steep slopes, all of them laughing and shouting to
each other, slithering on the packed snow, mock fighting with snow-
balls.

It was Alice who took the hand of the awkward child who was left
on the sidelines, who teamed up with him and drew him in. It was
she who saw to it that he named the snowman they built.

On the way home, walking behind Alice and Matthew, Dori realised a great and terrible truth. Whether he ever broke with her or not,
even if he never for an instant considered leaving her literally, something in him had already left her, and belonged to Alice again, even
more than before. Dori had had him only temporarily, charmed him
and made him forget his horror when he needed it, but that was all.
It was as inevitable as next winter that ultimately she would lose everything of him that mattered, be a wife only in that she had his name.

And others would see it. Other prying eyes would understand the
looks, all the words that were never said between them. Dori would
become the subject of gossip, barbed wit from her enemies, and far
worse than that, pity from her friends.

It was in a museum that she made her plan. Actually it was an
exhibition of South American jungle artefacts, arrows and such things,
a terrible bore for the most part. Of course it would leave a bitter
taste, but given the circumstances that was unavoidable. A little prep-
aration was necessary, but it would all be quite simple, really.

Alice could not say that she was happy that Christmas. She still loved
Matthew, and not all the work in the world, no matter how important,
altered that. But she had learned to live with the loneliness inside,

the dreams that always ached at the bottom of her heart, in the places within her thoughts she knew better than to seek.

Now, visiting him with Dori, being with him, talking as they had in the past, so easily and with instinctive understanding, the pain was acute. But it was also mixed with pleasure she would never deny herself. She would not stay away so long again. If she could not have love, at least she would have the courage to keep friendship, with all that it gave, and took.

She was dressing for dinner on Christmas Eve, a soft, slim blue-grey gown, very inexpensive, but nicely cut, when there was a knock on the door and without waiting for an answer, Dori came in. She was wearing sophisticated black, and with her mass of fair hair she looked radiant.

"I have a gift for you," she announced triumphantly. "I have absolutely made the decision and I won't change my mind."

Alice was hesitant about accepting, but a warmth of affection welled up inside her and she found herself smiling. Dori was not usually generous with her, but perhaps at last that was changing.

"Thank you," she answered. "What is it? Won't you keep it until Christmas?"

"No, you should wear it tonight." Dori was holding something half behind her back. Now she brought it forward, a black velvet jewel box about two inches long. Her smile widened as she opened the lid. Inside was the most exquisitely wrought brooch in the shape of a scorpion, the light rippling and burning in a dozen limpid aquamarines.

Alice drew in her breath sharply. It was the loveliest thing she had ever seen. It was amazing. She struggled for words, and could not find any. She looked up at Dori, trying to understand.

"It's . . . it's wonderful," she breathed. "Why would you give me this? It's your birth sign as well!"

"I just want you to have it," Dori answered. Her eyes were as bright as the stones. "Let me put it on for you. It goes perfectly with that dress. It'll set it off." She picked the brooch out of its box, very carefully, almost as if it had been a real scorpion. The clasp was already undone, it had been merely lying on the satin, not fastened through it as usual. She held it out, the darkly tarnished pin swinging loose. "Stand still," she ordered. "I don't want to prick you."

Alice took a step towards her to make it easier for her.

At that moment they both heard Matthew's voice in the corridor outside. "Dori!"

Dori froze.

"She's in here!" Alice called back.

Dori half turned, the brooch still held high, as if she intended to pin it on Alice first, before Matthew should interrupt them.

But she was too late, he must have been closer than she thought. He pushed the door. Dori swung around, flinging her arm behind her to conceal the brooch from him. Then she cried out, a high, sharp sound full of pain, as if she had been truly hurt, and the next moment she was staggering into Alice's arms, her eyes wide, her face stiff and blank. She tried to speak but her throat seemed not to move. Her head sank forward. Alice struggled to hold her up, but Dori's knees buckled and she gasped for breath, falling, already her skin blue about the lips.

"What is it?" Matthew said in disbelief, alarm rising in his voice.

"I don't know." Alice was startled and confused. Dori never fainted. "One moment she was fine. She had a present for me, the most beautiful brooch. It's . . ." Her eye travelled down and saw the dazzling blue scorpion on Dori's smooth, half naked back. The long pin was wedged deep into her flesh, a bubble of scarlet blood around it. Her swift movement had thrown her off balance and she had stabbed herself with the open pin as she was preparing to fasten it into Alice's dress.

"Dori?" Alice said gently, touching her sister's face. "Dori?"

But Dori did not move. Her breathing was slight, shallow, then it stopped altogether.

Curare, the South American Indian arrow poison, works very quickly. They called it 'the flying death.'

Later, Matthew understood what had happened, but in all their long, sweet years together, he never told Alice, for many reasons. Among them, he did not want to spoil her pleasure in the blue scorpion brooch. She wore it in memory of her sister's last generosity. Why shatter that?

# CONTRIBUTORS

**Peter Tremayne** is the pseudonym of Peter Berresford Ellis, a Celtic scholar who lives in London, England. He conceived the idea for Sister Fidelma, a 7th Century Celtic lawyer, to demonstrate that women could be legal advocates under the Irish system of law. Sister Fidelma has since appeared in eight novels, the most recent being *The Monk Who Vanished*, and many short stories which have been collected in the anthology *Hemlock at Vespers and other Sister Fidelma Mysteries*. He has also written, under his own name, more than 25 books on history, biography, and Irish and Celtic mythology, including *Celtic Women: Women in Celtic Society and Literature* and *Celt and Greek: Celts in the Hellenic World*.

**Lillian Stewart Carl** writes what she calls "gonzo mythology" fantasy novels, as well as mystery and romantic suspense novels. She began writing as a child growing up in Missouri and Ohio and has continued all her life, even while traveling to Europe, Great Britain, the Middle East, and India, among other places. He novels include *Dust to Dust*, *Shadow Dancers*, and *Wings of Power*. Her short fiction has appeared in *Alternate Generals*, *Past Lives*, *Present Tense*, and *Murder Most Medieval*. She lives in Carrollton, Texas, with her husband.

**Bill Crider** is the author of the Sheriff Dan Rhodes series, the first book of which won the Anthony Award in 1987. Crider's short stories have appeared in numerous anthologies, including *Holmes For The Holidays* and all the books in the celebrated Cat Crimes series. Recently he co-authored two books with Willard Scott, entitled *Death Under Blue Skies* and *Murder in the Mist*. He lives with his wife in Alvin, Texas.

**Jane Lindskold** is the author of more than forty short stories and ten novels—the most recent of which include *Changer* and *Legends Walking*. She lives in New Mexico where she writes, gardens, and enjoys the company of her husband, archaeologist Jim Moore. She is currently at work on another novel.

**Edward Marston** is the prolific author of plays, short stories, and novels, with his historical mystery *The Roaring Boy* being nominated for the Edgar award for best novel in 1995. He is currently writing two series, one featuring Nicholas Bracewell, a stage manager for an acting company in Elizabethan England, the other with Ralph Delchard and Gervase Bret, two men who travel England investigating land claims in the 11th century. His latest novel is *The Repentant Rake* , another mystery, set in Restoration England. A former chairman of the Crime Writer's Association in the United Kingdom, he lives in rural Kent, England.

**Brendan DuBois** is the award-winning author of both short stories and novels. His short fiction has appeared in *Playboy, Ellery Queen's Mystery Magazine, Alfred Hitchcock's Mystery Magazine, Mary Higgins Clark Mystery Magazine,* and numerous anthologies. He has received the Shamus Award from the Private Eye Writers of America for one of his short stories, and has been nominated three times for an Edgar Allan Poe Award by the Mystery Writers of America.

He's also the author of the Lewis Cole mystery series—*Dead Sand, Black Tide* and *Shattered Shell*. His most recent novel, *Resurrection Day,* is a suspense thriller that looks at what might have happened had the Cuban Missile Crisis of 1962 erupted into a nuclear war between the United States and the Soviet Union. This book recently received the Sidewise Award for best alternative history novel of 1999. He lives in New Hampshire with his wife Mona.

**Mat Coward** is a British writer of crime, SF, horror, children's and humorous fiction, whose stories have been broadcast on BBC Radio, and published in numerous anthologies, magazines and e-zines in the UK, US and Europe. According to Ian Rankin, "Mat Coward's stories resemble distilled novels." His first non-distilled novel—a whodunit called *Up and Down*—was published in the USA in 2000. Short stories have recently appeared in *Ellery Queen's Mystery Magazine*, *The World's Finest Crime and Mystery Stories*, *Felonious Felines*, and *Murder Through the Ages*.

**Marcia Talley**'s first Hannah Ives novel, *Sing It to Her Bones*, won the Malice Domestic Grant in 1998 and was nominated for an Agatha Award as Best First Novel of 1999. *Unbreathed Memories*, the second in the series, is a Romantic Times Reviewers Choice nominee for Best Contemporary Mystery of 2000. Both were Featured Alternates of the Mystery Guild. Hannah's third adventure, *Occasion of Revenge*, was released in August 2001. Marcia is also the editor of a collaborative serial novel, *Naked Came the Phoenix*, where she joins twelve best-selling women authors to pen a tongue-in-cheek mystery about murder in an exclusive health spa. Her short stories have appeared in magazines and collections including "With Love, Marjorie Ann" which received an Agatha Award nomination for Best Short Story 1999. She lives in Annapolis, Maryland with her husband, Barry, a professor at the U.S. Naval Academy. When she isn't writing, she spends her time traveling or sailing, and recently returned from the Bahamas where they lived for six months aboard *Troubadour*, their 37-foot sailboat.

**Jon L. Breen** is the author of six novels, more than eighty short stories, and two Edgar Award winning critical volumes. His most recent books are *The Drowning Icecube and Other Stories* (Five Star), the second edition of *Novel Verdicts: A Guide to Courtroom Fiction* (Scarecrow), and the anthology *Sleuths of the Century* (Carroll & Graf), edited with Ed Gorman. He also contributes "The Jury Box" review column to *Ellery Queen's Mystery Magazine*.

**Catherine Dain** is the creator of the Freddie O'Neal series, including the novels *Lay It On The Line* and *Lament for A Dead Cowboy*, both nominated for the Shamus Award. After receiving her graduate degree in theater arts from the University of Southern California, she worked as a television newscaster before turning to mystery writing. The first full-length Faith Cassidy mystery, *Death of the Party*, was published in 2000 by Five Star Mysteries. She lives in Ventura, California.

**Lawrence Block** is the author of Leo Haig, Bernie Rhodenbarr, Matthew Scudder, Evan Tanner, and most recently the John Keller mystery series. He writes all facets of the mystery field, from hard-edged mysteries such as *A Ticket to the Boneyard* and his most recent, *Even the Wicked*, lighthearted comedy capers like *Burglars Can't be Choosers*, to tongue-in-cheek adventure novels, including *The Thief who Couldn't Sleep*, and his excellent stand alone books, including *After The First Death*, *Random Walk*, aznd many others. Along the way he has been awarded the Nero Wolfe award (1979), Private Eye Writers of America Shamus award (1983, 1985), Mystery Writers of America Edgar Allan Poe award (1985), and the MWA Grand Master award (1994).

**Peter Lovesey** is well known to mystery readers the world over as the creator of Victorian age police officers Sergeant Cribb and Constable Thackeray. Other creations include using King Edward VII as a sleuth in another take on the Victorian age. In between these series he has written dozens of short stories, as well as several television plays. He has also won several awards, notably the Silver, Gold, and Diamond Daggers of the Crime Writers Association.

**P. N. Elrod** is best known for her supernatural detective series, *The Vampire Files*. She has authored and co-edited a number of novels and two anthologies, and co-writes the Richard Dun vampire series with Nigel Bennett. The character of Nick Tarrant is based on one of her friends. If she revealed his real name he'd just have to kill her.

**Simon Brett's** most recent books are in his new Fethering series, *The Body of the Beach* and *Death on the Downs*. He also created Charles Paris, an actor as well as amateur detective, who stumbles into the middle of crimes usually set against the backdrop of the London theater scene. Another series concerns the mysterious Mrs. Pargeter, a detective who skirts the edge of the law in her unusual investigations. He's also quite accomplished in the short form as well, with stories appearing in the *Malice Domestic* series, as well as the anthologies *Once Upon a Crime* and *Funny Bones*. A winner of the Writer's Guild of Great Britain award for his radio plays, he has also written nonfiction books and edited several books in the Faber series, including *The Faber Book of Useful Verse* and *The Faber Book of Parodies*. He lives in Burpham, England.

**Kristine Kathryn Rusch** is an award-winning fiction writer. Her novella, *The Gallery of His Dreams*, won the *Locus Award* for best short fiction. Her body of fiction work won her the John W. Campbell Award, given in 1991 in Europe. She has been nominated for several dozen fiction awards, including the MWA's Edgar award for both short fiction and novel, and her short work has been reprinted in six *Year's Best* collections. She has published twenty novels under her own name and sold forty-one total, including pseudonymous books. Her novels have been published in seven languages, and have spent several weeks on *The USA Today* Bestseller list and *The Wall Street Journal* Bestseller list. She is the former editor of prestigious *The Magazine of Fantasy and Science Fiction*, wining a Hugo for her work there. Before that, she and her husband Dean Wesley Smith started and ran Pulphouse Publishing, a science fiction and mystery press in Eugene. She lives and works on the Oregon Coast.

**Anne Perry** writes, "I was born in Blackheath, London in 1938. From an early age, I enjoyed reading and two of my favorite authors were Lewis Carroll and Charles Kingsley. It was always my desire to write, but it took 20 years before I produced a book which was accepted for publication. That was *The Cater Street Hangman*, which came out in 1979. I chose the Victorian era by accident, but I am happy to stay with it, because it was a remarkable time in British history, full of extremes, of poverty and wealth, social change, expansion of empire, and challenging ideas. In all levels of society there were the good and the bad, the happy and the miserable."